WADE RAWSON

Ruggedly quiet in the full vigor of his manhood, he embarks on a quest for gold that leads him on a wilderness adventure where danger lurks in the darkness and death may come with dawn.

KATHY BEDDOES

Radiantly lovely, she arrives in California to find herself a prospector's widow and dares to make her way on a man's frontier. Her brains, her beauty, and ultimately her voice become the toast of San Francisco.

JACK MARLOW

Unwilling to settle for the backbreaking life of a miner, he learns to turn a mean card in the gambling halls—and emerges a leader in San Francisco's burgeoning underworld.

SIMON ST. CLAIR

His Southern gentleman's airs hide the stone-cold heart of a ruthless killer. He wants Kathy Beddoes, and he stalks her from the panhandle to the waterfront to make her his own.

JUAN SOTO

His dreams of a better life in the American West are shattered when he sees his wife viciously murdered at the hands of a lynch mob. Now he finds solace in the burning fires of vengeance.

CALIFORNIA KINGDOMS

Robert W. Broomall

FAWCETT GOLD MEDAL • NEW YORK

A Fawcett Gold Medal Book
Published by Ballantine Books
Copyright © 1992 by Robert W. Broomall

Library of Congress Catalog Card Number: 91-92396

ISBN 0-449-14661-8

Manufactured in the United States of America

First Edition: June 1992

"O cursed lust for gold,
To what dost thou not drive
        the hearts of men?"

—VIRGIL

Part I

PANAMA

1

February 1849—the Chagres River

The river wound slowly, between jungle-clad banks. In the heat, steam rose from the water's surface. The air was alive with the cries of parrots and howler monkeys.

A boat was poled slowly upstream. The boat, called a bungo, was twenty-five feet long and made from a hollowed-out cashew tree. The two native boatmen wore cotton loincloths and straw hats. With long poles tucked under their shoulders, they pushed the craft along while their leader sang in fractured English:

> Oh! Susanna.
> You don't cry for me.
> I go to California
> With the bowl on my knee.

Across the bungo's stern stretched an awning of mango leaves. In the awning's shade were the passengers—eight men and a woman. They sat on the gunwales, knee to knee, with their bags heaped between them. They were Americans, and all but one were bound for California.

Wade Rawson sat up front, closest to the boatmen. Two months ago, Wade had been a law student. Now he was what the papers called an Argonaut. He had joined the mad rush for California gold.

Wade was twenty-four, tall, and sturdy. There was four days' growth of beard on his chin. Beneath his peaked leather cap, his wavy brown hair was tangled. He was pale and drawn from dysentery, and covered with mosquito bites. He wore a red flannel shirt, bandanna, worsted trousers, and high boots—all of them soggy with sweat. His new wool underwear had worn patches of his skin raw. He was sick of the broiling sun, sick of the blinding

3

rain showers, sick of the clouds of insects—*bichos*, the boatmen called them—that bit and stabbed and stung him until he thought he would go out of his mind. His only consolation was that everyone else was in the same condition.

Wade had sailed from New York twelve days earlier, on the steam packet *William Tell*. He had boarded this bungo in Chagres City two days before, bound forty-some miles inland to the village of Cruces. At Cruces he and the others would transfer to muleback for the final stage to Panama City. There, they had been promised, another steamship would be waiting to take them to San Francisco.

The bungo's pace was snaillike. There was little to do but observe the passing countryside. The green jungle was splashed with flowers in every imaginable color. There were flocks of parakeets, clouds of butterflies. There were fantastic creepers with red blossoms; there were festoons of ropelike vines. There were palm trees and banana trees, mangoes, teaks, and towering cedros, jumbled together in an explosion of life.

"This country hasn't changed in a million years," Wade marveled. "It's like we've left the nineteenth century and traveled back in time."

Beside him, Catesby, the railroad engineer, laughed without humor. Catesby was one of the bungo's two passengers who had not also been on the *William Tell*. He was gaunt and florid, with a perpetual sunburn. "You *have* left the nineteenth century," he said. "Only it's to hell you've traveled." He turned to the bungo's rear. "Pardon the language, ma'am."

Mrs. Katherine Beddoes nodded. Mrs. Beddoes had the bungo's best seat, where the gunwales were widest and she could rest her back against an awning support. She was prim and mousy-looking, with dark hair tied in a bun beneath her bonnet. She had been the only woman among the *William Tell*'s ninety-odd passengers, and the men felt uneasy in her presence.

Next to Mrs. Beddoes, the walruslike ex-Congressman George Shattuck said, "I won't argue your appraisal of the country, Catesby. It seems all too accurate. How the devil do you propose to build a railroad here?"

Catesby pulled a handkerchief from the pocket of his tropical whites. He took off his cork helmet and mopped his forehead. "Oh, we can build it, all right. It's getting started that's the problem. A full year I've been out here, and not a rail has been laid. I came with five men, engineers like myself. I'm the only one left alive.

One went mad and killed himself, the other four died from disease. We get our pick-and-shovel men by the boatload—Irish and West Indian, mostly—and half of 'em don't live to see their first payday. The fever takes 'em that quick. It's hard to find a dry place to bury all the bodies."

Catesby wiped the helmet's sweatband. "I tell you, they can talk about yellow jack and malaria, but Chagres fever is the worst. When the Chagres gets hold of you, it doesn't let go till you're dead."

That cast a note of gloom among the company. Fully a quarter of the *William Tell*'s passengers had come down with fever in Chagres, and three had died—including one who had booked passage on this bungo. Wade glanced uneasily at the dark-haired fellow in patched homespun who had taken the dead man's place. The new man's name was Marlow, and his face had developed an unhealthy flush.

Ex-Congressman Shattuck said, "Why don't you get out of Panama, Catesby? Go to California with the rest of us. That's the place to be these days. The greatest gold strike in history. Fortunes for the taking."

Catesby shook his head and put his helmet back on. "California's not for me. I've made a commitment here, and I'm bound to see it through. Meanwhile, we pay off the politicians and generals, and try to get things moving. That's where I'm bound now—to Panama City, to bribe some hero of the republic to get off his . . ." He looked at Mrs. Beddoes again, and he chose different words. "To exert himself and chase the *cimarrones*, the wild ones, for us."

Next to him, Captain Mitchell of the army rolled a cold cigar in his mouth—he had not lit the cigar in deference to the lady. "These *cimarrones*—they're some kind of bandits?"

"The worst kind," Catesby said. "Human life means nothing to them. They play the devil with our surveying and grading crews. Their leader is called Matachin—'the butcher.' "

Captain Mitchell scanned the surrounding jungle. George Shattuck squirmed and said, "Is there any danger to us?"

"I shouldn't think so," Catesby replied. "They don't usually bother river traffic."

Across from him, the elegant gambler Levelleire said, "Still, I'd feel better if we had sailed with the other bungos. For Mrs. Beddoes's sake, if nothing else."

Mrs. Beddoes spoke coolly. "Please, don't concern yourselves about me."

Levelleire nodded. He said, "Your husband is in California already, Mrs. Beddoes. Has he given you any indication as to the richness of the diggings?"

Mrs. Beddoes looked down demurely. Despite the ferocious heat, her traveling dress and jacket were buttoned to the neck. Her crinoline and petticoats must have been agony to wear, but she gave no sign of it. "Not really," she said. "He did . . . he did mention washing six hundred dollars from one pan. 'Twas from that pan that he sent me the money to join him."

Shattuck whistled. The others nodded approvingly.

"Yow!" The cry came from lumpy young Alex Baylor, who had been trailing a hand in the water. He jerked it back on board, just out of the yawning jaws of an alligator.

The rest of the passengers saw the beast and backed away.

From the bow of the boat, the lead boatman, Cristobal, laughed his infectious laugh. Cristobal was a frog-faced fellow with long, curly hair and a scarred cheek. "I must tell you, señores. *Los caimanos*, they are in this river."

"I wish you'd told me five minutes ago," Alex said, looking at his hand as though surprised to find all his fingers still there.

Cristobal laughed again. The other boatman, Ambrosio, was taller and quiet, with pronounced Indian blood.

The passengers stared at the half-submerged alligator. "What a monster," breathed Captain Mitchell.

"Look," said Catesby, pointing. "There's more."

At least a dozen of the scaly creatures lay on a narrow strip of beach, sunning themselves. As the Argonauts watched, one of the great reptiles stood and waddled into the water. It swam lazily toward the boat, as if to inspect it.

"A dollar says you can't hit him with your pistol," Alex Baylor told his brother Dan.

"Yes, Mr. Baylor, go ahead," said ex-Congressman Shattuck. "We could use a diversion."

The other passengers looked on in encouragement, roused from their heat-induced torpor. Even Mrs. Beddoes seemed interested.

Tall, red-haired Dan, an athlete of some repute, took up the challenge immediately. "You're on," he said.

"Stop the boat," Shattuck told Cristobal, gesturing. *"Alto. Alto."*

"Ah. *Alto. Si*, señor. *Prestimento.*" Cristobal gave a command, and the bungo slowly swung to, while the two boatmen braced it with their poles.

Shattuck said, "What about you, Mr. Marlow? Will you try a shot as well?"

Marlow, the fellow in homespun, carried a big .44 revolver in his belt. "No, thanks," he said curtly.

Dan Baylor's coat was with his bags. He reached inside it and drew out an oilcloth bundle, from which he unwrapped the small pistol. It was an expensive model, a .31-caliber Colt, with an engraved barrel. It had been a gift from his father.

Except for Marlow, the passengers were excited. The two boatmen looked like they'd seen this all before. They sat on the foredeck, passing a cocoa gourd full of rum and chatting in Spanish.

Dan checked the pistol's loads. He adjusted himself on the gunwale. The alligator was about thirty yards off. In the slow current, its eyes and the tip of its snout were visible above the water's surface. Dan cocked the pistol and extended his arm, closing one eye.

He fired.

The bullet splashed the water to the beast's left. The shot's echo was lost in the shrieks of thousands of birds that exploded into the air.

Alex hooted at Dan's miss. "Try again," urged Captain Mitchell.

Dan extended his arm. He cocked the pistol and fired. The bullet skipped off the flat surface of the water. There were more cries of birds, outraged screeches of howler monkeys.

"You owe me a dollar," Alex crowed.

Dan was mad. He didn't like to lose at anything. He fired twice more, missing both times. The racket of birds and animals made it impossible to think. He saw Cristobal looking at him, dark eyes filled with amusement, and he snapped, "What are you looking at? Do you think you can do better?"

Cristobal's eyes widened innocently. In broken English he said, "You let Cristobal shoot?"

That hadn't been Dan's intention, but now he said, "Why not? It might be good for a laugh."

He handed Cristobal the shiny new pistol. The little boatman hefted it, admiring it. He showed it to Ambrosio and said something in Spanish. The taller man laughed.

Then Cristobal braced his feet on the foredeck. He lifted the pistol smoothly, cocked it, and fired.

There was a roar. The alligator thrashed madly for a second, then vanished beneath the river's surface in a roiling mass of bubbles.

"Holy. . . !" breathed Alex.

"He did it," Captain Mitchell cried.

Ex-Congressman Shattuck shouted, "Bravo, Cristobal!"

Next to Wade, the dark-haired man named Marlow shifted uneasily. "There's going to be trouble," he muttered.

Wade turned. Before he could ask Marlow what he meant, Cristobal turned back to them. White teeth shone in his pockmarked face. "Is nice *pistola*," he said to Dan. "You give to Cristobal, no?"

"No," Dan said.

Cristobal grew firmer. "You give."

"No," Dan repeated, and he grabbed the pistol from Cristobal's hand.

George Shattuck tried to smooth hurt feelings. "Good heavens, Cristobal. You've taken everything of ours that isn't tied down already. Isn't that enough?"

This brought a good-natured laugh from Cristobal. He was so likable that the passengers had tolerated his little depredations. He shrugged and took up his pole. "Is good gun. I use again."

"We'll see," Dan said placatingly.

Cristobal turned to Ambrosio, "*Viente*, amigo."

The two boatmen stuck the long poles under their shoulders, and the bungo started upstream once more.

2

The bungo was bathed in an eerie green light formed by the canopy of trees that stretched overhead. As the stream narrowed, the current grew more rapid, and the boatmen kept to the shallows on either side. At one point the bungo was caught in a floating tangle of weeds and vegetation. Cristobal and Ambrosio had to cut it free, using axes and machetes. This took nearly an hour. The two boatmen sweated profusely in the heat and humidity. When they were done, they poled the bungo upstream and onto a sandbar. They stowed their poles on board. Then Cristobal took off his straw hat. He dropped his loincloth and leapt naked into the water, followed by Ambrosio. They swam out of earshot, laughing and splashing each other.

"Another *baño*," sighed Captain Mitchell, who was going to California to join the military government in Monterey. "That's the second one today. Three yesterday."

"They're the cleanest niggers on the river, if nothing else," drawled the gambler Levelleire, fanning himself with his low-crowned black hat. A six-shot pepperbox pistol was just visible beneath his pearl-gray coat.

Wade turned to Marlow. "What did you mean before, when you said there's going to be trouble?"

Heads turned. Marlow looked at Wade. His blue eyes managed to be cold and lively at the same time. Sweat poured down his flushed, unshaven face. "Don't you get it, college boy? How does a fellow like Cristobal, living in the jungle, become a dead pistol shot? It takes practice to get that good, a lot of practice."

Young Alex Baylor said, "Be serious, Marlow. Panama's practically part of the U.S. now. They see guns down here all the time."

"It was probably a lucky shot that got the gator," said his older brother, Dan, still miffed at being shown up by Cristobal. "He was probably aiming at one of the gators onshore."

Ex-Congressman Shattuck scoffed beneath his drooping mustache. "Are you suggesting that we have something to fear from Cristobal? The fellow's too simple."

"There's a lot I don't like about this voyage," Marlow said. "Why did this bungo get left behind the others in Chagres, for instance?"

"You know why," said the railroad engineer Catesby. "The original crew came down with fever. If Cristobal and Ambrosio hadn't volunteered their services, we'd still be in Chagres, waiting to get sick ourselves. Good heavens, man, we owe these fellows a debt of thanks, not our suspicions."

Most of the passengers muttered agreement with Catesby. Only

Mrs. Beddoes looked thoughtful, as though there might be something in what Marlow said.

"What do you think will happen?" Wade asked Marlow in a low voice. The other passengers had ceased paying attention.

Marlow said, "I don't know, but I bet it happens tonight. This is our last night on the river. Tomorrow we reach Cruces."

Water splashed alongside as Cristobal and Ambrosio returned to the bungo. Cristobal hauled himself aboard. The frog-faced little boatman stood on the prow, his naked body dripping. Wade saw Cristobal glance toward Mrs. Beddoes, and was it Wade's imagination, or did the boatman's affable grin become a leer?

None of the other passengers noticed except Mrs. Beddoes. Her face reddened. She refused to look into Cristobal's eyes, though. She refused to acknowledge his nakedness. She stared through him with cool disdain, as though he weren't there.

Cristobal's gaze flared up, then went out. He replaced his cotton loincloth and straw hat. Grinning his buffoon's grin once more, he picked up his pole. Ambrosio already had his.

"*Baño* good," Cristobal announced to the passengers. His long wet hair bobbed with his head. "We go now."

This announcement was greeted with a smattering of bored applause as the boatmen pushed the bungo off the sandbar.

Wade felt sorry for Mrs. Beddoes. It must be hard enough being in a hellhole like Panama, the only woman among all these men, without having Cristobal make eyes at her. Mrs. Beddoes caught Wade looking over. Wade smiled, to give her encouragement. To his surprise, she rolled her eyes and pulled a face. Wade grinned. Mrs. Beddoes grinned back. Then they both looked away, embarrassed by this exchange of intimacies.

The bungo continued its solitary course upriver. The green light lent its cast to everything—people, objects, water. The passengers were enveloped by the heat, by insects, by the smell of rotting vegetation.

Now and then Wade grew uneasy as he thought about what Marlow had said. Wade didn't know what to make of Marlow. He had no idea where Marlow came from or what he was doing in Panama. None of the passengers seemed concerned about Marlow's predictions of trouble, with the possible exception of Mrs. Beddoes. It was hard to tell what she was thinking.

In the bow, Cristobal sang:

Oh! Susanna.
You don't cry for me.
I go to California
With the bowl on my knee.

Late in the afternoon, as the jungle quieted, the bungo reached Calosoco, the riverside village where the passengers were to spend the night.

3

A mosquito brushed Wade's unshaven cheek. He slapped it too late. He felt the sting. In a few minutes there would be a lump on his cheek. It would have plenty of company.

Supper was over. Wade and the Baylor brothers were walking through the village. Calosoco was a cluster of bamboo huts built on stilts, located on the downstream side of a bend in the Chagres. The huts had open walls and conical thatched roofs. The stilts were to protect the buildings from the river's periodic floods. The streets were filled with garbage and old bones. They were populated by naked children, squawking chickens, and dogs that never stopped barking. Outside each hut were barrels of rainwater whose tops were alive with wriggling mosquito larvae. The water of the Chagres was muddy, and the natives found rainwater preferable for drinking. Outside the village were some indifferently tilled fields and a pasture. Everywhere, the jungle pressed close.

The three big gringos with their heavy clothing stood out among the smaller, lightly dressed villagers. The villagers paid them little attention, however. They had become used to gringos. In the last two months, nearly a thousand *norteamericanos* had passed through Calosoco on their way to California.

They were through the village quickly. The jungle barred progress beyond, so they turned back. They purchased a jug of papaya juice and returned to the hotel, which was a hut like the others, only bigger. They climbed the warped steps to the veranda, where a group of the bungo's passengers sat in wicker chairs, smoking cigars and drinking the gambler Levelleire's brandy.

Ex-Congressman Shattuck was holding forth, his walrus face red from heat and drink. He had been a minor celebrity in the East for having resigned his seat to go to California. "I tell you, California will be a state within the year," he said. "And I shall be her first representative to the U.S. Senate."

Captain Mitchell sat with his feet propped on the veranda railing. His blue uniform coat was unbuttoned. He laughed. "Well, you've got my vote, George. These are damn fine cigars."

"Agreed," said Mr. Levelleire.

Catesby, the railroad engineer, paid them little attention. He was too busy helping himself to the brandy.

At the veranda's far end sat Mrs. Beddoes, staring at the river. She seemed composed and calm. Wade wondered if she was that way by nature, or if it was an act to hide her fears and loneliness.

Wade and his friends went inside. The hotel was not large. The only furnishings were a dozen cowhide hammocks slung on poles. The floor was of cane, and it was full of roaches and spiders. Wade was pretty sure there were rats in the thatched roof as well.

Marlow was the only person inside. He had cleaned and oiled his pistol, and he was reassembling it. His battered cloth grip was by his side. The grip was his only luggage. Wade knew that it was not full, because he'd heard things rattle inside when Marlow carried it.

Marlow looked up as the three men came in. "Join us for a drink?" Wade said. He spoke more out of politeness than from a genuine desire for Marlow's company.

"No, thanks," Marlow replied. He looked more haggard than he had earlier. He finished reassembling the pistol and twirled the cylinder. He levered the hammer again and again, letting it down with his thumb. Satisfied, he rammed new loads of powder and ball into the chambers.

"You spend a lot of time with that pistol," Wade said.

"If you want it to work when you need it, you better keep it clean."

Dan Baylor, the athlete, couldn't resist a faint smile. "You're not still worried about Cristobal, are you, Marlow?"

Marlow looked at him sharply. "I ain't one for changing my mind," he said, and he went back to work.

Wade's trunk and leather hand grip, and those of the Baylor boys, were piled beneath their hammocks. Like Wade, the Baylors had money. Their father had made a fortune selling shoes to the army during the Mexican War. This trip to the gold fields was a vacation for them. Alex dragged out his trunk to use as a table. The three men put their tin cups on top, along with the papaya juice, a bottle of rum, and a tin of iced cookies that had been given to the Baylors by their mother.

"Ah, real American food at last," said Alex, stuffing cookies into his mouth.

They mixed the rum and papaya juice, and they guzzled it in the hot night. The mixture tasted smooth. It relaxed Wade. It made him realize how tired he was.

Sweat poured down Alex Baylor's round cheeks. He pulled at his red flannel shirt, which seemed to have gotten big on him. "The only good thing about Panama is that I'm losing weight," he said.

"Dysentery has that effect," observed his brother Dan, dryly.

"I'm starting to wonder if we shouldn't have gone to Europe, Dan, like we originally planned."

"Come on, Alex. This rush to California is a once-in-a-lifetime adventure. We'd never forgive ourselves if we missed it."

"Wouldn't we?" Alex said. "What about poor Bagley, dead of fever back in Chagres? He never even got to California. You think he wouldn't forgive himself for missing it? Who's to say we're not next?"

Wade said, "Get a hold of yourself, Alex. We've left the fever behind. A few more days, and we'll be out of Panama." He sneaked a glance at Marlow's flushed face, and he hoped that he was right.

Just then Wade felt something on his foot. He looked down. A large spider, brown and furry, was crawling on his boot toe.

Wade jumped up with a cry. Alex and Dan joined him. "Tarantula!" yelled Alex.

The three men backed away from the creature, which maneuvered its long legs toward them.

Marlow wandered over.

"Look out!" Alex told him. "It's poisonous!"

Marlow squashed the tarantula with his boot. "Not now, it ain't," he said.

Marlow wore his old slouch hat pulled low. The revolver was back in his belt. He scraped the tarantula's remains off his boot sole, and he kicked them into a corner. He looked at Wade and his friends, and he grinned.

"College boys," he said.

He walked out of the hut and down the steps to the village. Wade and the Baylor brothers looked at one another sheepishly.

4

When Wade and the Baylors were done with the rum and cookies, they went outside. Dan and Alex went down to the cook hut. Wade remained on the veranda. The evening air was steamy, like bathwater. Across the river the emerald green of the jungle had faded to a purple blur. On this side Wade could make out the rickety jetty, with the bungo tied at its foot. He saw the village canoes drawn up on the shore. He smelled the thick black mud of the riverbank, the perfume of flowers and sugar cane. He smelled the jungle, ripe with vegetation and rotting fruit. In the pasture, cattle lowed. Bats flitted from the palm trees at the jungle's edge.

Below, Wade saw Marlow strolling through the village. Marlow moved easily, but there was a noticeable wariness about him. For the life of him, Wade couldn't see what Marlow was worried about. "Sleepy" was too strong a word for Calosoco.

The party on the veranda was breaking up. Pitching their cigars off the porch, the men went into the hut to prepare for bed. Mrs. Beddoes rose from the chair and made her way to the veranda steps. She had removed her bonnet, but her dark hair was still in the bun.

Wade stepped aside as she passed. "Good night," he said, touching the brim of his peaked cap.

"Good night," she replied, smiling. Then she lowered her eyes and went down the steps. There were no facilities at the hotel for women, so Mrs. Beddoes was staying in a nearby hut with the hotel's owner and his family. Wade wondered how she felt there, alone, not speaking the language. Uncomfortable, he imagined. Afraid, even, though she was not the type to show it.

Wade joined the Baylor boys at the cook hut. The hut sheltered a brick oven, and it had a good view of the hotel, so that was where the guard would stay. The bungo's passengers had learned from experience to post a nightly guard to discourage light-fingered villagers.

Alex Baylor had first guard. He yawned. "I wish I hadn't drunk that rum."

Footsteps sounded behind them. It was Cristobal and Ambrosio. The two boatmen had girls on their arms. The girls' loose-fitting blouses barely concealed their breasts. The girls were giggling and laughing, leaning on their boyfriends.

Cristobal looked solicitous. To the Americans, he said, "You have need of something else, señores?"

Alex Baylor looked at the cold oven. "I want to make some coffee. How do you get a fire going here?"

The pockmarked little boatman grinned. "Cristobal take care of it, I promise. I get wood." He rejoined Ambrosio and the girls, and they set off into the growing darkness, singing:

> Oh! Susanna.
> You don't cry for me . . .

"Don't expect them back anytime soon," Wade told Alex.

"Come on, Wade," said Dan Baylor. "Let's go to bed. I'm beat. Good night, little brother."

Wade and Dan went back to the hotel. They climbed into their cowhide hammocks. Around them in the dim light were the coughings and stirrings of the other men. Marlow had not come back. Wade wondered where he had gone.

The tropic night descended like a curtain. The jungle erupted with noise. Insects chirped, monkeys yammered, a big cat cried. By the river, bullfrogs croaked, and alligators let out their peculiar roar. Wade lay on his hammock, fully clothed save for his boots and cap. The cowhide made his back sweat. The mosquitoes attacked him with a vengeance. They bit his eyelids and lips. They clustered in his ears and flew up his trouser legs. He swatted and swore, but he couldn't keep them off. There was something else in the hammock with him, too. Fleas. He felt them crawling on his legs and arms.

Wade sat up in the hammock. He swung his legs over the side. He put on his cap and groped for his boots in the dark. He tapped the boots upside down against his trunk. Something dropped out and skittered across the cane floor. He pulled on his boots and left the hut, taking his blanket with him.

He passed the cook hut, where Alex Baylor was fighting to stay awake. "Where are you going?" Alex said.

"To the bungo. Maybe I can sleep there."

Wade walked out on the jetty, taking his time in the dark so that he wouldn't fall through the places where the planks were missing. He came to the bungo. With the boat hook he searched for water snakes, as he'd watched Cristobal do, then he climbed into the craft and lay on the rough deck.

He had hoped that the slightly cooler air and running water would help keep down the mosquitoes, but they were as bad on the bungo as they had been in the hut. Wade struggled up, swearing. He scratched his numerous bites with one hand while he waved away the mosquitoes with the other. Around him was the racket of jungle and river. He saw Alex Baylor sitting by the cook hut, chin nodding on his chest.

Wade decided he might as well go up to the cook hut. If he couldn't sleep, he'd pull guard for someone who could.

He stood in the bungo, then stopped. Cristobal and Ambrosio had materialized from the deep shadows of the village. The girls were not with them. The two boatmen carried firewood. Cristobal's ax was slung over his shoulder. Ambrosio's machete was in his loincloth. Wade decided to stay put until they had left.

At the cook hut, something roused Alex Baylor from his stupor. He looked up and saw Cristobal and Ambrosio, and he stumbled to his feet.

Cristobal seemed surprised to see him awake. "*Buenas noches*, Señor Baylor."

"Hello," Alex said, rubbing his eyes. He had never been alone with these men before. He felt uncomfortable around them. He laughed nervously. "It's lucky you came when you did. Another minute, and I'd have been fast asleep."

Cristobal's dark eyes filled with humor. "*Sí*, señor. I think you would have been." He and Ambrosio stacked their wood in the oven. "Now you will have the coffee, señor. Like I promise."

Cristobal struck a flint and started a fire. He lingered, his ax on his shoulder, watching the flames grow. He and Ambrosio seemed hugely content. They must have had good luck with the girls, Alex told himself.

As if in answer to Alex's thought, Cristobal said to him, "You see the señoritas we with tonight?"

"Yes," Alex said. "I mean, *sí*."

"They were *buenas*, no?"

"*Sí*," Alex said. *"Buenas."* He felt more at ease now, and he laughed. *"Muy buenas."*

Cristobal and Ambrosio laughed along with him. Ambrosio stirred the fire. He put Alex's coffee can on the oven grate. Cristobal said, "They have girls like that in the Estados Unidos?"

Alex had never had much success with girls, but he said, "Oh, sure."

"Yes?" said Cristobal, wide-eyed. "Yes? Maybe I go there, then. What you think, Ambrosio? You want to go to there?"

The tall boatman shrugged.

To Alex, Cristobal said, "U.S. girls are *buenas*, yes?" He pantomimed the sex act and laughed. Ambrosio laughed, too. Alex thought the gesture crude, but he laughed along with them. They were only being friendly. Alex tried to sound like a man of the world. *"Sí, sí. Muy buenas."*

"Coffee ready," Ambrosio said.

Still smiling, Alex reached for the coffee can. As he did, Cristobal lifted the ax from his shoulder and struck him in the neck, nearly severing his head.

5

Alex fell without a cry. He bounced off the oven, twitched a second, then lay still.

In the bungo, Wade watched helplessly. His feet seemed pinned to the deck. He tried to yell, to scream a warning to Dan and the others, but no sound came from his throat.

From the cook hut, Ambrosio padded back into the shadows, as if on a prearranged mission. Cristobal stayed. He knelt and searched Alex's pockets. He found the dead man's purse and put it under his straw hat. He rose and gave a low whistle. From the darkness at the edge of the village, there was movement. Men appeared, some two dozen of them, wearing loincloths and cotton shirts. They were armed with machetes and old rifles, and they were running for the hotel.

Wade found his voice at last. "Dan!" he cried. "Dan, wake up in there! Dan! *Cimarrones!*"

Wade climbed from the boat. A pistol fired nearby. He saw the flash. It fired again. Wade thought the shots were aimed at him, but he kept going, running along the ill-built jetty. "Dan! Use your gun, Dan! Shoot them! They killed—"

Someone grabbed him off the end of the jetty and dragged him into the bushes. A heavy hand covered his mouth. He fought back, then a voice hissed, "Be quiet, damn you. They'll find us." The voice was Marlow's.

Wade stilled. He was breathing hard. "You've been out here all along?"

"That's right, college boy. I told you something was going to happen. I didn't want to get caught in it."

"Why'd you fire the shots? To warn the others?"

"Yeah. I owe them that much. But it's all I'm doing for them. They're finished. I've got a boat up the shore. You can come with me if you want. I guess I'm stuck with you."

There was gunfire from the hotel now. Wade and Marlow saw *cimarrones* swarming on the stairs. Wade got to his feet. "No, thanks," he said. "I'm going back."

Marlow got up, too. He grabbed Wade's arm. "I said, they're done for."

"What about Mrs. Beddoes?" Wade said. "Are you going to leave her for Cristobal?"

In the darkness Wade felt Marlow's intensity. Marlow said, "You're going to do the *honorable* thing, aren't you?"

"That's right."

Marlow hesitated. Then he let out his breath. "Come on," he said.

Marlow turned and started off, crouching low, heading back to the village and the gunfire. Wade followed.

* * *

In the hotel, two pistol shots awakened the sleeping Americans.

"What the. . . ?" somebody mumbled.

Catesby, the Panama veteran, knew what it was.

"*Cimarrones,*" he said, tumbling from his hammock. "Get your guns, if you've got 'em."

The other Americans jumped to the floor. They felt for their weapons in the darkness. Levelleire was first out the door, with his pepperbox pistol. He crossed the veranda and stopped. The *cimarrones* were approaching the foot of the stairs.

The bandits slowed when they saw him. Levelleire held his fire. The pepperbox pistol had little stopping power. It was useful only at point-blank range. Dan Baylor ran up beside him with his pocket Colt, then came Captain Mitchell with two dueling pistols, and Catesby with a big .44. "This damn thing is rusted through," Catesby swore. "It'll never work."

Below them, Cristobal moved in front of the bandits. "Don't stop, *muchachos*!" he cried. "After them!" He bounded onto the stairs with his ax. His men were right behind.

The Americans backed up, but Cristobal and his men came on too quickly for the Americans to get away.

"Fire!" yelled Levelleire.

The Americans began shooting. Levelleire fired his pepperbox pistol one barrel after the other. Men fell before him, but the rest of the bandits came on. Levelleire was still firing when Cristobal's ax cut him down.

Behind Levelleire, Catesby screamed in rage as he had misfire after misfire. He gave up on the big pistol, and he threw it at the *cimarrones*. He had the satisfaction of seeing it hit one of them in the face before he was hacked to pieces by their machetes.

Dan Baylor and Captain Mitchell scrambled back into the hotel, past ex-Congressman Shattuck, who was standing in the doorway. Shattuck had no weapon. He'd been watching in horror, his wet shirt plastered to his body. As the *cimarrones* came on, he fell on his knees before them, begging. "Stop! Please! I never did anything to you. I'll give you money. I've got friends in Washington. I can—"

A bandit placed a flintlock pistol to Shattuck's head and pulled the trigger.

In the hut, Dan Baylor had one shot left. There was no time to reload. Desperate, he ran the length of the building and vaulted over the open wall to the ground. Bandits outside saw him and gave chase.

Captain Mitchell stayed behind. He had fired only one of his dueling pistols. He stood at the ready with the other, and something in his attitude made the oncoming bandits stop. His steady gaze held them. Then, with utter contempt, he pointed the pistol barrel down and fired it into the floor.

The bandits did not know what to do. They had never seen this kind of behavior before. Turning his back on them, Captain Mitchell drew a cigar from his uniform coat and calmly bit off the end. He struck one of the new sulphur matches.

An old Brown Bess musket was pushed through the crowd. Cristobal held it. He fired.

Captain Mitchell staggered, but he hung on to the cigar and match. He drew on the flame, coughing from his wound. He got the cigar lit. Enraged, Cristobal grabbed another musket from his men. He fired that one, too.

The shot drove Captain Mitchell to his knees. His hand shaking, he raised the cigar for one defiant puff, but a blow from Cristobal's musket butt crushed his skull first.

The cigar fell to the cane floor with Captain Mitchell's body. Cristobal stamped out the smoldering cane with his bare foot. He looked around the hut. "Two of them are missing," he told his lieutenants. "Take some men and find them. The rest of you— bring these trunks outside. Open them and see what we have."

"*Sí*, Matachin," said one of the bandits, and they set to work.

Dan Baylor ran.

He ran for the fields, trying to outdistance the men behind him. He'd always been fast, the fastest runner in his school, but he'd never run a race like this before. He'd never run in heavy clothes and boots before, either. It was hard to get his breath in the heat, and the pistol in his hand threw off his balance. In the dark he stumbled repeatedly on the rough ground, but he managed to stay on his feet and keep going. Bare feet slapped the earth behind him.

He was almost at the tree line when a sudden spasm twisted his stomach in knots. His legs turned to rubber. He slowed and doubled over in agony. It was the dysentery. His stomach felt as if it were being torn apart. He kept moving, biting his lip, scuttling crablike toward the safety of the jungle. The *cimarrones* were right behind him now. He wasn't going to make it.

He turned. He cocked his pistol. He aimed his last shot at the lead bandit and pulled the trigger. The percussion cap went off, but the charge failed to explode. Sick, frustrated, out of bullets, Dan lowered the pistol and prepared himself for the blows of the machetes.

But none came.

Katherine Beddoes had heeded Mr. Marlow's prediction of trouble. She had gone to bed fully clothed. Her money and jewels were in a waterproof packet inside her dress. Now it had grown quiet inside the stifling hut. The jungle seemed unnaturally loud.

Katherine lowered herself from her rope hammock. She peered around the blanket that screened her from the hotel owner and his family.

The rest of the hut was empty. The family had left.

Katherine went cold. Mr. Marlow had been right. There was going to be trouble.

Just then she heard sounds from the cook hut. She recognized Cristobal's voice. There was a thud. Then an American was shouting. A pistol went off twice.

Katherine ran out of the hut and down the stairs. Instinctively she started for the hotel, to seek safety with the men. Then she stopped. She saw the *cimarrones* approaching, and she knew that their numbers would overwhelm any defense that the Americans in the hotel could make.

Where could she go? The jungle, she decided. She would lose herself in the darkness.

She turned back, and she ran straight into Ambrosio.

The usually sullen boatman grinned down at her. He took her arm in an iron grip. "Matachin wants you," he said.

Katherine knew that if she was ever going to get away, it had to be now. She bunched the knuckles of her free hand, and she punched the unsuspecting Ambrosio in the Adam's apple, the way her brother had showed her. Ambrosio bent over, choking in pain. His grip on her arm weakened, and she flew at him, scratching and kicking until he let go completely.

Katherine fled from the village. It was nearly impossible to run in her heavy crinoline and petticoats. Her legs tired quickly. Ambrosio was after her now. She could hear him gasping from the blow to his throat. He was gaining rapidly.

"Mrs. Beddoes!" said a voice. "Over here!"

Katherine turned in the voice's direction. As she did, a pistol exploded in noise and flame. Behind her, Ambrosio staggered. He dropped to his knees, cursing with pain.

In front of Katherine, a tall form loomed from the jungle. "Mr. Rawson," she exclaimed.

Wade touched Mrs. Beddoes's arm. Her wool dress was heavy with sweat. Her dark hair had come loose. "Are you all right?" he said.

"Yes," she replied, catching her breath.

Behind them, Ambrosio toppled onto his side. His curses became moans, then they stopped altogether.

Marlow came up. "Let's go," he told Wade and Mrs. Beddoes.

"Wait," said Mrs. Beddoes. "I have to take off these petticoats. I can hardly move with them on."

The two men looked away. They heard the rustle of linen.

While they waited, Marlow reloaded one chamber of his revolver. Wade marveled at the man's dexterity in the darkness. They were at the edge of the village. They could see torches around the hotel. The rest of the village was quiet. The inhabitants were either hiding, or they had fled into the jungle.

"The villagers must have known the *cimarrones* were coming for us tonight," Wade said bitterly.

"Good thinking, college boy," said Marlow. He had poured powder into the revolver's chamber; now he rammed a patch on top of it. "You don't think they were going to risk their lives for ours, do you?"

Wade and Marlow saw small groups of bandits moving through the village, checking the huts. "They're looking for us," Marlow whispered. "That gunshot got their attention." He pushed in a lead ball and seated it with the rammer. He placed a percussion cap on the firing needle. He rotated the cylinder so that one of the three loaded chambers was in firing position. He looked over his shoulder impatiently. "Are you ready, Mrs. Beddoes?"

"Yes," she said, joining them. "And call me Kathy, will you? This isn't the time to be formal."

"I'm Wade," said Wade. "And this is . . ." He didn't know Marlow's first name.

"Jack," Marlow informed him. "Now, let's go."

They rose and started off. They kept to the edge of the jungle, where the shadows were deep. Jack led the way, with Kathy in the middle. Wade brought up the rear, in case Mrs. Beddoes needed help. But she didn't. She was game, Wade thought. A lot of women would have been hysterical by now. They would have broken down, become incapable of action.

"Where are we going?" Kathy whispered.

"Downstream," Jack said. "I stole a canoe."

There was a halt while Jack scanned the open ground ahead. They saw the hotel's front clearly now. Torches lit the veranda and the street below. Bandits milled in groups. Bodies were sprawled on the steps, but no one paid them any attention. The Americans' trunks and bags were scattered about, along with the articles that had once been in them.

Kathy said, "Look, there's Cristobal."

They saw the squat bandit leader pacing back and forth. "He doesn't look happy," Jack said.

Cristobal—or Matachin, as he liked to be called—grew angrier by the moment. Where was Ambrosio? Where was that gringo woman? By all the saints, if Ambrosio was enjoying her for himself, he would pay. Mrs. Beddoes was Cristobal's share of the loot.

He stopped pacing. He took another of the sweetened biscuits from the tin box in his hand—"cookies," the box said they were called. Around him, his men still rooted through the gringos' belongings. They had begun drinking and fighting over small items, but that was to be expected. It had been a rich haul, and that could only add luster to Cristobal's reputation as a leader. True, men had been lost, but new men could be recruited. Cristobal should have been in an excellent frame of mind. But he was not. The only thing on his mind was Mrs. Beddoes.

Someone was coming. It was not Ambrosio. It was Cesar, the youngest and most ambitious of Cristobal's lieutenants. Cesar and some men were bringing in one of the escaped gringos, the red-haired one.

Cristobal forgot the woman for a moment. "Ah, Señor Dan Baylor," he said. He grinned. Cristobal was the master now. The gringo Baylor was doubled up with dysentery, wet with sweat and his own filth. Cristobal regarded the man's condition agreeably. "I bet you give me that *pistola* now, eh?"

Dan stood straight, struggling to maintain a shred of dignity. "What choice do I have? What do you want me to do, beg you? All right, I'm begging. Take the pistol. Take my money. Just let me live. Please."

Cesar was carrying the gringo's fancy pistol. He started to hand it to Cristobal. "I have reloaded it," he said.

Cristobal stopped him. "No. Let the gringo have it."

Cesar hesitated.

Cristobal motioned impatiently. "Do as I say."

Cesar handed Dan the pistol. Dan handled it uncertainly. Cristobal spread his arms, exposing his thick chest. "It is up to you, señor. You can shoot me, if you want to do that, or you can give the *pistola* to me. Then I know you really want me to have it. Otherwise, I do not want it. I mean it. I don't want it that way."

Dan swallowed. He looked around at the watching bandits. Then he took the pistol by its engraved barrel and offered it to Cristobal.

The bandit leader's pockmarked face was split by a smile. "Ah, *gracias. Gracias*, señor. My heart, she is no longer heavy."

Cristobal took the pistol lovingly. He reveled in its well-balanced feel. Then he cocked it, pointed it at Dan, and shot him in the forehead.

Dan flopped onto his back. His eyes were up in his head. Cristobal looked at his corpse and shrugged. "I told you I use it again."

Just then a bandit came running up. "Matachin! Matachin! Ambrosio is dead! The gringos have shot him!"

7

Jack Marlow didn't need to see more. "Run for it," he said.

Wade was on his knees, stunned by what he'd just witnessed. Jack shook his shoulder. "Come on, college boy. Go!" Jack grabbed Kathy's hand and led her off. Wade looked back to where Dan Baylor lay dead, then he ran, too.

Behind them were shouts, as Cristobal ordered out his men. "I want that woman," he cried. "Fifty *yanqui* dollars to the man who brings her to me."

Jack led the three Americans along a cane field. They could barely see where they were going in the dark. Kathy was hampered by her long dress and high-heeled shoes. With her free hand she held the dress up, lest she trip over it. Behind them was a yell.

Jack glanced back. "They've seen us."

They ran toward the river, straining with the effort, huffing for breath. Leaves like sword blades sliced their clothing and skin. Wade ran into a swarm of gnats. They filled his throat; they were in his eyes. He stumbled to a stop, gagging and spitting, unable to breathe or see.

Jack and Kathy came back for him. They grabbed his arms and shoved him on. "Hurry." Wade's feet moved, somehow. His eyes were full of tears and sweat and bugs. He couldn't see. He coughed violently as he ran.

They reached the riverbank and ran along it. Thick mud sucked at their feet and ankles. Their lungs burned. The jungle loomed close on the right.

"The boat's just up there," Jack gasped.

There was a flash ahead, a musket shot. The bullet buzzed by Wade's chest. The three of them halted.

"They found your boat," Wade said.

They saw men advancing on them from the direction of the boat. Behind them, the other pursuers were closing in.

"Into the water," Jack said.

They plunged through the mud, into the black water of the Chagres. It was colder than Wade had expected. He dipped his face in to wash the gnats from his eyes.

"Hold on to each other," Jack ordered.

The three of them linked arms and moved farther out. With his free hand Jack held aloft his pistol, powder flask, and bullet pouch. When the water rose to their chests, they halted. Behind them were shouts as the bandits reached the water's edge. A torch was lit. Another musket was fired. Wade did not hear the ball this time. The three of them must be invisible from the shore, he realized.

They heard Cristobal shouting orders. The bandits hurried back up the riverbank for the canoes waiting there. Jack said, "Can you swim, Kathy?"

"No," she said.

"We better not try to cross, then." Jack suddenly sounded tired. He was shivering as well. He said, "We'll float with the current. Wade and me will hold on to you, Kathy. Keep your legs moving. I know it's hard with shoes on, but it'll give you some steerage."

Jack stuck his pistol back in his belt. He jammed his powder under his hat to keep it dry, and he took Kathy's hand again. "All right. Here we go."

They pushed off, treading water. The gentle current caught them and carried them along. Wade thanked God they were below the rapids. His one arm was linked through Kathy's. With the other he paddled gently. Upstream, more torches were being lit. Wade heard splashes and the soft calling of men.

"Here they come," he said.

Just opposite them, on the shore, an alligator snapped its jaws loudly. The three Americans jumped. Kathy almost cried out. Another of the great reptiles snapped its jaws. There were scurrying, splashing noises as something entered the water.

Next to Wade, Kathy stiffened with fear. The three Americans hung in the water, treading just enough to maintain leeway, afraid that anything more would attract the alligators. They waited to be crunched by those powerful jaws. The menace was all the more frightening in the dark because they could not see it coming.

The bandits' boats were visible now, low, two-man dugouts spread in a line across the river. There were other men with torches in the bows. The boats came on slowly, searching. Wade's eyes darted from the boats to the surface of the water around him, waiting for the alligators to strike.

Wade heard another sound, a faint click. It was Jack's teeth chattering. Jack had the chills. He was shaking violently. His jaws were clenched, but he could not stop the sound.

From the boats came a startled shout. There was a collision, frightened voices. The bandits had found the alligators. Men pointed and talked at once. A sharp command from Cristobal quieted them. Cristobal waved the boats back into line and led them on.

Kathy caught Wade's attention. She flashed a worried look toward Jack. Jack didn't know where he was any longer. Wade paddled out in the water, caught the current, and let it drift him into the lead. The boats would be level with them in minutes. If they were discovered, it was death for Wade and Jack, worse for Kathy. They had to keep low in the water and hope that the bandits didn't see them. Jack could barely keep his head above water now. It was a toss-up whether the bandits would get him or he would drown. Kathy held him up, her face showing the strain. She couldn't hang on much longer.

Something loomed in the darkness ahead. A rock. There was a bungo wrecked on the rock. Wade remembered seeing it that afternoon on the way to Calosoco. He guided them toward the rock. He let the current drift them down on it. He was looking for the wrecked bungo, looking for something to grab on to.

He hit the bungo before he saw it, receiving painful blows to his chest and jaw. He caught on to the wrecked craft awkwardly. The bungo had been lying on its side, and Wade guessed that he had hit one of the gunwales. With one arm he held on to Kathy. He kept her and Jack from being swept along by the current. He gritted his teeth. His muscles cried out with the strain of holding her. With the other hand he inched himself down the side of the boat. His fingernails dug into rotten wood. He hoped there would be a space between the boat and the rock, where the three of them could wedge in unseen.

He reached the bungo's stern. Breathing hard, he moved along to the rock. Jack was dead weight. Wade could feel Kathy shifting to keep her hold on him. Wade made it to the rock. There was space for them. There was an eddy, too, which would help keep them afloat, but it was clogged with brush and deadwood that had drifted downstream and become trapped. The bandit canoes were close behind. Wade heard the splashes of their paddles. Reflected light from the bandits' torches already cast a faint glow inside the refuge.

''Put this in front of you,'' Wade whispered to Kathy, indicating the brush.

With their bodies they wedged Jack against the rock while they pushed the brush in front of them. Thorns tore their hands and cheeks. Wade prayed no water snakes were nested there, as he and Kathy built a screen between themselves and the river.

Wade motioned Kathy to stop. The bandit canoes were alongside the rock. Torchlight reflected off the water. It glinted through cracks in the brush screen.

Wade saw the boats now. Dugouts. Two men with paddles, another man in the bow, watching. There was a soft bumping as one of the canoes worked its way down the side of the wrecked bungo.

Wade and Kathy lowered themselves until only their faces remained above water. Jack was shaking so badly, Wade was afraid the bandits would hear his teeth chatter. Kathy jammed a finger into Jack's mouth. She held him tightly, trying to keep him still.

The canoe reached the bungo's stern. The man in the bow was humming ''Oh! Susanna.''

Wade and Kathy held their breaths. Kathy's lips moved in silent prayer.

The canoe turned into the eddy. The man in the bow held his torch close to the brush. It was Cristobal. In the torchlight, his pocked face was marked by deep pools of shadow.

Wade thought that Cristobal would surely see them through the brush. Wade dropped his gaze to avoid making accidental eye contact.

Then Cristobal nodded to his rowers. The canoe backed away from the bungo and moved downstream.

Wade waited until the bandits were well gone. He was shaking almost as badly as Jack. ''Come on,'' he told Kathy, and the two of them took hold of Jack. Pushing away the brush screen, they struck out for the shore.

8

With a start, Wade came to.

He lay in the mud. Hundred-foot-tall cedro trees blocked the sun, but from the brightness of the sky above the river, he guessed it was midmorning. Around him, the jungle vibrated with life. The Chagres lapped at his feet.

Then the events of the previous night came rushing back, and he came fully awake.

It had been no dream, he realized. Dan and Alex Baylor—all of them—were dead.

He heard a noise, a rasping, metallic sound. He turned.

Jack Marlow sat against a gnarled chunk of driftwood. He had broken down his pistol, and he was running a patch through the barrel. The pistol had gotten wet in the river, and it wouldn't fire again until it had been cleaned and oiled. Jack worked slowly. He'd had the fever bad last night after they'd left the river. His unshaven face was pale and gaunt. A lock of black hair hung across his forehead. His eyes had a haunted look.

"Fever down?" Wade asked him.

"For now," Jack said. "It'll be back."

"I thought you'd have slept longer."

"Can't afford to sleep. I have to keep moving. I've got Chagres fever, and it's going to get worse. If I don't get out of Panama—quick—I'm going to die."

Jack's eyes met Wade's and hung there a moment. Then Jack relaxed, and he grinned weakly. "Besides, somebody had to keep watch in case Cristobal and his boys came back."

Nearby, Kathy Beddoes stirred. There was a little bluff back of the river, and she had snuggled against it. She sat up. Her dark hair was loose, and she brushed it back from her eyes. She looked at the two men and smiled shyly. "Good morning."

" 'Morning," Jack said. He touched his battered hat brim.

29

"How are you?" Wade asked.

Kathy tried to sound chipper. "As well as can be expected, given the circumstances."

There was an awkward silence, then Wade said, "So what do we do now?"

Jack started putting the big revolver back together. "We walk," he said.

"To Cruces?"

Jack nodded. "We'll be safe there. There's a Colombian army garrison. We can buy mules and provisions and join the next east-bound convoy for Panama City—provided, of course, you got money for mules and provisions."

"My money's the one thing I do have," Wade said. "I was carrying it in my belt."

"I have mine as well," Kathy said, repinning her dark hair as best she could. Then she said, "May I borrow your knife, Mr. . . . Jack?"

Jack passed her his sheath knife. While he reloaded the pistol, Kathy hacked off the long hem of her skirt. "There," she said. "That's better. I can move my legs now."

Jack was done with the pistol. He stood and tucked it in his belt. "Better get a drink before we go," he said.

Wade rose, stretching his sore muscles. Both men gave Kathy a hand up. It was hot. The thick jungle blocked whatever breeze there might have been. The three of them smelled of sweat and the dirty river. Their hands and faces were swollen from insect bites. Their clothes were torn and bloodied. Their leather belts and footgear had developed mold from the damp. The stitching in their clothes was starting to rot. Wade had lost his peaked cap.

At the river's edge they got on their knees and drank. For once, the gritty water tasted good. Suddenly Kathy's shoulders shook.

Wade moved close to her. He started to put an arm around her shoulder, then stopped, unsure what to do. "Are you all right?" he said.

Kathy sniffed and nodded. "Yes."

"Go ahead and cry if you want. Sometimes it's better that way."

"No," she said. "I'm fine." She stood, and the two men rose beside her. With an effort she controlled herself. "I was just think-ing about those poor people back at the hotel. Mr. Catesby and the others."

"Worrying about them won't do us any good," Jack told her. "We've got to save ourselves now."

"Will Cristobal come back for us?" Kathy asked.

"Yes," Jack said bluntly. "I think he will. I think he'll come back for you."

Kathy stiffened.

"All right," Jack said. "Let's go. We'll keep to the bush. Cristobal's men will likely be watching the riverbanks."

"That's going to be a hard walk," Wade told Jack. "Can you make it?"

Jack's fevered eyes burned. "I can make it," he said.

Jack turned and started off. Kathy and Wade followed.

Upstream, the jungle became a swamp. The air reeked with rotting mangoes. The three Americans splashed through ankle-deep muck. They slipped and fell in it. They crawled over exposed mangrove roots. The *bichos* rose in clouds, devouring them. Their cuts burned from sweat. They were thirsty, and they scooped the dirty water into their mouths, trying to ignore its taste.

Wade's boots raised blisters on his feet. His wrinkled socks rubbed the blisters and made them break. Kathy's shoes burned her heels, but she knew that if she took them off, her feet would be cut to pieces. She loosened the top buttons of her dress against the heat.

Progress was slow. They could rarely use the sun as a guide, and they wandered the wrong way. At last the ground grew firmer, and they picked up a trail of sorts. The trail seemed to run parallel to the river, and they followed it, keeping a wary eye for the *cimarrones*.

The trail was narrow. They were slashed by razor-sharp leaves. They blundered into thorn-filled thickets from which they extricated themselves painfully. As they walked, they ate green plantains. They knew the plantains would make their dysentery worse, but they needed something in their stomachs.

After several hours they came to Calosoco. They gave the village a wide berth. Through the trees they glimpsed the fields, the pasture, and the huts.

Wade wondered what had happened to their dead companions. He wondered if the village priest had muttered over them. He wondered if they had been buried, or if they had been dumped into the river, food for the alligators.

Jack looked back over his shoulder. "Keep moving," he said.

Past Calosoco, it was Wade's turn to take the lead. His hands were shredded as he pushed through thorns and stands of bamboo. The day wore into afternoon. Sometimes the trail brought them in view of the river. They looked for signs of the bandits but saw none.

"I don't understand it," Wade said. "Where are they?"

"I don't know," Jack said. "But I ain't complaining."

Later Jack got the chills again. He could go no farther. He sat by the side of the trail, shaking. Kathy hesitated, then she sat beside him. She had never done anything like this, but she had to help. She took Jack in her arms, and she held him close, warming him with her body heat. He leaned against her, his head buried in her shoulder.

After a quarter hour the chills turned to fever, like the night before. Jack's forehead grew hot to the touch. Sweat poured out of him until it seemed there could be no more water in his body. He moaned, delirious. Wade found a creek nearby, and he brought back water in Jack's hat. While Wade held Jack's head, Kathy gave him water with cupped hands. She bathed his forehead and chest with a wet handkerchief. When the fever broke, Jack was left in a state of black depression, but by sheer force of will he fought through it. After a brief rest he was back on his feet, plodding along behind Wade and Kathy.

At dusk the three of them halted. There was no fire. There was no supper—their systems rebelled at the thought of more plantains. Water came from a muddy pool. Wade leaned against a bank of earth, too exhausted even to fend off the mosquitoes. His skin itched, his hair was tangled and dirty, his mouth tasted like a sewer. Ants crawled up his leg, and he didn't care. His companions lay nearby. Jack's eyes were already closed. Kathy's legs were tucked beneath her hacked-off skirt. With her willowy build, she seemed too frail for this wilderness. She didn't belong here.

In the growing darkness Wade and Kathy looked at each other awkwardly.

Wade tried to think of something to say. "It's funny," he began. "In the normal course of events, I doubt the three of us would ever have met. We're from different worlds." He waved a hand. "Now look at us."

Kathy smiled.

"How long has your husband been in California?" Wade said.

"About a year. He read Colonel Fremont's book, and he decided that California was the place to make our fortune. I waited in New York until he sent for me.''

"Then he was in California before the gold was found," Wade said.

"Yes. He was living outside Monterey when it happened. He was one of the first to join the rush. Right now he's in the southern mines, in a camp called . . . well, I shouldn't tell you what it's called.''

"Why not?"

"It's not something a lady says." Then Kathy looked around, and she laughed. "Of course, these aren't the most ladylike surroundings, are they?''

Wade laughed with her. "No. So what's the name?"

"It's called . . . it's called Sonofabitch."

Wade said. "Sounds very cosmopolitan."

Kathy raised her eyebrows. "I never pictured myself as a miner's wife, but if that's what Michael wants, I suppose I'm bound to follow." She sighed. "I wish I hadn't lost my trunk, though. I know it seems silly to be thinking about something like a trunk with all that's happened, but everything for our new home was in that trunk. There were items of sentimental value, things that can't be replaced. My wedding dress was in there." She paused, and her voice grew soft. "That trunk was the last link to my old life. Now I've lost it. Emotionally, I feel . . . adrift."

Wade nodded. "I've felt that way most of my life."

"What were you doing before you started for California?"

"Studying law. But only because I was expected to. My father's a big lawyer in New York." He laughed at himself. "I don't even know why I'm going to California, really."

"You're not going for the gold?"

"Oh, that's part of it. But it's more than the gold. It's being there. The experience. 'Seeing the elephant,' as they say."

Beside them, Jack snorted. "There's only one reason to go to California, and that's to get rich."

Wade and Kathy started. They hadn't known Jack was awake. "No," Kathy said. "I understand what Wade means. My husband was moved by the same kind of dream, I think. Something he couldn't quite control."

"That's it," Wade said. "It's like something I *have* to do. I don't really know why. I'm going to California, and nothing can keep me from it."

"Well," Jack said, "that's one thing you and I agree on." He snorted and rolled onto his side.

Neither Wade nor Kathy spoke. The jungle was loud around them. Each felt the other's closeness, and was comforted by it. Within minutes both were asleep.

9

They staggered into Cruces the next morning. Jack was on his last legs. He was getting by on grit alone. Wade and Kathy limped on blistered feet. Kathy's hair had come unpinned again; strands of it hung alongside her pale face. Their clothes were torn to pieces, falling off their backs.

Cruces was the transfer point for the Chagres basin. The river turned there, and traffic to Panama City proceeded overland. The town was bustling with military activity. Along the river wharves, Colombian soldiers and their equipment were being loaded into bungos. Another column of soldiers was marching out of town, headed downstream. The soldiers were Indians from the Colombian highlands. They were hard-bitten men, barefoot, in dirty white uniforms. Their harsh accents clashed with the soft Spanish of the Panamanians. They were led by a weary, one-eyed officer whose shoulders bore a major's red epaulettes. The major was a Frenchman, an adventurer named Leclerc, with a raffish goatee and eye patch. While the soldiers tramped by, the major and his staff questioned the three Americans about the attack on the bungo's passengers.

Wade did most of the talking. When he finished, Major Leclerc nodded sagely. "Yes," he said, "Cristobal Lopez Trujillo—El Matachin the people here call him. I've never met the fellow, but I expect to quite soon. Matachin has been a law unto himself for years, but the government has finally allocated men and money to end his reign of terror. It is a pity you could not have arrived in our country a few weeks later, *mes amis*. You would have been spared this unnecessary tragedy. If there is anything I can do for you. . . ?''

Wade shook his head. They were only a few steps from town now.

The major touched the visor of his battered kepi. *"Très bien. Madame, messieurs—*I bid you good day.''

"Bonne chance," Wade said.

The major and his staff wheeled their small horses and rode away, joining their men. The three Americans walked into town.

"That's why we didn't see any bandits," Jack said. "They got word the army was coming after them. They're on the run.''

Cruces was bigger than Calosoco, and the houses were not on stilts. Some of the more important buildings were made of adobe. There were dilapidated warehouses along the wharves. The narrow streets were jammed with wagons and crates of military goods. The smell of stables and animals was strong.

"I don't see any Americans," Wade said.

Kathy sighed. "The other passengers from the *William Tell* are probably in Panama City by now.''

"Maybe even out of the country," Wade said.

They went to the steamship office. The Pacific Mail Steamship Line kept an agent in Cruces to assist passengers in making connections. The agent was not an American, but a Panamanian named Sanchez. Señor Sanchez wore a linen suit in the heat. He smoked thin cigars and tried to seem important. He sat in a wicker chair and listened as Wade, with an occasional insert from Kathy, told the story of the Calosoco massacre and their walk to Cruces.

When they were done, Sanchez leaned back in his chair. He steepled his fingers. "Unfortunately," he said, "there will be no eastbound parties leaving—or arriving—here for some time. Our friend Major Leclerc has declared the lower part of the Chagres River a military zone. No traffic may move on the river without his permission. No travelers will be permitted to leave Chagres City until the bandit Matachin has been exterminated.''

"How long will that take?" Wade said.

Sanchez spread his fingers. "A week? A month? Major Leclerc is a thorough man.''

Wade could picture the American Argonauts in Chagres City backing up by the hundreds, dying from fever. "We can't wait that long," he said. "Mr. Marlow is sick. We have to get him out of the country. We'll go on by ourselves.''

He turned to Kathy. "Will you come with us, or stay here and wait for the next group of Americans?"

"I'll go with you," Kathy said.

"You will not be able to hire guides," Sanchez warned them. "All local labor has been commandeered by Major Leclerc to fight the bandits."

"It's only twenty miles to Panama City," Wade said. "We should be able to find our way. I mean, there's a road, isn't there?"

Sanchez laughed, "Oh, yes. A road. El Camino Real, the King's Highway. It was laid down over two hundred years ago, and no maintenance has been performed on it since. It is not a very good road, I think."

"Even so, the trip can't take more than two days," Wade said. "We'll take our chances."

"I must advise against it," Sanchez repeated. He stood to emphasize his point, gesturing with the thin cigar. "That country is extremely dangerous. There will be no one to help you should you get in trouble."

"There hasn't been anybody to help us this far," Wade retorted. "What's the difference?"

Sanchez looked put out, as if he did not think the gringo showed him the proper respect.

Kathy's soothing tone mollified him. "What he means, Señor Sanchez, is that because of this sick man, we're determined to go on. We would be most grateful if you would assist us with the arrangements."

Sanchez bowed stiffly. "I am at a lady's service, always."

Sanchez took them to a stabler, a huge, profane man who charged them one hundred dollars for four mules and their harnesses.

"Because of the military emergency, Señor Martinez is the only man in town with mules to sell," Sanchez said. "He is in a position to charge you whatever he desires. You would do well to take his price before he raises it."

Wade looked at the others. "Well?" He wondered how much of the hundred dollars Sanchez would receive back from the stabler.

Thus far, Jack had let Wade do all the talking. Now he cleared his throat. He beckoned his two companions out of Sanchez's hearing, and he said in a low voice, "I got to tell you something. I should have told you before, but . . . I got no money."

Wade stared at him. "None?"

"Not a cent. I'm sorry you went to all this trouble for me. I would have said something sooner, but you were doing so good, I hated to stop you.''

Wade was disconcerted. "How did you get to Panama without money?"

"I was working my way to California as a sailor. I signed on for a trip round the Horn, but my ship burst its boilers and had to put into Chagres for repairs."

"The Star of New York," Kathy said. "I remember seeing her in the harbor."

"The chief engineer said it would be months before she was put right. I couldn't wait that long, so I jumped ship."

"How did you get the passage money to Cruces?" Wade said. Jack grinned. "Let's say I got lucky."

Wade said, "I suppose you'd like us to lend you some money?"

"I can't deny I'd be appreciative," Jack said.

Wade turned to Kathy. "How much do you have left?"

"After we pay for the mules, about seventy-five dollars," she said.

Wade said, "I'll have a hundred and twenty-five." To Jack he said, "We can get you to Panama City, but we can't cover you all the way to San Francisco—that's a two-hundred-dollar passage."

"Just get me to Panama City," Jack said. "I'll do the rest."

Wade glanced at Kathy, who nodded. Then he said, "Come on. Let's get Sanchez and make the deal."

10

They left Cruces as soon as they could. The mules were old and tame. They gave little trouble. Three were saddled for riding. The fourth carried provisions and bedding.

From Cruces, the journey would take them across the Cordillera Central, the mountain range that snaked the length of Panama. The Cordillera began outside Cruces. The King's Highway, the Camino Real, was little more than a track through the jungle. In most places it was wide enough for only one person to pass at a time. There were no level stretches. The trail ran in two directions—up and down. It wound around narrow bends with death-defying drops to one side. The mules handled all this better than their looks indicated. They were slow but sure-footed.

The grade grew very steep. The scrawny mules tried, but they could not make it up carrying their riders. "We'll have to lead them," Wade said. "Can you walk up, Jack?"

"Sure," Jack said.

The three of them dismounted and started climbing. Wade went first, then Kathy. They led their animals by the reins. Wade led the pack mule as well. The mules were reluctant. They pulled at the reins. Wade hauled the stubborn animals by main force.

Jack fell way behind. Wade and Kathy waited on the trail for him to catch up. Kathy said, "Wade, I'm worried about Jack."

"I know," Wade said.

"I'm afraid he won't live through another attack of fever. Shouldn't he be getting one soon?"

Wade spread his hands. "I don't know. I think so. I think tropical fevers strike at specific intervals."

At last Jack caught up with them. "What are you two waiting for?" he rasped. "Keep going."

The hill seemed to go on forever. Wade's blistered feet screamed in protest. His shoulders burned from tugging the mules. His lower back hurt so bad that it went numb. Time and again he and Kathy stopped and waited for Jack to catch up. At last the trail emerged into a clearing. Jack and Kathy sat down, breathing hard. They drank from their canteens while Wade tied the mules.

They were atop one of the mountain peaks. Below them were ridge after ridge of emerald-green hills under a bright blue sky. Toward the Pacific, thunderheads piled above the jungle like towers of white fluff.

"Breathtaking, isn't it?" said Kathy.

"It would be a lot more breathtaking if we were on the far side, looking back," Jack said.

They rested awhile, then started down the other side of the hill. The path plunged back into the jungle. Around them were squawking parrots, screeching howler monkeys. The undergrowth rattled as small creatures crashed through it.

"I don't know what kind of king he was," Kathy said, "but he didn't have much of a highway."

"Just think," Wade said. "Over this trail passed silver from Peru, pearls and spices from the Philippines—the treasure of Spain's Pacific empire. They off-loaded it at Panama City on the Pacific, then walked it across the Isthmus to Portobello and Nombre de Dios on the Atlantic, for shipment to Europe."

Kathy said, "I always think of Henry Morgan's pirates leaping out of the bush to ambush them."

Surprised, Wade looked back over his shoulder. "You know about Henry Morgan?"

Kathy laughed brightly. "Yes. As a girl in the parish school I helped my brother with a library project about pirates. Just the subject for an aspiring young lady to learn about, don't you think?"

Wade grinned at her. Then he looked away. He felt guilty and ashamed. He was almost glad that the three of them had been forced to go to Panama City alone. It meant more time for him with Kathy. He could like Kathy. He could like her a lot.

"I don't remember you from the *William Tell*," Kathy said.

"I was in steerage," Wade explained. "I noticed you, though." Hastily, he added, "You were the only woman on board. You're not at all like you seemed on the boat. You were so cold, so remote."

Kathy laughed at herself. Her hair hung down all over, dirty and tangled. Her dress was torn, and in places her bare flesh showed through. One sleeve was coming off. "It's hard to be remote under these circumstances," she observed.

"It was more than that," Wade said. "You never talked to anyone."

Kathy hesitated, then she said, "I have to confess. What you were seeing was fear. I—I've never been away from home before. I've never even been away from my neighborhood. I felt so out of place on that ship, and I was terrified of making some dreadful social gaffe. I never spoke to anyone because I was afraid I'd be accused of flirting."

"What did your husband do in New York?" Wade asked.

"He was a clerk for the city."

"Have you been married long?"

"A little more than two years, but I've known Michael all my life. It was always assumed that he and I would end up together. I never really thought about marrying anyone else. Michael had a bit of education and a good job, and that meant a lot to my parents. They wanted me to have security—something they never had themselves.'' She laughed again. ''Heaven knows what they'd think of all this.''

Wade said, ''I bet they weren't happy when Michael left for California.''

''Not at *all*,'' Kathy said. She looked behind her. ''Jack, you've been awfully quiet—''

She stopped. Jack was starting to shiver again.

Kathy and Wade exchanged looks. They halted the mules and put their blankets around Jack, who slumped in the saddle. Jack's heavy revolver cut into his stomach. Wade took the pistol and stuck it in his own belt. They got back on the mules and kept going. At one point they heard Jack moan, ''Oh, Jesus.''

The chills stopped. The fever came on, burning to a red-hot peak. Wade and Kathy helped Jack dismount. They cooled him with water from the canteens. ''We can't wait here,'' Wade said. ''We'll lose too much time. There's supposed to be a village at the eight-mile point. If we keep going, we can make it before dark.''

''Jack can't ride,'' Kathy said.

''We'll tie him on,'' Wade told her. To Jack he said, ''Don't quit on us now, Jack. You've got to keep going.''

Jack looked at him with fevered eyes shrunk into his skull. He attempted to rise, and Wade and Kathy helped him. With much heaving they got him onto his mule. Wade took a length of rope from the pack and tied Jack to the saddle. Wade and Kathy remounted. Wade led Jack's mule, and they started on.

The going was slower than before. Wade hadn't done a very good job of tying Jack to the saddle, and there were fits and starts before they got it right.

At a brook they stopped to water the mules. Kathy came up beside Wade. In a low voice, so that Jack wouldn't hear, she said, ''Wade, what is he going to do in Panama City? He can't earn money for a ship out, not in his condition.''

''We'll worry about that when we get there,'' Wade said.

The village was at the crest of a low hill. It was more like a roadside farm. Another trail crossed from the north. There were a few huts on either side of the road, and a stable for mules.

The three rode in. There was no one around. A few chickens squawked in the road at their coming, but the rest of the village was quiet. The jungle had grown still as well.

Wade drew the pistol from his belt. He had never used a pistol, but its weight in his hand made him feel better. He looked at Kathy, and he could tell that she was uneasy, too.

"What is it?" she said.

"I don't know," Wade said.

There were noises. Out of the huts stepped men, seven or eight of them. They carried army muskets, and the muskets were pointed at the Americans. Some of the men were bandaged. All looked like they had seen hard times.

A last man stepped out of the late afternoon shadows.

It was Cristobal.

Cristobal carried Dan Baylor's pocket Colt. His straw hat was gone. His long hair was filthy and matted. He had been wounded in the shoulder. Blood seeped through his bandages and onto the dirty white army jacket that he wore. On the jacket's shoulders were a major's red epaulettes. Over his drawn, froglike face flashed a ghost of his old grin.

"Welcome, *muchachos*," he said.

11

Wade looked around, his thumb on the pistol's hammer. He cursed himself. He had walked right into this. He was no longer so glad that the three of them had come on alone. Cristobal's men had them surrounded—there was no escape. Wade recognized Cristobal's lieutenant, Cesar, among the bandits. Besides Cristobal, Cesar would be the one to worry about.

"*Por favor,*" said Cristobal. "Get down from your mules." His voice was weary. The long scar on his jaw stood out.

What choice was there? Wade and Kathy dismounted. Wade untied Jack, and they helped him to the ground. They rested him against one of the huts. Jack lifted his head with an effort. He looked up at Cristobal. The fever prevented him from focusing his eyes. "You son of a bitch," he said.

Cristobal might once have responded, but now he was tired. To

Wade he said, "Go easy with the *pistola*, Señor Williams. I want no trouble with you."

Wade took his thumb off the pistol hammer. "What *do* you want? Our mules? Our money?"

"I want the woman."

Kathy sucked in her breath. She and Wade glanced at each other.

Wade tried to be calm. He tried to be cold-blooded. Jack would be no help in this. Whatever had to be done, Wade must do it himself. He sneaked a look at Cesar. The young bandit's musket was trained on Wade, but his eyes were on his leader.

To Cristobal, Wade said, "What if we give her to you?"

Kathy stared at Wade in astonishment.

"If you do, then you and Señor Marlow are free to go your way," Cristobal answered. "You have my word on it."

"And if we don't?" Wade asked.

The bandit leader looked pained. "Look around you, señor. You are outnumbered. In the end, I will have this woman. I will pay a cost, though, and I am weary of killing. You yourselves have killed my oldest friend, Ambrosio. Ambrosio, from my own village. Ambrosio, with whom I first went into the jungle when we were little more than children. I have lost many men in this fight with the army. I must go to the mountains to rest and recruit new followers." He looked at Kathy. "And while I rest, I will have you by my side."

Kathy's mouth tightened. "I wouldn't count on that, señor."

"You have the spirit," Cristobal told her admiringly. "That is what first attracted me to you. A spirited mount is always the most enjoyable to tame."

"You won't tame me," Kathy promised.

The bandit leader smiled. "But you do not know my methods, señora. When I am finished, you will follow my bidding and be happy to do it." He turned to Wade. "Enough talk. Do you give me the woman, or do I take her from you?"

Wade hung his head. At first he tried to avoid Kathy's gaze. Then he looked at her helplessly. "What else can I do?" he asked her.

He turned to Cristobal, and he murmured, "All right. She's yours."

Kathy stifled a cry. "You—!"

"Bueno," Cristobal said, smiling and bobbing his head. *"Bueno."* He held out his free hand to Wade. "I must ask also for the *pistola.*"

Wade hesitated, and Cristobal spread his arms apologetically. "I need firearms for my men. The day when I could arm them with machetes is past. The rifles and *pistolas*, they are becoming as important, almost, as gold." He motioned impatiently. "*Por favor*, I must insist. Or there is no agreement."

Wade felt calm. It was as if the world were roaring about him, but he stood apart from it. "All right," he said. "I'll let you have it."

Wade raised the pistol, cocking it in the same motion. He pointed it at Cristobal and squeezed the trigger. There was a bang, and a hole appeared in Cristobal's forehead. Cristobal's eyes filled with surprise. As Cristobal fell, Wade whirled, cocking the pistol again. He was trying for Cesar, but even as he turned he knew he was too late. The young bandit had his musket leveled, his finger on the trigger. Just as Cesar fired, Kathy lowered a shoulder and drove into him, making his shot go wide. Before Cesar could recover, Wade shot him in the chest. Cesar staggered sideways. Wade cocked the pistol and fired again. Cesar's legs were jerked from under him, and he fell.

The other bandits had seen enough. They broke and ran into the jungle. The four mules ran as well, bucking and kicking. Wade ran after them. He saw some of the bandits capture them, leading them off. He fired a shot at the bandits and chased them into the bush.

"Wait!" Kathy cried. She caught up to Wade and grabbed his arm. "Let them go."

"But those mules. They have all our . . ."

"We'll never catch them now," Kathy said, holding on to him. "We were lucky this time. If we start another fight with those men, our luck might be different."

Wade's chest rose and fell. The madness drained from him. He looked at the two men that he'd shot. His mouth was suddenly very dry, and he wiped it with his free hand. After a second he turned back to Kathy. "Thanks. Cesar would have killed me if you hadn't run into him."

Kathy was trembling, but she forced a smile. "You know, I almost believed it when you told Cristobal you'd give me to him."

"I had to get him off guard somehow," Wade said.

"I wouldn't have blamed you if you *had* given me to him," Kathy said. "After all, you owe me nothing."

Wade looked into Kathy's hazel eyes. He wanted to say something, to tell her how he felt about her, but he was not sure how he felt himself. Was he falling in love with her? He had never been in love. Was this what it was like? But he couldn't love her. She was married. He felt guilty for even thinking about it. He felt unclean.

"It's all right," he said stiffly. "Anyone would have done the same."

Both Cristobal and Cesar were dead. Wade took Dan Baylor's brass-plated pistol from beside Cristobal's body, and he handed it to Kathy. He looked toward the huts, where Jack was staring at him.

"Nice work, college boy," Jack said. "There's hope for you yet."

"Thanks," Wade said. He didn't feel as though he'd done anything worthy of praise.

Jack could hardly hold up his head. "Now, check their pockets."

Wade stared at him.

"Go ahead."

Reluctantly, Wade searched the dead men's jackets. He found leather bags full of coins. There were watches and jewelry as well. "It's their share of the loot from Calosoco," Jack said. "I figured Cristobal would have it on him. Wait—what's that?"

Wade passed Jack a man's heavy diamond ring. "This belonged to Shattuck," Jack said. "Part of the profits from his years in office. It must have been too big for Cristobal to get on his finger." Jack stuck the ring in the breast pocket of his shirt.

"You're going to keep it?" Wade said.

"Of course I'm going to keep it. We're going to keep all of this. What do you want to do—leave it here for the next fellow? Throw it in the jungle for the monkeys?"

Wade said, "But . . . it's not ours."

"It is now. This ring will buy me passage out of Panama."

"He's right," Kathy said. "It wouldn't make sense to leave it."

Wade took a breath and nodded agreement. They divided the bandits' loot and stuffed it into their clothes. Kathy twisted the pocket Colt into a hole in her dress.

Jack sank back against the hut. His eyes were glazing over again. He was not looking forward to what came next. "I suppose we walk to Panama City from here?" he said.

"I wouldn't advise waiting for the train," Wade told him. He and Kathy gave Jack a hand up.

12

They moved along the jungle road. Wade was in the lead. He had taken Cristobal's machete, and he slashed at the undergrowth where it blocked their path.

Wade was shaking, not from fever, but from what he'd done to Cristobal and Cesar. He had killed them. True, they had intended to kill him, but that didn't alter the fact. He had shot them in cold blood. He had never believed himself capable of such a deed. He had never dreamed he would get the chance to find out.

He was a killer.

Bile rose in his throat. He swallowed to keep it down.

"Wade." It was Kathy, calling from the rear.

He turned. He had gotten way ahead of Jack. "He's too sick to go on," Kathy said.

Wade fought down his own feelings. "He has to go on. He'll die if he stops here. So will we, most likely."

Wade dropped back and gave Jack a shoulder. Kathy took Jack's other shoulder.

"Come on, Jack," Wade said. "You can do it. One step at a time. That's all it takes. There, that's good. Now another one. Keep going. That's it. One step at a time. Just keep doing that, and before you know it, you'll be in Panama City."

Jack hung on grimly, eyes fixed on the path ahead. The three of them fell into a rhythm, until they moved as one. They were filthy, skeletal, drawn with dysentery. Their clothing was in tatters. Wade's expensive boots were losing their soles. Jack's homespun shirt seemed to be melting away—every time Wade looked, there was less of it.

Kathy said, "It's a miracle you're still on your feet, Jack. I don't know where you get the strength. Is it California? Do you want to get there that badly?"

"I told you," Jack said. "I want to get rich."

45

"Getting rich and getting to California aren't the same thing," Wade said.

"For me, they will be."

"Is money that important to you?" Kathy asked.

"You bet it is," Jack said.

Wade trudged along, trying to ignore Jack's weight on his shoulders. "There's more to life than money."

Jack laughed. "That what they teach you in college? Well, the real world is different."

"What did you do in the 'real world'?" Wade asked.

"I did whatever I had to to survive."

"Did you ever break the law?"

"When I had to," Jack said. Jack saw Wade's reaction, and he sneered. "Go on, look down on me."

"I'm not—"

"Of course you are." Jack turned to Kathy. "You both are. You think I'm dirt."

Kathy said, "No, we don't, Jack. The fever has you—"

"The devil it does. I know what you think. But I don't mind, sèe? I'm not ashamed of what I done. You might have done the same—or worse. You just killed two men, Wade. And it was easy, wasn't it? Because you had to do it. You had to do it to live. Well, I had to do what I done. I had people depending on me—my ma, and my brothers and sisters."

"What about your father?" Kathy said.

Jack was grim. "My pa died years ago." The other two didn't expect him to say more, but he went on. "He was a construction laborer—he was Irish, and it was the only work he could get. One day a wagon rolled over his leg, broke it in four places. The drunken pig of a company doctor didn't set the leg right. There was infection, then gangrene. So Dr. Thomas—that was his name—cut the leg off below the knee. He was drunk for that, too, but he was the company doctor, and we couldn't afford no other. I helped hold Pa down. I listened to him scream. It turned out the operation was too late—the gangrene had spread above the knee. So good old Doc Thomas decided to cut off some more of Pa's leg—at the hip, this time. Fortunately, Pa died before that operation went too far.

"My ma was left with the six of us and barely a cent to her name. She took in washing to make money. She cleaned people's houses. Not rich people, neither, but people up the street—the Skelleys and the Andersons. People that didn't mind putting on airs and humiliating her. I was the oldest. It was up to me to get Ma out of that situation. Nobody would hire me for a regular job, so I did other things."

"Did your mother know what kind of 'other things' you were doing?" Kathy said.

"Not for a long time. I told her I did shift work for the railroad."

"And when she found out the truth?"

Jack said nothing.

After a while Jack went on. "Anyway, what difference does it make now? Ma's dead. My brothers and sisters can look after themselves. I'm free to make my own way. I've swore I'll never let myself be treated the way those people treated Ma. And I won't. I'll be better than all of them before I'm done."

After that Jack fell silent. They continued walking. Where the road was too narrow for all three of them, Wade helped Jack on by himself. On one especially steep grade he went back and helped Kathy as well. He put his arm around her, taking some of her weight. She sagged gratefully against him. They stayed that way to the top.

Night came over the jungle, almost without warning. The Americans dropped where they were, and slept beside the Camino Real. The nights were cool there in the highlands, and the three of them snuggled together for warmth. Later, when they were all asleep, Kathy's head slipped onto Wade's shoulder. He awoke once, but he didn't move her.

At dawn Jack's chills returned. It was the worst attack yet. Then came the fever. Jack's temperature shot up. Wade and Kathy gave him water. They bathed him, but it did no good. Jack became delirious. He moaned. His head thrashed from side to side.

Wade and Kathy slumped beside Jack, waiting for the end. Sadly, Kathy pressed Jack's hand in both her own. "What a rotten place to die," she remarked.

Wade said, "Anyplace you die is pretty rotten, I guess."

The fever seemed to have set Jack on fire. His skin was dry and brittle to the touch. His delirium deepened. He stopped thrashing. His pulse was almost nonexistent. His breath grew fainter and fainter, until he was struggling for each wispy gasp. Kathy squeezed his hand. "Fight it," she whispered. "Fight it."

Each breath seemed like it would be Jack's last. But each time he came back for another, then one more. "Fight it," Kathy urged him.

Gradually, almost imperceptibly, his breathing became deeper, more regular.

Kathy felt his forehead. "The fever's broken," she said.

Wade made a fist. "He beat it. By God, he beat it."

Jack slept, and in his sleep he refused to let go of Kathy's hand. It was as if he held a lifeline. When he woke he had a burning thirst. Wade gave him the last of the water from Cristobal's and Cesar's canteens. Then the depression came on Jack again, and he lay there, staring at a point in space, holding Kathy's hand.

Wade knelt beside Jack. He said, "We've been here a long time, Jack. We've got to go on."

Jack said nothing. He looked as if he were on the verge of slipping into a black void.

"Come on, Jack," Kathy joked. "You didn't come all this way just to die of a little fever."

Jack's lips tightened. He almost smiled. At last he croaked, "Help me up."

They got him to his feet. He dropped Kathy's hand reluctantly. They put their arms around him and started off.

It was past noon. The air seemed more humid than ever. The clouds that had been building for days moved in from the ocean. In the distance there was thunder and lightning. It came closer. The sky darkened. The wind picked up. A heavy drop smacked the palm fronds. Another. Then a lot of them, and all at once the three Americans were being battered by a terrific storm.

The rain soaked them instantly. It beat their faces. It whipped them. It washed away the dirt, the sweat, the blood. They leaned into it.

Around them thunder crashed. Lightning lit the darkness. The wind roared through the palms. A tree trunk snapped in two, with a sound like a cannon shot. The clay of the Camino Real became smooth as glass. The three of them slipped and slid as they walked.

"This is supposed to be the dry season," Wade shouted above the noise.

"Complain to the Pacific Mail Steamship Line," Kathy told him. "They make up the schedules."

There was an uphill stretch. Wade and Kathy struggled to keep their footing and walk Jack at the same time. They could hardly see for the rain in their faces. Then Wade slipped, and all three of them tumbled back to the bottom of the hill. They lay in the mud, exhausted, catching their breath.

Wade sat up. He thought about something Mr. Catesby had said.

"Do you know how long it'll take to get from Chagres to Panama City, once that railroad's built?" he asked his companions.

They stared at him.

"Four and a half hours," he told them.

Kathy sank back in the mud. "Four and a half *hours*? It takes us that long to get up a hill."

Wade looked at her, and he laughed. Kathy laughed, too. Then Jack joined in. The three of them laughed until they hurt. Around them the thunder and lightning had stopped. The rain became a steady downpour. When they could laugh no more, they got up and began climbing again.

This time they made it to the top. They half slid, half fell down the other side. At the bottom they encountered a rare level stretch, and their spirits picked up. Then they came to a stream.

The stream was in flood. There was a plank bridge. On the bridge's left side the hand rope had snapped. Some of the planking was smashed, and it dangled in the roiling water.

"It must have been hit by a rock or tree trunk, washed down by the flood," Wade said. "When we cross, it'll have to be on one side." He swore to himself. "A day ago this was probably a dry ravine."

Kathy said, "Can't we wait here for the water to go down again?"

Wade flicked his eyes toward Jack. "With *him*? Besides, who knows how long that will take?"

Kathy looked at the bridge again. "Do you think it's safe?"

"It'll have to be," Wade said.

Wade slipped his arm under Jack's shoulder. As they edged onto the bridge, Jack stopped him. "You don't have to do this, you know," Jack said.

"I know," Wade told him.

"I wouldn't do it for you."

Wade grinned. "So you say."

They started across. Wade went first, helping Jack. Then came Kathy. They shuffled along the right side of the bridge. They stepped carefully on the shattered planks, half expecting each step to be the one that broke the remaining ropes and sent them plunging into the water. Wade gripped the single hand rope as hard as he could. It was hard to reach around Jack's thick chest. The unbalanced bridge swayed wildly. It threatened to flip over. Each step seemed to take forever. Behind Wade, Kathy's eyes were half closed with fear. She refused to look down at the surging water. Jack held the hand rope as best he could, but he didn't have much strength. The bridge swung wildly. Jack fell back against Wade. He knocked Wade's right hand from the rope. For a moment Wade thought they were both lost, then his flailing fingers found the rope again. He pulled his hand onto it. He threw his weight against Jack, steadying him. His feet slipped on the wet planking.

Behind him, Kathy said, "Oh, God. You had me scared." She was down on one knee until the bridge stopped swaying. She breathed with relief—and with something more. Wade saw it in her eye, and she knew that he had seen it.

When the bridge had steadied, they went on. There was not far to go. Wade was within two steps of the other side. He had made it. He let out his breath.

Behind him was a loud snap, and a cry. He turned. A section of planking had given way. He saw Kathy in midair, in slow motion it seemed, arms waving back toward the broken bridge. Then she was under the bridge and in the water, whirling away.

"Kathy!" Wade yelled.

Wade heaved Jack across the remaining foot of bridge. He dropped him to the ground, then he jumped into the water after Kathy.

The water was cold, colder than the Chagres. It turned him, it buffeted him. He felt for the bottom, found none. He was swirling around. He bounced off something, and knew he was lucky his ribs weren't broken. He saw Kathy's dark hair ahead of him.

He swam for her, battling sideways to the current. He swallowed water. His stroke faltered, but he recovered. His arms were tiring. He bore down on her. She floundered against the current to get to him. She was close. He reached for her and missed. He reached again and caught her this time by the forearm. Still fighting the current, he pulled her to him and grasped her securely under the breast. They were plunged underwater, came up sputtering but still linked together. Wade stroked for the side of the stream. He kicked with as much strength as he had left. Soon the current's hold on them slackened. Wade saw a cove and swam into it.

They found footing at the cove's entrance. Kathy stumbled into the slack water and bent over, coughing and gasping for breath. She straightened as Wade joined her. What was left of her dress was sculpted to her. It revealed every curve of her body, the firm upthrust of her breasts.

They looked at each other. Then Wade took her in his arms and kissed her. She responded eagerly, hungrily. They pressed their wet bodies together, as if trying to make them one. They ground their lips. They dug their fingers through each other's matted hair.

Then they realized what they had done, and they drew back, trembling. It was all they could do to control themselves. Their breathing sounded loud even in the rain. Wade's heart battered his chest wall. He wanted to press Kathy to him. He wanted to kiss her again and never stop, and he knew that Kathy wanted the same.

"I . . . I'm sorry," he said at last.

"It was as much my fault as yours," Kathy said. She looked down as if she did not have the courage to face him, as if unsure of what she might do.

After a long second Wade stepped close to her again. "Kathy, I wish we had met . . ."

She raised a finger to his lips, quieting him. "I do, too. But we can't think like that, or we'll drive ourselves crazy."

"Your husband's a lucky man."

"Please. Don't talk about Michael. I don't know what my feelings are for him. Not anymore."

Wade held her hands lightly. "Why does it have to be like this?"

She shook her head.

"I'll never forget you, Kathy."

"I won't forget you, either," she said.

They stood that way a long moment. Then Kathy smiled slyly. "Hadn't we better get Jack?"

Wade laughed. "I guess we should."

They made their way back upstream, hand in hand. It was raining lightly now. Toward the south the clouds showed signs of breaking up. "There were times the last two days that I hoped we'd never get to Panama City," Kathy confessed. "I know it was selfish of me, with Jack so sick, but I couldn't help it."

"I've felt the same," Wade told her.

"Will we split up in Panama City?" she asked.

"I don't know," he said. "We *should*."

"Do you want to?"

"No."

They smiled.

They didn't talk anymore. They didn't have to.

Jack waited for them near the ruined bridge, sitting against one of the supports. When he saw them coming, he struggled to his feet. There was emotion in his face, but it was hard for him to put it into words. "I . . . I'm glad you're back, Kathy. Real glad." He glanced at Wade as if he wished Wade weren't there.

Kathy leaned her head against Jack's broad shoulder. "Thanks, Jack."

Jack looked like he wanted to say more, to do more. But he didn't. Maybe he felt ill at ease with Wade there—or maybe he, too, remembered that Kathy was married.

The three of them linked arms and started walking again. Less than two hours later the mountains suddenly dropped away, and they saw the distant spires of Panama City.

13

Panama City was a town of almost eight thousand people. Its massive ramparts had been built after the original city had been sacked by the pirate Henry Morgan in 1671. Outside the walls were hundreds of tents, most of them occupied by Americans. The Americans were cooking, holding cock fights, lazing about.

Wade, Jack, and Kathy came up the Cruces road. People stopped what they were doing to stare at them. The three newcomers were filthy, starving, half naked, and holding each other upright. They were covered with cuts and bruises, their faces disfigured by insect bites. Kathy's dark hair was long and matted. Her clothing was in total disarray.

"Lookit her, will you," the men nearby said. "Lookit that pistol in her dress."

Kathy had felt natural with Wade and Jack. Now she was embarrassed by the stares of these strangers. "At home I'd get locked up for looking like this," she said.

"You look fine," Wade told her.

The men pressed closer. "What happened to you all?"

Wade related their story. "This man is sick," he concluded, indicating Jack. "He needs to get on a ship right away."

That remark drew gales of laughter from the assembled Argonauts. "Get in line, sonny," said an older man. "Some of these boys been here a month."

"A month!" said Wade. "But the steamship line promised there'd be ships here to take us to San Francisco."

"There's ships, all right," said the old-timer, "but they're always full by the time they get here."

Wade said, "But we have tickets. They guarantee that—"

He stopped in the face of more laughter. The old-timer said, "I just used my ticket to roll me a *cigarito*. I reckon it's the only use I'll ever have for it."

"But Jack. He'll die . . ."

"He'll have lots of company," said a big southerner. "We got cholera here, and plague, too. They got them a real good graveyard going up on Ancon Hill."

"So what are we supposed to do?" Wade said.

"Get in line and wait," repeated the old-timer. "Now and again some gets on. Things go right, I figure to be out of here in three or four weeks."

The crowd began breaking up. Wade and his friends had outlived their value as a diversion.

An angular young man in a cutaway coat approached them. He had an open, friendly appearance, and his plug hat was pushed back on his head. "Excuse me," he said. "My name is Ralph Bannister. And there *is* one way out, if you're interested. Some friends and I are repairing an old cattle scow we bought at auction down the coast. We're going to sail her to San Francisco. Some of my friends are from Maine, and they know about boats. The rest of us are providing money and unskilled labor. We need more crew."

"I'm hardly a sailor," Kathy told him.

"You could help with the cooking," said the young man.

"San Francisco's twenty-five hundred miles," Wade said. "Will your cattle scow make the trip?"

The young man shrugged. "I don't know, to be honest. These Maine boys seem to know their business, though, and it's better than rotting here with fever and boredom."

"When do you sail?" Wade asked.

"In a week, perhaps."

Wade shook his head. "Mrs. Beddoes and I might be able to wait that long, but Jack here has to get passage out of the country right away."

"Yes, I see," said the young man. "Well, I wish you luck."

Bannister left. Wade and the others passed through the gate and into the city. The streets of Panama City were narrow and crowded. The shops all had signs in English, to attract Americans. The windows and balconies were decorated with ornate metal scrollwork. Refuse was piled high, causing a terrible stench. The ubiquitous barrels of rainwater stood on every counter. They passed a handcart carrying a dead Argonaut to the cemetery. The body was wrapped in a dirty sheet with the dead man's slouch hat on top. Two mourners followed behind. Jack stared after the little procession. Wade and Kathy tried not to look at him.

At an overpriced *fonda*, Wade and Kathy gorged on a beef stew called *ropa vieja*, rice cooked in coconut milk, and broiled red snapper caught that morning off the seawall. They washed it down with jugs of guava juice until their shrunken stomachs protested in pain. Jack just watched. He had no appetite. Afterward, they all purchased new clothes, then went to a bathhouse to get cleaned up.

Wade and Kathy were done first. They met on the street outside the bathhouse. Kathy wore a new blue dress and a wide-brimmed straw hat beneath which her dark hair had been washed and combed to a lustrous sheen, though in a looser style than before. Wade hardly recognized her. She had taken Dan Baylor's pistol from her old dress. She handed it to Wade, who put it in his belt, along with Jack's.

They looked at each other self-consciously. "It doesn't seem the same, does it?" Kathy said.

"No," said Wade. "It doesn't." Only that morning he had taken Kathy in his arms and kissed her. Only yesterday he had killed two men.

Jack rejoined them. New clothes and a cleanup only made him look worse. Time was running out for him, and there was nothing anyone could do.

Wade said, "We'd better see about accommodations for the night. Then in the morning, we can—"

"Ship!" came a cry. "There's a ship in the harbor!"

The cry was taken up throughout the city. Men began rushing toward the shore, shouting and pushing. "Come on," Wade said.

Jack touched Wade's arm. "I'll have my pistol back now." Wade handed him the big revolver, and the three of them joined the crowd headed for the beach.

The street ended at the Bovedas, the old Spanish seawall. Men crowded along the wall, jostling for spots. A few had telescopes trained out to sea. Far out in the bay, past the fishing canoes and the lines of pelicans riding the waves, the top masts of a ship could be seen.

"A three-master," said one of the men with the telescopes. "Yankee built, by the look of her."

A cheer went up.

"Why do they anchor so far out?" Wade asked his neighbor.

"Water's too shallow to come any closer," the man said.

The crowd on the seawall grew, spilling onto the *playa*, or beach, below. After a while a beetlelike shape with sweeping arms drew into shore from the direction of the ship.

"She's landing a boat!"

By the time the longboat's crew dragged their craft onto the *playa*, they were confronted with a wall of shouting, waving Argonauts. The seamen picked muskets from the boat and formed up. The officer, who wore a captain's frock coat, held a pistol.

"What ship is that?" men cried.

"The *Achilles*," said the captain, "formerly out of Boston, now based in San Francisco." The captain was a flinty, lantern-jawed New Englander who looked afraid of nothing.

"How many berths do you have?" men screamed. Some waved bags of coins.

"None," shouted the captain. "We're full up."

There was shouting, cursing, and moaning. Somebody threw a bottle.

"Even our decks are full," the captain told them. "There's no hope of taking on more. We've put in here only to deliver mail to the U.S. consulate."

The crowd moved closer to the boat. The nervous seamen presented their muskets.

Somebody yelled, swearing. "We'll make you take us to California. We'll swim out to your ship, and you'll have to let us on board."

The captain shook his pistol at them. "You do, and a bellyfull of lead is what you'll get."

The crowd roared its anger. They surged forward. The captain gestured, and half the seamen fired their muskets in a volley over the heads of the crowd.

That stopped the rush. It quieted the angry Argonauts, many of whom dropped to the sand in fear.

While the first seamen reloaded, the second group aimed their muskets menacingly. "The next volley will be into your guts," the captain warned. "I'll brook no interference with the operation of my ship."

The first group of seamen mounted guard over the longboat. The second group fell in behind the captain, who said, "Now, I'll thank you gentlemen to let us through."

Sullenly, the crowd parted. The captain and his escort, with muskets at half cock, marched up the beach and into the city. Wade and Kathy looked at each other dispiritedly.

"Where's Jack?" Wade said.

"Oh, God," Kathy said. "You don't think he's sick again, do you?"

"He must be," Wade said. He pictured Jack, delirious, lying in one of the filth-strewn streets. "Come on, we have to find him."

14

The *Achilles*'s captain, whose name was Adair, led his party into town. The clamoring crowd dropped behind them. After depositing the mail sack at the consulate, Adair left his men with instructions to meet him on the beach the next morning at dawn. Then he set off alone.

His path took him to the Calle Negro, a narrow street not far from Cathedral Plaza. It was almost dark. Weak lights from shuttered windows provided the only illumination on the street. The captain never noticed the shadowy form following him.

On the Calle Negro mingled the sounds of rough voices, laughter, and women. Somewhere a guitar strummed. Captain Adair went into a dilapidated cantina. Once inside, his New England flintiness seemed to fall away. His shoulders lost their rigidity. A smile broadened his face. The cantina's proprietor beamed and came forward. "Señor Adair, it is good to see you."

"How are you, Manuel?" said Adair. He looked around the

crowded, smoky room full of sailors and red-shirted Argonauts, with women in low-cut blouses sitting on their laps. "Where's Maria?"

"I get her," Manuel told him. "She will be glad to see you. She talks about you all the time. She misses you very—"

"Just hurry and tell her I'm here, will you?" Adair said.

Adair sat at a table in the corner. Manuel left him a bottle of rum and a jug of orange-lemon juice. Adair loosened his string tie and collar. He pushed his cap back on his head and poured himself some rum and juice.

A tawny young woman ran up to him. "James!" she squealed, and she threw her arms around his neck. She was sixteen.

Adair pulled the girl onto his lap and kissed her. He had not slept with his wife in over ten years, and these visits to Maria were what he lived for. She giggled as he nuzzled her neck. The giggles turned to sighs as he kissed her ear.

He stopped. A man had joined them at the table.

The newcomer was broad-shouldered, with a lock of dark hair that hung from beneath his slouch hat. His face was pale and feverish. His eyes were haunted. God only knew what was keeping him upright.

The newcomer pulled up a rickety chair and sat, smiling. "Evening, Captain."

Adair let go of Maria, who took another chair. "Who are you?" Adair asked.

"The name don't matter, Captain. It's what I want that's important. And that's passage north on your ship."

"No. Didn't you hear. . . ?"

"Save the speeches, Captain. I been a seaman. I know how things work. You can get me on board if you want. I'll make it worth your while."

Adair peered down his nose. "So will a lot of people. Men wealthier than you. But I'm not interested, d'ye hear? My ship's overloaded now. I wouldn't be carrying this many if the owners weren't making me. By all that's holy, if we run into rough weather, I'm worried that—"

Jack dropped a bag of coins onto the table. "The fare to San Francisco is two hundred and twenty dollars. There's four times that here."

"I've been offered more," Adair said. "Now, get out of here

before I throw you out. You can walk to San Francisco for all it interests me."

Jack looked around the dimly-lit tavern. No one was paying attention to them. He drew his pistol. He lay the pistol on the table, covering it with his arm. Still smiling, he spoke in a low voice. "You give me passage or you won't walk out of here alive."

Adair sneered. "D'ye think I haven't been threatened before? You won't shoot me."

Jack cocked the pistol. He shifted it so the barrel pointed toward Adair. In the lamplight, sweat glistened on his face. "I'll do it, Captain. I'll do it right now. If I don't get out of Panama, I'm a dead man, and I sure won't mind taking you with me. Hell, I'll be happy for the company."

Next to Adair, Maria stared, wide-eyed.

Jack went on. "You have a choice, Captain. Overload your ship a little more and make a tidy profit, or die right here."

Adair licked his lips. He realized that Jack was crazy enough to do it. "All right," he said. "You can go. We'll fix you a berth on the hurricane deck."

"Oh, I forgot to tell you," Jack said. "It ain't just me. There's three of us."

"Three—! But that's impossible!"

"I don't think I like that word," Jack told him. "Let me repeat. There's three of us. One is a lady. An American lady. My friend and I will accept accommodations on deck, but the lady requires a stateroom."

"It's impossible, I say. I don't have a free stateroom."

"I said, I don't like that word," Jack told him. Jack kept the pistol pointed at Adair. With his free hand he reached into his trousers pocket. He brought out Shattuck's diamond ring and sat it on the table in front of the sea captain.

"Pick it up," Jack said.

Adair did. He looked at the massive gold ring and its cut stones. "Where did you get this?"

"As a matter of fact, I found it in the jungle. What do you think of it's worth?"

Adair held the ring up to the light. "Five thousand, at least."

"I'd say that's a good guess. It's yours if you get the lady a stateroom."

Adair ran his tongue around the inside of his mouth thoughtfully. "There *is* a cabin with a greaser couple in it. They could be forced to move to the hurricane deck. They don't even speak English so what can they do about it?'' He looked at the ring again and made his decision. "Be on the *playa* tomorrow at dawn with your two friends. You can row out to the ship with me."

"Thanks, Captain. I knew you'd come around."

"How do you know I won't double-cross you?" Adair said.

Jack snatched the ring from the captain's hand. "I don't. That's why you don't get *this* until we're safely aboard and at sea. The money, you'll get on the *playa*."

"All right," Adair said. "Now, if you'll excuse me, I have business with the lady."

Jack rose, grinning. He flipped the captain a mock salute. "So long, shipmate."

Outside the tavern, it was night. Jack started down the dark street. He had to find Wade and Kathy. He'd start looking in nearby Cathedral Plaza. As he walked, he used the walls of buildings for support. He was short of breath. His muscles felt weak. He prayed that the fever would hold off till they were out to sea, where the fresh air would help cure him.

Cathedral Plaza was crowded with Americans. The air was heavy with the smell of unwashed men. There were people playing banjos and guitars, men dancing among themselves. There were men playing cards, drinking rum, smoking cigars. Others laughed and flirted with the native girls. Still others slept on the steps of the twin-spired cathedral, from boredom or drunken stupor, and passing natives who saw the sacrilege crossed themselves hurriedly.

Wade and Kathy were easy to find. Kathy was the only American woman in the plaza, and there was a crowd around her. Jack pushed his way through until he reached them. He grabbed Wade's shoulder.

"Jack!" said Wade. "Where have you been? We looked all—"

"Come on, amigos," Jack said. "It's time to *vamos*."

"What do you mean?" Kathy said.

"I mean we're leaving. Sailing on the *Achilles*."

"Are you serious?" Wade said.

"Yes. We leave at dawn. It's all arranged."

Wade and Kathy were stunned. "But how did you do it?" Kathy asked.

Jack grinned at her. "You just have to know how to talk to people."

15

The sun was not yet up when the seamen ran the longboat off the *playa*. The *Achilles*'s three new passengers laughed with delight as native bearers carried them through the surf and set them in the boat. Two hours later, the *Achilles* had weighed anchor, and they were standing across the bay with the island of Taboga hard on the starboard beam.

While Kathy was shown aft to her stateroom, Wade and Jack wedged along the ship's waist with the other deck passengers. There were men of many nationalities there, along with a few women, all headed north to strike it rich. They were sheltered from the elements by an awning that the crew had rigged from old sails and tarpaulins. They slept on their baggage and the mining equipment they carried with them.

The sun was up. Panama City was already lost to view. Only the green hills could be seen in the distance. For the first time in many days, Wade found the tropic air refreshing. Just the knowledge that he had escaped Panama seemed to have given Jack new strength.

Wade said, "Jack, I've been wondering. I don't know what your plans are, but . . . well, I wondered if you'd want to throw in together. When we get to California."

Jack looked at him. "Be a miner, eh?" He grinned slowly. "All right, college boy. You got yourself a partner."

They shook hands on it.

Kathy joined them. She'd taken off her bonnet, and the sea breeze ruffled her dark hair. Already there was color in her cheeks.

"How's the stateroom?" Jack asked her.

"Tiny," she said, "but it seems like heaven after the last few days." She looked around the crowded deck. "I wonder which of these gentlemen gave up his berth for me?"

Jack had told her that the stateroom had been surrendered by a man who had heard the story of her ordeal and taken pity on her. He shook his head. "I have no idea."

"I wonder why they hadn't done the same for some of these foreign ladies."

"These ladies haven't been through what you have," Jack said. "Anyway, they're greasers. Compared to the way most of them live at home, living on the deck of a ship is probably an improvement."

Kathy looked like she didn't agree. She started to say something, but Jack told her, "Don't worry. They paid their fare; they knew what they were getting."

Not far away, amid coiled ropes, baggage, and mining equipment, sat a dark-skinned man and his pregnant wife. The woman looked worried, and the man patted her hand in reassurance. Wade and the others paid them scant attention. They had no way of knowing that this was the couple who had been evicted from their cabin for Kathy.

Elena Soto was young and beautiful. Her face and dress gave evidence of good breeding, and she looked particularly healthy. She glanced toward Kathy. "I suppose that is the one to whom we have lost our cabin?"

"I suppose," said her husband, Juan. He was an eager young man with a red bandanna tied around his head. He came from a good family, but he had left them years before to mine for gold.

"It is not right," Elena said. "We paid our passage money."

Juan patted her hand again. "I know. I know. But it is only for a few days. Then things will be good for us, you'll see."

"I worry for the baby, Juan, here on the deck. What if the weather turns bad? What if I should fall sick and—"

"The weather will be good this time of year," Juan told her. "You worry needlessly."

Suddenly, Elena grimaced. She shifted uneasily.

"What is it?" her husband asked.

A strange look came over her. "The baby . . . he kicked me." Juan grew excited. "Really?"

"He has a hard kick. I am certain it is a boy."

Juan beamed.

Then Elena's face darkened again. "He will be born in a foreign land, Juan. Not in Chile."

"We will be in California only a short while. I am good at my trade of mining, you know that. With a strike as rich as this one, I'll be able to make a sizable amount in a short time—a year, perhaps. Then we will go home, and I will buy you the orange groves that I showed you outside Santiago, and I'll never wander again."

Elena smiled hopefully. "That would be good." Then she added, "Are you really glad I came with you, Juan?"

"Yes, of course, my darling. My only fear is that you are not used to a miner's life. You are a physician's daughter. You have known comfort, servants. What if your parents were right, and the mines should prove too rough for you?"

"I am your wife, Juan. Where you go, that is where I want to be."

Squeezing hands, they walked to the rail and stared north, toward California.

Part II

SEEING THE ELEPHANT

16

The two mules picked their way along the trail. Kathy Beddoes rode one. Wade Rawson and Jack Marlow drove the other, which was laden with supplies.

They were on the Miners' Trail, which ran from Stockton up to the diggings. It was warm and sunny, their fourth day out of Stockton, which they had reached by schooner from San Francisco. Before that had been the long sea voyage from Panama. Jack no longer suffered attacks of fever, but he had not regained his full strength. They had been camping early each night to give him more time to rest.

Kathy rode astride. There had been a time when sitting astride a mule would have embarrassed her. Now she thought nothing of it. The other mule clinked and clattered under its load—picks, shovels, crowbars, oversized flat-bottomed pans. These items were much more expensive at the mines, so Wade and Jack had purchased them in Stockton. They had purchased food as well—flour, bacon, coffee, sugar, salt, and beans. They were down to their last few dollars, both of their own money and that which they had taken from the bandits in Panama.

The trail was worn smooth from use by man and animal. All along it were discarded coats and boots, abandoned tools, packs, and coffeepots. There were bones of dead horses and mules. Here and there, among the trees or grassy hummocks, were little mounds. Some of the mounds had been dug open, apparently by animals, and their contents disturbed or dragged away.

The trail dropped over a ridge and into another valley, still green from the spring rains. In the distance they could make out the course of a river. Wade said, "That should be the Merced. That's where we're going."

Hooves sounded behind them. They turned to see a young man—

a boy, really—riding a mule. Large canvas sacks hung from both sides of the boy's saddle. The boy slowed his mule as he passed them. He stared at Kathy, and his jaw dropped. Kathy couldn't help but laugh.

The boy recovered. He was about nineteen, not tall, with large dark eyes and a smile that seemed to spill out of his ample mouth, as if he couldn't contain it. "I'm sorry for staring, ma'am, but I've never seen a woman in these parts."

"It's all right," Kathy said. "I'm used to being stared at."

The boy fell in with them. "You folks going to be miners?" he asked.

"They are." Kathy said, indicating Wade and Jack. "I'm here to join my husband. He's in a camp called Sonofabitch. Do you know it?"

"Know it? Sure I know it. It's at the head of Coleman's Creek. I'll be stopping there about suppertime. I'll take you there if you like."

"All right."

The boy looked to Wade and Jack. "You going to Sonofabitch, too?"

"I guess," Wade said. He looked at Jack.

"It's as good a place to start as any," said Jack.

They made their way toward the distant river. The boy said his name was Billy. He had been an apprentice pipe fitter in Providence, Rhode Island, but he had run away to sea. His ship had docked in San Francisco the previous summer. There he had learned of the gold strike, and he had deserted, along with the entire ship's crew—including the captain—and come to the diggings.

"Right now I carry mail for the boys at the mines," he said. "That's what's in these sacks. There's no post office up there, see, and lots of fellows haven't heard from home in a year. So I volunteered to go down to San Francisco and collect all the letters I could find for the boys. I'm charging two dollars a letter to bring them back." He laughed. "I'm making more doing this than I would from my claim."

Kathy said, "I wrote to Michael seven months ago."

"I probably got your letter in here, then. It sure didn't come up before. When we get to Sonofabitch, you can hand it to him yourself."

Wade said, "What are these mounds we keep seeing along the trail?" He pointed to one, visible through the trees.

"Graves," Billy said. "They're men who stayed in the mountains last winter and ran out of food. They tried to make it down to Stockton, but they died of hunger or sickness. The men who came up in the spring buried them."

Wade, Jack, and Kathy exchanged looks.

They crossed the Merced at a ford. The trail to the diggings ran up the right side, but right now the trail was alive with ragged, bearded men coming downriver. There were men on horseback and muleback. There were men carrying packs, men pushing wheelbarrows, merchants with mule trains full of goods. At the ford these men turned south, crossing the ridgeline toward the next river. Billy halted his mule. "Hey, friends!" he cried. "Where's everybody going?"

One of the miners called back. "They've found color on Mariposa Creek. Get there quick if you want the best claims!"

"How's the diggings around Sonofabitch?" Wade asked.

The miner looked back over his shoulder. "There's still good pay, but the best claims are taken."

Wade looked at Jack, then Kathy. "The Mariposa. If that's where the gold is, that's where Jack and I should be going."

Jack nodded, reluctantly it seemed. Kathy struggled to keep her face from falling.

"We're almost broke," Wade explained to Kathy. "We have to find gold quickly. Billy will see you to your husband."

This was the best way to end it, Wade realized. Better a clean break. He would just have been in the way once Kathy was reunited with her husband. He'd have been making a bad situation worse.

Kathy swung down from her mule. "This is so sudden," she said. "After all this time together."

She hugged Wade and Jack in turn. She fought back a tear. "I'm going to miss you two, you know that?"

They didn't answer. They didn't have to.

Kathy's hazel eyes searched Wade's briefly, desperately. There was so much they wanted to say but couldn't. Wade felt as if his heart were being torn apart. He and Kathy had managed to control themselves since that fateful day in Panama, but it had required a supreme effort of wills. They had known this moment lay at the end of their journey. Now they wanted to kiss each other good-bye, but they couldn't. Not with Jack and Billy looking on.

Jack turned away. He knew Wade and Kathy loved each other. He didn't care. Kathy liked him, too. She must. She could love him if given half a chance. He remembered the soft feel of her hands around his, the sensuous urgency of her voice when she had talked him back from death. He had fallen in love with that voice. It had kept him alive. To Jack, Kathy was the perfect woman. A lady. Anyone else, and he'd have gone into that shipboard cabin the first night and had his way with her. He was a gentleman, though, or he would be one day. Kathy was a married woman, and a gentleman must honor her vow. He'd have Kathy properly, or he wouldn't have her at all.

Kathy kissed each man on his bearded cheek. "Good-bye," she said.

Wade held her hands for a second. "Good-bye."

"Be seeing you," Jack said, more laconically than he felt.

Wade helped Kathy back into the saddle. It was his last time to touch her. A feeling of profound despondency ran through him. Then Kathy and Billy started off, fighting the current of miners coming down the Merced. Kathy's slender form bobbed to the rhythm of the mule. Once she looked back and waved. Then she vanished around a bend in the river.

Wade and Jack stared after her for a long minute. Then they urged their mule forward, and they joined the long line of men heading for the Mariposa.

17

Wade and Jack topped the ridge. To the east lay the towering Sierras. Between the ridge and the mountains stretched row after row of rugged hills, like waves on the ocean. The hills were dotted with chaparral and groves of oak. Wild oats grew in profusion. Below the two men, a river wound down from the mountains. In the sunlight the water sparkled. Birds were singing.

"It's beautiful," Wade said. "Like paradise."

Jack said, "Who cares what it looks like? As long as it makes us rich."

Up and down the river valley they saw men moving singly and in groups. They spread through the hills, up the streams, gulches, and arroyos. Tents sprang up like mushrooms.

Wade and Jack reentered the line of miners. The trail switch-backed down the steep ridge. In places the trail was so narrow that they had to hug the hillside lest they slip and fall to the bottom. As they descended, the valley looked different. The hills that had seemed so beautiful from above now hemmed them in on all sides.

They reached the bottom. Nearby, a merchant had staked out his line of mules, his *mulada*. He was selling food and mining supplies out of the animals' packs. Another merchant peddled bottles of whiskey from a wooden crate. The prices were astronomical—a dollar for a pound of flour, double that for bacon. Ten dollars for whiskey.

Jack whistled. "At these prices, we'll need to get rich just to keep eating."

Wade nodded. "We have to get a claim first."

"How do we do that?"

"How do I know? Follow the crowd."

They drifted upriver with the flow of miners. They passed men setting up tents and building lean-tos. Other men were digging holes and carrying dirt to wash in the stream. Wade and Jack tried to watch how to do it without looking too obvious.

After some miles the crowd of miners thinned out. Wade and Jack were almost alone when they encountered a man carrying a can of cooking grease. The man was English, and he offered to help them find a claim. "I was up at the mines last year, y'see, so I know a bit about it."

The Englishman's name was Sam Trumbull. He was short and burly, with a thick brown beard. He walked with a rolling gait, like a sailor. Tufts of chest hair poked over the top of his checked shirt. He and his partners had just gotten to the valley the day before.

Sam led them away from the river and up a narrow side stream. " 'Ere's a likely spot," he said. "Yer want to pick a place where the stream bends or drops. Where sediment's deposited, that's where yer find gold. It's 'eavy and it sinks to the bottom, yer see, so the best pay's down around the bedrock. Yer allowed a claim of twenty-five square feet a man, from the center of the stream back to the ridge. Put up stakes at the boundaries, wiv yer names on them. If yer gone more than three days wivout good reason, the claim's

considered vacant. Register ye claim wiv the alcalde, when we elect
one.''

Wade and Jack thanked Sam, who took his leave.

Though there were hundreds of men in the vicinity, Wade and
Jack felt alone among the hills. "It's so peaceful, it's hard to think
about work," Jack said.

"Look in your purse," Wade told him. "You'll start thinking
about work real quick.''

They picked what looked like a good place, and they marked off
a claim as Sam had suggested. They cut firewood, and while Jack
cooked their supper of pork and beans, Wade set up the tent. He
picked a level spot away from the stream. There was a clump of
brush in the way. He dug up the brush with his shovel and pulled
it out. He started to fill in the hole, then stopped. Something glittered in the dirt. Wade picked it up. He rubbed it and blew it clean.

"Jack! Look!"

Jack came over. Wade handed him the object. It was slightly
bigger than Jack's thumbnail, shapeless like a piece of chewed meat.
Jack held it up. In the fading light of afternoon it seemed to glow.

"So, that's gold," Wade said.

"Get the scales," said Jack.

Wade fetched the portable scales they'd purchased in Stockton.
The nugget weighed five and a half ounces. Wade figured in his head.
"At sixteen dollars an ounce, that works out to . . . eighty-eight
dollars. Forty-four for each of us. Jack, this is a good omen.''

They searched for more nuggets in the fading light but found
none. They finished putting up the tent, fed the burro, and ate
supper. "That's the end of the pork and beans," Jack said.

"That's all right," Wade told him. "We'll be eating oysters and
champagne soon.''

Darkness came, and Jack turned in. In the light of the dying fire,
Wade took a last look at the gold nugget. Then he lay down and
wrapped himself in his blankets. Outside the tent the night came
alive with the howling of coyotes. Wade heard distant laughter, and
shouts.

Jack was asleep quickly. Wade lay awake. He was thinking about
Kathy. Kathy was with her husband Michael by now. She was lying
in his arms. The idea upset him. He hated Michael. He knew it
was unfair, but he couldn't help it. He pictured Kathy before him
in the darkness—slender and pale, with hazel eyes and full lips,
and a smile that seemed for him alone. He heard once again the

bell-like richness of her laugh. Her image stayed with him a long time, then he drifted into an uneasy sleep.

18

The next morning they began to search for gold in earnest. They began outside their tent, near where they'd found the nugget.

They dug down to bedrock. It took them a while. They were sweating in the bright sun, and they took off their shirts. "Where's some more of them nuggets?" Jack complained, wiping his brow. "That's how I like mining gold—picking it off the ground."

Finally they struck bedrock. They knelt in their hole, which was about six feet square, and examined the rock. Sam had told them the rock was sometimes veined with gold, but here that was not the case. They picked up the loose dirt and sifted it. Wade thought he detected a faint glitter. They filled buckets with the dirt and carried them to the stream, ready to pan.

Panning, as Sam Trumbull had explained it, was easy. You mixed water with the dirt and swirled out a little of the mixture at a time. Since gold was heavier than dirt, this swirling, plus an occasional shaking of the pan, would make the gold settle to the bottom. When you had swirled out all the dirt, what was left in the pan was gold.

Wade went first. He filled his pan half full of dirt and squatted beside the stream. He dipped the pan in the ice-cold mountain water. He mixed the dirt with the water, breaking up the big clumps with one hand, throwing out the stones. The big flat-bottomed pan was heavy and unwieldy. It was hard to get a grip on the edges.

When he'd mixed the dirt and water, he swirled it around. As he swirled, he shook the pan to make the gold settle. Then he tipped the pan, letting small amounts of the mixture wash out. It was difficult getting the motion right. Sometimes he tipped the pan too hard, and too much mixture spilled out. Sometimes he did not tip hard enough, and nothing came out. Sometimes he balanced the pan wrong, and he sloshed icy water over himself. His thighs hurt from squatting. His wrists and forearms grew stiff. When the water was almost gone, he dipped in some more and started again.

As the contents of the pan diminished, his motion changed. He had to tip the pan more to get anything out. He saw a glitter in the bottom, and he grew excited. Then he swirled the pan too hard, and the mixture of gold, dirt, and water slid over the side and into the stream.

Wade sat stunned, holding the empty pan. "Your turn," he told Jack.

Jack didn't want the discomfort of squatting. He took off his boots, rolled up his trousers, and waded thigh-deep into the stream. Teeth chattering from the cold, he dipped his dirt-filled pan into the running water. The current was stronger than he had thought. It caught hold of the heavy pan, wrenched it out of one hand, and washed it empty. Jack turned behind him as if to catch the dirt before it floated downstream. But there was no chance of that.

"Good start," Wade said.

"At least I was quick about it," Jack told him.

Gradually, they got the hang of it. They worked through the day, bringing up dirt and washing it. Their backs hurt from shoveling. They raised blisters on their hands, and when the blisters broke, they wrapped strips of cloth around them and kept working. Their feet turned numb from the freezing water. Their noses ran. Their take of gold dust increased by tiny increments. The gold was mixed with heavy black sand, and they set the mixture in the sun to dry.

In the afternoon they were visited by a breezy-looking fellow named Quincy. Quincy led a mule with barrels of whiskey and brandy strapped to each side of its harness. On the mule's rump Quincy had painted the word "Saloon." Quincy's oversize coat was full of cigars and plug tobacco for sale.

"You got everything here but a whore," Jack said admiringly.

Quincy pointed at him. "You're right, sir. You're right. Perhaps I'll bring you one on my next trip."

Bearded miners appeared out of the hills as if by magic, with cups and bottles for Quincy to fill. Quincy charged a pinch of gold, or a dollar in coin, for a drink. Soon there was a small crowd, laughing and drinking and trampling all over Wade and Jack's claim.

Jack had no dried dust yet, so he used a dollar to buy a cup of brandy. Gentlemen were supposed to drink brandy. He sat on the lip of the hole, letting his legs dangle over. He needed a rest. He hadn't recovered his full strength yet. How could he, eating pork and beans and soggy flapjacks all the time? Soon—real soon—there wouldn't even be enough money for pork and beans. That nugget was going to disappear fast at these prices.

Wade kept working. He stood in the widening hole, breaking dirt with his pick. He looked up at his partner. "We're supposed to be *making* money," he pointed out, "not spending it. How much do you have left?"

Jack reached in his pocket. He held up a coin and flipped it. "One dollar. My emergency fund."

At the end of the day Wade and Jack took their dust back to the tent. Jack flopped on the grass, too tired to stand. Wade got the scales and sat beside him. "Let's see how much we made."

They spread their mixture of dried sand and gold dust on a blanket, then they carefully blew the sand away. They scooped the gold together into a small pile. The fine grains glinted in the late afternoon sun. Wade ran a finger through it, feeling its rough texture. He felt strangely attracted to it.

Eagerly, Wade put the gold on the scale. The pile looked small on the scale's big plate. Wade read the numbers closely. "It's a shade less than an ounce," he said. "I'd say we made about . . . six dollars each."

"Six dollars?" Jack moaned. "That's it?"

"Come on. That's more than you ever earned in a day—legally, anyway."

Jack cocked an eyebrow. "All right," he admitted, "you got me there. But look how we had to break our backs to get this ounce. When you figure it that way, six dollars ain't much. I'm going to be sore as hell tomorrow."

"Me, too," Wade said. "But it's a good kind of soreness. It makes you feel like you've really been working."

Jack said, "That's the difference between you and me. You've never done a real day's work before. I have, and I didn't exactly like it." He sniffed and wiped his nose on his sleeve. "I'm sick from standing in that damn water all day."

Wade carefully scooped the gold dust into a bottle. "We've got the hang of this now. We'll do good tomorrow."

"We'd better," Jack said.

19

"There's Coleman's Creek," the young mail rider Billy told Kathy. He looked over his shoulder at her with the same wide-eyed wonder he had shown earlier. "Sonofabitch is at the bottom of this canyon."

It was midafternoon. Kathy and Billy had left the Merced about an hour before. A shortcut, BIlly had said. Kathy was completely lost.

The mules picked their way down the side of the canyon. Kathy looked toward the bottom, but she could see nothing. Her heart beat faster. Her long journey was about to end.

Soon she would see Michael again. Michael, whom she had come all these thousands of miles to be with. It should have been a joyous moment. Instead, it was filled with guilt and sadness, because Kathy could think only of Wade. She tried to fight the guilt, to tell herself it wasn't her fault. She hadn't meant to fall in love with Wade. She had tried not to. It had just happened. She'd once believed that she loved Michael; now she was unsure. Hers had been the closest thing to an arranged marriage possible for a girl of her class. She had never really known another man. She'd had no idea what real love was. Now she knew. And she knew that she could never love Michael. He was a fine, decent man, but she would never feel about him the way she felt about Wade.

Poor Michael would be so excited to see her. And this was how she repaid him, by thinking about another man. And tonight, when she and Michael were alone together, whom would she think about then—him, or Wade? But she mustn't think about Wade ever again. She must put him from her mind. She must forget him. She must be a good wife to Michael. She must do her duty by him, even if duty was all that it had become.

After so long it was hard to remember what Michael looked like. Kathy tried to picture his face, the reddish side whiskers, the breezy charm. Michael was a good man, and that made her guilt harder to bear. He was attentive to her and thrifty. He'd come to California to give her a better life. She wondered what her new life with him would be like. His letter hadn't said anything about the living conditions, but they were bound to be primitive.

The path entered a belt of white oaks. Here and there were stumps where trees had been cut down. Ahead, Kathy heard muffled cries and banging. She saw more stumps, until, when they were within a quarter-mile of the canyon's floor, the entire hillside was denuded of trees.

"Here we are," Billy said.

Kathy recoiled in shock. The gold diggings were not the romantic woodland Eden of her imagination. Everywhere were towering mounds of dirt. There were shacks and garbage and wooden sluices running in all directions. There were pools of muddy water, piles of lumber. There were tin cans, pyramids of gravel and stone. Everything green had disappeared.

Men swarmed over the diggings. The air resounded to their cries, to the blows of hammer and saw. It smelled of wood chips and mud.

"Hey, look!" someone shouted. "A woman!"

"The mail's here, too."

"Who cares about the mail—there's a woman!"

Men stared at Kathy. They dropped their tools and followed her. She had grown used to this sort of attention since she'd left Stockton. At first she'd felt uncomfortable, but now, surprisingly, she found that she didn't mind it. In a way, she even liked it.

"Hey, Billy," cried one miner, "where'd you find her?"

"Man, oh, man," said another. "I must of died and went to heaven."

Kathy couldn't help but laugh. There was so much noise, so many shouted questions, she could hardly hear herself think. Billy was grinning widely.

The camp consisted of one street, churned with mud even in the dry season. Scattered along both sides of the street were log cabins, some with business signs hung out front. Behind the street were tents and wood-and-canvas houses, with similar dwellings scattered through the ravines and up the sides of the canyon. The street was busy even during the height of the workday, but all work halted at the sight of Kathy. Her arrival was the signal for a holiday. A procession of bearded men followed her, laughing and shouting.

Kathy's burro picked its way along the street, which was pocked with deep holes where men had dug for gold. The street was littered with discarded clothes, broken bottles, and empty sardine tins. There were worn-out tools, pots, and pans. There were bones and hides, the slops of men and animals. There was even a dead mule. Hogs and wolfish-looking dogs rooted through the mess, flies buzzed in clouds above it, and the heat made it all stink dreadfully.

The procession halted before the 1–2–3 Saloon, the camp's most substantial establishment. The crowd pressed close. The men were almost all in their early twenties. They were bearded and ragged. Many showed the debilitating effects of disease. They smelled as bad as the camp.

"Come on, boys!" Billy cried. "Give the lady some room!"

The mail, for which these men had waited months, was forgotten. "Who is she?" they yelled. "What's she doing here? Where's she from? Is she American?"

Billy raised both hands high. "She'll tell you who she is, if you shut up."

The men's voices died off, but not their excitement. Many of them were bouncing up and down on their toes, trying for a better look at Kathy. Kathy kept waiting to hear Michael's voice call her. She searched for him in the crowd but doubted she'd recognize him if he were in the same condition as the others.

"Go on, Miss Kathy," Billy said.

Kathy cleared her throat. The street grew quiet. "My name is Mrs. Michael Beddoes. I've come here to join my husband."

The miners looked at one another, shaking their heads.

"I don't know no Beddoes."

"Me, neither."

Kathy tried again. "He wrote me from this camp last September."

That produced more comment. "I only been here since April," said one man.

"Last September I was at Angel's Camp," said another.

For a moment, Kathy panicked. Where had Michael gone to? If he'd moved to another camp, she'd never find him. But he wouldn't have moved, not without good reason, and not without leaving her some kind of word.

Billy said, "Is Peach around? He'll know where Mrs. Beddoes

husband is." To Kathy he said, "Peach is the local alcalde, or judge. We call him to settle disputes, or when there's need for a miners' court."

"That's right," said the men. "Peach'll know, if anybody does."

A couple of miners started in search of this Peach. Kathy climbed off the mule, and there must have been a hundred pairs of arms eager to help her.

"Come sit," said someone. Kathy took the proffered seat on a bench beside a trestle table. The table was in front of the saloon, under a canvas awning.

"Drink, ma'am?" voices shouted.

"I'd like some water, if it wouldn't be too much trouble."

A half dozen men rushed to the camp well. The attitude of the remaining men toward Kathy was respectful, as though they were in a museum, studying a work of art. Some removed their hats.

Three or four tin cups were set before Kathy simultaneously. Water splashed over the sides onto the plank table.

"Thank you," she told the men, smiling.

She chose the cup that looked least dirty. The water was cold and refreshing. The miners pressed nearer to see her. Those in the rear stood on tiptoe and peered over the shoulders of those in front.

Billy said, "Here comes Peach."

The crowd parted for a spare, graying man of medium height. He appeared to be in his mid-forties, much older than most there. His clothes and face were plastered with mud. His old peaked cap was battered almost beyond recognition. His shoulders were slightly stooped, but his blue eyes twinkled. "Afternoon, ma'am," he said in a dry voice, touching the cap brim. "The boys tell me you're looking for your husband."

"Yes," Kathy said. "His name is Michael Beddoes. He was here last September."

Peach scratched his gray beard. "September, that was a long time ago. Michael Beddoes. Mike Beddoes." He shook his head, "No, I . . . wait a minute—I remember him now. Redheaded fellow. He's the one that opened Lucky Gulch. But . . ."

Peach's expression ranged from puzzlement to understanding in the space of a second. He looked at Kathy and let out his breath. "Ma'am, I got bad news." He paused. "Your husband is dead."

Kathy went cold all over. She put down the cup. "Dead? How?"

"Fever, as I recall."

"When did it happen?"

"A long time back, that's why it took me so long to remember the name. Last October it was, maybe even September. Early autumn, anyway."

"That means he died right after he wrote me," Kathy said. She sat back. "I've come all this way at the request of a dead man."

Things seemed to be spinning. Poor Michael. He had loved her so. And she had proved unfaithful to him—in spirit, if not in body. He had deserved better.

"I'm sorry, ma'am," said Peach. "We all are."

Kathy fought back a tear. She spoke as brightly as she could manage. "Well, Mr. Peach, I'm four thousand miles from home, I don't know anyone, and I haven't a cent to my name. Perhaps you can tell me what I should do now?"

20

Peach scratched his tangled gray beard. "Tell you what we used to do in Mexico when a woman came into camp. We'd each of us wash out one pan of dirt, and we'd give the gold from that pan to the lady. That would give her a stake." He looked around. "That sound about right, boys?"

The men shouted their agreement. "Sounds good to me."

"Me, too. Let's do 'er."

"Don't worry, miss, we'll get you fixed up."

The crowd started to break up, but Peach raised a hand. "Hey! Before we start, there's something else we got to do, and that's change the name of this camp. The present name ain't fittin' with a lady around."

A few in the crowd were disappointed. The name Sonofabitch made them feel properly raffish. But the majority agreed with the move.

"What'll we call it?" they said.

"How's about Widow's Diggins?" someone shouted.

"Lone Woman's Bar," another yelled.

The mail rider, Billy, said, "How 'bout Miss Kathy's Bar?"

"Kate's Bar," said Peach. "It sounds better. All right?" The majority agreed, and Peach said, "From now on, this camp is called Kate's Bar. You boys don't forget to tell your mamas that when you write home, or you won't get no letters."

"Speaking of which," Billy said, "let me give out what I got. I got other stops to make, you know."

The mail was distributed, and Billy collected his fees. The men— some happy at receiving mail, others disappointed at getting none— went off to raise Kathy's stake.

Billy remounted his mule. "Thanks, Billy," Kathy told him. "Will I see you again?"

"Yes, ma'am," said Billy, and his big eyes looked down shyly. "I guess you will. I intend to make this mail run my regular business. I've had enough of mining."

Billy rode out of the canyon. Peach stayed behind with Kathy. "I'll throw some gold in the pot, too," he promised her. "From what I got saved up."

"You needn't do that, Peach."

"It's all right, ma'am. I'm pleased to. It's the way we live up here. Everybody helps everybody else. It's the only way you *can* live here and stay alive."

"Why do they call you Peach?" Kathy said.

"It's a long story. I started mining gold in Georgia, twenty years ago. When I moved on, the boys at the next diggings started calling me the Georgia Peach. Later it just got shortened to Peach. My real name's Henry, but I can't remember the last time anybody used that."

"Twenty years?" Kathy said. "Surely you haven't been mining gold all that time?"

Peach looked embarrassed to admit it. "Gold and silver," he said. "I been a lot of places, from Dakota to Chile. Some of 'em I don't even remember anymore. This is the big strike, though. This is the one that's going to put us all on easy street. Last season at these diggings was the best I ever had." He cleared his throat. " 'Course, I spent near all my money with the boys in San Francisco over the winter. But this year's different. This year I'm saving my dust. I'm going to retire from mining, buy me a little *rancheria* down near Los Angeles or San Diego. Marry me one of them señoritas and settle down."

"Can you settle down after so many years of mining?" Kathy said.

Peach snorted. "I'm forty-two years old, and I got nothing to show for it, nothing but my dreams. I'm ready to quit, believe me."

Kathy was surprised at how she was sitting there, casually chatting with this stranger as if they were at home and he was an old acquaintance she had encountered on the avenue. Inside, she was a cauldron of fear and self-doubt. She was on her own, and she was scared to death about what was going to happen next.

"Have you ever been married?" she asked Peach.

The grizzled miner's blue eyes momentarily lost their twinkle. They took on a faraway look. "There was a girl, once, a long time ago. When I first left home. I even wrote her a few letters, as best I could, and she wrote me. I still have them letters somewhere. But I wouldn't go back till I'd made my pile, and . . . well, time drifted by. Pretty soon I'd been gone a year, then two. By then I had the gold fever. I was hooked. When the Georgia diggings died out, I didn't go home, but drifted on. After a while the girl stopped writing, or maybe it was me that stopped. I disremember now. I reckon she's long married, with growed children."

Kathy changed the subject. "Have you been here since the camp was founded?"

Peach's cheerful demeanor returned. He stamped a booted foot. "Near enough. At least one of them holes there in the street belonged to me. I've had three or four claims around here."

"Did you know my husband well?"

"Not real well. I don't think none of us knew him real well. He wasn't . . . he wasn't here that long."

Kathy looked away.

Peach added, "He seemed a pleasant fellow, as I recall."

"Yes," Kathy said quietly. "Michael was always pleasant."

Men began returning from their claims, with Kathy's gold. Some of the pans had produced but a few grains of the precious metal; others, more. The average was about fifty cents' worth. Somebody produced a leather pouch, and the men carefully poured their dust inside. Peach finished it off with a generous pinch from his own stash. The gold weighed out to nearly five and a quarter ounces. Peach figured up its value. "That's about eighty-three dollars," he told Kathy.

The miners cheered. "That'll get you going, Miss Kathy."

Peach said, "It's a good stake. It'll get you back to San Francisco. Or, if you want to stay here, you can invest it in one of the mines, or start a business.''

Kathy didn't know.

"Think on it," Peach told her. "Right now we got to get you a place to stay.''

Using Kathy's new money, Peach and some others went to Greenberg's Hardware Store. They bought Kathy a tent, blankets and camp cot. They set up the tent on a ledge of ground behind the camp's main street. Next, the owner of the camp's restaurant gave Kathy a free meal. The fare was substantial, if bland. Kathy ate it all. She'd been hungrier than she imagined.

When she was done, she said to Peach, "I'd like to see my husband's grave now, please.''

Peach shuffled his feet. "I'm afraid I don't know exactly where he's buried. Probably none of the boys that planted—I mean, laid him to rest, are still in camp. Men tend to get left where they fall up here, and there ain't much in the way of markers. Best I could do is show you his old claim.''

Kathy sighed and nodded. "All right.''

Peach took her up a gulch behind the town, accompanied by an ever-growing crowd of men. They came to an abandoned mine. There were a dozen similarly abandoned claims nearby. Michael's claim consisted of several large holes gouged out of the earth. There were mounds of dirt everywhere, along with old garbage putrefied by the summer heat.

Peach was apologetic. "It was worked over by other fellows after your husband died. This whole area's panned out now. Your husband had a lean-to, but it's gone.''

Kathy felt sad. Poor Michael, with all his aims and ambition. He'd always believed in himself so much, and now these piles of dirt were all there was to show that he had ever lived.

"It's getting late," Kathy told Peach. "I'd better retire now.''

This was a moment she'd been dreading. The crowd followed her back to the tent. "All right, boys," Peach told them. "Give the lady some privacy.'' The men backed away, but not far. Kathy raised a hand to them. "Good night," she said. She didn't know what else to do.

They waved back. Many removed their hats. "Good night, Miss Kathy.''

Kathy went inside, dropping the canvas flap behind her. Besides the cot, the tent's furnishings consisted of an overturned crate on which to sit. Kathy blew out the lantern. She shivered. It got cold up there at night. In the darkness the reality of her situation pressed in on her. She was alone, surrounded by hundreds of strange men. Outside the tent, crickets chirped. Wild animals called among the hills. She heard the faint rattle of camp utensils. She smelled meat cooking, bread baking. In the distance, someone was singing.

If only Wade were here, she thought. How ironic. Now she could have him, and he was lost to her forever. She wondered where he and Jack were, and what they were doing.

She heard faint noises outside. She swallowed. These men could break in and have their way with her, and there was no one to stop them. She crept to the tent flap and peeked out. Peach was sitting on the ground in front of the tent. Not far from him was Mr. Greenberg, owner of the hardware store. There were others as well. They had formed a protective ring around the tent. It looked like they were preparing to spend the night.

Kathy calmed down. She felt better now, reassured. She went to the cot and lay down, fully clothed, pulling the blankets over her.

Tomorrow she would begin a new life. Six months ago she would have begged the charity of these miners to get home. She would have gotten it, too. She could get it now if she wanted it. But she didn't want it. She was determined to be her own mistress. The only question was, how was she to go about it?

The problem of how to support herself was still on her mind when she awoke the next morning. The crowd of men was waiting for her when she emerged from the tent. They followed her as she went to the restaurant for breakfast. She sipped the bitter coffee, and as she watched the bearded faces peering at her, she had an idea.

Peach was with her, and she turned to him. "I think I know how I'm going to invest my money."

"How's that?" he said.

Her hazel eyes glittered mischievously. She got up and left the restaurant. She paraded down the muddy street, to Greenberg's Hardware Store, followed by Peach and the rest of the curious miners. She was enjoying this. She felt in control. Inside the store she purchased several pairs of scissors, a straight razor, and a leather strop, soap, and a bucket.

She came out of the store and looked at the expectant miners. Then she said, "All right, boys. Who wants a haircut?"

21

A long line formed. The miners sat on a boulder near the stream while Kathy cut their hair. They built a fire for her, and she kept fresh water steaming in the kettle for shaves. She charged the going price for everything at the mines—a pinch of gold dust for a haircut and beard trim, another pinch for a shave.

Most of these young men had not had their hair cut since leaving home. Their hair was long and tangled, stiff from months of dirt and sweat. Their beards were as bad. The men's once-robust bodies were run down from dysentery and the ague. Their skins were mottled. Many had bad or missing teeth from scurvy. Most were cheerful, though, certain that they would find enough gold to make their privations worthwhile.

While they waited their turns, the men played cards, talked, or dozed. Kathy hummed to herself as she worked. Music had been her favorite subject in school. Her dream had once been to play the piano, but there hadn't been money in her family for that sort of "foolishness," as her mother called it. The men nearest her tapped their toes to her upbeat tunes. Later, when she was tired, she hummed the sentimental favorite "Where Can the Soul Find Rest?" She didn't notice the men fall silent around her.

When she finished, a young man said, "That was pretty, Miss Kathy. Do you know the words?"

"What?" she said, surprised. "Why . . . yes, I know them."

"Would you sing 'em for us?"

"Sing?" she said.

"Please," said the man.

"Yes, please," echoed his bearded companions.

Kathy wasn't prepared for this. "Well, I don't . . ."

"Come on, Miss Kathy," they pleaded.

She didn't know what to do. She looked to Peach, but he was

grinning. He wasn't going to get her out of this. "Well," she said, "maybe. Just this once."

She cleared her throat. She started the song quietly, blushing, almost as if she were afraid of being heard. The men got out of line and crowded around, listening raptly. Those in back pressed forward. Kathy saw the effect she was having on them, and she grew more confident. Her voice became stronger. The high, sad notes of the song sounded somehow appropriate as they floated over the rough surroundings.

When she finished, the men were quiet. Some were misty-eyed, thinking of home. Kathy was half ready to cry herself.

"There now," she said, breaking the silence. "That's enough."

The men started to protest, but she cut them off. "No more. This isn't a music hall. I have a living to make."

By the end of the day Kathy was worn out. Her hands and forearms were sore. They were covered with bites from the fleas in the men's beards. The scissors had worn blisters on her thumb and middle finger. The blisters had broken, and there was blood on her hand. Her feet hurt from being on them all day. She had made over two hundred dollars. There was still a long line.

"I'm sorry, boys," she told the remaining men. "You'll have to come back tomorrow."

There was a chorus of groans. Then somebody said, "Will you cook for us, Miss Kathy? We'd pay you."

"We'll get the supplies," added his partner.

"How 'bout us?" said somebody else as the line broke up. "Will you cook for us, too?"

Before she could answer, Peach came to her rescue. "Miss Kathy's had enough work for one day," he told them. "I'm cooking for *her*."

Peach had been one of Kathy's first customers that morning. Shaved and with his hair cut, he looked years younger, and he was surprisingly handsome. Twenty years ago he must have been a real lady killer, she thought—or he would have been if he hadn't succumbed to gold fever.

Now his blue eyes twinkled in his tanned face, and he winked at her. "What say? I rustle up a mean plate of pork and beans."

Kathy laughed. "All right. I'll come."

She washed up and accompanied Peach to a tidy log hut shaded by oaks, with a shingle roof. "Your home is much cleaner than most around here," Kathy observed, looking around.

"It's a habit I picked up over the years," Peach told her.

They ate at a plank table out front, where they could enjoy the evening air. The pork and beans, cooked with molasses, were excellent. There were also potatoes, onions, and preserved corn, along with freshly baked bread, and tinned pears in syrup for dessert. All of it was washed down by coffee.

When she was done, Kathy sighed contentedly. "I haven't eaten a meal that good since I left New York."

Peach laughed. "I always figured, if I had to eat the stuff, I might as well learn how to fix it right."

The sun was going down. It had already disappeared in the canyon bottom, and the breeze had turned chilly. Peach poured more hot coffee. Kathy was glad to have it.

Peach pulled out a corncob pipe and tobacco. "Do you mind?"

"Not at all," Kathy said.

Peach filled the pipe and lit it. He said, "Another day or two like today, and you'll have made enough to get you back to the States."

"I'm not going back to the States," Kathy told him.

Peach raised his eyebrows, puffing the pipe.

Kathy said, "There's nothing for me there, not anymore. I couldn't stand living at home again with my mother trying to run my life. I've been through too much for that." There was also the faint hope that she might see Wade again, but she didn't tell Peach about that.

"What are you going to do?" he asked.

"I've been thinking about what the men were saying. Maybe I'll open a restaurant. You're not the only one around here who can cook, you know."

Peach brightened. "We could use another place to eat. A business like that's going to take planning, though."

"Perhaps you could help me with that," Kathy said.

The two of them worked out what Kathy would need to get started. The next day, while still cutting hair, she began making preparations. She hired a helper, a black man named Smoke. She bought a large open-sided tent and had it set up in a vacant lot on the camp's street. She purchased utensils and supplies. She hired men to build trestle tables and plank seats and peg them to the restaurant's dirt floor.

"Looks good," said Peach, who stopped in to check out her progress. "What'll you call it?"

"I don't know," said Kathy, who was scrubbing out a large kettle. "Kathy's Restaurant, I guess. How's that for originality?"

Two days later she was ready to open. It was Sunday, the day off at the mines. Men poured into camp from miles around. There must have been two thousand of them, and half wanted to eat at Kathy's Restaurant, just for the novelty of being served by a woman. They lined up in the street, waiting to get in. Kathy fed them in shifts. They crammed into the tent elbow to elbow along the plank seats. They wolfed down their food. The average time for a meal was five minutes, but Kathy couldn't keep up with the demand. She had workmen putting up an addition to the tent even as the men in the first tent were eating. She ran back and forth, sleeves rolled up, hair coming unpinned, sweat running down her face from the exertion and the steaming kettles of food. She cooked, cleared up, and cleaned. She supervised Smoke. She bought more meat from hunters at the rear of the tent.

At sunset she closed. Some of the miners asked if they could sleep over in the tent. They figured it was the cleanest place in town, and Kathy suddenly found herself in the hotel business as well.

She made her way home through the crowded camp street. Her presence was no longer such a novelty, and the men didn't follow her. Lamps twinkled like fireflies in the dusk. She carried the day's profits in a leather bag. Most of it was gold dust, but there were coins, too, from all over the world. She was exhausted but cheerful. She was a success, and she'd done it all on her own. It was a heady feeling. This might be an idyllic existence after all.

All sorts of grandiose ideas floated through her head. She would have a cabin built for herself, and a proper building for her restaurant-hotel. She would expand her menu. The first thing she wanted, though, was a bath. There was no question of bathing in the stream, not with all the men around, and anyway, the water was freezing. Tomorrow she would hire a cooper to build her a tub. She would fill it with steaming water, and—

She stopped. There was a light inside her tent. Peach or one of the men must have lit it for her so that she would not have to enter in the dark. It was a thoughtful gesture, though it did seem a mild invasion of her privacy. She opened the tent flap and went in. She stopped again, and a surprised gasp rose in her throat.

A man lounged on her cot, drinking from a bottle of port. He was a short, slightly built fellow, well dressed, with a neatly trimmed blond beard. As Kathy came in, he rose, fixing her with pale blue eyes. Beneath his blue coat she glimpsed a revolver handle. The man spoke softly, with an aristocratic southern drawl.

"Good evening, ma'am. I'm Simon St. Clair. Captain St. Clair to those that know me. I'm here for one of those haircuts."

22

Kathy was scared, but she tried not to show it. She replied curtly. "If you want a haircut, you can come back during the day, like everyone else."

St. Clair moved closer. He was handsome in a dissolute way. His accent was soft, menacing. "I'm here now."

"Not for long," she told him. "I'll trouble you to leave."

St. Clair said, "You're not bein' hospitable, ma'am. A pretty woman like you, that's not right. You need to learn some manners."

He grabbed for her arm. She moved back, out of his reach. "Get out," she said. "Get out or I'll have this whole camp on you."

St. Clair smiled insolently. "That's no way to talk to a man you're goin' to live with."

Kathy was contemptuous. "You must be mad. Why would I live with you?"

"Because a woman can't live alone up here. It's too dangerous. You need a man. You need protection."

"Protection from what?"

St. Clair smiled. "From me, if nothin' else."

Suddenly there was a long, thin-bladed knife in St. Clair's hand. He pushed its point into Kathy's nose. He put pressure on it. Kathy held her head back. There was nowhere to run.

"I could rip that pretty nose right off your face," St. Clair hissed. "It wouldn't bother me to do it, either. There's no one to stop me."

The knife was razor-sharp. Kathy could feel the blade prick the skin inside her nose. A drop of blood rolled down the back of her throat, choking her, making her cough. Her heart thumped with fear. St. Clair pinned her against the tent wall. He leaned in very close. She smelled liquor on his breath.

"I won't do it," he said. "Not yet. I don't like my women disfigured. I prefer that you come to me of your own will. And you will come to me. One way or the other, you'll come. And if I tell you, you'll work for me, too. You'll sell that body and make us some real money."

"And if I don't?" she breathed.

"You could have an accident," St. Clair said. "It happens all the time here in the mines."

Slowly, he withdrew the dagger. Kathy kept her head back, as if she could still feel the cold steel. St. Clair returned the dagger to his belt and picked up the bottle of port. He bowed mockingly. "Good night, ma'am. We'll meet again soon. You can count on that."

He turned and left the tent.

Kathy remained like she was, afraid to move, almost afraid to breathe. She trembled, sweating despite the nighttime chill. Her throat was so dry that she could not swallow. She realized how vulnerable she was in this mining camp. It had been nonsense to think that she had any kind of security here.

She moved away from the tent's side, still shaking. Another drop of blood rolled from her nose, and she wiped it on her sleeve. She could still feel the pressure of St. Clair's blade, even though he was gone. He had barely broken her skin, just enough to show her what he was capable of.

She lay on her cot. She did not extinguish the lantern. She did not sleep. She kept waiting for St. Clair to return. She kept wondering what she would do if he did.

But he didn't.

The next morning, she opened her restaurant, trying to act normally. The Sunday crowds were gone, but a lot of people who lived in town showed up for breakfast. She let Smoke get things in hand, then she went to Mr. Greenberg's store, where she bought a pistol and ammunition.

Next, she set out to find Peach. She inquired around the diggings until she found his claim. The claim was up a winding, rocky ravine. Peach was with his two partners. The three men had diverted a shallow stream, and they were mining a section of the streambed. The diverted water flowed down a wooden flume, with cleats in the bottom to catch the heavy, gold-bearing sand. The men shoveled dirt into the flume, picking out the rocks, breaking up the larger clumps with the blades of their shovels, letting the flow of the water wash the rest. Other groups of men were working at different places along the streambed and the hillsides.

Peach looked up as Kathy approached. He grinned, wiping sweat from his grimy forehead. "Good morning, Miss Kathy. I didn't expect to see you here." Then he noticed the pistol stuck in the waistband of her skirt. "Why the hog leg?"

"Can I talk with you?" Kathy asked.

Peach saw the look on her face; he heard the nervousness in her voice. "Sure," he said. He looked at his two young partners. "Let's break for a minute, boys."

One of the young men sat and drank water from a clay jug. The other lay on his back in the sun, tired.

Peach led Kathy off to one side, where they wouldn't be heard. In a low voice, he said, "What's the matter?"

"Do you know a Simon St. Clair?" Kathy said. "Captain St. Clair?"

"Captain St. Clair? I know *of* him. He's one of the dirk and bowie-knife crowd. They say he's come to Kate's Bar."

"He came to Kate's tent last night."

Peach let out a low whistle. "What did he want?"

"Me."

"That why you've got the gun?"

Kathy nodded.

"What happened?"

She told him. "He threatened my life if I don't live with him. He said I need protection and only he can provide it. He said I'll meet with an accident otherwise."

Peach rubbed a dirty hand across his mouth. "I was afraid something like this would happen."

Kathy said, "I'm sorry for coming to you with this, Peach. But I don't know where else to turn."

The grizzled miner patted her shoulder. "You did the right thing. I'm the alcalde, it's my job."

"That man scares me," Kathy said.

"He ain't one to get on the wrong side of, that's for sure. They say he killed a man in Weaverville, and another in Los Angeles."

"Who is he? Is he really a captain of something?"

"He was a captain of Texas Rangers in the war against Mexico. He was a real hero, they say, brave as a lion. Seems he had trouble with the bottle, resigned his commission in an argument over a woman. Before he came to California, I heard he hunted Apache scalps for the Mexicans in New Mexico and Chihuahua. He's supposed to have killed his first man when he was eighteen."

Kathy said, "What can I do about him?"

Peach wrinkled his brow. "Sounds like it's time to call a miners' court." Then he grinned. "Miss Kathy, you cost me more time off work than a case of the ague, you know that? I'm going to spread the word. Attendance at these things is voluntary. We call one, we never know how many'll show. We'll meet at Greenberg's store in two hours. I'll see you there."

23

Two hours later there were well over a hundred dirty, ragged men in front of the hardware store. In contrast to a few days earlier, most had trimmed hair, and many had only two days' growth of beard because Kathy had shaved them. They were restless and irritable because they'd left work to attend. It was money out of their pockets.

"What're we here for, Peach?" they cried.

"Who's on trial?"

"Captain St. Clair," Peach said.

That name produced murmuring and shuffling of feet. Peach picked out five good-size fellows. "Come on, we'll bring him here."

They looked first in the saloons, but St. Clair was nôt there. "Must be a little early for him to be up and around," Peach said. They found him in a tent, not far from the 1–2–3.

"Captain St. Clair?" said Peach, leading the men inside. The tent was dark. It smelled of liquor and tobacco and hair oil.

St. Clair was in bed. He came awake quickly, sitting up. He kept one hand under his blanket, and Peach suspected he had a revolver there.

"Who wants to know?" St. Clair said.

"The name's Peach. I'm the alcalde. You been summoned to a miners' court."

St. Clair looked at the five men. "On what charge?" he asked softly.

"You'll find out when you get there," Peach told him. "Get dressed, please, and come with us."

St. Clair hesitated, then smiled. "Sure, boys. I'll come. Give me a minute, will you?"

They waited outside his tent. When St. Clair appeared, he was wearing his blue coat with a clean white shirt and long bandanna. His wide-brimmed hat was brushed and centered firmly on his head. His boots were of fine quality. It was plain that he was no miner.

The five men accompanied St. Clair to where the crowd waited in front of the store. St. Clair lifted an eyebrow when he saw Kathy there. He gave her his insolent smile. Peach indicated a tree stump in the street. "Have a seat, Captain."

St. Clair sat, crossing his legs. "What's this all about, boys? I kill somebody I don't remember? I didn't think I had *that* much to drink last night."

A couple of the men laughed uneasily. Peach didn't. He said, "Miss Kathy, tell the court your story."

Kathy told the assembled men what had happened in her tent. As she talked, the miners got madder and madder. They felt protective of her, responsible for her. By the time she finished, they were ready for vengeance.

"Flog him!" somebody shouted.

"Cut off his ears!" yelled somebody else.

"Run him out of town!"

St. Clair looked around, smiling contemptuously. These men who were so brave collectively would be scared to face him one to one. He knew it, and they did, too.

"All right, all right," Peach said, motioning for quiet. "Let's hear what Captain St. Clair has to say." He turned. "Do you deny any of this?"

"We ain't afraid of you, St. Clair!" yelled somebody.

St. Clair spoke in courtly tones. "Certainly, I paid the lady a visit, though I wouldn't say it was quite so threatenin' as she makes out."

Peach had a hard time restraining his anger. "Did you stick a knife in her nose?"

St. Clair cleared his throat self-consciously. "Look, boys, I won't deny I was showin' off a bit. I'd had a bad run at cards, and too many drinks in consequence. Way too many drinks—I really don't remember all that I did. Whatever it was, I didn't mean anythin' by it, and I'm surprised the lady took it that way. Surely, in her profession, she's been approached by men before?"

Peach grew angrier. "Profession! Mrs. Beddoes is a respectable woman, St. Clair. She's lost her husband, and she's trying to make a living up here."

"Oh," said St. Clair. He looked as if he had made a mistake. "Well, I didn't know that. I thought she was a . . . your pardon, ma'am, but I thought you were a lady of the evenin'. I didn't know there was any other kind of woman up here. I certainly didn't know how you boys felt about her. I was just havin' fun."

"Fun, eh?" Peach didn't know whether to believe him or not. He scratched his stubbly chin, and he looked around. "Well, what should we do?"

"Hang him," shouted somebody. "He deserves it. If not for what he done here, for what he done in them other places."

Peach made a face. "Come on, MacReady. We can't hang a man just because of his reputation."

"Run him out of town, then," said somebody else. There was loud sentiment for that suggestion. The majority seemed behind it.

Abe Greenberg spoke up. He was a civilized man, well read. "I agree. I'd like to see St. Clair out of town. But he hasn't actually committed a crime. We're trying to bring American law to this wilderness. We must try to be fair. If we ran people out of town just for being drunk, there wouldn't *be* a town before long."

Peach sighed. He wasn't sure. At last he said, "I guess you're right, Greenberg."

The men didn't agree. "He insulted Miss Kathy!" one of them yelled angrily, and the others took up the cry.

"He won't insult her again," Peach told them. To St. Clair he said, "You're to leave Mrs. Beddoes alone, St. Clair. You're to say no more to her than 'good morning' or 'good evening,' and you be damn careful how you do that. We'll be watching you, and if you get out of line, just once, you'll be run out of this camp, and you won't have all your body parts with you when you go.''

Peach turned to the men. "Can everybody accept that as the verdict of this court?''

There was a lot of muttering, but the majority finally went along.

"You have anything to say, St. Clair?'' Peach asked.

St. Clair uncrossed his legs. "Of course I'll leave the lady alone. No one knows better than I how to treat a member of the fair sex.'' He rose, turning to Kathy and removing his hat. "I meant no harm, ma'am, I assure you. Between too much drink and a lack of knowledge, I misrepresented the situation entirely. My humblest apologies, and I give my word as a gentleman that it won't happen again.''

Kathy could almost believe he was sincere. Everybody was looking at her. What did she have to be afraid of, she thought, with Peach and the whole camp on guard against St. Clair? They would run St. Clair out right now if she pressed them on it, but then someone might get hurt, and she didn't want to be responsible for that. She still had nightmares about the men she'd seen killed in Panama.

Reluctantly, she said, "Very well. I accept.''

St. Clair smiled. For a brief second he fixed her with those pale blue eyes. Then he turned to Peach and the court, "I presume I'm free to go?''

"You're free," Peach said.

St. Clair nodded. He turned to Kathy and bowed. "Again, ma'am, my apologies.'' He put on his hat and strolled off to the saloon.

"Court adjourned,'' Peach said. "Let's all get back to work.''

Greenberg came up to Kathy. "I wouldn't worry about St. Clair, Miss Kathy. Men like that, they drift from camp to camp. He won't be around long.''

St. Clair didn't leave the camp, but he didn't bother Kathy after that. The few times she encountered him in the street, or in her restaurant, he went out of his way to be circumspect and polite. But every now and then, in an unguarded moment, she caught him watching her, and she wondered.

24

When new, the canvas tent had possessed a pristine whiteness. Now it was brown and frayed, patched with bits of calico. Around it were old bones, potato skins, tin cans, and other bits of garbage. Mounds of dirt were piled beside a series of nearby excavations.

Wade stuck his head from the tent fly, yawning. He crawled out of the tent, scratched a flea bite, and stretched. Like the tent, his flannel shirt and trousers were patched and mended. His boots were coming loose at the soles. A bushy brown beard covered his chin, and his unbrushed hair was down to his shoulders.

He took the two-gallon bucket and walked down to the stream. It was Sunday, but even on Sunday you had to get water early, before it became brown and undrinkable from men washing dirt in it. Already the day was warm. Birds were singing in the oaks, whose leaves had turned a shimmering yellow-gold. The wild oats that covered the hills had turned gold as well so that the whole valley seemed to have taken on the color of the mineral that lured men to it. Now and again gunshots sounded among the quiet hills as hunters pursued increasingly scarce game.

The stream was a trickle these days. It took a while to fill the bucket. When Wade returned to the tent, Jack was outside, building up the fire. Their fireplace was at the foot of an oak tree. Three feet up the trunk was an auger hole, into which a pick head had been stuck for use as a pot hook. Nails driven into the tree's trunk held the rest of their kitchen utensils.

"How's the water?" Jack asked, looking up.

"Low," said Wade. "It'll be dry soon. We won't be able to work. We'll have to move on or stay here and wait for the winter rains."

Jack filled the pot with water and started the coffee. "Thank

God for a day off from that digging.'' Beneath his shapeless hat, Jack looked like a scarecrow, ragged and run-down. His black hair was long and lank; his beard was tangled. In contrast, Wade seemed to thrive on this kind of life. He had filled out. He looked rugged and was suntanned. He was a different man from the one Jack had first met in Panama.

While the coffee boiled, Wade got out their ball of bread dough. He rolled out some and put it in one of the pans they used for washing dirt. When the fire had produced enough coals, he scraped them aside, put in the pan, and buried it. He took the remaining dough, added flour, water, and a little Seidlitz powder, pounded it all together and set it aside to develop the sour flavor they had become accustomed to.

''We going to wash clothes?'' Jack said.

''Maybe later,'' said Wade. ''I want to get into town and buy supplies before they're all gone.''

Jack scratched under his shirt. ''I'd kind of like to get these cooties out.''

''I'd kind of like to eat this week. We can wash when we get back. Anyway, I don't know if these clothes have another washing in them. I'm afraid they'll fall to pieces.''

When the bread was done, Wade took the pan from the fire. Jack turned their rocker—a machine looking like a baby's cradle that they used for washing dirt—on its side, and Wade put the bread on it. Jack began slicing the bread.

''This thing makes a good cutting board, anyway,'' Jack said. ''We paid more for the damn thing than we've ever made with it. The real gold mine is for the fellows that sell these things to us.''

They poured coffee. Flies buzzed around their molasses bottle. They had lost the stopper weeks before. There were dead ants inside. They poured molasses on the bread and ate.

''Another great meal,'' Jack said. ''Bread and coffee. Jail isn't any worse than this.''

''It'll get better,'' Wade promised. ''Every day like this brings us one day closer to finding the Big Lump.''

''The only big lump around here is the one between my shoulders for letting you talk me into this,'' Jack said.

''Oh, stop complaining. If it wasn't for me, we wouldn't have as much dust as we do. I do most of the work.''

''It ain't my fault I been sick,'' Jack said.

"It's not my fault you're lazy. How do you expect to get gold if you don't dig for it?"

"I don't know, but I'm thinking on it. I can tell you that much."

Wade crawled into the tent and came back with the half-gallon jar in which they kept their gold dust. With paint, they had marked eight levels on the jar. Number one, at the top, was optimistically labeled "Champagne and Oysters." Number eight, at the bottom, was "Half Rations." Right now the level of dust was just above number seven, "Pork Stew." They had never been past number six, "Pork and Beans."

Jack looked at the jar and shook his head. "All summer we been here, and this is what we got to show for it."

Wade took his leather pouch and poured most of the gold dust into it. He left the jar with the rest of the dust in front of the tent. No one bothered your stash up here. While Wade cleaned up, Jack pulled the silver dollar from his pocket and flipped it idly.

"You still have that thing?" Wade said.

"It's my good-luck charm, can't you tell? I keep it so I won't have any good luck."

"Come on," Wade said. "Let's get out of here."

They left the camp and made their way downstream, toward the Mariposa. All around them they saw other men heading the same way.

" 'Allo!" cried a voice.

They looked behind them, to see the bulldog figure of Sam Trumbull, laboring to catch up with them.

"Hello, Sam," said Wade. "Where are your partners?"

Sam snorted. "Timmy's decided to get some kip, and that bloody Oberg's reading 'is Bible. That's one 'ell of a way to spend Sunday, innit? Praying?"

Wade and Jack laughed. "Your purse deep?" Jack said.

"Deep enough," said the little Englishman. "Claim's about panned out, though."

"Ours, too," Wade said.

Sam said, "This 'ere'll be one of the last big weekends in camp. The lads'll start leaving soon, 'eading down to Stockton or San Francisco for the winter."

They reached the river. The path along it—and up and down the hillsides, where the banks were impassable—was so worn by now, it was like a road. Dust hung thick in the air, from the many men who passed along it, all headed into Oro Fino, as the camp was now called. There were men on foot, men on mules and horseback, feeding in from the gulches and ravines until they became a stream, like the river itself.

Oro Fino was situated near the river at the bottom of a trail that led down from the hills. Four months earlier, merchants had sold goods from muleback there, to men like Wade and Jack. Now a long street of tents and cabins and even a few frame houses stood on the site. On this Sunday the street was a babel of accents and languages. There were down-east Yankees, drawling southerners, flat-voiced frontiersmen from the Mississippi Valley. There were Irishmen, Englishmen, Frenchmen, Germans, Italians. There were Mexicans in bright serapes, Chileans in somber brown. Half-naked Indians rubbed shoulders with freed black slaves and swarthy Kanakas from the Hawaiian Islands. Here and there were Chinese, with pigtails and conical straw hats. It was as if the entire world had converged on California, drawn by the lure of gold.

There were men selling mules, men selling horses. There were men selling clothing and tools, and men selling drinks, all of them shouting to attract customers. There were gamblers with tables set up on the street. For every man who squandered a pouch of gold dust, there were five who could afford to do nothing more than watch the passing parade. There were wild yells, and the crowd gave way as a group of men racing horses galloped down the street. The mob closed in behind the horses once more, thinking nothing of it.

Sam Trumbull dropped off to have a drink with some of his countrymen. Wade and Jack were borne along by the crowd, taking in the sights, greeting acquaintances. "For a fellow that spends all his time working, you sure seem to know everybody," Jack told Wade.

Wade grinned.

Jack saw a garishly printed poster. "There's a bull and bear fight this afternoon. Two dollars to get in. What do you say?"

Wade shook his head. "Too cruel for my taste. Anyway, we don't have the money."

"We never have money for anything. God, I could use a bottle of whiskey and a few hands of cards."

"Unless you plan on spending that lucky dollar, you'll have to wait. Maybe next week will be better."

"You say that every week," Jack said. "Well, I'm tired of waiting. I'm tired of being dirty and hungry and not having five cents to my name. I was better off in Panama.''

From the next street there was an angry commotion. Shouts. Yells. People running. A tidal surge of men.

''What's going on?'' Jack said. ''Somebody actually find gold around this place?''

''I don't know,'' said Wade. ''Let's find out.''

25

Elena Soto was worried.

She was afraid the boy would come back. The boy and his friends had followed her home the night before, drunk, believing she was a whore. Juan had made them go away, but Juan was not here now, and she had seen the boy, whose name was Carney, in the main street a few minutes earlier. What was worse, he had seen her.

Elena had been in the street selling her meat pies. That was what she was reduced to these days, she who had once had servants and fine clothes and the best teachers in Santiago. Juan did odd jobs. Right now he was helping to build the stands for the bull and bear fight.

For the Sotos, coming to California had been a terrible mistake. Elena had lost her baby on the sea voyage north. After she and Juan had been forced to give up their cabin and move onto the deck, there had been a fierce storm. It had been cold and wet and rough, with the ship plunging in the swells. A great wave had smashed Elena across the deck, into the bulwarks and almost overboard. She had suffered a miscarriage, and had nearly died herself. Juan had been heartbroken over the baby's loss, but he'd sworn that everything would be better once they reached California.

At first it had been better. Juan was a skilled miner. He had made good wages. Then the *Norteamericanos* had passed laws designed to drive Mexicans—they considered anyone who spoke Spanish a Mexican—out of the mines. Juan had been barred from digging gold. He and Elena had been forced to move into this camp, where they took whatever work they could find—carpentry, cooking, selling drinks. They had no thoughts of fortune now, or of buying orange groves. They were just trying to save money for the passage back to Chile.

Elena peered out the door of the flimsy shack that served as her home. Santa Maria, there they were! The boy Carney and his friends. At the head of the street.

She retreated into the shack, pressing herself behind the thin walls. Had they seen her? Were they coming? It was impossible to hear them above the din of the town. Perhaps the boy was sober today. Perhaps he wanted to apologize for his behavior last night.

"Where's that girl! Goddammit, where's that girl!" Carney's voice. He was drunk again, coming down the street.

"Where are you?" Carney cried, slurring his words.

His three friends were laughing. "Find her, Carney," they said. "She's around here somewhere."

"This is a weekend you'll never forget," said another. "Your first drink and your first woman."

"First piece is the best piece," said the third. "And she's the best in town."

"Where is she?" Carney yelled, circling in the street. His face was flushed. His eyes were glazed. Beneath his thin beard he couldn't have been more than eighteen or nineteen. He was good-looking, refined even. He was probably a nice young man from a good home, but cheap whiskey had set loose a secret person deep inside him. His friends weren't in any better shape. None of them knew what they were doing.

The boy's voice suddenly became cajoling. "I brought more money today," he called out. "Here, look at this purse. It's worth hundreds. Come on." It grew rough again, frustrated. "You bitch!"

"Come on, *chiquita*," cried one of his friends. "You got a paying customer here."

"An American customer," added another.

"Do what he says or we'll run you out, like we did those other greasers."

Elena held her breath, looking through a chink in the wall. She prayed that Juan would get back soon—or did she? It was only by threat of violence that Juan had been able to make these men leave last night. They looked like they hadn't stopped drinking since then. Their mood could turn ugly in a hurry. If Juan came back, he might get hurt. She held her breath.

The men passed her house and went down the street. Elena let out her breath.

Then one of them turned. "Wait a minute. That's her place. I remember from last night."

"You sure?"

"Yeah."

Carney lurched over. He began banging on the door, shaking it with the force of his blows. "Hey! Hey, señorita! Hey, I know you're in there. Open up."

Elena was afraid the door would break in. She gathered her courage. "Go away," she cried.

Yells of satisfaction. "The game's been flushed," one of them crowed.

"Open up," Carney demanded.

Elena tried to keep the fear from her voice. "Go away, I said."

"Goddammit, you turned me down last night, but you're not going to turn me down again."

"I'm not a whore," Elena protested.

"Sure, sure. That's what they all say. What's the matter—my money's as good as anybody's."

"My husband will be back soon," Elena said. "I don't want trouble."

"Come on, *chiquita*," said one of Carney's friends. "Stop playing coy. We've got a virgin here, and he needs to be broken in."

"It's his birthday," said another. "And you're his present."

"He'll only be a minute," added a third, and all but Carney broke up laughing.

Their laughter seemed to enrage Carney. He rattled the door latch. "Open up, dammit. I want you, and I'm going to have you."

Elena was near hysterics. "Please. Go away." She wished she had learned English better so that she could explain herself, so that she could make these men believe her.

Carney threw himself into the door, smashing it open. Elena backed up with a gasp. Outside there were calls of glee.

"Please," Elena said, but Carney was not listening. His eyes were blank. Tomorrow he wouldn't remember any of this. He staggered toward her, mouth open, taking in her face, her body. "Come here," he said.

"Get out," she pleaded

"I said, come here." He lunged for her across the small room.

He grabbed her, drew her to him, kissing her, running his hands over her body. There were hoots from outside.

Carney held Elena tightly, kissing her, feeling her breasts, her buttocks. Running his hand under her dress. She fought him, pushing, scratching, screaming for help, but her cries were smothered by his kisses. The two of them crashed around the small room, knocking over furniture, breaking glasses. "Ride her!" cried somebody outside. Carney got a leg behind Elena's and threw her down. He climbed on top of her, lifting her dress. He reeked of whiskey. Elena pummeled his head and back. With a superhuman effort she pushed him off. She got to her feet and tried to run. He caught her by the leg and dragged her down again. As she fell, she reached out and grabbed the carving knife from the kitchen table. Carney straddled her, fumbling open his trousers. He pushed her legs apart with his own. He tore her dress open from the top, feeling her breasts. He bit through her ear. Blood flowed. He bit her neck. He banged her head against the floor, carried away by drink and passion, trying to enter her at the same time. Desperately, she stabbed upward with the kitchen knife. He seemed not to notice. She stabbed again and again, between his ribs, and suddenly he stopped his assault. A strange look came into his bloodshot eyes. He raised himself onto his knees. Something was dripping all over Elena. She pushed him off her. She got to her feet, hysterical.

"Hey!" somebody yelled. "She's stabbed him! The whore stabbed Brian!"

There was the sound of running feet. To Elena it was all a blur. Carney was still on his knees. Blood was spilling onto the floor. Then he toppled over. His friends were around him. "She killed him. The bitch killed him."

Yelling, shouting. The men grabbed her. She tried to explain to them in Spanish. She could not remember any English; her mind had gone blank. There was shouting from outside now. "Brian Carney's dead."

"Santa Maria, I was defending myself," she screeched.

Shouts rang up and down the street. "Brian Carney's dead. He was stabbed by a whore. She tried to rob him." A crowd gathered. Angry men, red faces.

"Hang her! Hang her!" they yelled.

"*Por favor*," she cried. "Please!" Where was Juan? He would help her. He would make it all right.

The crowd had become a mob. Men held her roughly. Somebody spit on her. "Hang the greaser bitch!"

Sobbing, she tried to explain, but nobody wanted to hear. Brian Carney was dead. Brian Carney, everybody's friend.

"My darling, what . . ." It was Juan.

"There's her pimp!" yelled one of Carney's friends.

"Get him."

"He's in it, too."

Men grabbed Juan. He resisted. One of them punched him in the face. He tried to fight back. Somebody else hit him. He sagged, blood coming from his nose.

"Trial! Trial!" the miners yelled.

It was happening too quickly for Elena to understand. There was the alcalde. She knew him, an ex-whaling captain named Sampson. The same man who had promulgated the laws ordering Mexicans from the diggings. Men were quickly chosen. A jury, the gringos called it. Carney's friends told what had happened. "Brian was just a kid. You knew him, he wouldn't hurt a fly. She's been leading him on for two days. Then, when she got him alone, she killed him."

Elena could not follow it all. She was sure they were not telling the truth. Even men who had not been there testified. "I was in Mexico with General Wool. I seen our boys killed by greaser whores, this same way." They were drunk. They were all drunk. Drunk and angry and shouting, even in the midst of the testimony. Juan struggled futilely against the gringos holding him.

The alcalde was asking for Elena's version of the story. She tried to tell. "He was raping me."

"You can't rape a whore," Sampson said.

"I'm not a whore!" she cried, but man after man rose and swore that she was. She was Mexican; she must be a whore. Blood dripped from her lacerated ear. The dead man's blood covered the front of her dress, or what was left of it. One of her breasts was exposed, and she pulled the dress up over it. She pleaded for these men to listen to the truth, but she could tell from Sampson's face that her pleas were not being heard, that her fate was sealed. Her words were drowned by shouts for vengeance. She was crying. She saw Juan crying, too.

Sampson looked at his jury. "Well?"

"Guilty!" they said.

"You heard the verdict," said the alcalde grimly. "There's only one sentence for murder."

"Hang her. Hang her," chanted the drunken crowd.

A bearded, rugged-looking miner with a faded shirt jumped onto an empty crate. "Wait a minute! Don't be hasty. Think this over. Find somebody that speaks Spanish, and hear what she has to say."

But the crowd was caught up in its own blood lust. "Keep out of this, Wade," somebody yelled. "Or we'll hang you, too."

The miner called Wade swore. "No, dammit! What you're doing is wrong, and I'm not going to—"

A bottle flew out of the crowd and hit Wade in the forehead. He crumpled and fell to the ground. Some of the men rushed at him, but his partner—a dark, lank-haired scarecrow—faced them with a revolver, and they backed off.

"What about the whore's pimp?" somebody asked Sampson. "What do we do with him?"

"Hang him, too," men cried.

Sampson said, "Was the pimp present when the crime occurred?"

"No," one of the dead man's friends answered reluctantly. "No, but he put her up to it, I'd swear."

Sampson faced Juan with his fists on his hips, as though he were still on his quarterdeck. "We'll let him live. But bring him along. Let him see what happens to murderers in Oro Fino."

"Help me, Juanito. Help me," Elena cried, even though she knew that Juan could do nothing. The miners laid hold on her and manhandled her down the street. Men were yelling drunkenly.

"To the old oak," Sampson ordered.

Elena couldn't believe this was really happening. It was like a dream. Any minute she'd awaken and find herself in her father's house, with the gentle music of the fountain in the courtyard and the servants bringing her coffee and iced fruit. Only it wasn't a dream, and she wasn't going to wake up.

The gringos dragged Elena to an old oak tree off the main street. Someone threw a rope over the lower limb. Somebody else produced a ladder for her to stand on. They pushed and hauled her up the ladder. She tried to fight them, but it was no use. They were too strong. She heard Juan's cries in the background. She heard men cursing him, hitting him.

She was standing on the ladder, looking at a sea of angry, sunburned faces. They were yelling as if they were at a sporting event, a bullfight perhaps, and she thought crazily to herself, now I know how the bull feels at the end. There was Juan, his face contorted with grief and hate and disbelief. Two burly miners pinioned his arms.

Someone put the rope around her neck. He drew it tight. The knot pressed behind her right ear. An hour ago she had been selling meat pies and wondering what to give Juan for supper; now she was going to die.

"Any last words?" said the alcalde, Sampson.

Elena composed herself. She did not want these gringos to see the daughter of Diego Marquez de la Guerra y Soveranez die in a cowardly fashion. She would show them how an aristocrat behaved. Below her, men gathered around the ladder, ready to jerk it from under her feet. She saw the expectant look on their faces. She would deny them that pleasure, at least.

She straightened herself, wiping tears from her eyes. "Yes," she answered. "I condemn you gringos and your country to perdition." She looked down at her husband. "Be brave, Juanito."

She smiled and waved contemptuously to the crowd. Then she stepped off the ladder.

"Elena!" Juan Soto strained at the strong arms binding him. He tried to tear himself free, to save her. He watched her kicking in midair and he thought he was going insane. "Elena! Gringo bastards, I'll kill you all!"

"Be quiet," somebody snarled. "Be glad it ain't you up there."

"Brian Carney was worth a whole country full of you grease-balls."

Somebody knocked Juan down. They began beating him, kicking him. He thought he was going to die, and he didn't care.

"All right!" It was the ex-whaling captain, Sampson. "That's enough, boys. Let him go."

Juan struggled to his feet. He was bruised. There was blood on his face. His clothes were torn. His bride Elena dangled from the limb of the oak tree, dead.

The miner who had tried to save Elena, the one named Wade, pushed his way through the crowd. Wade saw Elena's body, and he hung his head, "Oh, no. Oh, Jesus."

"Get out of town," Sampson told Juan. "Don't bring your whores here again."

Juan was too sick to argue. "What about . . . what about the body?"

"I don't care what you do with her," Sampson said. "Just do it quick and make yourself scarce." He turned to the crowd. "Boys, tomorrow we're going to have the biggest funeral in the history of Oro Fino. We're going to bury Brian Carney."

There was general assent. The camp's blood lust had been satisfied. Now there was mourning for their young friend Carney, along with the inevitable depression that sinks in after revenge has been extracted. By twos and threes, then in wholesale lots, the crowd drifted away. Soon all were gone save Juan, the miner called Wade, and his black-haired partner. The two men looked vaguely familiar to Juan. He might have seen them on the boat from Panama. The sun cast Elena's shadow onto the ground between them.

Wade looked at Juan, anguish in his eyes. "I . . . I'm sorry. I tried . . ."

Juan was filled with grief and rage. He did not want condolences. He had nothing to say. The black-haired man caught Wade by the arm. "Come on, Wade." He pulled Wade gently away, leaving Juan alone.

Juan climbed onto the ladder. With his knife he cut the rope. Gently, he let down Elena's body. The gringos had destroyed him. They had taken everything from him. He would leave Oro Fino, but he would make the gringos pay for what they had done. He would have revenge.

Elena's revenge.

26

An autumn afternoon's golden haze had settled over the hills. Wade and Jack trudged back from Oro Fino, carrying their rations for the coming week. Around them, other men were returning to their camps. Some had gotten drunk in town; some had lost all their money at games of chance. Some, like Wade and Jack, had lacked funds for anything but necessities. Almost all were thinking about what they had witnessed that day. It was a quiet procession.

"It makes me sick," Wade said. There was a purple swelling on his forehead where the bottle had hit him.

"Let it go, will you?" Jack told him. "You'll drive yourself crazy."

"I can't let it go. So many people just stood by and let it happen. How could they?"

Jack shrugged. "What were they supposed to do? It was legal, or as legal as it gets here. Those three boys were there when Carney was killed. We weren't. They saw what happened."

"Those three boys were so drunk, they couldn't see straight," Wade said. He shook his head. "It's Sampson I can't figure. He was such a big help to us when those Pikes tried to jump our claim. Now he does something like this."

"I guess he did what he thought was right," Jack said.

"I bet he wouldn't have done it if that woman and her man had been Americans. I bet none of them would."

"Look, Wade, I agree with you," Jack said. "I didn't like seeing that girl hang. But it wasn't our affair. You did all you could. One man can't fight a mob. You were lucky you didn't get killed yourself. Did you know the girl, or the man?"

Wade shook his head. "I've seen them around camp, but that's it." Then he added, "You know, it's funny, but I could swear I've seen them somewhere else, too."

"I was thinking the same thing," Jack said. "Can't imagine where it could have been, though."

They reached their tent. "Hey!" said Jack, running ahead. "Somebody's been here."

Their belongings were scattered about the front of the tent. Jack picked up the half-gallon jar they had left by the flap. The gold dust that had been inside was gone. "We've been robbed. Somebody stole our stash."

Wade looked into the tent. "Nothing else gone."

"Son of a bitch!" Jack swore. He started to throw the jar, then stopped. Broken glass was all they needed around the tent.

Wade sighed. "It's just not the same here anymore. Used to be, you could leave any amount of dust lying around, and nobody would touch it. Now somebody steals a few dollars' worth. There's different kinds of people coming in, that's for sure."

"How much we got left?" Jack said.

Wade pulled out his leather pouch. There wasn't much heft to it. "Two ounces, if we're lucky."

"Damn," Jack swore again.

They stood there for a minute, then Wade said, "Let's fix supper. We might as well feel sorry for ourselves on full stomachs."

Jack built a fire and put on the coffee. Wade sliced off some of the salt pork they'd purchased in town. They fried the pork and ate it with the coffee and the rest of that morning's bread. While they were eating, Wade said, "I been thinking, Jack. It's time to move on. Oro Fino's panned out. I was going to wait another week or so, but now I think we should go right away."

Jack looked up from his meal. "Where you plan on moving to?"

Wade dipped a piece of salt pork in molasses. "Farther up the mountains. We'll find a place that hasn't been worked yet. We'll build a cabin and wait for the rains to come."

"You mean, stay the winter?"

Wade nodded, chewing the pork. "We'll find a claim, and on days when the weather's good, we'll have water and we can work."

"What about food? We ain't got money for a winter's worth."

"We can buy about two weeks' worth. After that, we can hunt. From time to time we'll come down and buy extra supplies with the dust we find. It'll be a lot cheaper than trying to spend the winter in Stockton or San Francisco."

Jack chewed his food, thinking about what Wade had said. At last, he looked over. "I ain't going," he said.

Wade said, "What do you mean?"

"I mean, I ain't going. I ain't spending the winter in no cabin, and I ain't digging no more dirt. Not here, not anywhere. I'm tired of living like an animal, Wade."

"I'm not thrilled about it myself, but we've got to get some gold before we can do better."

"You'll never get it with no pick and shovel. You're playing a fool's game, Wade. There's gold in California, but it's back there, in the towns. That's where the fortunes are being made. Let some other sucker do the hard work."

Wade angered. "If you think being here makes you such a sucker, why don't you go right now?"

"Maybe I will," Jack said.

Jack drained his coffee. He began throwing his meager possessions in an old sack. He stopped. "You surprise me, Wade. I figured you for more brains than to stay a miner."

"I've kind of surprised myself," Wade admitted, no longer angry. "Finding gold didn't meant that much when I started. I never planned to stay out here. But now . . . I don't know how to explain it, but it's like I have something to prove. To myself, if nobody else. I have to prove that I can do it. It's become a challenge. I came here for gold, and I'm not leaving without it."

"You got the fever," Jack said. "You'll end up broke and broke down. You'll end up killing yourself. And for what? A couple dollars a day. Well, that ain't for me. I'm going to make me some real money."

"How? You've got no stake, no skills. What kind of work are you going to find?"

"I'll think of something."

Jack finished with his sack. Wade didn't seem unduly concerned. He said, "Where will you go?"

"Back to Oro Fino, for a start."

Wade took his leather pouch and tossed it to Jack, who caught it against his chest. "Take this with you," Wade said. "Buy yourself a few drinks. It sounds like that's what you need."

"That won't leave nothing for you," Jack said.

"That's all right. You'll be back in the morning, and then we'll both be broke."

"I'm serious, Wade. I ain't coming back."

"So you say."

Jack held out his hand.

Wade didn't take it. "Get out of here, will you? Get drunk, and get it out of your system."

Jack hesitated, then he threw the sack over his shoulder. "So long, Wade." He waved and started away from the camp.

Wade called after him. "And don't expect to get out of work tomorrow just because you've got a hangover."

27

It was nearly dark when Jack returned to Oro Fino. Along the main street, lights glowed in the purple dusk. Fiddle and accordion music could be heard. The afternoon's huge crowd was gone, but there were still lots of people in the saloons.

The street stank of vomit and urine and animal dung. Jack picked his way among bottles, tin cans, bits of clothing. Here and there a drunk was sleeping.

Jack had worked himself into a black mood. What was he going to do? He'd never had a trade. He'd never done anything but odd jobs—legal and illegal—and he didn't want to go back to that. Not if he intended to be a gentleman, like Ma had wanted.

He decided to have a drink and think it over. He went into Quincy's.

Quincy, who had started with two kegs of liquor thrown across the back of a mule, now owned the finest saloon in Oro Fino. The walls were timber, the roof canvas. Coal oil lamps hung from the rafters, casting deep shadows. The thick tabacco smoke made Jack's eyes sting. Its acrid smell mixed with the stench of unwashed men. The crowd was packed shoulder to shoulder. Some were drinking and talking. Others watched the action at the faro table. Still more were jammed in the far corner, clustered around something that Jack couldn't see.

Jack's mouth watered at the thought of a drink. It had been two weeks since he'd had one. He felt free all of a sudden, without Wade looking over his shoulder, worried that he would spend their money.

He pushed his way to the bar, which was an oak plank laid across two empty beer kegs. The plank was stained and splintered. Men had carved their names and initials into it. Quincy was there, in a white shirt and vest, with bushy side whiskers. The shirt was stained with liquor and tobacco juice.

"Hello, Quincy," Jack said. "Give me a brandy."

"Ah, there y'are, Jack," said Quincy, pouring the drink. "I've been thinking about you. I've got what you were asking for these many months ago. You see, I never forget a customer's requests."

"What's that?" Jack said, curious.

Quincy hooked his thumb toward the far corner. Through the smoke wreaths Jack saw what had attracted the crowd—two girls. Twin sisters, it looked like, done up in velvet with their faces painted. Men swarmed around them like ants around sugar, talking to them, buying them expensive drinks which they did not consume.

"The beauteous LeBeq sisters," Quincy said. "Direct from the salons of Paris—or is it the sewers? I always get confused with these Frenchies." He winked, and Jack grinned.

Beautiful the girls were not. Beneath the makeup they were rather plain, but they had good figures. Jack felt a stirring inside him. He hadn't gone this long without a woman since he was fourteen, prowling the back alleys of New York.

"Cuanto?" he said. "How much?"

"Well now, we have a special introductory price. Two ounces of gold dust or thirty dollars in specie. As a special favor, I'll let you go to the head of the line, Jack. You bein' the one that gave me the idea to bring them here, and all."

Jack looked at his drink. "I ain't got quite that much on me. I don't suppose you'd let one go for an ounce and a half?"

Quincy sighed. "I don't believe I could. Two ounces is a rock-bottom price, as they say. Anything less wouldn't be fair to the lovely ladies, them having come all these miles across the wine-dark sea."

"I'm out of it, then," Jack said.

"Ah, well, it's a shame, and that's certain. Perhaps another time."

"Yeah," Jack said. "Perhaps."

Jack paid for his drink with a pinch of gold dust. With a wooden blade Quincy swept the dust off the bar and into a funnel-neck jar. Jack knocked back the brandy, feeling sorry for himself.

He bought another drink and wandered over to the faro table. The house gambler was seedy-looking, with a dented top hat, dirty shirt, and a cold cigar stuck in one corner of his mouth. By way of contrast, Jack was reminded of Mr. Levelleire's impeccable appearance, even in the heat of Panama. Now, there had been a gentleman. Would Levelleire have been running a faro bank in one of these camps, had he lived? Jack wondered.

The action at the table was heavy. A large crowd watched. Jack took the pouch of gold dust from his pocket. Maybe he could win himself a stake, or at least enough for a turn with one of the LeBeq girls.

The croupier was dressed much like the dealer. In front of him was a Chinese box into which he placed the bank's winnings, and from which he paid out the losings. In the box were bags of gold dust as well as coins from all over the world. Jack bought some chips. His dust got him twenty-six dollars' worth.

The dealer rapped his knuckles on the table. "Bets, gentlemen."

The game of faro took a minute to learn and a lifetime to master. The first and last cards in the deck were dead. The dealer dealt the others in twenty-five turns of two each. The first card in each turn was a loser, the second a winner. On the table before the dealer was a layout of the thirteen denominations. Bettors placed their wagers on a card to win or to lose, regardless of suit. Bets paid even money. If two cards of the same denomination—or "splits"— came up, the house took one-half of all bets on those cards.

Jack laid five dollars on the jack to win. It lost.

Jack bet again, and again. He lost both times. His mood grew blacker, even as he continued to bet. For all his bold talk, he knew that Wade had been right. He would have to go back to the claim. He would have to dig for gold again. In the back of his mind he had known this would happen ever since he'd left Wade, and that made him all the madder.

Almost before he got started he was cleaned out. He turned away from the table, sticking his hands in his pockets dejectedly. He felt the silver dollar there. He pulled the dollar out. What the hell, he thought. How could it get any worse? He turned back.

"Bets, gentlemen."

He laid the dollar on the jack. The jack was his lucky card, though it had already lost for him twice that night.

First turn. Second turn. On the third turn the jack won. The jack of spades. The croupier pushed a dollar next to Jack's. Jack let it ride.

Another turn. The jack won again. Again Jack let his winnings ride. He had four dollars now.

Jack won again. He let his winnings ride a third time. This time he coppered his bet, for the jack to lose. It did. There were sixteen dollars in front of him. Suddenly there was a strange tingling in his body. He was on a run, and he felt that he could do no wrong. People were watching him. Some began betting with him, to take advantage of his luck.

Jack moved all his money to the seven. He won again.

A new deck of cards was shuffled and cut. Jack kept winning. Always, he let the winnings ride. His winnings and those of the players who bet with him were making a dent in the bank now.

A hundred and twenty-eight dollars. Two hundred and fifty-six. The croupier paid him in bags of dust. The other players stopped to watch. Everyone in the saloon crowded around the table. Even the LeBeq sisters and their admirers walked over. Those who had been copying Jack's bets dropped out, believing that he must lose soon.

Five hundred and twelve dollars. A thousand and twenty-four. Each time Jack won, the crowd shouted. Each time, the shout was louder. Across the table the dealer looked cool, though sweat glistened on his unshaven cheeks. He brought out a new deck of cards. No one else was playing . . . it was Jack against the house.

Jack won again. Another shout from the crowd. Two thousand and forty-eight dollars he had now. He let it all ride, betting the ten to win. The crowd held its breath.

Two by two, the dealer laid out the cards.

Loser . . . ace. Winner . . . four.

Loser . . . seven. Winner . . . ten.

The crowd's cheers rattled the rafters. The croupier pushed over more sacks of gold. The pile in the Chinese box had dwindled considerably. Jack looked at the dealer, but the dealer stayed calm.

"How much to tap the bank?" Jack asked.

The croupier fingered his remaining bags of dust. "Call it three thousand dollars," he replied.

The crowd was still as death. Jack toyed with his pile. The dealer's eyes were ice cold. He had that much in common with Mr. Levelleire. The dealer looked confident, too confident, as if the next card would be whatever he wanted it to be.

Jack smiled. "I think I'll keep what I got. I'm cashing in."

There were groans of disappointment from the crowd. They wanted to see the game played to a finish. Anger flashed in the dealer's eyes. Jack had not walked into his trap. The crowd's groans turned to cheers when Jack shouted, "Quincy! Drinks for the house!"

Thirsty men thronged the bar. Jack scooped up his winnings, putting the coins in his pockets and the bags of dust in his hat. He bowed to the frustrated dealer and croupier. "Thanks for the game, gents."

He left the table. "Hey, Quincy. How much for the girls? Both of them. For the night?"

Quincy squinched his mouth sideways in thought. "For you, Jack—say a hundred dollars each."

Jack tossed him a sack of gold. "This'll cover it. Use what's left to keep us in champagne."

Later, in bed, with the LeBeq sisters on either side of him, naked, Jack smiled contentedly and poured around of champagne.

"Now, this is what I expected California to be like," he said.

28

Wade was surprised when Jack didn't come back the next day. He hoped that no misfortune had befallen him. He couldn't picture Jack having gotten a job.

For the rest of the week Wade waited for Jack to return. By Friday he conceded that maybe Jack wasn't coming back after all. Meanwhile, the nights were getting colder, the days crisp. He would have to leave soon. He didn't want to winter in the mountains without a partner, so he supposed he'd go down to Stockton. He'd find work there, then come back in the spring. He didn't think about going home anymore, or finishing law school. Finding gold was the only thing on his mind.

He inventoried the camp, deciding what to take with him. It was hard to believe how much equipment and just plain junk he and Jack had accumulated. Rummaging in the tent, he came upon Dan Baylor's pocket pistol. He'd forgotten he had it. He never used it, and it badly needed cleaning. He considered selling it. Then he decided, no. This was one thing he wanted to keep. It would help him remember Panama—and Kathy.

" 'Allo, Wade. Planning to shoot someone?"

Wade turned to see the short, burly figure of Sam Trumbull, rolling down the gulch on his bandy legs.

Wade put down the pistol. "Hello, Sam. No, I'm just sorting through my things."

"Where's Jack, then? Not off digging by 'imself, is 'e?" Sam laughed at his own joke.

"Jack left," Wade said. "Said he's through with mining."

"Is 'e now?" said Sam, scratching his bearded chin. "Can't say I'm surprised."

"What brings you here?"

"I'm leaving as well. Me and me partners 'as dissolved our corporation, as you might say. Young Timmy and that Bible-readin' Dutchman Oberg is on their way to Stockton."

"Where are you going?" Wade asked.

The little Englishman shrugged. "Dunno. I'd like to stay 'ere this winter, to be 'onest. 'Old on to me money for a change. Maybe even make some more."

"I'm thinking about staying on, too," Wade said.

"Really? Got anything in mind?"

Wade told Sam his plan to go deeper into the mountains. " 'Ere, that don't sound 'arf bad," Sam said. "Need a partner?"

"Sure," Wade said. Then he added, "There's one problem. I don't have any money. I can't afford supplies or a mule, and that's what it will take."

Sam was unfazed. "I'm a bit flush at the moment. I'll spring for the gear."

"But that wouldn't be fair to—"

"Pay me back wiv what yer make this winter. Pay me interest if it bothers yer that much. I never complain about turning a profit."

"All right," Wade said. "It's a deal."

The two men shook hands on it. "When d'yer want to get started?" Sam said.

"The sooner the better," Wade replied.

"Capital. We'll go into Oro Fino first thing tomorrow and get what we need."

The next day was Saturday. Oro Fino was noisy and crowded. A lot of men were getting a head start on the weekend. Many were in town for a last spree before heading to lower ground for the winter. The town brought back bad memories for Wade. He saw the big oak tree, and it made his stomach turn. Didn't any of these men remember—or care—what had happened to that girl? Didn't any of them feel guilty?

Sam seemed to read his thoughts. " 'Orrible, them 'angin' that girl last Sunday, wannit? I was up the ovver end of town, I missed the 'ole thing. Everybody says she was a bad 'un. Still, they could 'ave 'andled it better, don't yer think?''

"A lot better," Wade told him.

With Sam's money, the two men bought a mule. They loaded the animal with flour, bacon, potatoes, onions, and coffee, as well as a bucket of grease, some paint, nails, canvas, and ammunition for the shotgun. When they were done, Sam said, "This'll last us a good three months. Winters is mild 'ere. By then there's bound to be a break for us to come back and get more.''

Wade said, "I want to look up Jack before we leave."

"Fair enough," Sam said. "I'll say good-bye to me mates in town while yer at it."

"Meet you here in half an hour,' Wade told him.

Wade set off. He wondered if Jack was even in Oro Fino anymore. He pictured Jack sick somewhere, or even shot and needing help. As he made his way through town, he asked among his acquaintances, until somebody said, "Jack Marlow? He spends most of his time at Quincy's, playing cards.''

Wade felt let down. He'd been worried about Jack, and here Jack was, gambling. He must be on a run of luck. Maybe he'd join Wade and Sam now that he'd had time to reconsider. Wade knew Jack. As long as he had money, he'd be too proud to come back unless he was asked.

Wade went into Quincy's saloon. It was noon. The place was hot and smoky and crowded. Diffused light shone through the canvas roof. The smell of sweat was strong. Wade shouldered his way to the bar. "Say, Quincy!"

"How are ye, Wade?" said Quincy. "Not like you to be in town on a Saturday. What happened, you find the Big Lump?"

Wade shook his head. "Seen Jack?"

Quincy looked around. "He was at the faro table a while back. I don't know where he is now.''

From down the bar, somebody said, "He went off with one of those French girls.''

Quincy looked at Wade and raised his eyebrows. "He's like to be a long time when he does that.''

"Damn," Wade said. To Quincy he said, "Tell him I was here looking for him, will you? Tell him Sam Trumbull and I are pushing on. Tell him I'll see him if he's still here in the spring, or if I get down from the mountains sooner."

"That I will," Quincy said. "And good luck to ye."

"Thanks," Wade told him. He left the saloon and went back to the grocery store.

Sam was waiting there with two bottles of beer. He handed a bottle to Wade. "Find 'im?" he said.

"No," said Wade.

Wade was thirsty. He drank the beer gratefully. In front of him, in the crowded street, he noticed an angular young man carrying a carpet bag. The young man was looking around, as though at a loss what to do. He wore the tattered remains of a cutaway coat, and what had been a plug hat was pushed back on his head. His good-natured expression looked familiar.

Wade stepped forward. "Haven't I met you before? In Panama?"

The young man stared quizzically, and Wade said, "You were sailing a garbage scow—no, a cattle boat—here, weren't you?"

The young man laughed. "That's right." He looked harder at Wade, then he said, "You're the one who came out of the jungle. With the girl who carried a pistol and the sick fellow."

"Right," Wade said. "And your name is . . ." He strained his memory. "Bannister! Ralph Bannister!"

The young man laughed again. "You have a good memory."

Wade stuck out his hand. "I'm Wade Rawson." They shook, and Wade said, "This is my partner, Sam Trumbull."

Ralph and Sam shook hands as well. "Hello, Sam."

"Pleasure, Ralph."

Ralph looked around. "Where's your two friends?"

Wade felt a twinge in his heart as he replied. "The lady joined her husband, on the Merced."

"And the sick fellow? Did he die?"

"No," Wade said. "We split up. What about you? I see your cattle boat made it all right."

Ralph laughed again. "Don't I wish. That tub started leaking even before we left Panama. It literally sank under our feet. We beached her in Mexico—not far from San Blas. We rotted in San Blas awhile, then caught passage north on a French barque. But the barque was so slow, and the food so putrid, we all got off in

San Diego and walked the rest of the way here. I've just now reached the gold fields. I left the last of my shipmates a day back.'' He chuckled ruefully. ''Now that I'm finally here, they tell me I should leave, because winter's coming.''

Wade looked at Sam questioningly. ''Three on a cradle's more efficient than two,'' Sam said.

To Ralph, Wade said, ''If you're not afraid of hard work, you can throw in with us for the winter.''

Ralph didn't think about it long. ''All right. I don't know anything about mining, though.''

''That's all right, Ralph,'' said Sam, clapping the taller man on the shoulder. ''We'll teach yer. Glad to 'ave yer aboard.''

With the last of Ralph's money Wade and Sam bought more supplies and loaded them on the mule. Then they went back to Sam's and Wade's camps, where they packed the rest of their equipment.

They left the Mariposa Valley by a trail they blazed themselves. As they topped the ridge line, Wade looked back. When he'd first seen the valley, it had seemed like paradise. Now the trees had been cut down. The once sparkling river had been dammed and diverted, its water was brown from dirt. Everywhere were rude dwellings, tossed-up earth, and garbage. The birds could no longer be heard for the noises of men.

Was this progress? Wade wondered. Then he turned and joined the others.

29

The three men left the miners' camps behind. They were in virgin wilderness. Wade led the mule. He wore his old boots, the ones with the floppy soles. He'd wait till they made permanent camp before breaking in his new ones. ''So far, most of the gold hunting's been done right along the Merced and the Mariposa,'' he told his new partners. ''If we get into the untested country between them, I think we'll find good diggings.''

"Sounds reasonable to me," said Sam Trumbull. "What d'you say, Ralph?"

The angular young man hiked along, the old plug hat pushed back on his head. "I'm a novice at this," he said. "I'll go along with whatever you fellows decide." Then he added, "Do we have to worry about Indians out here?"

"Nah," Sam told him. "The Indians 'as either been run off or killed. Them what survived is up in the mountains, where they won't be able to feed themselves this winter. That should kill the rest of them off right smartly."

"Sounds brutal," Ralph said.

"The march of civilization, my boy. The march of civilization. It's a bloody shame, but there's no stopping it."

They made camp that night deep in the forest. After supper they sat beside the fire, gazing at the frosty stars overhead. Sam lit his pipe from a dying ember. "This is the life, innit?" said the little Englishman, stretching. "Fresh air, not a soul for miles. Noffink like it in the East End, I can tell yer. Where are you from, Ralph?"

"Philadelphia," Ralph said.

"You 'ave a job there?"

"I was an apprentice daguerreotypist."

"A daggery-what? 'Ere, wait—yer mean one of them picture-taking chaps, don'cher?"

Ralph nodded.

"That's an odd kind o' work. 'Ow'd yer fall into it?"

Ralph cleared his throat. "What I wanted to be was a painter. You know, an artist. I even went to art school for a year. But I realized I didn't have the talent. So I decided to make the camera my paintbrush. I would record the world around me, and make an art of that."

Sam puffed his pipe. "Why'd yer come to California?"

"For the gold. At first, anyway. I wanted to make enough to start my own studio back home. But then, after I got here, I saw this great explosion of humanity, and I knew that I had to photograph it. As soon as I can earn enough money, I'm heading for San Francisco to buy a camera. I'm going to travel the mining camps and record everything I see. Who knows, maybe a hundred years from now, men will look at my plates, and they'll say, 'This is how it was.' "

Sam and Wade made approving faces. To Wade, Ralph said, "I

wish I'd had a camera when you and your two friends came out of the jungle. What a sight that was!''

Wade told Ralph the story of the Panama crossing, leaving out the part about himself and Kathy. Sam had heard most of it before.

When Wade was done, Ralph said, "What about you, Sam? What brings you here?''

Sam chuckled dramatically, and he rubbed his thumb against his fingertips. "Gold, mate. Filthy lucre. I was in Valparaiso, working as a factor for some London merchants. It weren't a bad life, but it was dull. There weren't much to do but watch sailors brawl and wait for the odd earthquake to 'it. Then I hears about gold in California, and I thinks, why not? Give it a chance. 'Oo knows, maybe I'll make me pile and retire as a bleedin' duke.'' He chuckled again. "Wouldn't that 'arf flip my old man.''

"What's he do?'' Ralph said.

" 'E don't do noffink now. 'E's dead. But 'e was a fish porter at Billingsgate Market, in London. So was 'is dad before 'im. Me mum's family was in the same trade—their family name was even Porter. My brothers are in it, too—them what's still alive.'' He shook his head. "I can still smell them stinking fish. I 'ate that smell. I can't eat fish to this day.''

"So you left?''

Sam nodded, pipe in his mouth. "Joined the navy. Served four years on H.M.S. *Asia*—H.M.S. *Arse'ole* we called it . That was a pleasure boat, I can tell you. Since then, I've knocked about, done a bit o' this and that. Now I'm a miner.''

They talked awhile longer, then Sam knocked his pipe on the sole of his boot, emptying the ashes. " 'Ere, we best turn in. Long day tomorrow.''

In the morning they pushed on. Wade wanted to keep a northeast course, but it was only by using his compass that they were able to maintain it in the rugged wilderness. Several times they took what looked to be promising turns, only to find themselves at an impassable cliff, or a sheer drop, from which they were forced to retrace their steps. In other places the hills were so steep that they had to unpack the mule and carry the baggage up or down, while the animal followed.

At last they came upon an old Indian trail, and they followed that. The trail wound deeper into the mountains, in the general direction they wanted. The oaks and sycamores were replaced by pines and cedars. The air was noticeably colder.

That afternoon the trail dropped into a deep ravine. It was wild and romantic, studded with tall trees and great boulders.

"What a place," Ralph said. "Like an Altdorfer landscape."

"Nobody's been here before us, that's for certain," Sam said, looking around.

Wade said, "There should be plenty of water here when the rains come. Plenty of game, too. Let's make some test diggings."

Wade and Sam dug in different spots along the bed of the twisting ravine, while Ralph watched. They brought up dirt from the bedrock and dry-washed it, tossing it in an old shirt, letting the breeze blow away the lighter sand. They looked at what was left. "There's color, all right," Wade said.

"You think this is the spot, then?" Sam asked.

"It looks good to me. What do you say, Ralph?"

Ralph shrugged. "All right."

"Sam?" Wade said.

"I'm game," said the Englishman. "I'm tired of walking, anyway. Reminds me of the time I—"

There was a tremendous crashing in the trees, just up the hill.

"What the—?" said Sam.

The crashing grew louder. It was coming their way.

Wade took the shotgun from the mule's pack. He handed Sam the pocket pistol.

"Is this loaded?" Sam said.

"No," Wade said, "but whoever's coming won't know that."

The crashing grew louder. The three men saw trees move. Then a huge dark brown bear emerged from the woods. The bear waddled into the open and stopped, looking in the humans' direction, sniffing the air.

"Christ, it's a grizzly," Sam breathed. He turned the mule away, clamping a hand over its muzzle. The animal trembled with fright.

Ralph wanted to run, but Wade grabbed his arm. "Don't. No sudden motion. Let him think we're no threat, and he'll leave us alone. I hope."

"Thank Christ we're downwind," Sam whispered. "I 'ope 'e don't smell that bacon."

"I hope he don't smell *me*," Ralph said.

The bear continued to stare at the three men, who remained motionless. Wade fingered the shotgun. He wondered what he'd do if the grizzly charged. The weapon was loaded with ball, but Wade didn't know how much use it would be against a monster like that.

Suddenly the bear reared up on its hind legs. Drool slobbered from its jaws. Then it dropped to all fours again. It snorted and shook its head. It turned away, ambling across the ravine and up the hill on the far side.

The three Argonauts let out their breath. Sam said, " 'E's come down from up 'igh, looking for food. It's getting cold up there. Winter's coming."

Now that the animal was gone, Wade could laugh, but one of his legs was still shaking. He said, "This is going to be our home for a while. Let's call it Bear Valley."

"It's not really a valley," stuttered Ralph, who was shaking even more than Wade.

"Maybe not," laughed Sam, clapping him on the shoulder, "but it was one 'ell of a bear."

30

On a level spot about halfway up one side of the ravine, they built their cabin. Wade and Sam were adept workers, handy with tools. Ralph was unskilled and a bit lost at first, but he was eager and a quick learner. They cut down trees, trimmed the logs, and laid them on their beam ends in a square. A door was sawed out of the front. A ridgepole with forks supported the roof, which consisted of two sheets of canvas, one six inches above the other, nailed to the walls. The top sheet was painted for waterproofing. The door was likewise formed by double sheets of canvas, weighted at the bottom to keep out drafts. They filled the chinks in the walls with branches, moss, and sod. Their beds were canvas sacks sewn together and stuffed with dried grass and leaves. The floor was packed down hard and covered with pine boughs.

When the cabin was finished, they found what looked like a promising pocket in the ravine bottom, and they began digging it out, setting aside the dirt to wash when the rains came. They supplemented their rations by hunting. As a boy, Wade had sometimes hunted with an uncle who owned a farm in Connecticut, but he'd never had to depend on his skills to set the table. He was surprised at how well he shot. At night the three men huddled by their fireplace, lost in the cold and the overwhelming quiet of the mountains.

Then, one morning, they awoke to the sound of rain rattling on the canvas roof.

They stood in the doorway of the cabin, watching the rain pour down. It rained all that day and into the next. By the second morning the ravine was running with water. Sam Trumbull drained the last of his coffee. "Well, lads. It's time we started earning our keep." He put on his coat and headed for the door. Wade and Ralph followed him outside, into the driving rain.

Ralph hugged himself. "It's freezing!" he said, and his breath turned to vapor.

"You'll get used to it," Wade told him. "It's perfect weather to break in these road smashers." He stamped his new boots in the puddles, getting them soaked and molded to his feet.

The three men went to their claim. With the dirt they had prepared, they worked the cradle, rotating jobs. One man shoveled dirt into the cradle's hopper, one poured water over the dirt with a bucket, and one did the rocking. The rocking motion broke up the dirt. The rocks were trapped in the hopper. The rest of the dirt washed below. It flowed down the cantilevered bottom, where the heavier gold was trapped against a series of riffles that had been treated with quicksilver to attract it. The rest washed out the tail.

About two hundred bucketfuls of dirt was all they could wash in the cold rain. When they'd had enough, they returned to the cabin, running there to warm up. They dried off before the fire and put on fresh clothes.

At the end of three days, they took the sand that had been caught on the riffles, melted off the quicksilver, and panned out the rest to get their gold.

"There's four and a half ounces for each of us," Wade announced when he'd finished weighing it.

Ralph whistled. "That's ninety-six dollars—twenty-four dollars a day."

"That's the best I've ever done up here," Sam said.

"Me, too," Wade said. "I was hoping for more, though."

Sam understood. "You want it all. You want the Big Lump."

Wade nodded. "We'll find it, too. We've got all winter."

Day after day the rain fell, with hardly a break. The wet and the cold began to take their toll. The men developed dysentery from a diet of game. They became afflicted with headaches and a severe ringing in their ears. Then they came down with fever. They dosed themselves with sulfate of quinine and went back to work. Eventually the quinine lost some of its power. Some days one of them stayed shivering in bed, some days two of them. Finally, all three were laid up, stoking the fire and wrapping themselves in their blankets.

"We'll be all right," Sam said above the noise of the rain and his chattering teeth. "We just need to see a bit o' the sun again."

With a shaking hand Wade opened a new bottle of quinine powder.

"Hurry," Ralph said. He was drinking tea made from oak bark, as hot as he could take it, to warm him and treat his dysentery. He spilled some down the front of his shirt.

"Lord knows what we'll do when this is gone," Wade said.

"The weather will break soon," Sam assured them. "It 'as to. There was never noffink like this last year."

But the weather didn't break. It kept raining. Veils of gray mist hung low over the mountains. Some days the men couldn't see across the ravine. Above them the clouds shifted and swirled, the smaller white ones roiling beneath the heavier monsters of gray and black.

Weeks passed, and still it rained. It grew too wet to work. The three men couldn't dig anymore. It was like shoveling soup. They sat despondently around the cabin. Their stomachs growled from dysentery. Their skins erupted with boils. Their hair and clothes became infested with lice. Water dripped from the chinks in the logs. The pine boughs sank into the mud of the floor. Their beds were wet. The flour turned moldy. The wet firewood produced too much smoke, making it hard to breathe. They couldn't leave their mule outside in the rain, so it stayed inside with them most of the time. There was just room enough for it to stand between the table and the beds. They stopped burying their garbage. They fed what they could to the mule and threw the rest outside the door, hoping it would attract an animal that they could shoot for food.

Sam carved a wooden checkerboard. He and Ralph played. Wade was down with fever. He wanted quinine, but they had to be careful about using it up. He listlessly turned the pages of one of Ralph's books, a well-thumbed copy of *Wieland*, by Charles Brockden Brown.

Ralph wasn't paying attention to the game. Sam double-jumped him, taking his king. "Damn!" Ralph said. He smashed his fist on the table, overturning the board and markers, frightening the mule. Ralph pushed himself from the table angrily while Wade steadied the animal.

"Easy on," Sam told Ralph. "It's only a game."

Ralph was breathing hard. He calmed a bit. "I'm sorry," he said. "It's this rain. It's driving me mad. It never stops."

He sank onto one of the benches, pulling at his thin beard. "Look," he told his partners, "we've made some money. Maybe we should . . . maybe we should go back."

There was silence. Ralph and Sam looked to Wade. At last Wade said, "I'd like to stay. I'm convinced we're near a rich vein of gold here. If we keep prospecting up the ravine, I think we'll find it. But we'll put it to a vote. We won't stay unless everybody agrees on it. If one of us wants to leave, we all leave."

"How rich a vein?" Sam asked.

"Real rich," Wade told him. "The Big Lump. Enough to make us all wealthy. It's right around here, I can feel it."

Wade looked at them. "What do you say?"

Sam said, "I'm willin' to stick it out a bit longer. 'Ow about you, Ralph?"

Ralph hesitated. Then, reluctantly, he said, "All right. I guess I can take it if you two can."

"Attaboy, Ralph," Sam said. "Yer won't regret this, I can tell you."

Christmas came. As if by divine decree, the rain let up.

"Maybe the worst is over," Sam said, looking out the door.

Wade shot a hare for their Christmas supper. It was the first fresh meat they'd had in days. It was Sam's turn to cook, and he turned the hare and a bit of bacon into a stew. He fried a small potato and an onion, and he split them three ways.

"Not exactly the 'oliday feast," he apologized, "but we 'as to stretch the vegetables. We're getting low."

The three men sat at the table. Next to them the mule munched its scanty grain ration. Sam produced a flask of whiskey, and Wade grinned. "You've been holding out on us," he said.

"No, I swear," Sam told him. "It was Saint Nick. 'E left it in me stocking."

Sam poured them each a drink. He raised his tin cup in a toast.

"Merry Christmas, lads. God bless us, every one, as Tiny Tim would say." They drank. "All right. Tuck in."

Ralph bit into a chunk of bacon, and he winced. "Ow!"

"Gums 'urt?" asked Sam.

Ralph nodded.

"Mine, too," Wade said.

Sam said, "We're getting scurvy."

"Oh, great," said Ralph. He felt his teeth, which were loose. There was a drop of blood on his finger.

"Noffink we can do about it," Sam said. "It's from not 'aving vegetables."

They finished the meal, sopping up the remains of the stew with their bread. When they were done, Sam poured more drinks. "Pity we can't celebrate the 'oliday wiv summat special."

Wade said, "Wait a minute, I have an idea."

From his pack he bought out Dan Baylor's old pistol. "We'll set this off. Each person gets two shots." He began loading it.

"There yer go," Sam said. "First person what 'its the moon wins a toffee."

Ralph was still feeling his teeth.

Wade finished loading the pistol. "Ready?" he said.

"Ready," Sam said. "Come on, Ralphie."

Ralph cheered up a bit. "All right."

"That's the ticket. It's Christmas, after all."

The three men squeezed past the mule and went out of the cabin. There they stopped.

It was snowing. The world had turned white.

Ralph looked scared.

"Don't worry," Sam told him. "This is California. It won't last."

31

In Oro Fino it was raining. The streets were ankle-deep in mud. There were puddles a man could swim in. The town was rapidly becoming depopulated. Every day saw more men departing for lower ground.

It was Christmas Eve, and the jollification had started early. Men drank, laughed, and sang, even those who did not usually indulge in such pursuits. With the bad weather, no one could work. There was nothing for them to do but hang out in the saloons and gambling halls, whether or not they had money to spend.

The inside of Quincy's saloon was hung with pine wreaths and garlands. Some Germans had put up a tree in one corner and decorated it, but Quincy wouldn't let them put candles on it for fear of fire. The saloon was permeated with a damp chill, with only the body heat of the crowd to dispel it. The usual cloud of tobacco smoke hung over the room, but Jack Marlow was getting used to that.

Jack sat at the faro table, dealing. He was clean-shaven. He wore a plain coat, hickory shirt, bandanna, corduroy pants, and high boots. He was working with a used layout and card box. He'd bought the outfit from a gambler up the street who was getting a new one. He didn't have a croupier. The fellow he'd been using had left for Sacramento.

Since breaking up with Wade, Jack had spent his time playing cards in the various houses around town. He'd gotten the job at Quincy's the previous month, after the house dealer came down with food poisoning and died. Jack had dealt before, but always in friendly games, never for a living. Right now he was getting by, but that was all. He wasn't making the kind of money he aimed for. In the last week or so he had started feeling at home in the dealer's chair. He was beginning to think of himself as a professional gambler. He modeled himself on the suave Mr. Levelleire, from Panama, though he had a long way to go before he reached that gentleman's attainments.

Jack felt out of sorts among the raucously happy miners around him. Christmas had meant something to him once, when his father was still alive and the family was together. Now it was just another day. There was a time when he had tried to get excited about it, but he couldn't. Now he didn't even try anymore.

On this gloomy afternoon, Jack couldn't have been merry even if he wanted to. Luck had been against him all day, and his bank was not capitalized to withstand much more. Another hour, maybe even a half hour like this, and he'd be tapped. He'd be out of a job, too, because Quincy didn't want anybody dealing for him who couldn't turn a profit.

As he played, he eyed the men around the table, looking for a mark. His eye rested on a genial fellow in glasses, Doc Billington. The doc was only half paying attention to what he was doing. He was drinking, looking around, talking to his friends. This was probably the first time he'd played faro—it was the first time Jack had seen him play, at any rate. Billington was the only doctor for miles around. He charged an ounce of dust for most procedures, and on some days his line was plenty long. He could afford to lose money.

Jack waited for an opportune moment. The doctor was betting big. His chips spilled off the card on which he'd bet, so that one might think they were intended for the card opposite. He slid a pile on the five to win, at least seventy-five dollars. Two turns later Jack dealt a six to lose. Jack glanced up. The doctor wasn't paying attention. Jack dealt the next card, completing the turn.

"The ten wins," he said.

He paid off the winners and raked in money from the losers. As he swept off the losing bets, he took the doctor's money with him. Amid the hurly-burly of the crowd, and people placing new bets, no one noticed.

"Next turn, gentlemen. Bets, please."

Jack dealt the next card. "Queen," he said. "The lady's a loser." He moved a button on the case keeper.

"Hey, wait a minute." It was Doc Billington, looking befuddled, peering through his thick glasses. "My money was on the five last turn, not the six."

Jack played another card. "Deuce wins," he said. He moved another button on the case keeper. He paid off on the deuce. There was no action on the queen, so nothing to rake in.

"I said, my money was on the five," Doc Billington repeated.

"No, it wasn't," Jack said nonchalantly. "All bets in?" he asked the house. He started the next turn. "Seven. Seven loses."

"Yes, it was," said Billington, refusing to concede.

Jack tried to stay calm. How had this fool caught him? He worked the case keeper. "You may have thought it was, sir, but it wasn't. A common mistake."

He dealt again. "Seven again. Split." He took in half of the bets on that card. He'd stacked those sevens in the deck. It was about time for them to turn up.

"The mistake was yours," the doctor insisted. "You took my money wrongly."

Men all over the saloon were looking. Cold sweat trickled down Jack's back. Billington was just drunk enough to be obnoxious, a first-time player who thought he knew everything. Jack wished he could admit his mistake and give back the money, but he couldn't. If he did, everybody in the house would be claiming the same thing. Jack would be tapped before the deck was out. He tried to imagine how Mr. Levelleire would have reacted to a situation like this. He spoke much more coolly than he felt. "I must repeat, sir. You're mistaken."

Doc Billington smacked his open hand on the table. "Dammit, Marlow, give my money back."

Jack ignored him, starting the next turn. "Ace of hearts, gentlemen. The ace loses."

"You're cheating, Marlow!"

The crowd quieted.

"Come on, Roy," said one of the doctor's friends.

"Let it go," said another, trying to pull him away.

But the furious doctor wouldn't budge. Jack looked up. His cold eyes bored into the bespectacled eyes of his accuser. "That's not a word to use lightly, sir."

"I don't use it lightly," Billington said. "You're no good, Marlow. You can't even cheat properly. Why don't you get a real job?"

"Doc," said somebody, "calm down."

"Jesus, Roy . . ." said another.

"Are you going to give my money back?" Billington demanded.

"No," replied Jack. "Like I said, you're—"

Billington jammed a hand in his coat pocket.

Instinctively, Jack went for the pistol in his waistband. As the doctor pulled his hand from the pocket, Jack cocked and fired the pistol in one motion. The .44's roar was loud in the smoky saloon. The bullet caught the doctor square in the chest. He lost his footing, as though he'd slipped on something. His arms windmilled as he tried to regain his balance. Then he crashed face first onto the heavy table and slid off.

Jack scraped back his chair and stood, pistol cocked and ready to fire again. The idiot, why had he done that? The crowd was in an uproar. Jack's hand was shaking, but he tried not to let anyone see it. He moved around to the front of the table. There were men bent over the fallen doctor. "Give him air," somebody shouted. Blood welled from a small hole in Billington's chest. He was breathing, but just barely. One lens of his glasses was cracked.

Quincy pushed his way through the crowd. His cheeks and nose were red from drink as he bent over the doctor. "Christ, Jack, ye've killed him."

Jack stared. "There's . . . there's so little blood."

"Blood or not, he's dead," Quincy said.

"It was self-defense," said Jack. "He was going for his gun."

Quincy felt in the doctor's coat pocket. A strange expression came over him, and he drew something out.

It was a pipe.

"He wasn't going for a gun, Jack. He was going for this. Oh, Jack, ye've made a bad mistake."

Jack felt his face go white. His tongue was dry. Some of the crowd were in shock. Others grew angry. "Doc don't even own a gun. Everybody knows that."

There were murmurs of agreement. Jack stepped back nervously, covering the crowd with his pistol.

Somebody said, "You son of a bitch. Doc Billington was a grand fellow. He cured me of the bloody flux last summer. And you killed him."

"It was an accident," Jack protested. "I . . . I didn't know . . ."

"You killed him, you bastard."

In the background, men were calling for the alcalde. "There'll have to be a trial," Quincy told Jack sadly.

Jack remembered all too well the kind of justice he was likely to get from the alcalde.

Angry miners closed in on Jack. He stepped back again, pistol leveled. "That's far enough."

Tempers were rising. People poured out of the saloon, crying,

"Doc Billington's been shot." Jack saw only one end to this, and it wasn't a good one. With one hand he snatched his half-empty pouches of gold dust from the table and stuffed them into his coat pocket, still covering the crowd with his pistol.

Angry voices shouted, "You won't get away, Marlow. Hand over that gun."

"The gun, Marlow." It was Sampson, the stern ex-whaling captain who served as alcalde.

There were too many people between Jack and the front door. He'd never make it out that way. There was no back door. Jack looked to Quincy for help, but he saw from the expression on the saloon keeper's face that he wasn't going to get any.

The crowd inched closer. Jack flourished the pistol at them. That stopped them for a moment, but only for a moment. They were working themselves up for a hanging. There probably wouldn't even be a trial. Men edged around him. It was only a matter of seconds before they rushed him.

Jack flourished the pistol again. "Get back," he ordered. Then he turned and ran to the rear of the saloon. He tensed himself, praying, and with all his strength he smashed into the building's wood and canvas wall. He shattered a breach in it. Desperately, he pushed himself through, shredding clothes and flesh on jagged splinters of wood. There was a cry, and the crowd was after him. He turned and shot into them blindly. He heard someone scream. He ran down the alley behind the saloon, sliding in the mud, losing his hat, pouches of gold spilling from his pocket. Sobs rose in his throat. Behind him there were shouts as men crushed through the opening in the wall, widened it, and came after him.

He ran as fast as he could. He prayed he did not lose his footing in the mud and fall. If he went down, it was death for him. Shots were fired at him now. Bullets zipped by. Bullets hit the puddles. Jack reached the head of the alley and looked back. He fired his pistol into the oncoming mob. Somebody staggered. He had three shots left. He left the alley, running into the main street, which was in an uproar. He splashed down the street, hoping there was a horse in town. The churned-up mud sucked at his feet as if it, too, were trying to capture him. Rain slanted into his eyes. He saw a horse in front of the hardware store. He ran for it, gasping for breath, the mob after him. Men in the street saw what was happening and moved to intercept him. He brandished the pistol at them, and they backed away.

He reached the horse. It was only looped to the rail, thank God. He knocked the reins loose and mounted in one motion. The mob was close. He fired at them. The horse bucked at the shot and at the unfamiliar rider in the saddle. Jack hung on, wheeling the frightened animal in the street. The mob was coming on again. They were shooting at him. He fired again, and started the horse out of town. The horse went at a slow gallop, slop flying everywhere. Bullets cracked around him. He reached the end of the street and started up the long grade out of town. Behind him, he heard curses and yells as a pursuit was organized. Rifle shots followed him up the grade. Bullets splintered the trees; they whined off rocks. Jack urged the horse along, but there was no making speed on that grade. At last he reached the top. Breathless, he looked back once, then he headed west, a fugitive from justice.

32

On Christmas Eve, Kathy Beddoes stood in the doorway of her restaurant, watching the rain lash the puddles in the street. The creek at the canyon's bottom had become a gushing torrent. Its roar was so pervasive that she hardly noticed it anymore. Behind Kathy, her helper, Smoke, and a team of volunteers were decorating for the Christmas party. The restaurant had done no business that day, nor had there been any the day before. Only those who had stocked up on provisions could afford to remain at the placers, and even they worried about being trapped by continued bad weather. There was no more food to be purchased in camp, at any price. Heavily laden mules and wagons could no longer be brought up the treacherous mountain trails.

Watching the rain, listening to its melancholy rhythm on the canvas roof, Kathy thought about Wade. She wondered if Wade had gone back east at the end of the autumn as he'd planned. By this time next year he would be a lawyer, moving in society, making a name for himself.

And she. . . ? She had no idea.

Her thoughts were interrupted by the sight of Captain St. Clair toiling up the far side of the street, head bent against the slanting rain. St. Clair tipped his hat brim to Kathy with that insolent manner of his. Then he went on his way.

St. Clair had deserted his tent for an abandoned cabin outside town. He divided his time between the tent and the 1-2-3 Saloon, where he ran a monte bank. There was no action at the gaming tables, though. There was no reason for a man like St. Clair to remain in Kate's Bar. Kathy could not understand what kept him in town. Unless . . .

Unless he was waiting for her.

There was a cold feeling in the pit of Kathy's stomach. It was not the first time she'd had this thought. She'd seen more and more of St. Clair lately. He'd made a habit of parading outside the restaurant, of casting bold looks at her. But if he still desired her, what was he waiting for? She didn't know.

Christmas was celebrated with a sing-along. The entire camp gathered at Kathy's restaurant. In the spirit of nondenominational fellowship, Abe Greenberg, the hardware store owner, donated three tubs of champagne punch. The grizzled alcalde, Peach, led the chorus. Everyone joined in, even Greenberg.

Because of the weather, Kathy wore a man's coat and high boots with her dress. Her dark hair, usually braided for convenience, had been brushed out in honor of the holiday. She was surrounded by ruddy-faced, bearded miners, and her soprano lent a lilting counterpoint to their bass and tenor. The music transported her back to other Christmases, to other sing-alongs. Christmas had always been a happy time for her, a time for home and family. She remembered her one Christmas with Michael, in their tiny flat on Washington Street, before he'd gone away to California. Her life had seemed so ordered then, her future so certain. In her wildest dreams she couldn't have imagined that two years later Michael would be dead and that she'd be living on her own in a wilderness mining camp. Still less could she have imagined being happy in such a situation.

After the singing, somebody unlimbered a fiddle, and there was dancing on the restaurant's packed-earth floor. Kathy took a mandatory turn with each of the men, then they danced with each other, half of them tying handkerchiefs around their arms to designate themselves as "women."

Red-faced, puffing for breath, Kathy left the dancing and joined

Peach and Greenberg on the side. She noticed a knot of men meeting among themselves, talking earnestly, looking her way.

"What's that all about?" she wondered aloud.

A delegation of the miners approached. They moved hesitantly, almost apologetically. They halted in front of Kathy. Their leader looked around for support. "Go ahead," the others urged. "Go on."

The leader, a prematurely balding young man named Hudson, cleared his throat. "You sure sing pretty, Miss Kathy."

"Thank you, Mr. Hudson. That's very kind."

"No, ma'am. Just telling the truth. And the fact is . . . well, we've got a proposition we'd like to put to you. Me and the boys here."

"Yes?" Kathy said.

Hudson twisted his shapeless straw hat in his hands. "We'd like you to sing for us. A regular concert, like. We'd pay you, we'd pay you real good. Everybody from camp would come. Everybody from all the camps around, if you wait for the weather to turn. There's a lot of us homesick, Miss Kathy, and it sure would make us feel good."

Kathy glanced at her friends. Peach was grinning. Greenberg looked strangely subdued. Kathy started to dismiss the request. She had told these men that she was no music-hall performer. But the idea did have an appeal. She remembered the power she'd felt when she'd sung for the men once before.

"Go ahead," Peach told her. "Do it."

"Please, Miss Kathy," said Hudson.

"Yeah, please," chimed in the others. Men all over the room watched, waiting for her answer. Kathy took a deep breath. She would never have said this if she hadn't had a few cups of the champagne punch.

"Very well," she began, and she was drowned out by cheers and yells.

"When? When?" the men demanded.

"When I've had time to digest what I've gotten myself into," she joked. "A few weeks, anyway. I've never done this sort of thing before. I have to build up some nerve."

"You promise?" they said.

Kathy took a deep breath. "Yes. I promise." She shut her eyes. She was afraid that she was going to make a fool of herself. But she also felt a tingling of anticipation, and that was something else she could never have imagined two years ago.

Kathy watched the celebrating miners dispatch the rest of the champagne. Abe Greenberg had the tubs refilled. Then he brought Kathy and Peach more punch. He did not drink himself.

"One might think you're liquidating your stock," Kathy told him.

Greenberg looked guilty. "I am. I'm leaving for Stockton in the morning."

Peach was wide-eyed. "You're kidding," he said.

Greenberg shook his head. "No."

"When did you decide this?" Peach said.

"Two days ago. I am sorry that I didn't tell you, my friend. It was a mistake. But I didn't want to create a panic in town."

Kathy said, "What about your store?"

"It's empty," Greenberg said. "The champagne was all that I had left. I'll come back in the spring with new supplies and reopen it."

Kathy and Peach exchanged looks. "We'll miss you," Kathy said.

Greenberg shrugged. "It's business. I can't make money if I don't have anything to sell." Then he added, "You should consider leaving yourself, Kathy."

Kathy said, "I have supplies to last myself and Smoke through the winter."

"If there's shortages, who knows what might happen?" Greenberg said. "It could become dangerous here."

Kathy scoffed. "These men wouldn't—"

"Who knows what starving men might do? Besides, you don't need this kind of life. You've made money. You could open a thriving business down below."

Kathy thought for a moment. "No," she said. "I feel at home here. I have plans. It's hard to see how I can do better somewhere else."

Peach put an arm around her, grinning. "That's right. What would Kate's Bar be without Kate? You're a civic institution. Why, I bet you've had at least one marriage proposal from every man in town."

"Everyone but you," Kathy said.

"A few more glasses of Abe's champagne, and I may surprise you," Peach said.

Kathy left the celebration soon after. She returned to her cabin by herself, wearing a man's hat for protection against the never-ending rain. She moved carefully down the side of the street, picking her way around the deeper puddles and avoiding the abandoned gold pits in the center, which had flooded, and into which an unwary person might tumble and drown in the dark. She passed ruined cabins and tents deserted by owners who had fled to lower ground.

A shadow loomed ahead of her, and she started. It was a smallish man, muffled in a military-style greatcoat. He leaned against the awning pillar of an abandoned saloon. As Kathy came up, the man stepped away from the pillar, blocking her path.

It was Simon St. Clair.

St. Clair touched the brim of his slouch hat. "Good evenin', Miss Kathy."

She avoided his eyes. "Good evening," she replied, trying not to sound nervous.

She tried to move around him, but he moved with her, cutting her off.

"I heard you singing," he said.

"Yes?"

"Very pretty."

"Thank you. Now, if you'll just—"

"Oh, come now, Miss Kathy. I was hopin' we could be friends."

She replied frostily. "I'm afraid that's impossible, Captain. You know why."

He held his hands wide. "That? That was just a misunderstandin'."

"I don't consider physical threats upon my person a misunderstanding, Captain. And I'll thank you to remember the promise by which you were allowed to remain in this community. You seem to have forgotten that promise. Have you also forgotten the consequences of its violation?"

St. Clair smiled. "There's not as many men to enforce those consequences as there used to be."

"Peach is here," she told him. "That's enough. Now, please let me by."

She moved around him once more. Once more he blocked her. He leaned in close, and in the dark his pale blue eyes seemed to glow. "I haven't forgotten a thing. Not a thing." The last words were spoken in a whisper. It was as if he were undressing her with his voice.

Kathy swallowed in fear. Then St. Clair stepped aside, bowing. She walked by. "Merry Christmas," he said.

That night Kathy decided to leave. She no longer felt safe from St. Clair. Peach could not guard her twenty-four hours a day.

She was too late to go with Abe Greenberg, who left at dawn. She bought a mule, packed her things, and got ready to join the next group out. Smoke had no desire to test the unknown racial climate down below, so he volunteered to remain in charge of the restaurant.

Two days later, Greenberg reappeared in camp, haggard and splattered with mud.

"What happened?" Kathy said.

"The trails below are washed out," Greenberg told her. "The ferry at Wilkin's Gap is closed. I'm afraid we're stuck here until the rain stops."

The new year was seen in with an artillery barrage. The remaining population of Kate's Bar gathered in the main street and set off their revolvers and shotguns, firing enough ammunition to start a small war. One of the men was slightly wounded when a spent bullet fell back to earth and hit him in the shoulder.

Peach got roaring drunk. "It's 1850!" he shouted, weaving in circles, holding a bottle aloft. "Mark it on your calendars, you sorry sourdoughs. This is old Peach's last year in the mines. Come next fall, I'll be a gentleman of leisure. A *haciendado*, or whatever them Mexes call it. While you boys is butt-deep in mud next year, looking for that Big Lump, I'll be riding over my domain, giving orders to my *vaqueros* and *peones*."

"Have you saved that much?" Greenberg asked.

Peach winked. "I got me a bit."

When the party broke up, Kathy and the others warned Peach to be careful walking home.

"Careful?" he cried. "I was born careful." He waved to them. "I'll see you boys in a day or two, when my hangover wears off."

Kathy went home and slept. Early next morning she was awakened by a banging on the door. "Miss Kathy! Miss Kathy! You better come."

Kathy threw her coat around her and opened the door. It was the miner named Hudson. "What is it?" she said, blinking sleep from her eyes.

Young Hudson was crying. He was out of breath from running. "It's Peach, Miss Kathy. He's dead."

The blood drained from Kathy's face. "What?"

"Some of the boys found him a little while ago. In one of them abandoned pits in the street. He must have fallen in on his way home and drowned."

Kathy felt numb. "Oh, God. I knew someone should have walked him back."

Kathy threw on her boots and dress and hurried out. By the time she got there, Peach had been pulled out. His body lay in the street, next to the flooded pit. His face was covered by someone's coat. Kathy sank to her knees in the mud. She reached out, touched the dead man's shoulder, and closed her eyes.

They buried Peach that same day, on a windswept hillside, with gusts of rain whipping their faces. They had a hard time finding a place dry enough to dig a grave. The men put up a headboard, and on it Kathy had them carve "Henry." Nobody knew Peach's last name. Nobody knew where he had come from, or if he had any family that could be notified. In Peach's cabin Kathy had found the old letters from his girlfriend. The letters were neatly tied with string. They gave evidence of many readings. The ink on them was faded; the paper was worn thin. Kathy hadn't read the letters. She hadn't even looked at the girl's name. It had seemed like an invasion of the dead man's privacy. She buried the letters with Peach.

"I couldn't find his stash of gold," she told Greenberg. "It's not in his cabin."

"He must have hidden it," Greenberg said. "It's probably buried in the woods. Most likely, it will never be found."

Everybody that was left in Kate's Bar attended the funeral, with one exception. Abe Greenberg led the prayers for the dead man's soul. Then the body was lowered, and the grave filled in with mud. The handful of mourners made their way back to town.

As she trudged down the muddy street, Kathy saw Simon St. Clair standing in front of the 1–2–3 Saloon. St. Clair looked at her and smiled.

Suddenly, Kathy knew that Peach's drowning had been no accident. She had a good idea what had happened to his gold dust as well.

And she knew that until the rain ended, she was trapped there, at the mercy of Peach's killer.

33

Kathy knew that St. Clair wouldn't wait long to move on her. She knew that she would get no help, either, with Peach dead. Greenberg and the few remaining men in town were scared to death of St. Clair. Whatever she was going to do, she would have to do it on her own, and quickly. She must act before St. Clair did. She must somehow get him off guard and put him at a disadvantage.

Late that afternoon she approached him, in the 1–2–3 Saloon. He was alone at a table, laying out cards. There was no one else in the building but the owner. St. Clair's eyes widened as Kathy came in. She pulled out a chair and sat beside him, looking at him frankly. "Captain, it's time you and I came to an arrangement."

One corner of St. Clair's thin mouth turned up. He fixed her with those pale blue eyes. "Well now," he drawled. "I knew you'd come around in the end."

"I'm not stupid, Captain. I know when to cut my losses. Do you still wish to be friends?"

His mouth turned up still more. "Very good friends."

"Then perhaps you'll join me for supper tonight, at my restaurant."

St. Clair inclined his head. "I'd be delighted, ma'am."

"The fare will be rather plain," she said. Then she added, "The main course, at any rate."

"I always was partial to desserts," St. Clair told her.

"Shall we say six o'clock?"

"I'll be there." St. Clair touched her cheek with his finger. It took all her effort not to jerk away with revulsion. "You're a smart lady, Miss Kathy."

"You've given me no alternative."

"That's right. I haven't."

"Until six, then." She smiled and left.

They dined alone, by candlelight. St. Clair looked boyishly handsome. His blond hair was combed back and pomaded. His silk bandanna was carefully knotted at his throat. He was freshly shaven and he smelled of bay rum. He'd already been drinking. Kathy wore a clean, plain dress. She'd brushed out her hair, and its lustrous highlights burned red in the candle's gleam.

"You look most fetchin'," St. Clair told her when he arrived.

"Thank you, Captain. I'm sorry I've nothing fancy to wear."

"I'll buy you things," he said. "I'll buy you necklaces and earrings, satin dresses that shimmer in the moonlight."

"How poetic," Kathy said. "Do you have that kind of money?"

St. Clair smiled. "I do now."

Kathy thought about Peach, floating in the abandoned pit. She thought about his missing gold. "Yes, I imagine you do."

As she led St. Clair to the table, he grabbed her arm. "I've waited a long time for this evenin'," he said.

She disengaged from his grasp and smiled coquettishly. "Sometimes the best things are worth waiting for. Don't you agree?"

They sat at the long table. Kathy had cooked the meal herself. There was preserved beef with canned mushroom sauce. There were potatoes, canned vegetables, and canned peaches. For this camp, at this time, it was a feast.

Kathy poised a bottle. "Wine, Captain?"

St. Clair nodded. "Call me Simon."

Kathy filled his glass. "It's lucky that Mr. Greenberg had a few bottles of this St. Julien tucked away."

St. Clair cut his meat in a neat, almost dainty fashion. He tossed down glass after glass of the wine. Kathy said, "Your accent suggests that you're from the South, Simon."

St. Clair's pale eyes were alight. He couldn't take them off her. His speech was husky with desire. "I'm from Georgia, originally. My father was a lawyer in Atlanta. He bought a plantation outside the city. We spent our summers and holidays there."

"It sounds lovely. Why did you leave?"

St. Clair shrugged. "I killed a man in an affray over cards. A matter of honor, you understand."

"You weren't arrested?"

"I hid with friends until the scare blew over. Then I went to Texas."

Kathy could imagine it. His friends had probably been too scared to turn him in. They had probably been glad to have him out of the area. She tried to sound like she was fascinated by his story. "They say you're very brave."

He nodded, in arrogant recognition of his own prowess.

"Have you killed many men?"

He smiled slightly. "It depends on what you mean by many. And if you consider Mexicans and Indians to be men."

He told her about his exploits in Texas and Mexico. He bragged about hunting Apache scalps for the Mexican government. Talking about himself seemed to make him more excited. He didn't want to know anything about her. Kathy kept pouring him wine. When one bottle was empty, she opened another, then the next.

At last he pushed aside his glass. "Let's do what we came for," he said.

He stood and came around the table. She rose to meet him, trying not to let her fear show. He embraced her. They kissed. He wrenched a fist into her thick hair and pulled, just enough to make it hurt, just enough to let her know what was in store for her. She took the offensive, sticking her tongue in his mouth, darting it in and out. He made animal sounds of desire and tried to press her onto the trestle table.

She pushed away. "No. Not here. My cabin."

His chest was rising and falling. His voice was hoarse. "All right," he said.

They put on their coats and walked into the rain toward Kathy's cabin. She took his arm. He kissed her and said, "You and I are going to be a great team, Kathy."

They reached the cabin and went in. Kathy lit a lamp. In one corner of the small room was an iron bedstead. "Now do you see why I wanted to come here?" she said. "I had the bed brought up from San Francisco. It's my only concession to the money I've made."

St. Clair tossed his wet coat on the floor. He went over to Kathy. He slid off her coat and began to unbutton her dress, kissing her with wine-foul breath.

With difficulty she fended him off. She smiled from under half-lowered lids. "No," she said. "We'll do it my way. I promise you, I'm going to make this a night you'll never forget."

St. Clair was hooked. In his drunken state he believed that she had succumbed to his charms. Kathy pushed him across the floor to the bed. "Lie down," she told him.

He lay on his back, and Kathy straddled him. She unbuttoned

his shirt and slid it off. He reached up for her, but she stopped him. "My way, remember?" Her long hair brushed his chest. She felt him moving with urgency; she heard his hoarse breathing. She slipped the pistol from the waistband of his trousers. "I don't think we'll need this."

She laid the pistol on the floor, well away from the bed. She took St. Clair's long dagger from its sheath and put it on the floor, too. Then she got out some cords of silk that she'd prepared earlier. She'd had to cut up her best chemise for them. She looped one cord around St. Clair's wrist and tied it to the bedstead.

"Hey, what. . . ?" he said.

She tied a cord around his other wrist. "Have you ever done it like this?"

"Y-yes, but not for a long time."

"Then you're in for a treat," she said.

"I don't like having my hands tied."

"Trust me," she told him.

He did. He would go along with anything she proposed. He grinned. "You didn't learn this by keeping house for some store-keeper husband. I was right about you all along, wasn't I?"

She smiled back. "I had to tell these rubes something, or they'd have been all over me. I came here to meet a man all right, but he wasn't my husband."

St. Clair laughed. "I knew it. I knew it. Why'd it take you so long to warm up to me?"

"You never made it worth my while before."

He laughed harder. "Well, I sure did that, all right."

"Like I said, I'm not stupid. Now that you've got me, I want you to know that you're getting the best."

She got off the bed.

"Hurry," he said, stretched out. "It's cold in here."

"I'll warm you up. Believe me."

She started to unbutton her dress. "Close your eyes."

"I want to watch you undress," he said.

"I don't like men watching me take my clothes off," she said. "It's an affectation of mine. I want you to see what you're getting all at once." She leaned over him and ran a fingernail lightly down his bare chest. "All right?"

"All right," he breathed.

"Now close your eyes."

He did. He lay there, licking his lips. He heard the rustle of her dress, the petticoats and chemise. He smelled her in the cold room, clean, no perfume, just woman scent, and it was enough to send his drunken brain spinning out of control. For months he'd tried to visualize her naked. Now it was coming true. He was scarcely able to breathe in anticipation.

"All right," he heard her say. "You can open your eyes now."

He opened his eyes.

The first thing he saw was that she was still dressed. The second thing was that she was holding a pistol. The pistol was cocked, and its muzzle was pointed between his legs.

He rose against his silken bonds. "What the. . . ?"

"Stay where you are," she ordered. Suddenly her voice was hard. "Did you really think I'd give myself to you? After what you did to Peach?"

She had hidden the pistol on a shelf earlier, in preparation for this moment. Her finger curled around the trigger.

"Be careful how you hold that thing," St. Clair warned. "It might go off."

"That's the idea," she said.

St. Clair lay back down. In the lamplight, droplets of sweat glistened on his face and chest.

"Are you warmed up now?" Kathy said.

"What do you want from me?" St. Clair said. Some of his drawl had faded.

"I want you to swear that you'll leave this camp and never come within five miles of it again. I want you to swear it on your honor as a gentleman."

St. Clair squirmed. Once a gentleman gave his word, no matter to what purpose, honor would make him hold to it.

"When am I supposed to leave?" he croaked.

"Right now," Kathy said.

"But this weather. I could die before I—"

"So much the better."

St. Clair grit his teeth. "And if I won't swear?'

She moved the pistol a fraction of an inch closer to his crotch. "If you don't swear, they're going to be calling you Captain Stumpy."

"You wouldn't," he said.

"Try me." Kathy's eyes were fierce. "I'll count to five. One . . ."

St. Clair's sneer started to crumble.

"Two . . ."

St. Clair breathed more quickly.

"Three . . ."

St. Clair swallowed.

"Four." Kathy's finger tightened on the trigger. "Fi—"

"All right," St. Clair said. "Jesus, I'll swear."

"On your honor? As a gentleman?"

"Yes. Yes. Just don't . . ."

"Say it!"

"On my honor. As a gentleman. I swear I'll leave Kate's Bar and never come back. Just get that goddamn gun away from my—"

Kathy stood. "Then go."

St. Clair sat up, pulling the silk bonds loose from the bedstead. His lips were white with rage. He looked like he wanted to tear her apart. But he'd given his word, and he was bound to it, and that made him angrier than anything else. "Can I put on my shirt?"

"Do it outside," she said.

St. Clair reached to the floor for his weapons.

"I said nothing about taking those," Kathy told him.

"What if I meet a bear, or robbers?"

"Use your charm on them," she said. "Now, get out before I forget myself and shoot you for the fun of it."

St. Clair glared at her for a moment. Then he kicked open the cabin door and stamped out into the rainy night.

Kathy stood in the doorway, watching him go. She trembled, not because she'd been scared of St. Clair, but because she had wanted to pull the trigger. She had wanted to shoot him. She had never thought she could feel that way about anyone, and that feeling scared her more than St. Clair ever had.

34

"Will it ever stop snowing?" Ralph asked.

Wade looked out the canvas door for the dozenth time that day. "The law of averages says it has to, eventually."

Sam Trumbull wasn't so sure. "I 'ad a cousin once. 'E said all laws is made to be broke."

"What happened to him?" Ralph said.

" 'E broke too many, and they sent 'im to Australia."

It was February. It had been snowing for the best part of two weeks. This current blizzard was in its third day. The wind howled around the cabin.

The three men were starving. They had used up nearly all their provisions, and the snow had driven what was left of the game down the mountains. They hadn't seen a rabbit in a week. They were ragged and emaciated, their gums blackened by scurvy. Their teeth were loose and falling out. Their legs were swollen, so that they walked with difficulty. They were light-headed from lack of food. They dreamed about food. No one thought about gold anymore. Food consumed them. They would trade all the gold they had ever mined for a good meal.

It was cold inside the little cabin, smoky from the crude fireplace. It stank as well, both from the smell of unwashed bodies and from the corner that the men were forced to use as a latrine during the blizzard. Sam sat at the table, playing checkers against himself. Ralph was too weak to get out of bed. He lay with his back against the wall, wrapped in blankets, sketching. On the cabin walls were tacked his pencil drawings of imaginary—sometimes nightmarish—landscapes and city scenes.

"We should have left at Christmas," Ralph said.

Near the door, Wade felt guilty. "It's my fault," he said. "I talked you two into staying."

They had never found the rich vein. When they had exhausted

their supplies, finally ready to pack up and go, it had started snowing, and they'd been trapped.

Sam was philosophical. "Look, we agreed we wouldn't stay unless everyone wanted it. We're all equally to blame. In a way, we're lucky. If we'd left at that last break in the snow, we'd 'ave been caught outside in this."

Ralph's pencil scratched over the paper. He was using a book for a rest. Sam got up and looked over his shoulder. "That's a wicked-lookin' cove yer drawing.'Oo is it?"

"You," Ralph said.

The picture looked remarkably like Sam, though the little Englishman couldn't have known that, not having a mirror. It showed the dark circles under Sam's sunken eyes. It showed his once-jowly cheeks hanging in folds. "Cor, mate, that's depressing," Sam said. "Draw summat else, would yer?"

"All right," Ralph said. He'd grown unusually calm the last few days. He began working with a new scrap of paper. The face of a woman took shape. The woman was beautiful; her oval face was framed by hair in fashionably curled ringlets.

"I know *that* ain't me," Sam said.

"It's my sister, Faith. I've got four sisters. Faith's the oldest. She used to practice her kissing on me. Drove me crazy."

Sam whistled. "She can practice on me anytime she wants."

Ralph put the picture down. "I doubt I'll ever see her again. I doubt I'll see any of them."

" 'Course yer will," Sam told him. "We'll get out o' this. It's just a bit o' snow."

"Is it time to eat yet?" Ralph asked. Wistfully, he added, "I wish we had some more of that mule meat."

Sam said, "Yeah, that was tasty, wasn't it?"

They had kept the mule alive as long as they could. It had been a faithful beast, and they'd refused to slaughter it. But the snow had made it impossible for the animal to find grass, and its grain was gone. They'd fed it their bedding, then old flannel shirts, even Ralph's plug hat, but at last the poor mule had starved to death. Its stringy meat had provided meals for a week. They'd boiled off the bones for broth, but all that was gone now.

It was Sam's turn to cook. "What's on the menu?" Wade asked him. "Steak? Turkey with dressing?"

Sam held up a mostly empty sack. "Flour and water, mate. 'Eavy on the water, easy on the flour. Seidlitz powder's gone. We can't even make bread."

"How about flapjacks?" Wade said.

"No grease to fry 'em."

"Wait a minute," Ralph said. He eased himself from his bed. He stumped across the room on his grotesquely swollen legs. From the bottom of his knapsack he brought out a can. "I don't know why I've kept this so long, but maybe you can use it." He tossed the can to Sam.

Sam read the label. " 'California Gold Grease?' "

Under his layers of dirt and beard Ralph blushed. "I bought it back east. According to the directions, you're supposed to rub it all over your body, then roll down a 'gold-spangled hill.' It's got secret ingredients so that gold and nothing else will stick to you."

Sam opened the can and sniffed its contents dubiously. "Grease is grease, as one Mexican said to the other. Let's 'ave a go."

He started to prepare the flapjacks. There was a time he'd have picked the mouse droppings out of the flour, but he didn't bother anymore. They hadn't seen the mice lately, or they would have eaten them.

Wade put on his coat. "Where you going?" Sam asked.

Wade didn't answer. There was a strange look in his eyes. He took his mining pan and went outside. He moved to the lee side of the cabin, where the snow was not as deep. He stayed next to the cabin because he was afraid that if he moved away from it, he would get lost in the blizzard and freeze to death. He fell to his knees and cleared away the snow. When that was done, he pulled up the dead grass and weeds he found there, and he filled his pan with them. He brought them back inside.

"What's that?" Sam said.

"Spinach," said Wade. "Spinach with butter."

He brushed off most of the dirt, then he threw the greens in a pot and boiled them. The scurvy had given the men such a craving for fresh vegetables, they were able to persuade themselves the mess actually was spinach, though it took a longer stretch of the imagination to add the butter. They ate the greens with the flapjacks. They shoveled the flapjacks down, ignoring the horrid taste imparted to them by the gold grease. The greens were tough and fibrous, but the three men chewed them with rotting teeth and forced themselves to swallow. They drank the greenish water from the boiled grasses and pretended it was tea. The food sent spasms of pain through their shrunken stomachs. Everyone was sick. But they had survived another day.

The next morning the snow stopped.

The three men raised a weak cheer. The clouds parted; the sun beamed through. The light was so strong that they had to avert their eyes, which had been weakened by months of gloom.

Their initial joy was quickly dispelled. "Two weeks ago this would 'ave been lovely," Sam said, "but now what do we do? Ralph 'ere can barely get to the door.'E'll never make it to Oro Fino."

Ralph was braced against the doorway for support. His lower legs and feet were so swollen that he wasn't able to lace his shoes. Tears made little tracks down his grimy face. "Go without me," he told them in a voice surprisingly bereft of emotion.

"Don't play the 'ero," Sam said. "We're all in this together."

Wade said, "One of us will have to go for supplies and come back, Sam. The other can stay and take care of Ralph."

Sam looked at Wade. "You're in better shape than I am. You go. Tell the truth, I ain't sure I could make Oro Fino, either. Not anymore."

Wade nodded.

Ralph said, "What if it starts snowing again?"

"That's a chance I'll have to take," Wade said. To Sam he said, "How long can you hold out here?"

Sam tried to be cheerful. "At the going rate of one-'alf flapjack a day—five days."

"I'll be back in four," Wade promised.

"We'll be 'ere," Sam said dryly. "Ralph will likely 'ave turned this place into the Sistine Chapel by then."

Wade said, "I'll leave you the shotgun. With the snow stopped, maybe you'll get a squirrel, or a rabbit."

Sam fried two big flapjacks for Wade. Wade rolled them up and put them in his coat pocket, along with a pouch of gold dust to buy supplies in Oro Fino. He wrapped his boots with strips of oilcloth and stuck the pocket Colt in his waistband. He rolled up a blanket and tied it around his shoulder with string.

Wade stood in the doorway with Sam and Ralph. He could read their thoughts. Would the weather hold? Would he reach safety? If he did, would he make it back?

He shook each of their hands.

"Good luck," Ralph said, trying not to look afraid.

"See yer in four days, then," Sam said, as offhandedly as if Wade were going to the local for a pint of beer.

"I'll be back," Wade promised again. He didn't know what else to say.

Then he pushed aside the canvas door, and he went out into the snow.

35

With the thick mantle of snow, everything looked different than it had on the journey northeast from Oro Fino. Wade recognized no landmarks. He could find his way only by using his compass. With his bowie knife he marked his trail on the trunks of trees. From each hilltop he took an azimuth toward a landmark that he picked out. Then he shot a back sight toward Bear Valley. He was fortunate that there was a distinctive mountain, higher than the rest, with a scoop out of one side, that he could use to guide him on his way back. In the distance he made out a depression that he took to be the line of the Mariposa. But there was much rugged country to be covered first.

It was hard walking in the snow. Wade felt it especially in his thighs, due to the unnatural motion of lifting his legs. He hadn't had much exercise during his months in the cabin, and that didn't make his task any easier, nor did his weakness from scurvy and lack of food. Wearing extra layers of shirts and a heavy coat, he soon worked up a sweat in the bright sun. He took off his coat and the scarf he'd wrapped around his ears.

The sun's glare off the snow hurt his eyes. He squinted. He averted his gaze. He pulled his hat brim low, but nothing worked. Still, that bright sun meant good weather. It meant he had a chance. He anxiously scanned the skies for signs of another storm. If a blizzard caught him in the open, it was certain death.

He came to a swiftly running stream. The stream had been dry last October, when he and his companions had made their trek out of Oro Fino. There was no way of telling its depth. Wade took off his boots, pants, and drawers. He held them over his head and plunged in. The freezing water took away his breath. As the water level reached his chest, he lost his footing, slipped, and was almost swept downstream by the rapid current. He struggled for balance, all the while holding his clothes over his head, trying to ignore the streambed's sharp rocks that cut into his feet. He steadied himself, leaning against the current; he continued across, testing each step, lest he fall into a deep spot. When he reached the other side, he climbed onto a sun-splashed rock and jumped in place until he was dry and warmed up. Then he put on his clothes and started off again, slogging through the snow.

He struggled up the sides of mountains. Going down, he let himself slide in the deep snow. Then he snagged his foot on a covered rock. The foot snapped beneath him, and he went tumbling down the side of the hill. He lay in the snow at the bottom, moaning, holding his ankle. If it were broken, it was the end of him. He felt it gingerly through the oilcloth and boot. He didn't think it was broken. Sprained, though, and that wouldn't help. He levered himself to his feet. A wave of pain passed over him. He put weight on the foot. More pain. He kept going, biting his lip, limping along. After a while the sprain warmed up, and he didn't feel the pain as much, but he knew it would worsen once he stopped.

As the afternoon waned, the temperature began to fall. The sweat on his body and clothes froze. He put on his coat and scarf again. Toward evening a thin layer of clouds set in. The sun glowed from behind the grayness with a yellow luminescence. As the sun sank lower, it reddened, and the sky and the snowy world beneath it were tinged pink. It was quiet, peaceful, still. Cold.

Wade spent the night in a hollow, out of the wind. With much effort he found burnable wood and he built a small fire, taking care to site it far from the trees, so that the overhanging boughs wouldn't dump snow on it and put it out. He sucked on snow to ease his thirst, and he ate part of a flapjack. Then he wrapped himself in his blanket and covered himself with dead leaves that he'd dug up for insulation from the cold. He lay near the fire, watching the flames dance in the darkness, listening to the crackle of wood in the vast stillness, and he fell asleep.

When he woke, everything was gray. Dawn, it must be. Time to get up. But he didn't want to get up. He wanted to lie there. A pleasant numbness was edging out the cold. It felt so good not to be cold anymore. He wanted to close his eyes and drift into that comforting numbness, but something in the back of his mind told him that if he did that, he'd never come back. That he'd be dead. He didn't care. What was death, anyway? Death seemed natural. It seemed like a friend, come to take him from the awful cold.

Then he thought about Sam, and Ralph. They were waiting for him. Their lives depended on him. If it wasn't for his greed, they wouldn't be in this mess. He couldn't let them down. He had to get back. Death was the coward's way out.

He stirred. With difficulty he emerged from his blanket and covering of leaves. He stood, resting his weight on his good leg. His limbs were stiff. He could barely move them. His thighs screamed with pain. His teeth and gums ached. There was ice on his eyelids and beard. He had a headache from the sun's glare. Fumbling with frozen fingers, he rebuilt his fire. He finished his first flapjack and had a few bites of the other. He stuffed the remainder of the second flapjack into his coat pocket, then he stood and started off. With his first step his sprained ankle buckled under him, and he gasped in pain. He stiffened the ankle and hobbled along.

The second day was a blur. More mountains. More streams that hadn't been there last fall. More sun's glare off the snow, splitting his head apart. One step at a time, he told himself, just like he'd told Jack Marlow in Panama. One step at a time. That's all it takes. Keep doing that, and before you know it, you'll be in Oro Fino. One step at a time. His mind went blank to everything else. He lost track of time and distance. He took compass sightings mechanically, as though in a fog. When he came to an impassable cliff, he stopped and cried, and the tears ran down his cheeks to join the ice in his beard. Then he turned and went around.

He blazed a trail for the return trip, if he lived to make one. Nothing around him looked familiar. Was this the way they had come, months ago, on those beautiful autumn days? He realized he was talking out loud to himself, and he laughed, a mad, cackling laugh.

He wished Kathy were there. Was she happy, wherever she was? He hoped so, for her sake. He wondered if she ever thought about him. He wondered if she even remembered him, if she remembered that day in Panama. . . .

Why torture himself? Why make this trip worse than it was? He would never see Kathy again. It was useless to think about her. He couldn't stop thinking about her, though. He supposed he never would.

Another night. Another campfire. Another gray dawn. Wade ate most of his remaining flapjack. The nauseating taste of the gold grease fouled his mouth. His head throbbed from the snow's glare. He started off again. One step at a time.

As he reached lower elevations, the snow was less deep. He made better time. He recognized where he was. This was the trail he and his partners had followed out of Oro Fino. At last he paused on a ridge line, and the Mariposa Valley was spread out below him. He felt suddenly warm. It was like coming home. He made his way down from the ridge. He began to pass abandoned miners' camps. He saw evidence of human activity—snow-covered mounds of dirt, garbage, deforested hillsides. He had never thought such sights could make him happy.

He reached the river and followed it downstream. He saw Oro Fino before him. He had made it. He munched the last of his flapjack in celebration.

Oro Fino's churned-up main street was covered with snow. There hadn't been traffic on it recently. There didn't seem to be anyone around. Buildings were deserted. Trash was everywhere, along with mining supplies and items of clothing, all as if hastily abandoned.

He reached Pappas's grocery store and stopped. The store was a blackened ruin. A layer of snow covered the charred boards.

Down the street he thought he saw movement in the doorway of Quincy's saloon. He started forward. "Hey. . . !"

There was a rifle shot. The bullet zipped past.

"Keep away!" called a voice from the saloon.

"What's going on?" Wade cried. "Where's Quincy?"

"Gone," returned the voice.

Wade thought he recognized the voice. "Is that you, Sampson?"

"Yeah," replied the alcalde.

"This is Wade Rawson."

"Hello, Wade. Didn't recognize you."

Wade started forward.

"That's far enough," Sampson cried.

"What's the matter here?" Wade repeated. "What happened to Pappas's store?"

"Pappas was holding back supplies, trying to get higher prices. One night some men—we don't know who—killed him. They looted his store and burned it. There's only eight of us left in town, and we're forted up here. Everybody else has gone down below.''

"Why don't you go, too?" Wade said.

"We've got good claims, and we don't want nobody jumping them while we're gone.''

"Look, Sampson, I've got two partners higher up, and if they don't get something to eat, they're going to die. I've got to get food to them in a hurry.''

"Sorry," Sampson said. "We can't help you.''

"Didn't you hear me? I said they're going to die. They're eating grass up there. They've got scurvy.''

"We've got scurvy here, too. I don't know if we've got supplies to last *us*, much less give some away. Try down below, at Oak Flats.''

Wade stood in the street. He felt let down, foolish, angry. If Sampson had showed himself now, Wade might have shot him. There was no time for emotions, though. He had to get moving. Oak Flats was nearly a day's walk. Wade was already a half day behind schedule. Ralph and Sam would be running out of food about now.

Wade turned away from the saloon and limped out of town.

That night he slept in an abandoned cabin, sheltered from the cold and with wood for a fire. He reached Oak Flats the next morning. Oak Flats was as short of supplies as Oro Fino had been. There was nothing to be had. Wade's heart sank. He remembered seeing the graves of men who'd died from starvation. That was how Ralph and Sam were going to end up. He did not think of his own condition yet.

Then he met five men who'd had enough of the bad weather and were heading for lower ground. They were traveling light, and they had to get rid of some supplies. For a steep price Wade was able to buy twelve pounds of flour from them, along with six pounds of beans, three pounds of rancid bacon, and two pounds of very small potatoes. He also persuaded the men to part with a half pound of coffee.

As the five men left, Wade sat in the snow by the side of the trail. He ate one of the potatoes raw, gnawing on it like a rat, grunting with satisfaction. He glanced around furtively as he ate, as though someone might spring out of the ground and steal his prize. There was blood on the potato from his sore gums and teeth. Though old, the potato was too hard for him. So he cut it into pieces and sucked on it. When he finished one, he ate another the same way.

He stuffed the provisions in his knapsack. What he had would keep him and his partners going another few weeks, until spring arrived and the game returned, or until Ralph and Sam were strong enough to come down from the mountains.

He started back. Walking had been hard before. With twenty extra pounds on his back, it was harder. His sprained ankle throbbed. It was swollen, and rubbed against the inside of his boot. Wade limped along, telling himself that he was past the halfway point now, that each step brought him closer to being finished, to rest.

He passed through Oro Fino at midday. He went down the back street, away from Quincy's saloon. He kept his pistol out in case the men in the saloon saw him and tried to take his food.

No one tried to stop him, though. He left the Mariposa. The return trip was mostly uphill, and that made it harder on his exhausted legs. The snow grew deeper. Above him, the clouds were building. Another storm was coming. Desperately, Wade sought shelter. He found it under a rock overhang, just as the snow began to fall. For a day and a half he was trapped there. He was freezing, tired, unable to make a fire. He ate the rancid bacon raw. He melted snow in his mouth, mixed flour with it and swallowed it. There were piercing spots of pain in his eyes from the snow's glare. His muscles felt drained of strength. He thought about Sam and Ralph back at the cabin. They must have run out of food long since. They must have given up on him as well. They must have thought he'd died on the trip or decided not to attempt the journey back. No, he said to himself. He was being unfair to them. Sam and Ralph had faith in him. Just as he'd have had faith if it were one of them. They wouldn't give up. They'd count on him to come through. If they weren't already dead.

The storm stopped. Painfully, Wade stretched his frozen joints. He crawled out of his hole and kept going. Up to now, he'd been able to follow his own tracks, but they'd been covered by a foot of new snow. He had to resort to the compass again, and the trail he'd blazed on the tree trunks. Each time he topped a ridge line, he looked toward the scooped-out mountain. The pain in his eyes and head had him seeing double, but the mountain did not appear to be getting closer.

That night he was able to build a fire. He roasted bacon over it on a sharp stick. He felt guilty for eating, because he knew Sam and Ralph needed the food. He roasted another one of the potatoes, too. When he was done, the potato was burnt on the outside and raw on the inside, but he didn't care. He felt even guiltier about eating the potato, because potatoes contained something that alleviated scurvy. But his craving for the vegetable was too powerful for him to ignore.

Another day of walking. How many days had he been gone? He didn't know. His legs hurt so badly that he had ceased to feel them. He had passed beyond the barrier of pain and cold. He was going strictly on will. It was as if it were all happening inside him, as if the world around him didn't exist. It was like a dream, a nightmare from which there was no awakening.

One more night in the mountains. He was close to Bear Valley now. He was going to make it. But would he be in time?

The clouds started rolling in again after dark. Wade couldn't sleep for watching them. Would he beat the storm?

The next morning he stumbled along as best he could, one eye on the sky. The gray deepened, then turned white and heavy, promising snow. Suddenly, Wade was limping down the last long incline to the valley. He saw the cabin. A thin column of smoke curled from the rude chimney.

"Hey!" Wade called, staggering, falling toward the cabin. "Hey! Ralph! Sam!"

There was no answer. Maybe they were asleep.

"Ralph! Sam! I'm back! I've got food!"

He reached the cabin. He pushed aside the canvas door.

Sam sat by the cook pot, hunched over a piece of meat that he'd been eating. They must have found game, Wade thought. He said, "Sam, thank God you're—"

Something in Sam's look stopped him. It was a furtive look, guilty. The eyes had a feral quality.

Wade stepped all the way in. He followed Sam's gaze across the room. Ralph Bannister lay on the table, naked save for a rag thrown across his genitals. His mouth was open, revealing brown, rotted teeth. His bones showed through his skin; his stomach protruded from starvation. His eyeballs were rolled up in his head. One arm lay flat at his side, the other was draped at an odd angle across his chest, its stiff, clawlike fingers half closed. A portion of his thigh had been cut out, halfway above the knee, revealing the bone.

Wade's stomach twisted. Bile rose in his throat. He struggled to keep it down.

"When did he die?" he asked Sam softly.

Tears rolled down Sam's bearded cheeks. "Yesterday. I been sittin' 'ere, starin' at 'im, ever since. I tried not to do this, Wade. I tried. But I didn't 'ave no choice. I'd 'ave died, too." His hands shook, the dead man's partly-eaten flesh in them. "If yer'd only come back sooner. If yer'd come back when yer was supposed to."

Wade was shaking, too. Then Sam rose angrily. "You think I'm 'orrible, don't you? You think I'm some kind of monster. I know you do, I can see it in yer face. Well, it was eat this or die meself. Tell me what you'd 'ave done in my place. Go on, tell me!"

Wade could not tell him. His brain refused to imagine himself in that situation. "I don't know," he said honestly. "I just don't know."

Part III

EL DORADO

36

Spring 1850

Jack Marlow rode into the camp called Coyote Diggings, on the Stanislaus River. Coyote Diggings was an older camp, settled in '48, the year gold had been discovered. It looked like most of the other camps Jack had seen—a wide, straggly main street with tents and cabins scattered back into the hills on either side.

It was a warm, beautiful afternoon. Fluffy clouds drifted high in the sky. Yellow and blue wildflowers painted the hills in splashes of color. Overhead, a flock of geese headed north, honking. The rainy season was over. The mining camps were filling up again. Old buildings were reoccupied, new ones went up. There was traffic in the streets, optimism in the air.

Jack still had the horse he'd stolen in Oro Fino. Mules were more practical in this rugged country, but he'd kept the horse out of vanity. There was no law in this part of the world, no communication from camp to camp. There was no way to tell the animal was stolen, no way that its owner could ever recover it.

Jack didn't feel sorry for Doc Billington. The damn fool should have had more sense than to accuse Jack of cheating of cards. He'd gotten what he deserved. Since being chased out of Oro Fino, Jack had drifted from camp to camp. He had eked out a living as a gambler, dealing faro out of hand. He was down to his last few dollars, but he had been in that position most of his life. He was used to it. His clothes were worn and travel-stained, but he took pains to keep himself freshly shaved, as befitted his new profession.

In front of him there was a commotion, coming from a saloon. There were loud voices, a man's and a woman's. The man was cursing, the woman yelled back spiritedly. A crowd had gathered in the street, near the saloon's door. Suddenly the man appeared, dragging the woman by her long reddish hair. She screamed in pain. She wore a dark blue dress and red stockings, with red ribbons on her sleeves and green ones in her hair. The man was of medium build and thick-chested with curly hair and long side whiskers. His face was crimson with anger. "Hold out on me, you bitch."

"I told you, King, it was a tip. I got a right to keep—"

"Don't tell me about your rights."

The man called King swung the woman by the hair and threw her into the muddy street. Her ribs hit the stump of a tree, and she grunted in pain. King charged into the street after her. He pulled her up by the hair again and began pounding her with his fists in the ribs and stomach. She yelled out, "No, King! Stop!" She tried to fight back, but she wasn't strong enough. No one moved to help her. King smashed her in the eye, in the nose and mouth. There was blood all over her face.

"This is what happens to a bitch that don't play square with me."

He hit her again, and she fell to the ground. He started kicking her.

Jack jumped off his horse and pushed through the crowd, many of whom were whooping with enjoyment. After all, she was only a whore.

"Let her alone," Jack said.

The pimp turned. There was blood on his fists. "Who the hell are you?" he demanded.

"Most folks call me Jack."

"Yeah? Well, let me tell you, Jack, I'm a businessman, and right now I'm tending my business. So why don't you keep your damn nose out of it?"

King turned back to the girl and got ready to kick her again.

Jack said, "Lay another foot on her, and the only thing you'll be tending is a broken head."

King turned back. His mustached upper lip curled. "Oh, yeah?" he said.

Jack started to reply, when King's left fist flashed out and caught him on the chin, knocking him backward into the crowd.

Jack shook his head and got back up, fists raised. King threw the left again. Jack went to block it, but it was a feint, and the right hand that followed it caught Jack flush on the cheek, splitting his lip and knocking him down again. The crowd yelled and hooted. Jack found himself lying next to the girl. Her voice was mushy through a blood-filled mouth. "You're not doing so good," she said.

"I'm just getting started," Jack told her.

As Jack got up again, King rushed him. Jack tried to scramble aside, but King grabbed him around the waist and took him down. They rolled around in the mud. King went for the pistol in Jack's waistband. He wrenched it out. Jack gripped King's gun hand in both his own. King was hitting Jack with his free hand. Jack could not shake the pistol loose. King was trying to cock it. Jack sank his teeth into King's wrist. King howled and dropped the pistol. With his free hand King grabbed Jack's hair and pulled hard, yanking Jack's head back. Jack's eyes watered with pain. The two men scrambled in the mud. King tried to get the pistol back. Jack kicked it away. He let go of King's hand and drove an elbow into his stomach. King relaxed his grip on Jack's hair. Jack pulled himself loose and got to his feet, breathing hard. The pimp got up, too, his massive chest heaving like a bellows. His face was redder than before. King came on. Jack caught him with a left and a right, and knocked him skidding onto the seat of his pants.

King rose slowly. He pulled something from his pocket and flipped it open. It was a straight razor.

"I'm going to give you a new face," King said.

Before Jack could draw his own knife, King charged. He brought the razor up in a wide, slashing movement, he was too quick for Jack to back away. Jack caught the razor blade with his bare hand. He yelled with the pain, "Shit!" Letting go of the razor, he fell onto his back. He tangled his feet with King's and threw him over. As King came up on his knees, Jack drew his bowie knife from behind his back. He plunged it into the pimp's neck and twisted. Blood gouted, spraying Jack.

King stayed on his knees a moment, wide-eyed. He swore wordlessly. Then he fell over in slow motion. He lay on his side, legs jerking, blood still spouting from the wound in his neck.

Jack screwed his eyes shut with pain. He shook his bleeding hand. He went down on his elbow, holding his wrist. He hoped the tendons weren't severed. He took a handkerchief and wrapped it around the hand. The bandage quickly turned red.

He got up. There was blood in his mouth from his cut lip, and he spit it out. To the crowd he said, "Better tell the alcalde, if you got one."

"Don't worry none about the law," somebody said. "That King Poulteney was a bad fellow. Nobody'll miss him."

Jack went over to the battered girl. She was on her hands and knees, vomiting into the mud. Blood ran out her nose. Tears mingled with the blood and dirt on her face. Jack knelt beside her, wincing at the damage. He felt her side gently.

"I'm all right," she said, trying to shake him off.

"Yeah, I can tell," Jack said. "Your ribs ain't broke, anyway."

She said, "What about . . . what about King?"

"He's found himself another kingdom."

"Great," moaned the girl. She sat on the ground. "Now what am I going to do?" She shuddered with pain, and Jack put an arm around her. He looked at the watching crowd. "She have anybody to take care of her?"

Men shook their heads. "She's the only whore King had left. Looks like you're stuck with her."

Jack swore under his breath. Just what I need, he thought, a beat-up whore, he thought. Aloud he said, "Well, we can't leave her here." He saw a two-story hotel across the street. "Some of you men help me carry her to that hotel."

The men hesitated. Jack rose and yanked some of them out of the group. He was hurt and angry, and he didn't feel like fooling. "God damn you, help me pick her up. Be gentle about it, too."

Before they could act, a bearded man stepped forward. "That's my hotel, mister, and I'll tell you right now—the room's two dollars a day. Three for a whore. In advance. Two dollars for board, if that's what you want."

Jack went back to the dying pimp. He went through King's clothes till he found his money bag. He tossed the money bag to the hotel owner. "He's paying for it," Jack said. He worked his bowie knife from King's neck. He cleaned the blade on the dying man's broadcloth coat, then he returned the knife to its sheath.

He went back to the group of men. "Now, help me move her."

37

Jack and three men carried the beaten girl across the street to the hotel. "Room Seventeen," the hotel's owner told them, pointing upstairs. "And don't make a mess."

"Send up a bottle of good brandy, would you?" Jack asked.

"Get it yourself," the owner said. "There's no room service for whores."

In the room, they laid the girl on the bed. Jack motioned the other men out. "Thanks, boys," he said.

Jack got a basin of water and a cloth. He cleaned the girl up, wiping blood, vomit, and dirt from her face. Even with her swollen eye and mouth, he could see that she was attractive. Her reddish hair was clumped with mud.

She opened her good eye. "Thanks, mister," she mumbled.

"Yeah," Jack said. She was pretty beat up. He wondered how long he would have to take care of her.

She tried to get up.

"Rest easy," Jack said, holding her down. He adjusted the sack that passed for a pillow. He lifted her head and gave her a drink of water. "What's your name?"

"Brandy. Brandy McCall. And you're Jack, right?"

Jack nodded. "Jack Marlow." He kept working on her face. "He beat you good. What'd you do?"

Brandy sipped more water. She winced as Jack touched a sore spot. "Fella gave me more than the usual price. I kept the difference. King didn't like it."

Suddenly her face paled. She looked faint. Jack laid her back down on the pillow. "Rest now," he said. "I'll be back later. You got any clothes or anything you want brought over?"

"My stuff's at Pasqual's boardinghouse, behind the Brass Elephant Saloon. You can't miss it."

"All right," Jack said. "You close your eyes."

He adjusted the pillow again. The girl fell asleep quickly, and Jack slipped out.

It was late afternoon when Jack returned. Brandy had just awakened. She sat up in bed, in obvious pain. Jack carried in her trunk. "The fellow at the boardinghouse said you owed him money," he told her. "I let him have King's bags as payment."

He set the trunk down, shaking the pain out of his bandaged hand. Then he stepped into the hall and brought back two more items. "Here's a can of hot beef soup, from the restaurant. And a bottle of brandy."

The red-haired girl looked touched. "Thanks, Jack."

Jack shrugged. He didn't tell her he was doing this only because nobody else would be bothered with a stomped-on whore.

He poured her a glass of brandy. "Pour yourself some, too," she said.

"Thanks."

She managed to smile through her swollen mouth. She had an engaging smile, marred only by a gold tooth on the upper right side. "How's that hand?" she asked him.

"It's all right."

"You haven't fixed it, have you?"

"Not yet," Jack said. "I—"

"Take off the bandage."

"I'll fix it later. It's all—"

"Take it off."

Jack gave in. He unwound the bandage, which was stiff with dried blood, turning wet again where the cut had reopened from carrying the trunk.

Brandy looked at the deep cut, and she made a face. "Damn that King. Give me a wet cloth."

Jack obeyed. Brandy swung her legs over the side of the bed. She blinked as a wave of dizziness swept over her. She fought it off and said, "Give me the bottle, too."

Jack said, "I swear. It's not that bad . . ."

"You get gangrene, and you'll lose that hand, Jack Marlow. Being with King, I've seen my share of razor cuts. I know what I'm talking about. Now, do what I say."

Reluctantly, Jack handed her the brandy.

"Open your hand," she said.

She wiped off the cut with the wet cloth. Then she tilted the bottle and poured brandy into the open wound.

Jack sucked in his breath. It felt as if he'd been stuck with a red-hot poker. His legs weakened.

Brandy said, "Look in my trunk. Take out a clean petticoat and cut a bandage from it with your knife."

When Jack had finished that, Brandy dabbed at the cut again with the wet cloth. "You ought to have this sewn, you know."

"I can't find a seamstress," Jack said. "And don't you go volunteering, neither."

Brandy wrapped the strip of petticoat around the cut and knotted it. "There," she said.

That bit of effort had tired her. She sat back in the bed and sipped the brandy. "Ah, that's good." She spooned the hot soup into her.

Jack explained, "I didn't think you could handle solid food with that mouth."

She looked up at him. "I must—"

There was a knock, and the door opened. Two bearded miners stood there, hats in hand. The one in front shifted from foot to foot. "Begging your pardon, Miss Brandy, but we was wonderin,' are you ready to work yet? We're in kind of a hurry, see, and we was hopin' you could fit us in before . . ."

Jack strode across the room. He turned the two men around and kicked them down the stairs. "Get out of here."

He went back to the bed. He looked down at Brandy, and they both laughed. "Oh," she said, holding her side. "It hurts to laugh. The funny thing is, King probably would have made me take them on."

She had some more soup. "I really must thank you for all you've done for me."

Jack shrugged. "It's nothing."

"You know that's not true. I didn't see people lining up to help me out there this afternoon. Only you. Why'd you do it?"

Jack took a slug of his drink. "I don't know. I think maybe it was because I watched a girl get lynched last year. A friend of mine tried to help her, but I didn't. I've always felt bad about that. She would have hung anyway, but I should have tried. I should have done the right thing. I guess I saw King beating you, and I was reminded of that."

"Well, whatever your reasons, thanks. I'd like to do something for you in return."

Jack snorted. "Like what? Work for me?"

"If that's what you want. I'm between employers."

Jack shook his head. "I'm no pimp. If you want to do something for me, hurry up and get well, so I can be about my business."

"Which is?"

"Gambling."

Brandy raised her eyebrows in amusement. "You?"

"What's wrong with that?" Jack said.

"A real gambler would laugh at you. No wonder you don't make any money."

"Who says I don't make money?"

"Nobody has to say it. They just have to look at you. You don't look like a gambler. You don't have the right shirts and cravats. And that coat—it looks like you've been sleeping in it."

"I have been," Jack said.

Brandy sipped her drink. She eyed him appraisingly. "Maybe that's how I'll repay you. I'll teach you to be a gentleman. You seem like you have potential."

"What do you know about it?" Jack asked.

"More than you, obviously. I've been around some of the biggest gamblers in the East. What's your game—faro?"

Jack nodded.

"Maybe I can help you there, too. What do you say?"

Jack drummed his fingers on his leg. Being taught by a woman was something he'd never figured on. Still, there might be something in it. "All right," he said. "When do we start?"

"Right now. Get a deck of cards and we'll practice dealing. When I'm able to get out of bed, we'll do the rest. Who's your lookout?"

"I ain't been using one."

Brandy smiled. "You've got one now."

"Hey, wait. I just said you could help me. I didn't say nothing about us working together."

"You don't have to. We'd be perfect. I need a job, and you need all the help you can get."

"Tart-tongued, ain't you?" Jack said.

"Why not? I'm a tart. And stop saying 'ain't.' If you want to be a gentleman, speak like one."

Jack sighed. "And your share of this little arrangement will be . . . ?"

"Half of the profits. Agreed?"

"Do I have a choice?" he said.

"No," she said. "You don't. Now get the cards."

38

For the next three days, while she recovered from her beating, Brandy showed Jack how to play faro. She taught him how to deal, how to stack a deck, how to slip in extra cards, how to shave the cards' edges so that he would always know what was coming next.

Jack was surprised at how much she knew. Even more surprising, he found himself able to relax around her. It had been a long time since he'd had anyone to talk to.

"What's your real name?" he asked one afternoon while they were taking a break.

"Elizabeth," she said.

"Pretty name."

She shrugged.

"How long you been in the game?"

She thought. "Twelve years now. Since I was thirteen. It seems like all my life. Pretty much has been, I guess."

"Where are you from?"

"Maine, originally."

"Why'd you leave?"

"My father was a drunk. He used to beat my mom and me. I couldn't stand it anymore, so I ran away. I ended up in Boston, living on the streets, stealing, eating out of garbage bins. Selling myself. A fellow took me in. He treated me nice, bought me clothes. Made me a whore. What I didn't know then was that once you're in, you can't get out. They won't let you. I worked for that fellow a long time. Then he sold me to King."

"Sold you?" said Jack. "You mean, like a slave?"

Brandy nodded. "Welcome to the wonderful world of whores," she said.

"How'd you end up in California?"

"King liked to move around. He heard about the gold strike and figured it was his chance to get rich. He brought us around the Horn. We've only been here a couple months.''

"They said you were his last girl."

"There were four of us to start. One died at sea, one killed herself, and one died of fever a few weeks back. I was King's meal ticket.''

"Pretty stupid, beating up your meal ticket.''

"Pimps are like that. You have to have 'em to keep the tricks from killing you. But they're always beating you up themselves. They say King beat a girl to death once. I don't know if it's true or not. He had a bad temper, but I guess you know that.''

Jack flexed his bandaged hand. "Yeah. King give you that gold tooth?''

She shook her head. "A customer did it, years ago. It's a hazard of the trade. I'm lucky I haven't had worse done to me.''

When Brandy was able to get around, she took Jack to a general store. She picked out two new suits for him, along with some shirts and cravats, a silk top hat, and new boots.

"I can't afford this,'' Jack said.

"I've got some money,'' she told him.

"I can't let you spend your—''

She shushed him. "I owe you this much for what you've done for me, besides, I'm going to share the profits of what you make. I look at this as an investment. If it works, I won't have to whore again.''

After buying Jack the clothes, Brandy showed him how to wear them properly. She cut his hair. As best she could in the short time they had, she taught him how to walk, how to sit, how to speak proper English. She taught him to sip his drinks, not guzzle them. She made him get rid of the big .44 revolver and substitute a smaller pistol, a .31-caliber five-shot that slipped easily, and unnoticed, into the waistband of his trousers.

At the end of it all, Jack looked at himself in Brandy's hand mirror.

"What do you think?'' she said.

"It don't—it *doesn't*—look like me, or at least the way I remember looking, the last time I had use of a mirror.''

"Now for the big test,'' she said. "Are you ready?''

Jack stretched against the stiffness of the boiled shirt and its cellulose collar. "As ready as I'll ever be.''

That night Jack and Brandy went to the Cozy Home Saloon, the biggest establishment in town. Brandy said you could rent a table and run an independent game there. Jack wore his new outfit with the top hat tipped low over his eyes, as was the style. Brandy had on the blue dress and red stockings. The hem of the dress ended at her knees, showing her shapely legs to good effect. The front of the dress was scooped low, revealing the pale swellings of her breasts. Her red hair was piled high and decorated with green ribbons. She wore dangling earrings and a fake diamond necklace that sparkled in the lamplight. Until then Jack hadn't realized how attractive she actually was. Her bruises were nearly gone. What was left was covered by makeup, so that it hardly showed. Jack guessed that she'd learned early how to use makeup that way.

They paused at the saloon door. Jack was nervous. "Thirty-five dollars is a hell of a small bank," he said.

"It's all we have," Brandy told him. "It'll be enough, you'll see. They'll be too busy looking down my dress to notice what you're doing with the cards."

She was right. They started with a five-dollar limit on bets, and they never looked back. Brandy was like a magnet. Men flocked to their table. Brandy made sure she bent low every time she raked money in or paid it out. She kept all eyes on her. Jack could have pulled cards out of his sleeve, or even out of his hat, and he didn't think anyone would have noticed. The money rolled in.

At first Jack felt stiff with his new persona. He had to remind himself to sit straight, to speak slowly and grammatically. His bandaged hand bothered him. Then he remembered Mr. Levelleire, the elegant gambler from Panama. He tried to think how Mr. Levelleire would have acted. After a while he began to fantasize that he was Mr. Levelleire, and suddenly everything fell into place. He was having a good time.

It was stifling in the saloon. Strands of Brandy's red hair worked themselves loose, and she pushed them back. There was a sheen of sweat on her neck and on the exposed tops of her breasts.

"Take a break, Brandy," cried one of the miners. "I'll give you fifty dollars to go out back with me. It'll be like old times."

"Fifty hell," swore another. "I'll give you a hundred."

"A hundred and twenty-five," said a third, a bearded giant. "Come on, Brandy, that's a lot more than we paid for you before."

Brandy laughed at them. "Sorry, boys, I'm not for sale."

"You mean not right now," somebody said.

"Maybe not for a long time," she said. "You'd better find your-selves another floozy."

The woman-starved miners turned to Jack. "What do you say, Marlow? What's it worth to you to put her back to work?"

"Name a price. We'll meet it."

"The sky's the limit."

Jack and Brandy exchanged looks. Jack could see fear in her eyes. He knew that she'd do it if he told her to. "She *is* working," Jack told the men.

"You know what we mean."

"And you heard what the lady said. Now, place your bets, gen-tlemen, or make room for those who will."

When the game was over, Jack escorted Brandy back to the hotel. Brandy carried the layout, along with two fat bags of dust and coins that represented their winnings. Somewhere behind them a concertina played. Laughter issued from saloons and gaming halls. In the distance there was pistol fire as exuberant miners celebrated or shot each other, or both.

"Well, how was I?" Jack said, proud of himself.

Brandy made a face. "You need a lot of work, partner. There were a couple times there . . ." She shook her head. "It's a wonder you haven't been shot or hanged by now."

"It has been tried," Jack admitted. "Still, it was a good night. The best I've ever had."

She looked at him, into his eyes, as though searching for some-thing. "Me, too," she said.

They reached the hotel and climbed the stairs to the second floor. Brandy paused at the door latch—there was no sense putting locks on these flimsy doors. It was dark, with only the weak glow from a whale-oil lantern at the end of the hall. Brandy looked up at Jack. He smelled her perfume—expensive stuff, just a whiff. He smelled the rose scent she used in her hair. He saw the soft curve of her neck where it met her bare shoulders. His pulse was suddenly pounding.

"Well . . ." she began.

Jack pulled her to him. He kissed her hard, his strong arms holding her close. She kissed him back. Maybe it was the first time she had really kissed a man. The gold bags and card layout dropped from her hands to the floor. Their bodies pressed close in the warm hallway.

"I want you," Jack whispered hoarsely.

"You've got me," she said.
They went into the room.

39

Kathy Beddoes waited nervously behind the curtain of the makeshift stage. On the other side of the curtain she heard the crowd—impatient, chanting, full of anticipation.

It was Sunday afternoon, and Kathy was giving her long-awaited singing performance. The 1-2-3 Saloon, the largest building in Kate's Bar, had been turned into a theater. A stage had been constructed at one end of the room. Admission to the show was a pinch of gold dust or one dollar a head. Kathy peeked around the curtain. From the looks of the audience, she stood to make a good deal of money. The diggings had filled up quickly once the weather had turned good, and every man in the neighborhood seemed to be in the saloon, or fighting to squeeze through its doors. A lucky few sat or stood on the bar. The rest were crammed shoulder to shoulder, drinking and talking and calling for Kathy.

Money was the least of Kathy's considerations just then. She wanted only to get through the show without making a laughing-stock of herself. She wished Peach were there to give her support. Kate's Bar wasn't the same since he had been killed.

At one end of the stage, a fiddler, a Tennessean named Daven-port, sawed away, keeping the audience occupied until the show's star made her appearance. He would be her accompanist. It would have been nice to have had a piano, but how would they ever get a piano up here?

"Ready when you are, Kathy," said Abe Greenberg, who had helped organize the show. Greenberg and one or two others who'd been lucky enough to be allowed backstage were looking at her, waiting.

"In a second," Kathy said. Her stomach roiled. She wished she hadn't done this. Why had she promised? Why couldn't they just let her alone to run her restaurant and hotel?

On the other side of the curtain the men began clapping and stamping their booted feet in unison. The building shook.

Kathy brushed imaginary specks of dust from the starched front of her blouse. She smoothed her gray skirt. She wore no costume, nothing unusual. She was just being herself. After all, this was a one-time affair.

She couldn't stand there forever. She nodded to Greenberg. "All right. Let's get it over with."

Greenberg and Finn, the saloon's owner, pulled on the ropes. With a creaking of hooks the curtain opened. The stamping stopped. There was wild applause. The fiddler began playing Kathy's entrance tune, "Old Dan Tucker."

Suddenly, surprisingly, Kathy's jitters were gone. The heck with it, she decided. She had to do this, so she might as well have fun with it. She bounded onto the stage doing a sailor's hornpipe. The audience loved it.

When she finished her impromptu dance, she began singing. She had worked out her songs in advance. She sang old favorites and popular hits of the moment, starting with a mix of tunes from George Christy's Minstrels and upbeat rollickers like "Polly Wolly Doodle," "Oh, What a Row, What a Rumpus and Rioting," and "The Rival Beauties."

> At dancing school I next was sent,
> All muffled up with care.
> Where I learned to dance a minuet
> As graceful as a bear.

She followed these with ballads like "Scenes That Are the Brightest," "I Dreamt I Dwelt in Marble Halls," and "Kathleen Mavoureen." Whatever doubts she'd had about her abilities to hold an audience had vanished. She was in total control. She scarcely heard the applause. It was more what she felt from that sea of faces—a supportive encouragement that enabled her to do whatever she wanted, to lead the audience wherever she wanted them to go. She fed off that encouragement; it gave her confidence. It made her feel five feet off the floor.

After the ballads came more upbeat tunes, miners' favorites like

"Hangtown Girls," "There's a Big Pile Coming, Boys," and "On the Banks of the Sacramento."

> Then blow, you breezes, blow!
> We're off to Californi-o.
> There's plenty of gold,
> So I've been told,
> On the banks of the Sacramento.

For the show's finale, the fiddler stopped playing. Kathy stood alone at center stage. A cappella, she sang "Where Can the Soul Find Rest?"

A hush fell over the audience, just as it had when she'd sung the song while cutting the men's hair. Her clear, strong voice carried to the farthest reaches of the building. She heard men crying, thinking of home and family.

> Tell me, ye winged winds, that round my pathway
>> roar,
> Do ye not know some spot, where mortals weep no
>> more,
> Some lone and pleasant dell, some valley in the
>> West,
> Where free from toil and pain, the weary soul may
>> rest?
> Faith, hope, and love, best boon to mortals given,
> Waved their bright wings and whispered, "Yes, in
>> heaven."

With the last words her voice dwindled to a whisper, then faded. For a moment there was silence. Then the room exploded with applause. As it did, the fiddle struck up once more, and Kathy launched into the anthem of the 49ers, "Oh! Susanna." She danced across the stage, clapping her hands in time. The bearded, ragged men wiped the tears from their eyes, and they clapped and sang along with her at the top of their lungs.

> Oh! Susanna.
> Don't you cry for me.
> For I'm going to California
> With my washbowl on my knee.

On the song's last beat, Kathy stopped dancing. She stamped one foot dramatically, and on the spur of the moment she hiked her skirt well above her knee. Show them some leg, she thought, even as she realized how wildly unlike her this was.

That last gesture brought down the house. Kathy bowed amid applause and cheers. She waved to the audience. She blew them kisses. People threw money and flowers—she couldn't imagine where they'd gotten those—onstage. Kathy felt a glow inside her. She'd never felt anything like it before. It was an elation that seemed to well up from inside of her and spread itself over the whole building.

Men pressed to the edge of the stage. Kathy came over to them. They offered congratulations, touching her outstretched hands.

"Miss Kathy! Miss Kathy!" A gaunt, tallish miner waved his hand at her, trying to get her attention.

"What is it?" she said above the uproar.

"My name's Steve Tillmon, Miss Kathy," the miner cried. "I'm the alcalde from Skunk Flat. We'd like you to put on a show for us, too."

"We want you, too," cried another man, a dapper fellow with a forked beard, "in Ellisville. We'll guarantee you a full house."

"So will we," countered the Skunk Flat alcalde.

Kathy didn't know what to say. She was still overwhelmed by her reception. She was still out of breath from her performance. "When?" she asked.

"Whenever you want," said the man from Skunk Flat.

"Soon," said the dapper fellow from Ellisville. "As soon as possible."

Kathy thought for a moment. She had enjoyed herself more than she had thought she would. "Why not?" she said. "All right, I'll do it."

"Which camp?" both men cried at once.

"Both," she told them.

"When?"

Kathy nodded to the Skunk Flat alcalde. "You asked first. How about next Sunday?"

The man let out a howl of glee.

"And Ellisville?" said the fellow with the forked beard.

"The Sunday after," Kathy told him.

The two men leapt with joy. Other miners told Kathy how they would travel to Skunk Flat and Ellisville to hear her sing again.

She grinned at them all in wonderment. Maybe this wasn't going to be a one-time affair after all.

40

Kathy's concerts at Skunk Flat and Ellisville were roaring successes. Men lined up for hours to get into her shows. The turnouts were so big that second shows were added in both camps. On two Sundays, Kathy made over a thousand dollars.

After the Ellisville show, there was a reception in her honor. All the camp bigwigs were there, fighting to be introduced to the beautiful Mrs. Beddoes. She shook a hundred hands; she learned a hundred names, most of which she quickly forgot. Half the men propositioned her on the spot, to be met with polite but firm refusals.

She had finally gotten a moment to herself, near the buffet, when she was approached by one of the show's organizers. It was the dapper man with the forked beard. He wore a plum-colored coat, top hat, and striped pants, all of which had seen considerable use but still managed to look stylish.

"Mrs. Beddoes, might I have a word with you?" Up close, the dapper fellow was surprisingly young and eager. The beard made him look older than he was.

Kathy said, "Yes, Mr. . . . Storey, wasn't it?"

"That's right. Ned Storey. You have a good memory."

"You did a good job putting the show together."

"Thank you. I hope I'm not being presumptuous in asking, Mrs. Beddoes, but have you received offers to sing elsewhere?"

Kathy laughed. "I've received three within the hour. There may be more coming."

"What do you intend doing about them?"

"I'm not sure, to be honest. I never intended my singing to go this far. I did it only as a favor to the boys back in Kate's Bar."

"Do you enjoy singing?" Storey said.

"Yes. Yes, I do."

"Do you want all this to end?"

Kathy thought. "No," she said at last, "I guess I don't. I'm having too much fun with it. Why do you ask?"

Young Mr. Storey twisted one end of his forked beard. "I'll be blunt with you, Mrs. Beddoes. I'd like to become your—your manager."

"Manager? That sounds so professional."

"I think you should approach this in a professional manner. You need someone to guide your career."

Kathy arched an eyebrow the way she did onstage. "And you can do that better than I?"

"Respectfully, ma'am, I believe I can. If you'll allow me, I'll handle your engagements. I can get you more money than you're getting now, I'm sure of it. I'll make all the arrangements for your travel and lodgings. Most important, I'll oversee the receipts, and make sure you aren't being cheated."

"I see," Kathy said. "And for this you would charge . . . ?"

"A percentage of your earnings. Say . . . twenty?"

"Say, ten," Kathy told him in a tone that brooked of no negotiation.

Storey considered, then he spread his hands. "All right. Ten."

Kathy added, "How do I know that *you* won't cheat me?"

"You have only my word. There are dishonest managers, all too many. I can only promise that I won't be one of them."

Kathy said, "You have experience in the field, I presume?"

"I used to work at the Park Theater, in New York."

"Really?" Kathy's eyes lit up. "My husband used to take me to the Olympic, to see the Tom and Jerry shows, but we could never afford the Park. That was only for the swells. What did you do there?"

Storey cleared his throat. "Actually, I was a ticket taker."

Before Kathy could say anything, Storey went on. "Please, Mrs. Beddoes. It's true my experience has been on a lower level, but I watched and listened. I know how the business works. I'll do a good job for you. I won't even ask for a written contract. If you're not happy with my services, you can dismiss me at any time. I believe you can be a big star."

"Oh, come now," Kathy said.

"It's true," Storey said. "Don't you see how these men react to you? You're special."

Kathy said, "I must tell you, I feel silly about all this. I'm not a star. I'm not even sure what I'm doing here."

"You will be a star, Mrs. Beddoes. Mark my word."

Kathy sighed. "I don't know about that, but if I'm to continue singing, I will need help with the bookings and money and such. That much has already been made clear to me." She held out her hand. "Very well, Mr. Storey. You're hired."

The dapper young man shook her hand, grinning behind his beard. "You won't regret this, Mrs. Beddoes. I promise you."

"Please, call me Kathy."

"All right, Kathy. And I'm Ned."

"What are you doing out here anyway, Ned? You're a long way from the Park Theater."

"My dream is to one day have a theater of my own. I came west hoping to find enough gold to make that dream a reality. Unfortunately, I'm not cut out to be a miner. I've been supporting myself at odd jobs, barely staying alive." His expression picked up. "But now—now things are going to be different. I know they are."

Ned threw himself into his job. He had Kathy performing every Sunday. Through the spring and early summer the two of them traveled the southern mining camps—from Bladderville to Hell's Delight, from Ground Hog's Glory to Red Dog. Kathy played in saloons, in tents, in the open air by torchlight. Everywhere, she received the same riotous reception. At Ned's urging, she now wore an off-the-shoulder velvet gown of bottle green. Ned had it made for her by a Chinese man he knew. Her hair was held in place by a golden tiara. She kept her act basically the same, only changing some of the songs and adding a few jokes. The ending never changed, the a cappella rendition of "Where Can the Soul Find Rest?" followed by "Oh! Susanna." It always had the same effect. If someone had told Kathy a year before that she'd be showing her legs to hundreds of strange men every week, she'd have called them sick in the head. Now she thought nothing of it.

Ned had handbills printed and distributed throughout the mines, advertising Kathy as "Kate Beddoes, the Toast of the Mother Lode." All her time was now spent on her career—traveling, rehearsing, meeting the public and signing autographs. Her trips took her farther and farther from Kate's Bar, until she was never there anymore. She was forced to give up her restaurant and hotel.

The money Kathy made was astronomical. Ned bumped her admission price to a dollar and a half, then two dollars a head, and the concerts were always sold out. Kathy found that the money didn't mean that much to her. The joy of performing, of entertaining, was what attracted her. She lived for the applause.

The Fourth of July found Kathy in Sonora, unofficial capital of the southern mines, where she was to give a concert at the opera house. She and Ned got there early. They stood outside the stone building, which had been decorated with American flags and bunting for the holiday.

"This will be the first time I've sung in a real theater," Kathy said.

Ned looked at her. "Nervous?"

She nodded. "For the first time, I feel like a professional. Like the singers I've watched in theaters just like this."

"You are a professional, Kathy. You're the star of the show. You even have a dressing room."

She still looked worried, and Ned put a reassuring arm around her shoulder. "Don't worry. You'll do fine."

Men from all over the district had descended on Sonora for the holiday. There were horse races, bullfights, and gunfire all day long. The theater opened at dusk. The men had to check their pistols and knives at the front door, and if the management was still suspicious, they had the patrons searched by a group of bouncers. Inside, the opera house had a hardwood stage with velvet curtains. There were boxes and muraled walls with plaster scrollwork. There were other acts on the bill—jugglers, an aging Shakespearean, a minstrel show, an Italian puppeteer. Kathy was going on last. She was the one everybody had come to see.

Kathy sat backstage in her cramped dressing room. She was nervous, as always, before a performance, but it was a different kind of nervousness this time. She could no longer delude herself that she was doing this as a favor to the boys. Her hands shook as she brushed her hair and put on her makeup. She heard music from the act in progress. She heard boos as well. She wondered how she would feel if those boos were ever directed at her.

There was a knock on the door, and she jumped. "Five minutes, Kathy." It was Ned.

Kathy left the dressing room in a fog. She nearly got lost backstage. She tripped over some scenery and almost fell. From the audience she heard the rhythmic hand clapping and stamping of feet. It had never sounded so loud before. Her mouth was dry. She wished she'd never come here. There was a blur of people wishing her luck. She tried not to let them see how scared she was. Then the curtain opened, and she was doing her hornpipe to "Old Dan Tucker."

Suddenly the magic struck, and she was as good as she had ever been—better, even. At the end, after Kathy sang "Where Can the Soul Find Rest?" and "Oh! Susanna," she showed her legs, and she was so happy that she turned around and shook her rear as well. She thought the audience would tear down the house. They made her sing two encores. She was showered with applause. Someone handed her a dozen long-stemmed California roses. She bowed and left the stage with a wave and a blown kiss.

She hurried backstage to the plaudits of the crew and the other acts. Ned hugged her. "That was great, Kathy. Great. Get dressed, and we'll go to the reception."

Kathy nodded. She was laughing and crying at the same time. "All right." She'd gotten used to these receptions. She'd have to put in an hour or so, then she could have a late dinner and go to her hotel room for some much-needed sleep. Tomorrow she would pack and be off for the next engagement.

She carried the roses into her dressing room, feeling a mile in the air.

Behind her, the dressing room door slammed shut.

Kathy turned, and she dropped the roses.

Simon St. Clair lounged against the wall, grinning at her.

41

"What are you doing here?" Kathy said.

St. Clair moved away from the door. He still had the slim, boyish figure, the thatch of blond hair. Under his pale brows his eyes were bloodshot, his skin pasty, as if he'd been drinking heavily. He said,

"I should have thought that was obvious, Miss Kathy. We're goin' to finish that little supper of ours."

"You swore you'd stay away from me," Kathy told him.

St. Clair's voice was soft. "I swore I'd stay away from Kate's Bar. You're not in Kate's Bar now, are you? If you'd made me promise to keep away from you entirely, I would have. But you didn't. That was a bad move on your part."

Kathy closed her eyes and silently cursed herself.

St. Clair went on. "It was a long, cold walk to the next camp, Kathy. I had a hard time getting myself established again. But I managed. I always do. Ever since that night, I've been thinkin' about you, hopin' I'd run into you again. And guess what? I just did." He chuckled. "You humiliated me, Miss Kathy. You degraded me. And that's what I'm goin' to do to you. You're comin' with me, and you'll do everythin' I say."

"And if I don't?" Kathy said.

"I'll kill you. It won't bother me to do it. I'll enjoy it after what you did to me. I won't make it an easy death, either. In fact, I may kill you anyway. It depends on how you perform."

"Perform?"

St. Clair grinned. "Didn't I tell you? You're givin' another show tonight. A private show, for me and my friends."

"But there's a reception. I've got to—"

"No, you don't." He grabbed her arm. "Let's go."

He pulled her from the dressing room. For a small man, he had a strong grip. He steered her down the narrow hall toward the opera house's back door.

"Kathy!" It was Ned Storey behind them.

"One false word, and I'll kill you," St. Clair whispered to Kathy. "I'll kill him, too." Kathy believed St. Clair would do it. Drink seemed to have driven him completely mad.

Ned hurried up to them. "Kathy, where are you going? The reception—they'll be waiting for us."

"The lady has a previous engagement," St. Clair told him.

Ned said, "Look, I'm her manager, and she has to—"

Kathy said, "Please, Ned. It's all right. I—I'll explain later." She just wanted Ned to go away before he did something that got them both killed.

St. Clair bowed curtly to Ned. "Your servant, sir." He led Kathy outside. The astonished Ned could only watch, unsure what to think.

St. Clair dragged Kathy along the dark streets full of holiday revelers. Surprised men recognized Kathy and whispered among themselves. They recognized St. Clair and backed away.

St. Clair took Kathy to a saloon—Kelley's, she thought the name was. She barely had a chance to read the sign, St. Clair was walking so fast. He propelled her inside. It was dim, smoky, filled with rough-looking men and women. There were Mexicans, Frenchmen, well-heeled gamblers, and whores. They welcomed St. Clair.

"Christ, look who he's got with him."

"How'd you do that, Simon?"

"She's a prime piece, ain't she?"

In one way, the aristocratic St. Clair seemed out of place among these low types. In another way, he seemed right at home. With his free hand he snapped his fingers at the bartender, who produced a bottle of port. Someone passed the bottle to St. Clair. He drank, blotting his lips with the back of his hand. "Gentlemen, and ladies," he said, "let me introduce the celebrated Kate Beddoes, singer and dancer extraordinaire."

The assembled men and women cheered.

"Miss Beddoes has kindly *consented*"—St. Clair paused for the laughter—"to give a special—a very special—performance of her show."

More cheering and laughter.

St. Clair shoved Kathy toward one end of the saloon. The crowd gathered around. St. Clair found a chair and placed it in front of the crowd. "Professor?" he said.

An old man stepped up with a fiddle. The man's bulbous nose was veined from drink. His face was covered with carbuncles.

"Your accompanist, ma'am," St. Clair said.

Kathy tried to hide her fear. Faces leered at her. There wasn't a friendly one among them.

St. Clair turned the chair around. He sat astride it. He draped his arms over the back, pistol in one hand, bottle in the other. "By the way," he said. "For this performance, you're going to show more than your legs. A lot more."

Cheering came from the men.

"Do you understand?" St. Clair said.

Kathy said nothing. St. Clair smiled, enjoying himself. "Who knows, maybe you'll give some of my friends a special treat after the show."

There was whistling, shouts of appreciation. Men vied for St. Clair's attention. "Don't forget me, Simon."

"You can't make me do that," Kathy told St. Clair.

"I can make you do anything I want," St. Clair said. "Now, get on with it."

The carbuncled old professor looked up at her. "What tune, dear?"

Kathy's mind reeled. How could she get out of this? St. Clair would kill her if she didn't do what he said. " 'Old—Old Dan Tucker,' " she mumbled.

The professor limbered up his screechy fiddle.

"Hello, Kathy," said a deep, firm voice.

A miner had moved to the front of the crowd. He looked out of place in this room, where not many people made an honest living. He was tall and broad-shouldered, with a mane of uncombed hair and a tangled beard. His hair protruded willy-nilly from the missing crown of his straw hat. His clothes were a series of connected patches. On one foot was a boot without a toe, on the other, a kind of rawhide moccasin. His trousers were held up with rope suspenders. There was something familiar about the way the man stood, something familiar about his blue eyes.

Kathy started. "W-Wade?" she said.

Wade smiled. He looked bigger somehow, and there was a presence about him that hadn't been there before.

"Who the hell are you?" St. Clair demanded.

"A friend of the lady's," Wade replied. He didn't look at St. Clair. His eyes were fixed on Kathy, drinking her in the way a man dying of thirst drinks water. "I was passing through Sonora, Kathy. I saw the handbills, the name. I didn't think it could be you, but I had to see. I spent near my last few dollars getting into your show. I tried to see you backstage, but you'd . . ."

St. Clair spoke impatiently. "That's quite touchin', friend, but we're not interested in your problems. You're interruptin' a private performance here. Either keep quiet and watch, or get out."

For the first time, Wade seemed to notice St. Clair. He fixed him with a steady gaze, then turned back to Kathy. "Is that your husband?" he asked coolly.

Kathy didn't know what to say. She feared for her safety, but she feared for Wade's more. "N-no," she said.

"Where *is* your husband?"

"Michael's dead, Wade. He was dead before I got to Sonofa-bitch. Ever since then, I've been—"

"You ask a lot of questions, friend." The chair scraped the floor as St. Clair stood and faced Wade. "Too many questions. If I were you, I'd leave while I could."

"Please, Wade, do as he says," Kathy beseeched.

Wade stared at St. Clair.

St. Clair said, "Didn't you hear me, friend? I said get out."

Wade said, "This is a public house, *friend*. I'll get out when I'm ready. Right now I'm talking to the lady."

"You get out now or I'll shoot you." St. Clair took another drink from the bottle, then set it aside. The pistol hung ready in his hand. "And I have a room full of witnesses to say it was self-defense."

Kathy said, "He means it, Wade. He's crazy."

Wade said nothing. St. Clair laughed. "That shut you up, didn't it? Look at you. What kind of a man are you? You don't even carry a gun. Any time you choose to dispute with a gentleman, sir, you'd best come armed like one. Now, get out."

Wade stared at St. Clair for a second. Then he turned and walked away. The crowd parted to let him through. Some of them laughed at him. Kathy watched his broad shoulders disappear in the mass of people. Tears rolled down her cheeks. To have found him after all this time, only to lose him again. It was too cruel. She had a final glimpse of him picking up his pack. Then there were too many people in between for her to see him anymore.

St. Clair turned back, dismissing Wade. "Now, Kathy—or Kate, as you call yourself—where were we?"

"The legs!" somebody shouted. "We want to see her legs."

"Hell, we want to see everything," shouted somebody else, and the room exploded with laughter. "Take it all off!" Even the whores thought it was funny. They liked to see a girl like Kathy humiliated.

"You heard them," St. Clair said. "Take off your clothes." A smile crossed his thin lips. "This time I'll keep my eyes open."

There were hoots and cheers from the crowd. They pressed closer, to see.

"You heard me," said St. Clair. "Take off your clothes."

"No," Kathy said.

St. Clair pointed with the pistol. "I told you what would happen if you didn't obey me."

"I don't care. Go ahead and kill me. I won't take off my clothes. Not for you or for any of your friends. I won't sing for you, either."

There was anger from the crowd. St. Clair's pasty face reddened. "Take them off, or we'll take them off for you. you little—"

Suddenly the room fell silent.

St. Clair turned. Wade was back. There was a pistol in the waistband of his trousers. Kathy recognized the brass-plated weapon that had once belonged to Dan Baylor, in Panama.

"I'll finish my talk with the lady now," Wade told St. Clair.

St. Clair snarled. "Friend, you just made a big mistake."

St. Clair raised his pistol. Wade drew. There were three shots in a flurry. Kathy screamed. St. Clair staggered. He fired again into the floor. Then he pitched forward onto his face.

The room was silent. Powder smoke floated in thin wreaths. Wade turned his pistol on the crowd. "Anybody else want some?"

No one said anything. No one moved.

Still covering the crowd, Wade reached his other hand behind him. "Come on, Kathy. We're leaving."

Kathy took his hand. She couldn't believe Wade had fought St. Clair and lived. The two of them walked out of the saloon. The crowd parted for them sullenly. Wade picked up his knapsack and slung it over one shoulder.

Outside, another crowd had gathered. Ned Storey was there, looking worried and distraught. He must have followed Kathy from the theater at a distance. "Kathy, thank God you're safe. What happened in there? Are you all right?"

She nodded. "I'm fine. Just a bit shaken."

Ned looked at the bearded, hairy miner with Kathy. He looked at the pistol in the miner's hand. Kathy said, "This is Wade Rawson. We traveled across Panama together. Wade, this is Ned Storey, my manager."

Wade nodded. Now that it was over, he looked pretty shaken himself.

Ned cleared his throat. "I don't suppose you'll be going to the reception after all this?"

"No," Kathy said. "Make excuses for me, will you, Ned? Everyone in town will know about this within an hour. They'll understand."

Ned backed off. Kathy and Wade started walking again, still hand in hand. All around them people were talking and pointing. "There they are. Kate Beddoes and the man that killed Captain St. Clair."

Wade said, "Where shall we go?"

"Where are you staying?" Kathy said.

Wade looked sheepish. "I'd planned to camp in that grove of live oaks just north of town."

Kathy shook her head. "Change your plan. You're staying with me."

42

They went to Kathy's hotel room. They sat up late into the night, talking.

Kathy told Wade all that had happened to her since they had separated on the Merced. Wade told her about his experiences mining for gold. He told her about splitting up with Jack and the winter in Bear Valley. He told her what had happened to Ralph Bannister.

Kathy put a hand over her mouth. "Oh, God. That sounds awful."

Wade stood and walked to the window. "It *was* awful," he said, looking out.

Kathy rose and stood behind him. "Then what?" she said softly. "Where is Sam now?"

Wade let out a long breath. "Sam was never right in the head after that. He got quiet, jumpy. He couldn't eat. He couldn't sleep at night. He couldn't get out of his mind what he'd done. We split up the gold dust we'd mined. We sent Ralph's share to his family in Philadelphia. Sam said he was taking his and going back to England. Whether he did or not, I don't know. He left me in Oro Fino."

"What have you been doing since then?"

"I don't think I was right in the head, either," Wade said. "Between what we went through up there and what happened to Ralph, something snapped. I spent all my money on liquor, trying to forget. I was drunk most of the last four months. I sobered up only because I ran out of money to buy booze. When I came through

Sonora, I was headed back to the mountains to find another claim and start working again.''

Kathy moved closer. "Are you right in the head now?"

Wade turned around. He put his hands on her shoulders and looked into her hazel eyes. "Yes. I am."

He ran his fingers through her hair. "I never thought I'd see you again, Kathy."

"Or I you. But I never gave up hope."

"Me neither. There was never a day I didn't think about you. Never a night I didn't dream of you. Sometimes, on the way back to Bear Valley in the snow, you seemed so close I could almost touch you, and I wanted to cry."

Kathy said, "We won't be parted again, will we?"

"No," Wade said. "Never." He leaned down. He kissed her lightly, his lips brushing hers. They looked at each other. Then they embraced and dissolved into a long, lingering kiss.

When they parted, Wade stepped back. "I feel guilty about touching you. I'm filthy. I must look awful."

Kathy drew him to her again. "I don't care," she whispered.

43

"I want to marry you," Wade told Kathy sometime during the long night.

"I want to marry you, too," she said. "But even if we're not married, as long as we're together, that's all I need." She giggled girlishly. "Doesn't that sound sinful?"

"You've changed," Wade said.

"Maybe. Or maybe this was the real me all along, and that other woman was a lie. You've changed, too, you know."

They reminisced about how they had met in Panama. "I wonder what happened to Jack," Kathy said. "You've no idea, do you?"

"No," Wade said.

"Poor Jack. He was a strange man in a lot of ways."

"He was a good friend. He was in love with you, you know."

Kathy lowered her eyes. "I was afraid that he was. He'd never have admitted it to me, though. It would have violated his concept of how to be a gentleman."

Wade sighed. "He was so determined to be rich. Well, good luck to him, wherever he is."

There was an inquest the next day into St. Clair's death. A few words from Kathy cleared Wade of any blame. "Indeed, you've done the community, if not all California, a service," the judge concluded.

Kathy gave Wade the money for a bath and a new outfit. With the long hair and beard gone, and new clothes, Wade looked like a different man. Then it was time to leave for the next town.

Ned Storey had his own and Kathy's mules packed while Wade bought a mule for himself. When Wade showed up in front of the hotel, Ned looked worried. "He's not going with us, is he?"

"He'll be going with us for as long as he wishes," Kathy said.

Ned looked askance. He said no more, however, and the three of them started out of town, to a great sendoff from the populace.

Those first days on the road were as close to paradise as Wade and Kathy could imagine. They traveled leisurely, lost in themselves. They camped under the stars. They went for long walks in the woods. Wade cooked and set up camp. At night he and Kathy slept in his tent. Ned was forgotten, an afterthought, and it made him more nervous by the minute. Wade represented a threat to him, someone who might take Kathy away. If Kathy should marry this miner and leave the stage, where would he be?

They reached their destination, Gopher Creek, near the Tuolumne River. There, everything changed. A man had been killed over Kathy, and that gave her a new aura of danger. She had become more than a star. She was a celebrity, the biggest in the southern mines. Wade's celebrity was nearly as great. Crowds followed the two of them everywhere. It was nearly impossible for them to find privacy. The crowds for Kathy's shows were larger and more raucous than ever. She was feted with endless receptions and surrounded by people seeking her autograph. Newspapers wanted interviews with Wade about how he had killed St. Clair. He turned them down. Denied first-hand accounts of the affair, the papers made up their own, more lurid ones. Each succeeding stop on the circuit was just as bad.

Two weeks later, Wade and Kathy were in a camp called Sullivan's Bar, having lunch in a restaurant. A crowd had gathered at a respectful distance, watching them, but Wade and Kathy had grown used to that. Now and then a bolder person would venture forward for an autograph, but glowering looks from Wade usually kept them back. No one wanted to anger the man who had killed Captain St. Clair.

Bearded young Ned Storey came into the restaurant, looking excited. "Kathy," he said, approaching their table, "great news!"

He sat, waving a piece of paper. "I've just had this by mail rider. It's an offer from the Civic Opera in Stockton. For a week's run at the end of September. They're talking a thousand dollars up front, against three-dollars-a-head admission, but I'm sure I can get you more than that. And if you do well there, we're guaranteed an offer from Sacramento later on." Ned pounded a fist on the table in glee. "This is it, Kathy. The big time, like I told you. Nothing can stop you now."

At first Kathy was as thrilled as Ned, then she saw the look on Wade's face.

Ned went on. "I'll tell them yes, of course."

"When do they have to know?" Kathy said.

"We want to get it settled as soon as possible. That way we can fill your calendar for the remaining time."

Kathy nodded. "Ned, would you leave us for a bit?"

Ned looked puzzled.

"I'll talk to you in a little while."

Ned looked from one of them to the other, worried. Then he shrugged, rose from the table, and left.

Kathy and Wade sat silently for a moment. Wade fiddled with his spoon. "Come on," he told her at last. "Let's get out of here."

They sneaked out the back door. Wade led Kathy into the hills. They followed a narrow trail, walking on a carpet on pine needles. The trail led them to a hillside that provided a spectacular view of the distant Sierra Nevadas, and the undulating hills in between.

A large, rounded boulder jutted out of the hillside, and the two of them sat on it, taking in the scenery. At last Kathy said, "You're unhappy, aren't you?"

Wade looked toward the far-off mountains. "When we're like this, I'm the happiest man alive, but . . ." He turned. "I feel useless, Kathy. I feel like a kept man. And all this talk about me being a gunman doesn't make it any better. The paper in Gopher Creek said I'd killed ten men."

"Do you want me to quit singing?" Kathy said.

"I don't have any money to support you. I don't have a job. Everything I have, you give me. I guess that's why I feel like a kept man. I am one."

"Wade, what's mine is yours. You know that. What kind of work do you want to get into? The law?"

Wade shook his head. "I couldn't sit in an office anymore. I was thinking about transportation. A stagecoach service, express mail. God knows it's needed up here. A business like that requires a lot of capital to start, though."

He paused, staring into the distance again.

Kathy said, "It's more than money, isn't it?"

Wade nodded. "I want to take another shot at the mountains, Kathy. I think I know where to find the rich vein."

"You can't let it go, can you?" Kathy said quietly.

Wade was grim. "It's a challenge. No, it's more than that. It's personal now. It's between me and those mountains. I won't let them beat me. All that suffering, all those dead men—the Baylor brothers, Ralph, Sam Trumbull gone out of his mind—it can't have been for nothing. The rich vein's out there, and I'm going to find it. I owe it to them, if nothing else."

"You've got gold fever," Kathy said. "You've got it bad." She remembered Peach. "It can be fatal, you know."

Wade said nothing.

Kathy said, "That's why you didn't go back east, isn't it? The gold fever?"

Wade turned. "That was part of it. But there was you as well. I wasn't going to leave California as long as there was a chance I might see you again."

Kathy said, "So what do I do? Come with you?"

Wade touched her cheek. "It's no life for a lady up there. You know that. Anyway, you don't want to quit singing, do you?"

Kathy smiled. "No. I want to try Stockton, Sacramento if I can. The big time, like Ned said. I guess I feel like you. It's a challenge. Right now I'm riding a star, and I want to see how far it can go."

Far off, they saw a hawk circling. It dived.

"All right," Wade said. "I'm going back to the mountains for one last try. Win or lose, I'll be back for you at the end of the season. I'll meet you in Stockton in November."

Kathy nodded. "The Civic Opera will know where to find me." Then she said, "Oh, Wade, I'm going to miss you. I just found you again, and already you're leaving."

"It's for the last time," he promised.

"When will you go?"

"As soon as I can get an outfit together. Tomorrow probably."

"Then we'd better make our time together count," she said.

Wade lifted her into his arms. He twirled her around, grinning. "Let's give ourselves something to remember."

She arched an eyebrow. "Something sinful?"

"Absolutely."

44

Wade bought a burro, tools, and supplies, and he started back for the country between the Merced and the Mariposa. He believed that the previous year's mistake had been in not going high enough. If the gold was washed down from above, it stood to reason that the rich vein was somewhere in the high country. He would start at the scooped-out mountain and work his way upward.

His path took him through Bear Valley. He passed the cabin where he and his partners had spent the past winter. It had been used by other men since then, and was in bad shape. Seeing it brought back many memories. He walked up the grassy hillside where Ralph Bannister was buried. The grave was already overgrown with weeds. The weather-stained wooden marker had fallen over. Wade straightened it and tidied up the grave. Then he moved on.

Past Bear Valley he didn't run into any miners. He was on his own. For the rest of the summer and into the fall he prospected for gold. There was no problem finding water; the heavy snows had left the streams full.

Everywhere, he found gold. In one place he estimated that he might have washed out twenty dollars a day, but it was not enough. It was not the Big Lump.

Deeper into the mountains he went, guided by his compass, relying on it to find his way back. He crossed a swift-flowing stream on a fallen pine tree, leading his reluctant burro.

Then he stopped finding gold. He dug, he washed, he got nothing but float. He wondered if he had somehow missed the rich vein, gotten above it.

October passed its halfway point. Oak, ash, and sycamore leaves turned color and began to fall. The nights grew cold. Wade ran low on supplies and ammunition for his shotgun. Finally there came a day when he was forced to admit that it was over. He had been beaten. The mountains had won.

He prepared to start back. He needed food for the trip. He shot a deer, but he only wounded the animal. The deer leapt forward and vanished in the woods. Wade followed the trail of blood. The trail ended at a steep ravine. Below, Wade saw the deer, twitching weakly.

Swearing, Wade clambered down the ravine's side. He reached the bottom and slit the deer's throat, putting the animal out of its misery. As he dressed the carcass, his practiced eye roamed the sides of the ravine out of habit. He saw outcroppings of reddish quartz.

He left the deer. With his knife he began to dig near one of the outcroppings, along the bed of the ravine. He soon struck bedrock. He scraped the rock. It was veined with a blackish clay. His heart pounded as he pried out the clay. On the bottom he saw a yellowish glitter.

He sank back on his heels, looking around the ravine. "This is it," he said. "Jesus God, this is it!"

He began laughing madly. The sound echoed off the ravine and surrounding hills. He threw his hat in the air.

"I've done it! I've done it!"

There was little time to celebrate. He had to work fast. He should have been halfway to Stockton already, but he couldn't leave. He was going to be late for his appointment with Kathy, but she wouldn't mind. Not when she saw the fortune he was bringing back with him.

He moved his camp to the edge of the ravine and he began digging, taking gold from the bedrock with his knife and pick, working his way along the vein. Much of the gold was in flake and nuggets. Dust he obtained by drying the black clay and blowing away the sand.

This was it, the Big Lump. And it was all his. There wasn't another miner within fifteen miles. He laughed while he worked. He sang to himself, making up nonsense songs, cackling as he watched his pile of gold grow.

When his supplies ran out, he lived on game. He developed scurvy, but he'd had scurvy before, just as he'd had the boils that broke out on his body, and the headaches and fever that racked him. He could face them. He could tough it out. There were thousands of dollars up here, millions maybe. What was a little sickness, a little hardship, against that?

The rains came, and he hardly noticed. He kept working. Gold was the only thing that mattered to him. He lost track of the days. November passed. December came. He got caught by an early snow. That sobered him up, much as he'd sobered up from his drinking binge after Ralph's death. He was out of food, save for some dried meat. The snow had driven away the game.

Wade had to get out. All this gold was no use to him if he starved to death.

He loaded his burro and started back. He kept the heavy bags of gold on his person. It was hard going in the snow and cold. He was not dressed for it, not prepared for it. His second day out, he awakened in camp to find the burro gone. Footprints in the snow told the reason. The animal had been stolen by Indians, no doubt for food. There was no time to go after it. Wade had to get to lower ground, and in a hurry.

Weakened by hunger and fever, he marched on, abandoning everything that had been on the burro but his ammunition. He came to the pine tree across the stream. The pine's trunk was slippery with ice and snow. Wade moved carefully along it. Below him, the stream raged. One slip, and he was dead, if not from drowning, then from the freezing water. The wind whistled down the canyon, making his task harder. He shook his fevered head, trying to clear it. Ice and snow on his eyebrows made it hard to see. The roaring of the stream was loud in his ears.

His heel slipped. He tried to recover, overbalanced, and fell. He caught himself on a broken branch, hooking one leg over the trunk.

As he did, something fell out of his coat pocket. His compass. He grabbed for it with his free hand, but it was already gone, vanished beneath the swirling water.

He hauled himself back onto the tree trunk. He continued across, sliding this time, not trying to stand. He reached the other side. He couldn't find the path he'd followed from the Mariposa. It was buried by snow. He couldn't take a sighting of the sun because it was hidden by clouds. He trudged on in what he could only hope was the right direction.

Without his compass he was soon lost. Nothing about this country looked familiar, but whether that was because of the snow or not, Wade couldn't say. He decided to return to the stream and follow it down to where it connected with the Mariposa or the Merced. He had not gone far when his path was blocked by steep walls of rock. In trying to detour around, he once more got himself lost. He couldn't find the stream. It was snowing again, and visibility was down.

That afternoon the snow stopped briefly, and Wade managed to shoot an eagle. He was so hungry that he tore off the feathers and tried to eat the bird's dark flesh raw, but it was bitter and almost impossible to chew. He cooked the bird that night over a small flame. It tasted worse, if anything, and it gave him dysentery, but he forced himself to eat.

The next morning he found himself walking through barren granite uplands. There was no possibility of game there. He had nothing to eat besides what was left of his eagle. He found a lone cedar tree growing out of the rock. He hacked off some of the bark and chewed that.

He no longer knew where he was. He was trying to get back to the stream, but he had no idea where that was, either. It started snowing again. He wandered aimlessly. His head and eyes ached. He was feverish, cramped with dysentery. He knew he was going to die. How ironic, he thought. He was carrying a fortune, and it was useless to him.

He sang tunelessly. He fell down a hill in the snow. He got up and kept going. He heard something. Bells. The bells seemed to be welcoming him. But to where? They sounded like cathedral bells. But there was no cathedral nearby. Or was there? Maybe they had built one since he had ascended the Mariposa. Anything was possible in California.

He moved toward the sound of the bells. Things were spinning. It was hard to focus his eyes. The bells were very loud.

Then everything went black.

45

Wade struggled up from the depths of unconsciousness. There was breath in his face. Then movement next to him. Something snuggled against his side. He smelled pipe tobacco. Broth simmering.

He opened his eyes. He was in a cabin on a bed of pine boughs and leaves. The thing by his side was a dog, black and white, long-haired, of mixed breed. The dog looked over its shoulder at Wade, then put its head back down, making little sounds of contentment.

A man stood over Wade, a big man in his late twenties with an enormous black beard. The man had a pipe in his mouth. "Ah," he said. "Our visitor wakes." He spoke with some kind of accent, French it sounded like.

The man felt Wade's head and cheeks with a touch that was surprisingly gentle for one of his size. He said, "The fever, it is down. We thought you were going to die, monsieur, but, it seems, you will not."

Wade suddenly remembered his gold. He felt the bed around him. The bags were gone. So was his coat.

The big man smiled, puffing his pipe. "Your gold is safe. It is in the corner with your coat and weapons."

Wade struggled to sit up.

"Be careful. You are still weak."

The big man was right. Wade lay back down, breathing deeply from that little bit of exertion. Next to him the dog stood on the bed. It sniffed Wade's face, then began licking his mouth.

"Roland!" said the big man. *"Arretez!"*

The dog sat. There was the rhythmic slapping of its tail on the bed. It lifted a paw to Wade, who scratched its chest. "How long have I been here?" Wade said.

"Five days," said the big man. "It was Roland, here, who found you. We were hunting, he and I, and he discovered you lying in the snow. I thought at first you were dead. We brought you back here. It was—how do you say—touch and go for a while with you. You had the delirium."

Wade swallowed. His throat was parched.

"You would like a drink?" the big man said.

"Please."

The man brought Wade a tin cup full of water. Wade sipped gratefully. He said, "You're French?"

"Belge," the man replied. "Belgian. I am called Jean-Claude Merlot. And you?"

"Wade. Wade Rawson."

Jean-Claude sat on a stool next to the bed. "What were you doing out there, Monsieur Wade?"

"Trying to get to lower ground. I got lost."

Jean-Claude nodded, puffing his pipe placidly.

"Are you a miner?" Wade asked him.

"In my way, yes. Though, it is certain, I have not had your success. Still, I have my claim, and it keeps me busy when the weather permits." He rose. "You are hungry. Have some soup."

Jean-Claude ladled broth from the simmering pot into a hand-carved wooden bowl. "Do you live here by yourself?" Wade asked him.

The Belgian shrugged. "I had three partners, but they left at the end of the autumn. I decided to stay on. I have food here, and Roland, and my books for company. I am content."

He handed Wade the bowl, along with a wooden spoon. Wade tasted the broth. It curled his tongue.

"I must apologize," Jean-Claude said. "The soup is made from bear meat. Bear steak is quite good, but, for some reason, bear soup, it is . . . well, you may taste for yourself. It is all I have, however, because of the snow. You have been taking it for some days."

Wade forced himself to take some more. "I'd thank you," he said, "but thanks seem inadequate. I'd be dead if it weren't for you."

"And Roland," Jean-Claude added with a twinkle in his eye.

The dog was sniffing the soup. "Yes," Wade said, "and Roland."

Wade thought about Kathy. What must she think had happened to him? He had to get to her. "I've got to get out of here," he said. "I mean, I don't want to be more of a bother to you than I've already been. I'll leave as soon as I can."

Jean-Claude relit his pipe, which had gone out. "I am afraid you will be with us for some time, monsieur. You are not in condition for the travel."

Wade slumped. It was true. He was weak and feverish. His legs were black and swollen from scurvy. He had an attack of panic. He was helpless in the hands of this man. There was nothing to stop Merlot from killing him and taking his gold. But if he was going to do that, he would have done it by now, surely? He could have left Wade to die in the snow, if it came to that. The panic subsided.

"Besides," said Jean-Claude, "it is still snowing. It will be some time before any of us can travel. It is all right. Roland and I shall be glad of the company. Eh, boy?"

As if in answer, the dog curled itself against Wade once more and went to sleep.

46

Wade spent the rest of the winter with Jean-Claude. The two men talked long hours. They played chess and checkers. Jean-Claude lent Wade his extensive collection of books. Most were in English—works by Prescott, Thackeray, Dickens, translations of Dumas.

"No wonder you speak the language so well," Wade told him, looking them over.

"Yes," said the Belgian, "I am very interested in your country. Everything is so free here. A man can make himself whatever he wants. In my country, one's life is based on who one's parents are. Schools, jobs, wife—it's all worked out for you.''

"That's what brought you here, the freedom?" Wade said.

"After a fashion. I am a younger son. You understand, that means I inherit little from my father. I was provided with a bit of education, then I went off to Paris to make my way. I became apprenticed to a printer there. It was my idea to one day publish my own newspaper. Then came the revolution. The 'June Days'—you have heard of them, no? I became a known enemy of Louis Napoléon. As you may well understand, that was not a good thing. I had to leave France. Just at that time there came news of the gold finds in California. So here you see me.''

"Do you miss Belgium?" Wade asked.

Jean-Claude nodded gravely. "Oh, yes. One day I will go back. But it takes money, you see, to make one's way there, if you don't have the family connections. It's the same all over." He rubbed his thumb against his two middle fingers, and winked. "You have to have the money."

When the weather permitted, Jean-Claude took Roland and went hunting. Even with the snow he managed to snare an occasional hare or rabbit. Wade got used to hearing his cheery whistle as he set out or came back, shotgun tucked beneath his arm. When Wade grew stronger, he went along. "Roland is a good dog," Wade said as they trudged through the snow one day. "Where did you get him?"

"I found him in the woods, lost."

"Like me?" Wade said.

"Yes. Like you."

That day the two men shot a deer. "A sure sign of spring," Jean-Claude said. "Soon you will be able to travel."

The Belgian's words made Wade think about seeing Kathy again. Then he thought about all the gold that remained to be dug up, and what he and Kathy could do with it. He pictured Kathy in fancy clothes and a big house, all the things she'd never had. He was already four months late going back to her. Would it be worth taking a few months and digging out more gold? He was close to the claim. He would never have a chance like this again.

They walked back to the cabin. Wade carried the shotguns. Jean-Claude carried the dressed deer carcass on his shoulders. Roland bounded ahead, sniffing around.

"Jean-Claude," Wade said hesitantly, "you know—you must know—that I've found a rich vein of gold."

"Yes, I know that."

"You've never mentioned it," Wade said.

"It's not my business," the Belgian told him.

"What would you say to going partners in it with me?"

"I thought you were going below," Jean-Claude said.

"I've decided to work up here one more season. There's too much gold. I can't just walk away from it. You've been a good friend, and I'd like you to share it with me. It's the least I can do to repay you. What do you say?"

Jean-Claude was philosophical. "I don't turn down gold, I'll admit it. I'm a miner."

Wade grinned. "Does that mean yes?"

"I believe it does." The Belgian laughed. "We will go partners, as you say."

"There's one problem. I might have trouble finding my claim again without a compass."

"I have a compass."

"Good. Now, there was a stream with a fallen pine tree over it that I used as a bridge. If I find that tree again, with your compass I can find the mine."

Jean-Claude chewed his pipe. "I know these mountains well. There are several fallen trees across streams. We will look at all of them."

"One more thing," Wade said. "I was supposed to meet someone—a lady—in Stockton last November."

"Kathy?" said Jean-Claude.

"How did you know?" Wade said.

"You talked about her. While you had the delirium."

"You didn't tell me."

"Like I say, it's not my business."

"I need to get a message to her," Wade said.

Jean-Claude nodded. "There is a camp. Tough Luck, it is called. The mail rider stops there. We will need supplies for the spring. Write your lady a note, and you may mail it when we go there. I myself am looking for mail. A year I've been here, and I've had no news from home."

March came. The snow melted. A notice had been left that the mail rider would be in Tough Luck the first Saturday of the month, and that was when Wade and Jean-Claude arrived. Tough Luck was a collection of tents and shacks on the Merced side of the divide, inhabited by a rougher than usual set of men. Wade and Jean-Claude bought their supplies, taking care to pay only with gold dust. If they used Wade's nuggets or flakes, it might attract unwanted attention.

The mail rider arrived in the afternoon. It was Billy, the young man whom Wade had met almost two years before. Billy rode a horse now instead of a mule, and he carried a pistol in his belt.

Jean-Claude was excited as Billy rode in, but he got no mail, to his disappointment. "Perhaps next time," he said. It sounded like a phrase he had used more than once.

Billy didn't remember Wade or Jack, but he remembered Kathy. "Kathy Beddoes? Sure, I remember Miss Kathy. How could I forget her? She's the most famous woman in California. Heck, you might say I was the one that got her started. I was the one that took her to Sonofabitch. I was the one suggested changing the camp's name to Kate's Bar. I've had more fellas buy me drinks because I know Kate Beddoes than you can imagine. I've paid to see her sing three times. And that was you with her that day, huh?"

Wade nodded. "It was me."

"What was your name again?"

"Wade Rawson."

Billy's ample mouth opened wider. "Not the Wade Rawson that killed . . ?"

"Captain St. Clair, yes." Wade shuffled his feet, embarrassed. "Look, that's something I'd prefer to forget. I've got a letter here for Mrs. Beddoes. It's important that she get it."

Billy grinned. "Fan mail, huh? From an old friend?"

A touch of impatience entered Wade's voice. "Mrs. Beddoes and I are going to be married."

Billy's eyes opened to an extent Wade would not have believed possible. "You're going to marry Kate Beddoes? I don't believe it."

"I don't care if you believe it or not. Just get the letter to her."

Wade gave him the letter, scratched in pencil on Jean-Claude's paper. Billy looked at the address. "Well, she ain't in Stockton, Mr. Rawson, I can tell you that much. Last I heard, she was playing Sacramento. Took the town by storm, too."

"It says Please Forward on the envelope," Wade pointed out.

"So it does," Billy said, looking again. He held out a brass thimble. "That'll be four dollars in coin, or fill this with dust."

Wade dipped the thimble into a small pouch of gold dust. "Your price has gone up since we last met."

"I ride express now as well as mail," Billy explained. "I carry gold to San Francisco for the boys, to be banked. It's more dangerous, so I charge more." He tapped the pistol in his belt.

When no one was looking, Wade slipped a gold nugget into Billy's coat pocket. "That's to make sure it gets forwarded."

Billy peeked in the pocket without letting anyone see. The nugget was good-sized. "Consider it delivered," Billy said.

Billy mounted his horse and set off for his next stop. Wade and Jean-Claude loaded their supplies on a freshly purchased mule and prepared to leave Tough Luck. Jean-Claude led them out of town in the opposite direction from his cabin.

"Why are we going this way?" Wade said.

"We must be careful that we are not followed," Jean-Claude told him. "There are men who do not trouble to find their own claims. They follow someone who has found gold and set up a claim next to his. Some of them just kill the man and steal his claim."

Wade said, "Have you been followed before?"

"I am followed every time I'm here. We are being followed right now, I'm certain of it."

Wade looked back. "I don't see anyone."

"You won't," Jean-Claude told him. "Do not worry. We will lose them. I always do."

47

Billy rode from camp to camp, stopping only to deliver the mail and make his pickup. He took his meals in the saddle. He had a lot of ground to cover. He had posted his schedule at the beginning of the previous winter, and it was a matter of pride to him that he keep to it.

Billy was making more money as a mail rider than he had ever dreamed of as a miner. Now that he'd begun taking gold dust to the banks in San Francisco, his profits would be greater than ever. Because of the gold's heavy weight, he could work only the camps along the Merced's drainage area on this trip. Then he'd go to San Francisco, pick up more mail, and visit the camps along the Mariposa. After that would be the Tuolumne, then the Mokelumne and the Stanislaus, if there was time left in the season. Even if he hit every camp in the southern mines—and that was unlikely—the north would be left unserviced. There were other mail riders, Billy knew, but none as good as he. None who rode express, and none who kept to a schedule like he did. His goal was to own a mail and express service throughout the California mines—regular service, not just one trip a year. But for that he would have to hire men, and why would men work for him when they could go into business for themselves and keep all the profits? And if they did work, what was to keep them from drifting on once they'd made a few dollars?

These problems occupied his mind as his horse paced the chaparral-choked hills. It was a desolate stretch. The once-thriving placers along here had been worked clean, and the miners had moved on. The bustling camps had become ghost towns. Billy didn't have another stop for miles. He wasn't paying attention to what he was doing.

He started as a man rode out of a brush-filled draw directly into his path. The man sat a beautiful black horse with an ornate, silver-chased saddle. He wore a red silk headband and an earring, and he held two revolvers on Billy.

"Please, señor, halt your horse," said the man.

Billy didn't know what to do. He carried a revolver now, but he'd never thought he'd have to use it. He knew there was danger in carrying gold dust, but the danger had always seemed more potential than real.

"Please, señor," repeated the bandit. "Or I shall be forced to shoot you."

Billy's mind raced. The bandit's revolvers were cocked. Billy would never be able to draw and fire before the bandit did. He couldn't turn and ride away, either. The bandit was too close. He'd shoot Billy out of the saddle before he got ten yards.

Billy reined in and raised his hand.

The bandit grinned engagingly. *"Bueno."*

Billy was red-faced with anger and frustration, along with shame at having been taken unawares. What would happen to his business now? How would he repay the miners for the gold dust he was going to lose? The reputation of which he had been so proud was going to be destroyed.

"Now," the bandit said, "take your pistol, please. Remove it from your belt with your left hand, slowly, and throw it to the ground."

Billy did as he was told.

"Now give me the bags. The ones with the gold."

Billy lifted the gold bags from the flat horn of his Spanish saddle. He handed them to the bandit. "Hey," he said suddenly, "I know who you are. You're Juan Soto, the famous Mexican bandit."

"I am Chilean," the bandit corrected proudly. "Why must you gringos lump us always together?"

Billy shrugged. "I don't know."

Soto hung the gold bags on his own saddle. Billy went on. "They say you're like a Robin Hood, or something. That you steal money and you give it to poor Mexicans—and Chileans—and all. Is that true?"

The bandit smiled. "No."

"Oh," said Billy.

"But it makes a good story, yes?"

"Yeah." Billy smiled, too. "I guess it does."

Soto saluted Billy with one of the pistols. "Adios, amigo."

"Adios," Billy said. He was already thinking of the stories he'd have to tell about this. He had met the two most famous individuals in California—Kate Beddoes and Juan Soto. How many people could say that? Surely there would be a way to make money off that. Maybe even enough to pay back all the miners whose gold dust he'd lost. He could sell his story to the—

"By the way," Juan added, "my wife Elena sends you a message."

"Your wife?" Billy said, wrinkling his brow. "I don't understand. A message from where?"

"From heaven," Juan said. He fired both of the pistols into Billy's chest. The young mail rider toppled off his horse, dead. The horse galloped away, terrified by the shots.

Juan stuck the pistols in the red sash he wore around his waist and rode off. Billy's horse was eventually found by a party of indigent miners, who sold it to buy food. So that no one would think they'd stolen the animal, they threw the saddle and the mail sacks away.

48

It was early morning when Juan Soto rode into Coyote Diggings. It had taken him the best part of two days to get there. He had ridden through the nights, stopping to sleep only when too exhausted to go farther. He didn't like to sleep anymore, especially at night. At night he had the dream. The dream was always the same. He was back in Chile, mining for gold along the Copiapo, with the snow-capped volcano Ojos del Salado in the background. His day's work was over, and he was walking back to his cabin. Elena was waiting for him, waving to him with their infant son in her arms. He ran to her, and just as he got there, he saw the terrible rope burn around her neck. The dream ended, and he woke up in a cold sweat.

Juan had not been active around Coyote Diggings. Those who came in contact with him on his visits there thought of him as a lowland *haciendado* with interests in the local mines. He stabled his black horse, Pizarro. The horse and its silver-chased saddle were part of his growing legend. They might one day give away his real identity, but he would not surrender them. They were objects of vanity, a quality he had discovered only since becoming an outlaw.

He strolled down the main street to a saloon, The Black Jack. A sign with the jack of spades painted on it hung over the plank sidewalk. The Black Jack was the biggest, most popular saloon in Coyote Diggings. It featured the best liquors, the best cigars, the best women and games of chance in the southern mines.

At this early hour, men were rolling kegs of beer through the saloon's open doors. Inside, two Chinese swept the floor, which was littered with used decks of cards, bottles, and cigar butts. A group of young boys had sneaked in. They picked up some cards and some old chips, and they started playing faro on the floor.

"All right, you boys, beat it," said a woman's voice. The boys got up and scampered out the doors, past Juan.

Brandy wore a plain blouse and skirt. Her red hair was pinned up. "Put one of those kegs behind the bar and tap it," she told the brewery men. "The rest goes in the back."

She returned to the bar, where she'd been helping the bartender take inventory as he stocked his liquors. She seemed tireless. She must have been up late last night, and here she was hard at work again. A couple of her girls lounged sleepily at a corner table, drinking coffee and eating French pastries.

"Wash this bar down when you're finished," Brandy told the bartender, prying loose one of her inventory sheets from the woods. "It's sticky."

"All right," said the bartender.

Brandy looked up and saw Juan, who bowed. "Señorita Brandy. *Buenos días.*"

She nodded without enthusiasm. "You're looking for Jack, I suppose."

"Is he awake yet?" Juan said.

"He's awake. He's in the back." She returned to her inventory.

Juan went into the back room, where he found Jack Marlow going over the books. Jack wore a suit of pearl-gray broadcloth. He had grown a thin mustache. His hair was slicked back save for an unruly lock that still tumbled over his forehead. As he read, he worked his stiff left hand, opening and closing it. It had become such a habit that he no longer realized he did it.

"Hello, Juan," Jack said, looking up. "Didn't figure on seeing you this soon. You have good hunting?"

"Very good," Juan said. He placed a sack of gold dust on Jack's desk. "The usual arrangement?"

Juan and Jack had become acquainted on one of Juan's earlier visits to Coyote Diggings. Juan had been seeking a permanent hide-out, and Jack had been willing to oblige—for a percentage of Juan's take. Juan was no trouble. He didn't drink or chase women. He spent his time reading or playing an occasional game of monte.

"Sure, Juan," Jack said. "The room's always ready for you." He hefted the leather sack. "How many jobs did it take you to collect this much?"

Juan grinned. "Just one. I robbed a mail rider. I heard he was carrying dust from the mines to San Francisco."

Jack pushed a box of cigars across the desk. Juan took one and lit it. He looked over Jack's shoulders. "You're working on your accounts?"

"Just looking them over," Jack said. "Brandy keeps them. She does a damn good job of it, too. She's the one that runs this place, not me. She's got a head for business."

"She is in love with you," Juan said.

"Who, Brandy? No, she's just grateful for what I've done for her."

"I tell you, amigo. I have had a woman love me, and I know the signs. She loves you."

Jack remembered Juan's wife, Elena. He remembered what had happened to her. Juan didn't recognize Jack from that day in Oro Fino when his wife had been hanged. Jack had changed too much. Jack had never told Juan that he'd seen him before.

"Brandy's not the type to fall in love," Jack said at last. He pushed the ledgers aside and lit a cigar for himself.

"So," Juan said, "business is good, no?"

"Not as good as I'd like," Jack said.

Juan looked surprised.

"I want more, Juan. I'm tired of this two-bit mining camp. I want big money, enough to go to San Francisco and start a business there."

Juan smiled broadly. "You know, amigo, I have been thinking the same."

"You thought how to do it?" Jack said.

"Yes," said Juan. "I believe I know a way it might be accomplished. It will require men, though."

"I can get men," Jack said.

"Good." Juan puffed his cigar and leaned close. "This is my idea."

When Juan had gone to his room, Brandy came in to see Jack. "What did he want?" she said.

Jack shrugged. "Business. He's got a way for us to make more money."

"Why go into business with him? We're making plenty."

"You know how I feel about that," Jack told her.

Brandy sighed. "Yes, yes. And you know how I feel about Juan. I don't like him."

Jack laughed. "I'm not particularly fond of him myself."

"I don't like you associating with him, Jack. He's going to get you into trouble."

"It won't be the first time I've been in trouble," Jack said. "I can handle it."

49

Wade showed Jean-Claude the claim. "Well, what do you think?"

The Belgian nodded sagely, examining the bedrock where Wade had uncovered it. "It's a rich vein, that's true. There is enough here that I can go back to Belgium, to my city of Namur, and be a man of substance."

"Substance? You can buy the whole town," Wade said. "We'll have to work quickly, though. If we're discovered, there'll be five thousand men up here inside of two weeks."

Jean-Claude said nothing.

"You're not exactly jumping up and down with excitement," Wade observed.

"Ah," said Jean-Claude. "A lot may yet happen, my friend. I could take fever and die. I could be robbed. I could be sailing home, and my ship could sink and the gold be lost at sea. No, when I am safely docked at Le Havre or Antwerp, and I am at the bank watching my gold being deposited, that is when I shall get excited. For now, what is required is that we begin to work."

Through the spring and into the summer Wade and Jean-Claude mined the rich vein. They dug along the ravine, scraping the bedrock, breaking flakes and nuggets out of the quartz. There was water in the ravine now, from the melting snow, and they washed the paydirt, using Jean-Claude's cradle.

They built a cabin at the top of the ravine, on Wade's old campsite. Every day they climbed down to work. Each evening they climbed back. On Sundays they took the dog, Roland, and went hunting.

Jean-Claude remained phlegmatic about his new riches. He dug or helped Wade work the cradle, barefoot, pants rolled up, puffing his pipe, now and then whistling. He could labor from dawn to dusk and at the end of the day be good for another ten hours, while Wade was exhausted.

At night the two of them weighed their take. They divided it and each put his share in a hiding place. Jean-Claude hid his in a hole he had hollowed out beneath the chopping block. Wade's was in an auger hole he'd made in a gnarled cedar near the cabin. These spots were quickly filled, and they had to find more.

On a long evening in June, Wade and Jean-Claude got together their earnings to tally them up. There were bags and bags of gold. It took the two men a long time to weigh it all.

"I've got just short of four hundred pounds," Wade marveled when he was finished. "That's—Jesus, it's a hundred thousand dollars, more or less."

"Yes, and it's about eighty-five thousand for me," said Jean-Claude.

Wade said, "It's been a hell of a season already, and that vein's barely touched."

"Mmm," said the Belgian, puffing his pipe.

Wade dipped his hand into a bag of nuggets. He sifted the rough lumps of gold through his fingers. He watched them glint in the candlelight. This was what he had come to California for. This was what he had suffered scurvy and fever for, watched his friends die for. Shiny rocks.

"What is it?" Jean-Claude said.

"I don't know," Wade said. "I have all this gold, and . . . and suddenly it means nothing to me. Nothing. It was finding it that was important. The actual possession—being rich—is nothing. The only thing that means anything to me is Kathy."

He stood and walked around the tiny cabin, running his fingers through his hair. "I should have left this place a long time ago, Jean-Claude. I never should have come here at all. I never should have left Kathy. She means more to me than all the gold in these mountains. God, what have I done?"

Behind his black beard, Jean-Claude's blue eyes were bright. "I've been wondering how long it would take you to realize that."

"I should have realized it long ago. How could I have been so stupid?"

"Gold's reflection is bright," Jean Claude said. "It can blind a man to many things, not the least of which is the truth. And the truth is that of all things in life, love is the most important.''

"Why didn't you tell me that before?" Wade said.

"Because it is the kind of lesson one must learn for oneself or one does not learn it at all. What will you do now?"

Wade suddenly felt a great urgency. "I've got to get out of here. I've got to get back to Kathy."

"When will you go?"

"As soon as possible. Tomorrow. The devil with the gold. You take it.''

Jean-Claude raised a hand in caution. ''You would be foolish to leave your gold, my friend. You have earned it by honest labor. It gives you and your lady a stake for your future. Listen. You will need two mules to carry so much gold. I must get supplies for the next months. While I am in Tough Luck I will buy you the mules.''

"I'll go with you," Wade said.

"No. You must stay and guard the claim. I will let you keep Roland. He is a good watchdog.''

The next day Jean-Claude set out for Tough Luck. There, he purchased supplies for himself and Wade, as well as two mules. The purchase of the two animals attracted attention, so when Jean-Claude left town, he took more care than usual to throw off anyone who might be following him. He gave the slip to all of his trackers— all but one.

50

The late afternoon sky had turned dark. In the distance, thunder rumbled. The smell of rain was in the air.

The dog Roland pricked his ears. He growled. Then he ran out to the edge of the pines, barking.

Jean-Claude looked up from the shirt he was mending. "What is it, boy? Eh?''

The dog ran back and forth, from the woods to the cabin, barking furiously.

"Someone coming, is it?" Jean-Claude said.

There was an open space in front of the cabin. Beyond that, visibility was limited by a belt of cedars and pines, and a large outcropping of rock. Jean-Claude stepped inside the cabin. He took his pistol from a wall nail and stuck it in his belt. He loaded his shotgun with ball. The dog was still barking.

"*Assez*, Roland. *Arretez*." Jean-Claude stood just inside the cabin door, waiting. The dog alternately sat and stood beside him, scratching the floor, crying, growling, wanting to go after whatever was out there.

"Roland," said Jean-Claude, holding him back.

He saw movement on the path that ran down through the trees. Men showed themselves. Six of them. They were on foot, carrying rifles, with pistols in their belts. They had no packs and no mule, which meant they must have left their horses elsewhere, which meant they hadn't wanted to be heard. The dog had given them away, so they approached boldly.

Jean-Claude leveled his shotgun. "*Arretez*, messieurs."

The men stopped.

"What is it you wish?" Jean-Claude called out.

The men's leader, a well-dressed fellow with a stiff left hand and an unruly lock of dark hair, said, "We're miners, looking for a place to spend the night. We don't want to be caught out in this storm that's coming."

The men started forward again, but Jean-Claude said, "I do not believe that you are miners, monsieur. Remain where you are."

The men stopped again. They spread out, fingering their weapons. Their leader spread his arms. "Come on, friend. All we want is a dry place to spend the night. Hell, we won't even stay the night if that's what you want. Just let us get out of the rain. We've got some whiskey we'll share with you."

Jean-Claude said, "You are lying. You believe there is gold here, and you wish to take it. You have followed me from Tough Luck. I saw your companion with the red headband when I was in that camp. My congratulations, monsieur. I did not think that anyone could trail me."

Juan Soto bowed, smiling. Juan had made the rounds of the mining camps, disguised as a day laborer, swamping saloons and washing dishes, all the while keeping his eyes and ears open. In

Tough Luck he had heard about the Belgian. A lot of men thought the Belgian had a rich claim, but no one had been able to follow him. Juan had followed him, though, using skills developed while on the run, using skills he'd acquired in Chile, pursuing Indians who'd stolen his equipment.

Next to Juan, Jack Marlow cried out, "Where is your partner?"

"What makes you think I have a partner?" Jean-Claude replied.

"That's the word in Tough Luck," Jack told him. "And if you don't have gold, why did you buy two more mules?"

"My first mule died, and I thought his replacement should have companionship."

"Really? Then why do I see three mules behind your cabin?"

"Perhaps you suffer from multiple vision," Jean-Claude suggested.

One of Jack's men, a round-faced, heavyset fellow named Gary, said, "What are we waiting for, Jack? Let's get this smartass."

Jack motioned Gary quiet. To Jean-Claude he said, "All right, so we want your gold. Give it to us, and we'll be on our way. Nobody will get hurt."

"I am afraid that is impossible, monsieur," Jean-Claude replied.

"Come on," Jack said, trying to be reasonable. "You can't win. What's to stop us from camping here and waiting you out? You have to sleep sometime."

"Go ahead and camp, if that is your wish. I shall not object."

The six men continued to spread out. The leading one had edged near the right side of the cabin, trying to get behind it.

Jean-Claude said, "That is far enough, monsieur. Any more, and I shoot."

Suddenly Jack said, "Take him, boys!"

The men rushed the cabin. Jean-Claude fired at the one on the far right. He fell sideways. The others kept coming. Jean-Claude fired the shotgun's other barrel. The ball grazed Gary's temple, and he dropped to the ground. Jean-Claude fired the pistol. The other claim jumpers dropped as well. They crawled to cover behind the trees, except for Juan, who dodged behind the rock outcrop.

Jean-Claude grabbed Roland by the collar. "Get out, Roland. Find Wade. *Allez! Allez!*"

The black-and-white dog scampered out the door in the direction Wade had taken. Jack and Gary fired pistols at him, but they missed, and the dog disappeared among the trees.

The claim jumpers turned their fire on the cabin. Bullets peppered the log structure. Jean-Claude took cover just inside the door, where he could see when they rushed him again. He reloaded his shotgun and pistol, but he didn't fire back. He didn't have ammunition to waste. The man he'd shot didn't move. He was either dead or too badly wounded to matter.

There was a lull in the firing while the claim jumpers reloaded. Jack cried, "Come on, give it up. You don't have a chance."

Jean-Claude made no reply. The sky was very dark. The wind had picked up. If he could hold out until the storm broke, he had a chance.

Jack tried again. "Give us the gold, and we'll go in peace. It's not worth your life."

Jean-Claude said nothing.

By the trees, a skinny, sharp-faced claim jumper named Paul said, "What do you want us to do, Jack?"

"Let's burn him out," said Gary.

"No," Jack said. "If we burn him, he won't be able to tell us where the gold is."

"We'll find it after the fire goes out," Gary said. "Gold don't burn."

"It's not in the cabin," Jack explained patiently. "It's buried out here somewhere. We'll never find it without him."

"Why don't we camp here and wait him out, like you said?" Paul asked.

Jack shook his head. "That won't work, and he knows it. It's going to be dark soon. That storm's ready to hit. He could get away in the darkness and slip down the ravine. If he knows this country as well as I think he does, he could cause us a lot of trouble, especially when his partner shows up. No, we'll have to rush him. Get ready."

Around them the thunder grew louder. Lightning flickered among the hills.

"Hey," said a dirty-looking young man named Brian, "where'd Juan go?"

"He's working his way behind the cabin," Jack told him. "He should be there by now." He looked around, cocking his revolver. "You boys ready? Let's go."

The four men broke from cover. They ran toward the cabin, firing their pistols. Jack lagged behind the others. If anyone was going to get shot, he didn't want it to be him.

Jean-Claude propped himself on one knee. He fired the shotgun. Brian stumbled. He fell on his face and did not move. The other claim jumpers dove for cover as Jean-Claude fired again.

"Goddamn fancy shooting for a foreigner," he heard one of them say.

Jean-Claude hastily reloaded his shotgun. The claim jumpers commenced a slow, steady fire at him. They were closer now. Their shots were more accurate. Wood splintered around him. Dirt kicked up. He hugged the doorway and waited for his chance. It was nearly dark now. Lightning flashed, momentarily blinding the combatants. Thunder boomed. The wind filled the air with loose dirt. A few minutes more, and it would be dark enough to make his break. One of the claim jumpers crawled forward. Jean-Claude fired his pistol at him. The man scuttled backward. It was hard to see for the dust swirling into his face. It would be just as hard for the claim jumpers to see him when he ran for it.

Jean-Claude tensed himself. The next lightning flash, and he would go.

Unnoticed by Jean-Claude, Juan Soto had made his way to the rear of the cabin. Unheard because of the gunfire and the storm, he knocked loose some mud chinking between the logs. He looked through and saw Jean-Claude. The Belgian was standing, ready to run. Juan pushed his pistol through the crack.

Lightning crashed. Jean-Claude made a break.

Juan fired, hitting Jean-Claude in the back of the thigh. Jean-Claude dropped to the floor, grabbing his leg and yelling with pain. The rest of the claim jumpers rushed forward. Jean-Claude lunged for his dropped weapons, but Jack got there first, and he kicked them out of the Belgian's reach.

Jean-Claude lay in the doorway, holding his wounded leg. Jack stood over him, smiling. "Now we can have our little chat."

Jack looked at his men. "How are the others?"

"Eric's dead," said Gary angrily, stanching blood from his forehead.

"So's Brian," said Paul.

"Go wait for the partner," Jack told Paul and Gary. "You know what to do if he shows up."

The two claim jumpers moved off. While Juan lit a lamp, Jack looked around the small cabin. The wounded man had a partner, all right; there was no doubt about that. There was gear for two men. Jack spied a case of wine. He lifted one of the bottles. "Saint Emillion," he said. "Good stuff. What's this for?"

Jean-Claude bit his lip in pain. "It's for drinking."

Juan kicked the Belgian in the face. Jean-Claude's mouth filled with blood. At least one tooth tilted at an unnatural angle. Blood dripped into his black beard.

"Let's try again," Jack said. "What's it for?"

Jean-Claude spit blood onto the dirt floor. "A celebration. My partner and I. This is his last night in the mountains. He's leaving."

"Where is your partner now?"

"He went for a walk."

"You expect us to believe that?" Jack said.

"Believe what you wish, you swine. He went for a last look around."

Jack and Juan glanced at each other. Juan shrugged. "It could be true."

The wind whistled around the cabin. The lamp flickered with the gusts. Jack sat on the edge of the table. "Now," he said to Jean-Claude. "The gold. Where is it?"

Jean-Claude hesitated. It was hard to talk with the blood in his mouth. He let out his breath. "The chopping block, outside. Look underneath."

"And your partner's?"

"That first cedar to the right of the rock. In an auger hole near the big knot."

Juan went to check. As he did, lightning flashed. Thunder rolled across the mountains. Trees bent in the wind. The first drops of rain beat the dry earth. Suddenly the heavens opened, and rain poured down. Lightning and thunder crashed and crashed again.

Juan came back, soaked, with two bulging sacks.

"And the rest?" Jack said to Jean-Claude. "Where is that?"

"That is all, messieurs," said the Belgian. "There is no more."

Juan kicked Jean-Claude in his wounded leg. The big man arched his back and cried in pain.

"Don't make this hard on yourself," Jack said. "I don't want to kill anybody. I know there's more gold, and I want it. Tell us where it is, and we'll let you go. We'll even patch that wound for you."

Rain lashed the cabin, coming through the open doorway, getting Jean-Claude wet. He said nothing. He knew they were going to kill him. His only hope was to hold out long enough for Wade to return. Wade must have heard the shots. He must be on his way.

"You'll talk in the end," Jack promised. "Do it now, and spare us all a lot of pain. What do you say?"

"Go to the devil," Jean-Claude told him.

Jack shook his head. He nodded to Juan. "Go ahead."

Jack turned away. He couldn't watch. He took one of the wine bottles and broke off the neck on the side of the table. He poured the red liquid in a tin cup and drank. He hadn't wanted to come on this expedition. But if he hadn't, what was to keep Juan and his men from keeping the gold for themselves and disappearing into the vastness of California?

The process was short but bloody. The Belgian's screams were muted by the thunder and lightning of the storm. The guttering candlelight threw obscene shadows on the wall. When it was over, Jean-Claude had revealed all his and his partner's hiding places.

"What shall I do with him?" Juan asked.

Jack forced himself to look. He recoiled at the sight. Jack had killed men before, more than he cared to remember, but he had never done anything like this. Where he came from, you just shot them—bam—and it was over. It was business. But this, this was brutality for its own enjoyment, the work of an unhinged mind. It was far beyond anything Jack could have imagined. Still, he had come to California to get rich. If this torture was what it took to make the Belgian tell his secrets, so be it. Jack was not going to let anyone—or anything—stand in his way. He said, "Put the poor bastard out of his misery."

Juan drew a pistol from his silk sash. He shot the Belgian in the head. The body jumped, then was still.

"Let's get the gold," Jack said. "Hurry, before the partner comes back." Maybe they could get away without killing anyone else.

Jack and Juan carried the gold into the cabin. "It is a fortune," Juan said, shaking off the rain.

Juan was right. Everything Jack had ever wanted was now within his grasp. He and Brandy would go to San Francisco. He would be a gentleman.

Before leaving, Jack and Juan rummaged through the cabin in case there was gold they had overlooked. The dead man's partner's knapsack sat on his bed, packed for travel. Jack opened it and dumped out the contents. An object caught his eye in the candle-light. He picked it up.

It was a pistol, a brass-plated pocket Colt, .31 caliber.

Jack went cold. He knew this pistol. He'd handled it before. He'd taught its last owner how to load it. He turned it over. The initials D.B., for Dan Baylor, were scratched on the bottom of the backstrap.

Jack knew who the dead man's partner was.

"Juan!" he cried. "Get the men! Tell them not to—"

Over the thunder he heard gunshots, close by.

51

Wade ran toward the cabin. The dog went ahead of him, unseen in the darkness and rain.

Wade couldn't go at full speed. The wet ground was slippery, and he was afraid of blundering off the path and getting lost. Occasional flashes of lightning helped illuminate the way.

He had remained in camp a few extra days to dry deer meat for the journey back. Carrying so much gold, he intended to bypass as many towns as he could on his way to Stockton, where he could deposit the gold safely in a bank. Today, his last day here, he'd climbed the highest peak in the neighborhood, some four miles from the cabin. He had gone to say good-bye to the mountains. They still held an attraction for him. They always would. He'd stayed later on the peak than he'd planned, fascinated by the spectacle of the approaching storm, the play of lightning and cloud over the hills. Then he'd heard distant gunshots, and he'd started back. He'd run into the dog Roland on the way, and he'd known there was trouble.

The shots had ceased some time ago. Wade had no idea what had happened. He could only hope that he was in time to help.

He sucked in air. The shotgun he carried banged his thigh. Wind and rain beat at his face. Thunder exploded around him. His boots skidded on the wet ground. His clothes were heavy with water. He tripped over something in the darkness and fell.

He entered a belt of pines and cedars. The cabin was not far. He glimpsed its light through the trees. He heard a single pistol shot ahead. He speeded up, crying from the exertion.

Suddenly he was hurled to the ground, stunned. He recalled seeing flashes, and he thought for a moment that he had been hit by lightning. Then the real lightning crashed nearby, and he realized that he'd been shot.

He felt numb. He tried to move. Waves of pain washed over his chest and side, and he almost passed out. He gritted his teeth and dragged himself off the trail into a clump of manzanita bush. He lay there without moving.

He heard boots going back and forth in the mud. They were looking for him. Somebody hacked at the bushes.

"I can't find him," said a man's voice.

"He's got to be dead," said another. "We shot him point-blank."

"We'd have to stay here till dawn to find the body," said the first. "Come on, let's go tell the boss what we done. Get out of this rain."

Wade heard laughter as two sets of footsteps receded toward the cabin.

He must have passed out. When he came to, something was rasping his face. It was the dog, Roland, licking him. The thunder and lightning had moved farther east. The rain was now a steady downpour. It sounded oddly peaceful after the violence of the storm.

"Hello, Roland," Wade said. He tried to stand, but he had to stop because of the pain. He couldn't be sure, but he thought he was carrying two bullets. He came to his hands and knees, crawled to a tree, and used it to haul himself up. The blood rushed from his head. He got dizzy and had to bend over to keep from blacking out.

At last he straightened. He staggered to the cabin. The dog trotted ahead, looking over its shoulder to make sure Wade was coming. The cabin was quiet. A light burned inside.

The dog scratched open the door, then came back to Wade's side, unwilling to go on by itself. Wade slipped in the mud. He caught hold of the cabin's corner. He paused, catching his breath. He worked his way to the door and went in.

There was blood everywhere—on the walls, the floor, the furniture. Wade saw Jean-Claude. He saw what they'd done to him. He leaned against the doorway for support, trying not to be sick. He had never seen anything so horrible. Jean-Claude must have talked before he died. That much punishment would have made any man talk. Wade knew the gold was gone. It didn't matter.

Wade remembered how Jean-Claude had saved his life, how he had cared for him. He vowed to find the men who had done this. He vowed to kill them.

The dog whined beside the body, frightened. The room was spinning. It was hot, stuffy. Wade saw that his shirt was covered with blood. The blood had soaked into his trousers as well. He reeled back outside. The air cooled his face, but it didn't stop the spinning. He stumbled once, then he fell in a puddle and was still. The rain beat down.

Part IV

THE CITY

52

November 1851

Kathy Beddoes wanted to make a strong impression on her opening night in San Francisco. She had been heralded as a sensation, but San Francisco lived on sensation, and she intended to give its residents something to remember.

She'd had a special costume made for the occasion. It was an off-the-shoulder green velvet gown, the type she usually wore. This one, however, fastened down the front with snaps so that it could be taken off in one quick movement.

That night, the Jenny Lind Theater, on Portsmouth Square, was packed. The boxes glittered with men in evening dress and ladies in satin and jewels. Ned Storey, Kathy's manager, said that the tickets had sold out in less than an hour. For the first time, Kathy was working with an orchestra.

The audience expected Kathy to end her show with a glimpse of leg. It had become her trademark. They were ready for it when she performed her a cappella rendition of "Where Can the Soul Find Rest?" Tonight, they got something different. When the moment of sad silence passed, and the orchestra launched into "Oh! Susanna," Kathy pirouetted and popped out of her gown, revealing herself in a sequined corset, her long legs encased in flesh-colored tights. As she sang and danced across the stage, the crowd—the men, at any rate—went wild. The ladies were scandalized. Many of the men sang along with her. Others rushed the stage. They would have carried her off bodily had they not been prevented by a force of bouncers hired especially for the occasion.

After the performance Kathy retired to her dressing room, which was buried in flowers and invitations to parties and receptions. She sat in her chair, catching her breath, drinking water. She'd expected Ned to be waiting for her. She wondered where he could have gone.

He was probably accepting the congratulations of the management or lining up more work.

There was a knock at the door. Kathy threw on a robe. "Ned?" she said.

There was no answer. Kathy opened the door, then stepped back. Before her was a dark-haired man in evening clothes, holding a bouquet of yellow roses.

"For the Toast of the Mother Lode," he said gallantly. "Now the Toast of San Francisco."

Kathy stared at him a moment, then she cried, "Jack!" and she threw her arms around him.

Jack embraced her as well, then they drew back and looked at each other. "Kathy," he said. "I would never have believed it was our demure Mrs. Beddoes onstage, if I hadn't seen it with my own eyes."

"There are times I don't believe it myself," Kathy told him. "And look at you, dressed to the nines, with a fancy mustache and haircut. You said you were going to get rich, and it looks like you have."

Jack grinned. "I have my finger in a lot of pies."

"Such as?"

"Well, among other things, I'm your new manager."

Kathy stepped back. "Manager? But Ned . . ? What about . . ?"

Jack laughed. "That boy? I bought him out a few minutes ago. Made him a damn—a darn fine offer for your contract, too." The offer had been made with a pistol pointed at Ned's head, but Jack didn't tell Kathy that.

Kathy said, "I never thought Ned would do something like that."

"Oh, don't worry about him. He's been taken care of quite generously. You're in San Francisco now, Kathy. You're on another level. Young Mr. Ned got you this far, but I have the contacts and clout as well as the money to keep you on top. We're going to build our own theater so that all the money we bring in will be ours. No more splitting the profits."

Kathy looked bewildered. Jack laughed again and put an arm around her shoulder. "But first tell me how a girl like you ended up running around a stage in pink tights."

Briefly, Kathy told him her story. "One engagement leads to another. I've had no real control over it. I spent last winter in Stockton and Sacramento. This season I toured the northern mines.

In September Ned received the offer for me to come to San Francisco." She shrugged. "And here I am."

Kathy had other exciting news. "Guess what, Jack? I've seen Wade."

A strange look came over Jack. Kathy supposed it was because of the way the two men had ended their partnership. "It was July of last year," she went on, "in Sonora."

"Yes, I know," Jack said. "Wade shot that St. Clair fellow. It was in the papers. That was how I learned you'd become a singer. I confess, if Wade hadn't been mentioned, I'd have thought it was another Kate Beddoes."

"We're going to be married," Kathy said. She smiled. "I guess you knew we were fond of each other. He went back to the mines for one more season. He was supposed to meet me in Stockton a year ago, but I missed him. I've left messages for him at every stop I've made. I keep waiting for him to catch up to me. I don't know what's happened to him."

Jack took a turn around the small dressing room. Then he stopped, and he looked into her eyes. "Kathy, I've got bad news. Wade is dead."

Kathy gasped. "He can't be."

"He is."

"How . . . how do you know?"

"I was still up at the mines when they found out. It happened last spring. Apparently Wade and his partner were killed by claim jumpers. They must have found a rich claim, and they were robbed."

Kathy sank onto her chair.

Jack went on. "A party of prospectors found the partner's body. He was a Frenchman, I believe, and Wade was known in the district as his partner. Wade was famous for having killed St. Clair, so the news got around."

A spark of hope leapt into Kathy's eye. "What about Wade? Was his body. . . ?"

Jack shook his head. "Not as far as I know. But that doesn't mean anything. It was probably dragged off by animals."

Kathy shuddered at the thought. "But there's a chance, isn't there? He might be alive?"

Jack put a hand on her shoulder. "Kathy, that was months ago. If he was still alive, don't you think you'd have heard from him by now? Don't you think somebody would have?"

Kathy's head sunk onto her chest.

Jack knelt beside her. He took one of her hands in his. "I'm sorry to be the one to tell you, Kathy."

Her eyes brimmed with tears. "All this time I've been waiting for him, and he's been dead. It's just like it was with Michael, my husband." She smiled wistfully. "At least he found his rich vein. That meant a lot to him."

"I know," Jack said, and he stood. "Look, Kathy, you can't dwell on the past. What's done is done. You have to look to the future. I say this as an old friend as well as your manager."

Kathy was tight-lipped. She didn't say anything.

"Now," Jack went on, "you go and get dressed. They're throwing a big party for you at Tortoni's. I know it's big, because I arranged it."

53

They left by the theater's back door. Kathy noticed that Jack's left hand was stiff. There was an ugly scar on the palm. "What happened to your hand?" she asked.

He looked at it. "Oh, nothing. I got into a fight. Hazards of the profession."

"What *is* your profession?" she said.

He grinned. "You'll see in a minute."

He steered her onto Portsmouth Square, the heart of the city. The paved square was lit with whale-oil lamps. It was crowded with men and carriages. The buildings fronting it were ablaze with lights, their doors filled with patrons coming and going. Jack led Kathy into a building to the right of the Jenny Lind. The sign across the front said The Black Jack. On it was painted a jack of spades.

The crowd near the door made way for Jack and Kathy. The Black Jack was an immense, ornate gambling house. There were mirrors on the walls, crystal chandeliers on the ceiling. The polished bar was trimmed in brass. The room was mobbed. There were men in evening clothes, dusty fellows in from the mines, and men wearing every manner of dress in between. The few women were fancily trussed up whores. The tables were piled with bags of gold dust and coins.

"There's more money here than I've ever seen in one place," Kathy said, looking around in amazement.

"On a good night there may be a half-million dollars on these tables," Jack told her.

"My God," Kathy said. "It's very impressive, but why bring me here?"

"Because it's mine."

Kathy's eyes widened. "You own this?"

"That's right."

"But where did you get the money?"

Jack faltered for a second, then he recovered. "Let's say I got lucky."

Kathy looked around once more. "So you're a gambler now."

"Yes," Jack said. He added, "You don't think there's anything wrong with that, do you?"

"No," said Kathy. It was a measure of how much she'd changed since leaving home that she meant it. "You must be quite good."

"I get by," Jack said, and he laughed.

Jack had reason for his good mood. He had just finished a war with the Australian gangs—the "Sydney Ducks," the newspapers called them. The Australians had demanded tribute from The Black Jack, and from the high-toned brothel that Brandy ran next door. They had threatened to burn out Jack or to kill him if he refused to pay. Jack had refused. It had been a war of back-alley stabbings and shootings, of men found floating in the bay or Mission Creek. Jack had survived several attempts on his life, but he'd done little of his own dirty work. He had used Juan Soto—or Menendez, as he now called himself—for that. It was a job that Juan had enjoyed. After burying a number of their men, the Australians had called a truce. They had decided to leave Jack's businesses alone and seek easier pickings elsewhere.

By now Kathy had been recognized and surrounded. Men were having her autograph their shirts, their hats, pieces of paper, anything they could get their hands on.

"There's Brandy," Jack said, and he beckoned with his hand. "Brandy! Here's someone I want you to meet."

Kathy saw a red-haired woman coming through the crowd, pushing her way easily, as though she'd done this sort of thing all her life. She was good-looking in a hard way. She wore a low-cut dark blue dress with red ribbons and red stockings. She stopped in front of Kathy, looking her up and down.

Jack said, "Brandy, this is Kathy Beddoes."

"The singer?" Brandy said, and Kathy glimpsed a gold tooth.

"That's right," Jack told her. "Kathy and I came to California together. Across Panama."

"This is the one you told me about," Brandy said.

"Yes. Kathy, this is Brandy McCall, my partner—the partner that does the work."

"How do you do?" Kathy said, sticking out a hand.

"My pleasure," Brandy replied. She did not take the hand, and Kathy withdrew it.

Brandy went on, "So, Jack's your new manager, huh?"

"That's what he tells me," Kathy said. "It's all happened so fast."

"With Jack it usually does."

Jack laughed. "Don't let that tart tongue bother you, Kathy. She's this way with everybody." He winked at Brandy as he took Kathy's arm, "Come on, let's get to Tortoni's. You don't want to be late for your own party."

After supper and the reception at the restaurant, Jack walked Kathy back to her rooms at the St. Francis, the town's most expensive hotel.

"San Francisco's changed since we were here in forty-nine," Kathy marveled. "I remember all the ships crowding the bay, and how we had to be rowed across the cove to shore. Now the cove's not even there anymore."

"They filled it in," Jack told her. "They threw in chaparral and dirt from the hills, garbage, rotted timber—anything they could think of. Land's worth too much money here. Where they don't have it, they create their own. There's thirty thousand people in the city now, about seven times what was here when we came through. It's about thirty times what was here a year before that. Remember Happy Valley, where we set up our tents? There's factories there now, and houses. It's amazing, this city. No place like it on earth. Every couple months it burns down, and they build it right up again, bigger and better."

They had reached the hotel's lobby. "I'll take my leave now," Jack told Kathy. "What are your plans for tomorrow?"

"I'd like to find Ned and say good-bye to him," she said.

Jack cleared his throat. "He's already left town. I guess he's in a hurry to invest the money I gave him for your contract."

"That doesn't sound like Ned," Kathy said.

Jack shrugged.

Kathy went on. "In that case, I'm free until rehearsal."

"Good," said Jack. "I'll call on you after breakfast."

For the next month Jack monopolized Kathy's time. There were carriage rides along the shore to Seal Rocks. There was rowing on Lake Merced. There were horseback rides over the new plank road to Mission Dolores. There were steamboat excursions across the bay to the Contra Costa, and picnics at Martinez with its spectacular view of the Strait of Carquinez. When the weather turned bad or cold, as it frequently did at this time of year, the two of them repaired to rest houses to warm up over toddies or mulled wine. At night there were balls and dances, and dinners at the best restaurants. Kathy hardly met anyone in the city except for Jack. Indeed, people seemed to keep an arm's length from her, but she was so busy with Jack that she didn't notice. From time to time Jack took her to The Black Jack. She was well received there, but she felt out of place, uncomfortable. It was not an establishment frequented by respectable women, and Jack's friend Brandy plainly did not like her.

Kathy's run at the Jenny Lind was extended. The crowds were still sold out. When she wasn't with Jack, she spent her time rehearsing and giving interviews. Jack was working with architects on plans for her theater. He even talked about starring her in a legitimate stage play.

One morning in early December, Jack called for her and said, "Come on. There's something I want to show you."

He had a carriage waiting. They drove through the packed, muddy streets. It was sunny, but the wind made it seem colder, and Kathy pulled her coat's fur collar up around her neck. Around them were the noises of the city—the rumbling of heavy wheels over planks, the jingling of harness and bells, whistles, curses, the neighing of animals, the cries of vendors, the tunes of organ grinders and street musicians. There were smells of mud, of manure, of coal smoke and wood smoke. The carriage made a slow passage up California Street to Nob Hill, where it stopped.

A great house was under construction on the hill. As yet there were few structures on the city's hills, and the building site, like the street, had been blasted out of the hillside, and a plank road laid down. The house was nearly finished. It had a half-dozen chimneys, a porticoed entrance, and a graveled carriageway. When complete, the house would look over the city and bay. It would dominate them.

"It's magnificent," Kathy said. "Who is it for?"

Jack took off his hat. The wind ruffled his dark hair, blowing the unruly lock across his forehead. He looked at her earnestly. "Well, I hope . . . I'd like to think it's for you."

"I don't understand," she said. "What do you mean?"

"I mean, I'm building it, and I want you to live here with me. I want you to marry me, Kathy."

Kathy was taken aback. "It's . . . it's so unexpected," she said.

"I love you, Kathy. I've always loved you."

"I know you have," she said.

"Then say you'll marry me. Maybe you don't love me now, but you will in time. I'll be good to you, Kathy. I'll give you the world. I promise, you'll never find a man who loves you more."

There had been such a man once, Kathy thought. But he was dead. Jack could help her forget Wade. He could help her put the pain behind. It was a rushed decision, but that was the way things were done in California.

"Will you do it?" Jack said.

Kathy looked into his eyes, and she smiled. "Yes," she said. "I will."

54

They were married right away. There was no sense waiting.

The wedding was at St. Francis Church. It was a cold, foggy December morning. Kathy wore a gown of shimmering white lace with a crown and veil to match. She was driven to the church in an open carriage drawn by matched white horses. The band of Engine Company Number Four—"California Four"—led the way, playing the "Radetzky March." The rest of the firemen, in their full dress uniforms, marched alongside the carriage as an escort.

The church was full. Jack wore a gray morning suit with top hat. His best man was a Latin named Juan Menendez. Kathy had seen Juan once or twice at the club, but she'd never spoken with him. During the ceremony she caught him looking at her strangely.

After the service Jack and Kathy ran a gauntlet of thrown rice to the carriage. They drove through the crowded streets to their new house, where the reception would be held. The fire company's band went first, playing "Hangtown Girls," "Oh! Susanna," and other selections that Kathy performed onstage. Kathy and Jack planned to spend the night at the house, then take the coastal steamer to Monterey for a week-long honeymoon. They would be back in San Francisco for Christmas.

Band playing, the carriage rolled up California Street. It turned onto the graveled driveway and halted by the porticoed entrance. As the band struck up "Home Sweet Home," Jack handed Kathy down. "Welcome home," he told her.

The firemen formed an honor guard. Jack lifted Kathy in his strong arms. He carried her between the rows of firemen and through the open front doors. Inside, he set her down. It was the first time she had been in the house. The richness of the furnishings took her breath away. "It's a palace," she said.

"It's your palace," Jack corrected.

A liveried butler took Jack's hat. A maid took Kathy's white shawl. Other servants waited to assist the arriving guests, while Jack gave Kathy a quick tour of the house. The grand staircase was made of carved French oak, with polished silver handles on the doors. The walls were decorated with paintings and statues. Rich carpets lined the floors.

Jack showed Kathy the drawing room with its walls of embossed velvet. From there they went to the billiard room, then the library, whose wainscoted walls held books piled shelf on shelf.

"Have you read all these?" Kathy asked.

"I haven't read any of them," Jack admitted. "But they look nice."

Next was the music room, done in rose and satinwood. Its centerpiece was an ebony piano with mother-of-pearl keys. Kathy couldn't resist sitting at the piano. She ran through the opening bars of "Where Can the Soul Find Rest?"

"It has a lovely sound," she said. "I only wish I could play better."

"Take lessons," Jack told her. "We'll get the best teacher in San Francisco."

He heard sounds of revelry, and he gave Kathy a hand up. "We'd better go and greet our guests."

As they walked down the carpeted hall to the ballroom. Kathy said, "All this must have cost a fortune, Jack. Do you have that kind of money?"

"The Black Jack is the biggest gambling club in San Francisco. Plus, I've got investments everywhere and they're all paying off—real estate, the iron works, a plank road company, river transportation, a wharf. Have I forgotten anything? Oh, yes, the gasworks."

"Gambling's been very profitable for you."

Jack could almost deny to himself the real way he'd made his fortune. "Gambling and winning," he told her. "There's a difference."

The guests were waiting in the ballroom, where they were being entertained by a group of black singers from the club, the Ethiopian Serenaders. In one corner a string orchestra tuned its instruments. Around the walls, sideboards were heaped with food and drink. There was champagne, wine, and brandy punch with ice from the Sierras. There was beef and elk, deer, mutton, plover, salmon, and trout. There was oyster omelette and turtle soup. A tiered wedding cake decorated the head table. The blue and white table settings were from Haviland of France.

Jack introduced the guests. They were all his friends. Kathy didn't know anyone in San Francisco. There were lawyers, politicians, businessmen, flashy gamblers. There were also miners, workingmen, and anyone who happened to have stopped by the house. Jack didn't know half of them, and he didn't care. Today everyone was welcome.

"There aren't many ladies," Kathy whispered to Jack at one point.

"There aren't many ladies in San Francisco," Jack pointed out.

"I don't see your friend Brandy here."

"She isn't coming. She's sick."

"How long have you known her?"

Jack raised an amused eyebrow. "Jealous?"

"Curious. She's very good-looking, after all."

"Brandy and I are partners, nothing more. I did her a favor once, and in return she's helped me with my businesses."

Juan Menendez was there, staring at Kathy from the corner of his eye. He made her feel uneasy.

"Who is Juan?" she asked Jack.

"Who? Oh, my best man. He works with me."

"Why does he look at me like that?"

Jack didn't know. "He probably wonders what kind of girl could have gotten me to the altar."

Kathy wanted to ask exactly what Juan did for Jack, but the orchestra struck up the "Hofballtanze," one of the Viennese waltzes that were San Francisco's current rage. Everyone looked to the newlyweds. Jack bowed to Kathy. "I believe the first dance is ours."

Kathy curtsied in reply. Jack led her onto the floor. He wasn't used to dancing, especially in front of an audience, but he made a bold show of it, leading Kathy around the floor the way Brandy had taught him.

"You dance well," Kathy told him.

"I'm a gentleman now. Gentlemen are supposed to dance well."

When the dance was over, Jack kissed her gallantly, to great applause. Then others took the dance floor. Kathy got some punch while Jack accepted the congratulations of his cronies. When Kathy returned, she heard Jack talking to Juan. His voice was bitter. ". . . Brannan, George Oakes, Bill Coleman. They're good enough to come to my club, but they're too good to come to my house. I won't forget this."

Then Kathy walked up, and Jack broke into smiles once more. "There you are." He held out a hand. "Come with me."

He led her out back of the house, to the stables. He took her into the stalls, where he showed her a string of blooded riding horses. "My wedding gift to you."

Kathy was taken aback. "Why, they're lovely, Jack." She stroked a muzzle.

"There's more," Jack said.

In a shed at the rear of the stables was a carriage, a phaeton, glossy black with gilt trim and a red leather interior. On the doors were painted the initials KM.

Kathy turned to him, shaking her head in wonderment.

Jack said, "I told you, Kathy. Nothing's too good for you. Nothing ever will be."

He took her in his arms and kissed her. Kathy felt a twinge of guilt. She thought about what might have been with Wade. Then she put the guilt from her mind. It was time to start a new life. She had started so many new lives since leaving New York.

They put their arms around each other's waists. Jack led her around the side of the house. The sun had burned away the fog. From this spot on top of the hill they had a view over the city and the sparkling bay to the mountains across the Golden Gate.

Jack said, "Are you happy, Kathy?"

"Yes," she said. "Very."

"I'll make sure you stay that way." Jack remembered growing up in the slums, living in a small room with his family. He remembered his father and the way he had died. Now he stood in front of his mansion. "I've done it, Kathy," he exulted. "I've done everything I said I'd do. I've got money, social standing, a grand house."

He turned. "And now I have the thing I wanted most. You."

He kissed her again, tenderly. "I've dreamed about this from the moment I first saw you. I never allowed myself to think my dream might come true. But it has. You've made me the happiest man in the world."

"I'm glad," she said.

"Our children will be born in this house. They'll have everything we lacked—money, education, prestige. Maybe they'll go to Europe and marry nobility—who knows?"

He looked at her. She could feel him tremble with desire. "There is one more room I want to show you," he said.

"Which one?"

"The bedroom. Now."

"Wouldn't that be bad manners? I mean, shouldn't we wait until our guests are gone?"

Jack grinned. "I've learned one thing, Kathy. When you're rich, you can make your own rules."

55

Christmas Eve. The Metropolitan Theater was staging a gala performance of *The Bandit Chief*, starring Mrs. Ray of the Royal Theater, New Zealand. The play had been a hit in Sacramento and the mining camps. Tonight it was making its San Francisco debut.

The theater was hung with wreaths and garlands for the holiday. There was not a seat unsold. Early arrivals commented on the new curtain, whose painting showed a panoramic view of San Francisco and the Golden Gate.

Jack and Kathy had tickets for the first balcony, the most expensive seats in the house. Jack was ruddy-faced with excitement, like a child. It was the first time he'd looked forward to Christmas since his father had died. He wore his best evening clothes. Kathy wore a low-cut burgundy gown with tiered skirts trimmed in gold lace and embroidery. Her hair was swept upward with side ringlets. She wore a dazzling jeweled necklace, jeweled earrings, and long white gloves.

Because of heavy traffic, Jack and Kathy were one of the last couples to arrive. They made their way to their seats. In the pit, in the boxes and second balconies, eyes turned. People pointed. There was a buzz of conversation. Jack couldn't help but smile. Some of the bolder men waved at Kathy, who nodded to them.

They took their seats among the cream of San Francisco society, where they continued to create a stir. Necks craned for a view of the beauteous Mrs. Marlow.

"They're looking at you," Jack whispered to Kathy.

She nodded. "Perhaps this gown was a bit too daring. I'm not onstage tonight."

"Nonsense," Jack said. "You're a star. You're always onstage."

In front of them sat Judge Elden Mason and his wife, Abigail. Judge Mason was a long-nosed dyspeptic fellow with frizzy side whiskers. Defeated for election to the Senate from Connecticut, he'd come west to civilize the godless Californians. His wife was high-minded and serious, the kind of woman who had never really been young. She believed that she and her small circle of friends had been anointed as San Francisco's social arbiters. Mrs. Mason wore a somewhat dowdy, high-necked lace gown with embroidered flowers and flared sleeves. Her eyes popped at Kathy's décolletage. Kathy's jewels made Mrs. Mason's look paltry as well, and that did not add to the older woman's enjoyment. Every few seconds she whispered urgently in the judge's ear, scandalized by Jack and Kathy's presence.

At last the brow-beaten judge turned to Jack. "Excuse me, sir, but you're disturbing this assemblage."

Jack crossed his legs, amused. "And what would you have me do about that, sir?"

"I would have you change seats," said the judge, "or, better yet, leave the building."

"I'm afraid that's not possible," Jack said.

"You don't belong in this section," the judge told him.

"That's not what my tickets say."

The judge was disdainful. "You belong in the pit, Marlow, with the rest of your kind. Frankly, I'm surprised you have the nerve to sit here."

"Maybe I like the view," Jack said.

"Nonetheless, I insist that you leave. You're bothering the ladies."

"Really?" Jack turned to Kathy. "Am I bothering you?"

"No," she said.

"You see," Jack told the judge. "Here's a lady, and I'm not bothering her. Now, you do what you like, Judge, but I purchased these seats, and I intend to stay."

Frustrated, Judge Mason turned away. He and his wife engaged in animated whispers, his wife doing most of the talking.

Kathy leaned in to Jack. "What was that all about?"

"They don't like the fact that I'm a gambler," Jack explained. "They don't think I should be allowed to sit near them."

"I thought everyone in San Francisco was your friend."

Jack shrugged. "Maybe not everyone."

Judge Mason turned back to them. His voice was officious. "I must again request that you leave. You offend the decent people of San Francisco by flaunting yourself in such a manner. I'm not afraid to say it, Marlow. You are part of this city's criminal element. You're the type of person we're trying to drive out.''

Jack grinned. ''I could say the same about you.''

Kathy chuckled at that.

The judge looked at Kathy and reddened. To Jack he said, ''It's bad enough you show yourself here, but you have the nerve to bring your whore with you.''

Jack's grin faded. He gripped the arms of his chair, knuckles white. Beside the judge, he saw Mrs. Mason looking smug.

Everyone in the theater was watching the argument. Kathy had never been talked about in this way. Her first reaction was outrage, then hurt. Why would anyone say that about her?

Jack leaned forward. ''Judge, I don't mind you saying things about me, but I get upset when you start talking about my wife. Mrs. Marlow and I are going to watch this play. We have no intention of leaving or moving our seats, or anything else you might have in mind. So I'd advise you and that horse-faced bag of bones to mind your own business.''

Mrs. Mason let out a gasp of outrage. She fanned her face with a program.

The judge stood, his voice rising. ''By God, sir, if you were a gentleman, I'd call you out.''

Jack rose opposite him. ''If my wife weren't here, you wouldn't have to call me out. I'd have tossed you over that railing by now.''

The judge clenched his fists. ''I'll not be talked to in such a manner.''

''Do something about it,'' Jack dared him.

The judge stood for a moment, his thin chest rising and falling. Then he turned and extended a hand to his wife, who stuck her nose up in the air. The judge spoke loud enough for the entire audience to hear. ''Come, my dear. We won't sit with common criminals and strumpets. I advise all decent people to follow our example. Send a message to the management of this theater, and to the city. Their kind will not be tolerated.'' To Jack he said, ''I'll see you again, sir.''

Jack's voice was cold, deadly. ''Yes, Judge. I believe you will.''

The judge and his wife trooped up the aisle and out of the theater. Four or five more couples followed. Some people laughed at them. Everyone else stayed put. There was a small round of applause for Jack, which he did not acknowledge.

Jack turned to Kathy. A tear ran down her cheek. Jack sat again and took her hand. "Those people have ruined your Christmas, darling. I'm sorry."

Kathy looked at him. "He called me a whore. Why? What did I ever do to him?"

"Nothing. Don't pay attention to people like that."

"And he said you were a criminal. Where do they get these ideas? You've never broken the law, have you?"

Jack shook his head. "The only law we've broken is having money we weren't born with. To Mason and his kind, that makes us worse than criminals. It makes us upstarts. They think their little world is a closed circle. Well, we just busted that circle wide open. Now, relax and sit back. The play's about to begin."

56

Jack waited for the right moment to get his revenge. He didn't have to wait long.

Three days after Christmas, a thick, oily fog settled over San Francisco. Visibility was measured in feet. Traffic slowed to a crawl. The streets were snarled. Whale-oil lamps glimmered dully through the murk. People were shadows on the sidewalks.

It was dusk. Jack waited outside the bar of the Bank Exchange on Washington Street. His top hat was pulled low over his eyes; his features were muffled by the collar of his heavy greatcoat. In his coat pocket was the brass-plated Colt that had once belonged to Wade Rawson. Around him, the city was heard rather than seen.

Judge Mason came here every day for a late lunch and drinks with his cronies. At last the bar door opened, and the judge came out, momentarily silhouetted against the bright light inside. He was alone.

Jack stepped out of the fog. "Good evening, Judge."

Mason was startled at first, but his reaction quickly turned to contempt. "What do you want, Marlow?"

"An apology."

The judge snorted. "For you?"

"For my wife. You called her a whore, and I can't allow that."

"Why not? It's true."

Jack held his temper. "You know that's not so."

"I know nothing of the sort. She's a music hall 'entertainer,' isn't she? And she consorts with you. What more proof does one need?"

Their voices were muffled by the mist. Still, a few passersby had stopped to look. Judge Mason went on. "How do you think she made her living in the gold camps before she became famous?"

"She ran a restaurant," Jack said.

"Of course she did. They all say that. You know the truth as well as I do. Now, let me pass."

The judge started by Jack, who blocked him with his arm.

"Take your hand off me, Marlow," said the judge.

"Not till I get that apology. No—not till my wife gets it. You're going to my house to deliver it in person."

"I'll die first," said the judge.

"That is an option," Jack told him.

The judge looked down his long nose. "You don't frighten me, Marlow. You or your kind."

Jack pushed the older man against the wall. "Damn you. Apologize, or I'll . . ."

"I will not apologize." Perhaps emboldened by the liquor he had consumed, the judge drew himself up. "Furthermore, I'll repeat what I said before, in case you didn't hear. Your wife is a whore. She has no doubt slept with hundreds of men. For all I know, she's slept with animals as well. Now, let me . . ."

Jack pulled the brass-plated Colt from his coat cocked it, and fired it into Mason's heart. The judge backed into the wall, looking surprised, then he sank onto the plank sidewalk. Blood welled through his coat.

Jack knelt beside the judge. Quickly, as he had planned, he slipped a second pistol from his coat pocket and put it in the judge's hand. He stood and looked around. There were people watching, but what they had seen in this fog he couldn't tell. Three were close to him—a Spanish-looking woman, a bearded man with a laborer's cap, and a man in a top hat.

Jack brazened it out. "Get a policeman," he ordered.

A crowd gathered, attracted by the shots. In the street, traffic slowed even more. There were angry shouts from teamsters and hack drivers. Jack stamped his feet in the cold, trying to warm them. He blew on his gloved hands. Soon a man in a long overcoat ran up, led by the bearded laborer. The man opened his coat, revealing a policeman's badge.

"What's happened here?" he said.

Jack told him. "This man and I had an argument. He drew a pistol on me, and I was forced to shoot him." He handed the brass-plated Colt to the policeman. "I'm afraid he's dead."

The policeman looked at Jack closely. "It's Mr. Marlow, isn't it? I'm sorry, sir, but I'll have to take you to the station house."

"That's all right," Jack told him. "I understand."

A second policeman came up. The first one said, "Send for the coroner, Ted. You'll likely find him at Denison's Exchange, or The Black Jack on the Square. After that, take statements from the witnesses, if there are any." He turned. "Mr. Marlow?"

The policeman led Jack off through the fog. Behind them, the crowd closed around the dead man.

57

Kathy soon heard what had happened. The news was all over the city. Kathy ordered her carriage made ready. "Take me to the county jail," she told her driver.

It was dark. The fog had grown thicker. The carriage crawled through the crowded streets. Kathy leaned out the window. "Can't you go any faster?" she asked the driver.

The liveried driver, a black man, looked down from his box. "With this fog, I'm lucky to go at all, ma'am."

By the time they arrived at the jail, there was a large crowd outside. This was no rabble. They were well-dressed men and women—pillars of society, some of them. Elden Mason had been a respected, if not a particularly well-liked, member of the state Supreme Court. He had been a leader of the city's growing reform faction. A lot of people were angry at his death. There were calls for vengeance.

"San Francisco's been ruled by gamblers too long," men cried. "It's time for the honest people of this city to stand up and be counted."

"Don't wait for the courts," others shouted. "We'll get no justice from them. We have to make our own justice."

"Call out the vigilantes! They'll know what to do."

There were shouts of agreement. "The vigilantes. Send for the vigilantes."

Kathy was worried.

"Do you want me to wait, ma'am?" asked the driver as he handed her out.

"No, Charles," said Kathy. "Seeing our carriage here may only make these people angrier."

Kathy went inside the jail building. Armed policemen—young and nervous—stood guard at the front door. "Do you think there will be trouble?" Kathy asked them.

"We're afraid of a lynching party," one of them admitted.

An older man said, "If we make it through tonight, we'll be all right. These mobs usually calm down after a while."

There weren't many prisoners in the jail. Kathy found Jack in a cell, drinking champagne and playing monte with his guards. The cell door was wide open.

Jack seemed happy to see her. "Why don't you join us? Help yourself to the champagne. There's a case of the best. There's cold ham, too, if you're hungry. And soda crackers."

Kathy said nothing. Jack turned to the guards. "Excuse us, will you, boys? We'll finish our game later." He winked at them. "Give you a chance to win your money back."

The guards left, and Kathy entered the cell. "Is this how they usually treat prisoners here?" she said.

"The ones that can pay for it," Jack replied, kissing her.

"You don't seemed worried," Kathy told him.

"Why should I be? I shot Mason in self-defense. No jury will convict me."

"It may not go to a jury, Jack. The people outside are talking about lynching you. Maybe that doesn't worry you, but it worries me."

Jack drank some champagne. "They're just letting off steam. It won't last."

"Why did you have to confront Mason in the first place?" Kathy demanded. "Why didn't you just forget what he said, like I asked you to at Christmas? Why couldn't you put it out of your mind? I did."

Jack grew serious. "I couldn't forget, Kathy. He insulted you. As a gentleman, I couldn't let that pass. If I had, people would have believed it was true."

"Who cares what people believe? You and I know it wasn't true. That's what's important."

"No, it's not," Jack said. "I won't have you run down, by Elden Mason or anyone else."

Kathy gave up. "I'm not going to argue about it. What do you want me to do about getting you lawyers and running your affairs while you're in here?"

"That's been taken care of," Jack said.

Kathy was surprised. "By whom?"

"Brandy."

Kathy gave him a look. "You've already seen her?"

"She's my partner, Kathy. Of course I've seen her. She's arranged the best attorneys in San Francisco for me. She's the one who sent the champagne and food. Here, let me pour you a glass."

Kathy stared at him.

"For God's sake, Kathy. Don't take it personally. Brandy and I have been through this sort of thing before. She's my business partner, and this is business. Go ahead, have some champagne."

"No, thanks," Kathy said. "I have to go out."

"Where are you going?"

"Business," she told him.

58

"Are you sure you won't have some tea?" Brandy asked.

The girl named Maria trembled. "No."

"Why not?"

"I think you are trying to poison me."

"Why would I do that?" Brandy wanted to know.

"Because of what I saw. The same reason you brought me here."

They were in the basement of Brandy's establishment on Portsmouth Square. Maria had been brought there by Juan Soto. She had been dragged off the street, kidnapped. Juan sat on a crate in one corner, swinging a leg idly, staring at Maria. It was dank in the basement. Somewhere, water dripped.

Brandy smiled. "You're a smart girl, Maria. Your employer is lucky to have a maid as smart as you. Do you like your work?"

"*Sí*. Yes, it is all right."

Brandy paused. She picked up a heavy leather bag and sat it on the wooden crate that served as a table, next to the teapot. The bag jingled with coins. "Here is a thousand dollars, Maria. It's yours."

Maria looked at the bag. She looked at Juan in the corner.

"There is one condition," Brandy added. "Do you know what that is?"

"*Sí*. I think."

"What?"

"That at the trial I say that Señor Mason, the judge, he drew the pistol on Señor Marlow first?"

Brandy smiled. "That's very good, Maria."

Maria said, "And if I do not take this money?"

Brandy laughed. "Then you'll just have to drink the tea."

Maria was so scared, she could hardly speak. "I take the money."

"I thought you would," Brandy said. "All right, Maria. You can go. I've enjoyed talking with you."

The Mexican girl put a hand on the money bag. "Thank you." Relief showed in her face. She hadn't expected to leave the house alive.

"If you ever need a job, see me," Brandy told her.

"Yes, señora. Thank you." Maria took the bag full of money and stood.

"Up those steps. One of the girls will show you out."

"Yes, señora."

"Oh, and Maria?"

"Señora?"

"I'll see you at the trial."

Maria nodded and left.

As Maria's footsteps faded on the stairs, Brandy turned to Juan. "That's one taken care of."

"Unless she goes back on her word," Juan said.

"She won't. She's not that stupid."

"What about the other two witnesses?" Juan said. "Has your man at the district attorney's office learned who they are?"

"One's named Templeton," Brandy said. "He's a businessman with a warehouse on Pacific Street. The other is a German, a baker, I believe. We're supposed to have his name tomorrow. You can pay them a visit."

"What if they won't do what we want?"

"Explain the consequences to them."

"And if they still won't do it?"

Brandy just looked at him.

Juan nodded with a faint smile.

Brandy shuddered inside. She had never liked Juan, though she had to admit he had his uses. He didn't like her, either, but he respected her, the way he respected Jack. He seemed to have no emotions. The only thing he really enjoyed was killing. How did a man get that way?

Brandy rose from the overturned box on which she had been sitting. "What was Jack thinking of, gunning down Judge Mason? Was he trying to make work for us?"

Juan shrugged. "I asked him if he wanted me to take care of Mason, but he said it was something he had to do himself."

Brandy shook her head. "Jack and his damn sense of honor. Well, the lawyers are here. Let's not keep them waiting."

They went upstairs into the brothel's richly furnished parlor, where a number of well-dressed men were waiting, pouring whiskey from crystal decanters. Prominent among these men was Colonel Edward S. Espenshade, who, before coming to California, had been the most noted trial attorney in the South. He was there with two associates, as well as some men on Jack and Brandy's payroll.

The men stood as Brandy walked into the room, followed by Juan. Brandy smiled. "I'm sorry to have summoned you here at such short notice, gentlemen. Colonel, it's a pleasure to meet you." She shook his hand.

Colonel—the title was honorary—Espenshade cleared his throat. "I won't beat around the bush, ma'am. Defending your, er, partner, will be an unpopular case. Extremely unpopular. To take it on, I'll have to charge much more than usual."

"How much?" said Brandy.

"Twenty thousand dollars." Espenshade looked smug. He thought he had priced himself out of the market.

Brandy didn't blink an eye. She rang a bellpull. The establishment's majordomo, a huge black man named Percy, appeared. He leaned low, and Brandy whispered something to him. He left and returned a minute later, carrying a silver tray on which were a checkbook, ink, and a pen. Brandy dipped the pen in the ink and wrote out a check. She blew on the check, then gave it to Percy, who set it on the table beside Espenshade.

"That is a draft on Page, Bacon, and Company for ten thousand dollars," Brandy said, "made out to you. You'll get the rest when the case is won. You're the man we want, Colonel, and we mean to have you at any price."

Espenshade looked at the check. His mouth twitched.

"Oh, did I mention?" Brandy said. "Your fee also includes a year's free use of my girls for you and your colleagues."

Espenshade looked at his associates. "Your girls are reputed to be the best in San Francisco," one of them said.

"It's more than repute," Brandy assured him.

Espenshade cleared his throat again. He struck a distinguished pose. "Very well. What are the facts of the case?"

Brandy told him about the Christmas Eve incident at the theater. "Tonight Mr. Marlow approached the judge, perhaps injudiciously, for an apology. They had words. The judge drew a pistol, and Mr. Marlow was compelled to defend himself."

Espenshade nodded. "What are the real facts?"

Brandy's voice grew frosty. "Exactly as I have given them to you."

"I've heard differently," Espenshade said.

"You've heard wrong."

"They say the state has witnesses."

"So do we."

"Reliable ones?"

"They will be found so."

"Very well," Espenshade said. "I will be back in the morning. I'll start preparing the case, then." He pocketed the check and rose, followed by his associates. "Until then, good night, um, madame."

Brandy smiled, revealing her gold tooth. "That's all right, I don't mind the term. Good night to you."

Brandy rang the bellpull. Espenshade and his colleagues were ushered from the drawing room by the majordomo. When the door closed behind them, Brandy turned to the rest of the men in the room.

"I didn't know we had witnesses, Brandy," said one, a sharp-eyed lawyer named Kasmarek.

"We don't yet," Brandy told him, "but we will. Hire some, as many as you can. Respectable men, too, not the usual loafers and barroom loiterers. Make sure they have their stories straight."

"How much can we spend?" Kazmarek said.

"As much as it takes."

"Anything else?" asked Kazmarek's partner, a bearded dandy named Russel.

"Yes," Brandy said. "As soon as a jury's chosen, I want you to get to them. Persuade them to vote for acquittal. Bribe them, threaten them if you have to. But be discreet about it."

"What about the judge?" Russel said.

Brandy smiled. "I'll take care of the judge, whoever he is. I know them all."

She turned to a man with ink-stained cuffs and huge waxed mustaches. "Johnny, I've heard that the *Alta* will be out tomorrow with a front-page editorial. It'll be the usual moaning about how San Francisco is being run by gamblers and harlots, how our leading citizens can be murdered in the streets with impunity—blah, blah, blah. You know the kind of thing—we could write it ourselves, we've seen it so many times. I want you to get our story in the *Chronicle*."

Johnny, who was the *Chronicle*'s deputy editor, looked amused. "And our story is?"

"Judge Mason made a play for Mrs. Marlow. He tried to seduce her—unsuccessfully, of course. His actions caused the arguments at the theater and in front of the Bank Exchange. Jack was defending his wife's honor. He demanded that the judge leave her alone. The judge had been drinking, and in a fit of rage he pulled a pistol on Jack."

Johnny looked even more amused. This was a game to him. "That story would be a lot better if the judge had actually *fired* at Jack."

Brandy shrugged. "You can't have everything. If you think of something better, go ahead and use it, but check with me before you put it in print."

The lawyer Kazmarek spoke appreciatively. "You leave nothing to chance, do you, Brandy?"

She said, "No, I don't. I want to walk into that courtroom knowing what the verdict . . ."

There was a commotion outside the door. Voices were raised, one of them a woman's. The other belonged to Percy, the major-domo. Percy said, "You can't go in—"

The door opened. Kathy Marlow stood there.

The men in the room looked at each other, then at Brandy. They rose.

Percy came in behind Kathy. He said, "I tried to stop her, Miss Brandy, but . . ."

"It's all right," Brandy told him. "Come in, Mrs. Marlow." To the men she said, "You can go."

The men filed out, bidding Kathy and Brandy good evening. Juan Soto went last. He paused and looked at Kathy close up. Again there was that strange expression in his eyes. Then he left.

Brandy said, "Please, Mrs. Marlow, have a seat. Percy, clear away these glasses and bring Mrs. Marlow some tea."

Percy raised an eyebrow.

"The real tea," Brandy said.

Percy cleared the decanters and glasses. Kathy sat on the edge of a chair, red-faced with embarrassment. She said, "I—I looked for you at the club. They said I could find you here. As many times as I've passed this building, I didn't know what kind of establishment it was until I saw the girls in the front room. I didn't know you owned it."

"I own half of it," Brandy corrected Kathy. "Your husband owns the rest."

"Jack?"

"He's your husband, isn't he?"

Kathy didn't know what to say. "He never told me."

"I expect there's lots of things he never told you."

"Like what?" Kathy said.

"Ask him."

"Like the real relationship between you two?"

"Mrs. Marlow, what brings you here?"

"Jack told me you were arranging his defense. I want to find out what you're doing."

"I'm doing what has to be done," Brandy told her.

Percy came back with the tea. Kathy waited until he'd poured it and left again. She was angry. "The point is, *I* should be handling the arrangements. As you so cleverly pointed out, Jack *is* my husband."

"Yes," said Brandy. "And frankly, that presents us a problem. One man has already been killed over you."

"That was different," Kathy said indignantly.

"I'm sure," said Brandy, in a tone that indicated quite the opposite. "Nonetheless, it makes it hard for us to present you as the outraged maiden, if you see what I mean."

"No, I don't see what you mean, and to be honest, I don't see why you have to present me as anything."

"Because we have a court case to win. There's work to be done. Money to be spent."

"Spent on what?" Kathy said.

"Alms for the poor, what do you think? Witnesses. Jurors."

"You mean bribery?"

Brandy shrugged.

"Why are you bribing witnesses if Jack is innocent?"

"If Jack were innocent, we wouldn't be bribing them," Brandy said.

Kathy went rigid in the chair. After a second she said, "But I thought Judge Mason drew a pistol on him?"

"Your loyalty is commendable," Brandy said dryly. "But at the moment it's what a judge and jury think that interests me."

Kathy's head was spinning. "You mean . . . Jack murdered the judge?"

"Come now, don't act so innocent. Of course he did."

"But . . . why?"

"Because he loves you."

Kathy looked away. She felt as if she'd been punched in the stomach. "I . . . I had no idea."

Brandy studied her. After a second she said, "You really didn't know, did you? You never even guessed."

Kathy was pale. She shook her head.

Brandy suddenly felt guilty. "Maybe you aren't the kind of girl I thought. Maybe I said more than I should have."

Kathy said, "Has Jack . . . has he done anything else like this? Been involved in other crimes, I mean?"

Brandy shook her head. "Like I said, I opened my big mouth too much already."

Kathy went on. "Why are you doing all this for him? It can't be just because he's your business partner."

This time Brandy said nothing.

"You love him, don't you?" Kathy said.

Again Brandy was silent.

"Of course," Kathy said. "I should have known. No wonder you've never liked me."

After a second Brandy stood. She looked out the window at the fog-bound night. "Yes, I do love Jack. You can't imagine how much. I'd do anything for him. Anything." She turned. "Have you ever felt that way about a man?"

"Yes," Kathy admitted.

"But not Jack?"

"I—I hope to feel that way about Jack in the future. I've known him for some time, but our marriage was so sudden."

Brandy went on. "Once, I thought Jack loved me, too, but I guess I was wrong. The time I spent with him in the diggings is the only time I've ever really been happy in my life. I didn't want him to come to San Francisco, but he insisted. He's ambitious. He's always got to have more, always got to have the best. Now he has you."

"I'm sorry," Kathy said.

"Why? You've got nothing to be sorry about. You won. I'm a big girl. I can take care of myself. I've got money now, and my business investments. I don't have to sell my body anymore. I have a lot to be thankful for. And I wouldn't have any of it if it weren't for Jack. He's done a lot for me, and I intend to stand by him. All that matters to me is getting him free."

Kathy nodded slowly. "I think I've underestimated you, Brandy. Or maybe I just never tried to understand you."

Brandy laughed mirthlessly. "Yeah, well, I guess I did the same with you. Hell, it's not your fault Jack liked you best. Who could blame him? When you get down to it, I'm just a whore. Look, those things I told you about Jack. Don't tell him I told you, huh? He'll think I did it because I was jealous. I thought you knew what happened. I thought you were putting on an act."

"I won't tell," Kathy promised. She rose. "I'd better be going."

Brandy moved toward the door. "I'll see you out."

"That's all right," Kathy said. "I can find my own way."

"No, I'll walk you," Brandy said. Then she smiled. "Please. I insist."

59

Jack's trial began just after the new year. The bright, crisp January day reminded Kathy of October back home. There was a large crowd outside the courthouse. Half of them seemed to have come for a glimpse of Kathy, the other half to voice their dislike of Black Jack Marlow and anyone associated with him. As Kathy was led into the courthouse, she was greeted by jeers. "Whore!" people cried. "Slut!"

Kathy turned in surprise. She was used to the crowd's adulation, not its abuse.

Inside, the courtroom was just as crowded. Heads turned as Kathy took her seat behind the defense table. Tongues whispered.

The trial did not last long. The state had three witnesses. One, a merchant, had unexpectedly left town. The second, a Mexican maid named Maria, changed her story on the stand and swore that Jack had acted in self-defense. Kathy looked across the shocked courtroom at Brandy, who hung on to every word of Maria's testimony. Near Brandy sat Juan Menendez, a faint smile on his face.

The state's third witness, a German baker, had disappeared.

Jack's lawyers produced a number of witnesses, all respectable workingmen, who testified that Elden Mason had owned the pistol later found in his hand. Other witnesses, just as respectable, swore that they had heard Mason threaten Jack. Still others, the most respectable of all, testified that Mason had drawn his pistol first on the evening in question, and that Jack had fired in self-defense. The prosecution was outraged, but there was nothing they could do. The judge repeatedly overruled their objections. The jury was out less than fifteen minutes. They came back with a verdict of acquittal. Jack was a free man.

The courtroom broke into pandemonium. News of the verdict spread swiftly to the crowd outside. An angry tumult could be heard. Inside there was shouting and cheering. Men clapped Jack on the back. Others swore and cried fraud. Jack looked smug, as if he'd never been in doubt about the verdict. Kathy felt mixed relief and . . . she was not sure what.

Jack came through the bar and kissed Kathy. "I told you no jury would convict me," he said. In a lowered voice he added, "God, I missed you while I was in jail."

Brandy came up, and Jack hugged her, too. "Brandy, you were fantastic."

Brandy looked like the happiest person in the world. She beamed at Kathy. Somehow Kathy felt closer to Brandy than she did to Jack.

"Celebration at The Black Jack," Brandy shouted to the courtroom. "Free drinks!"

That brought a cheer. The county sheriff, a smallish, ex–Texas Ranger named Hays, shouldered his way through to Jack and said, "I ordered your carriage brought to the back door, Mr. Marlow. You'd better leave that way. That mob out front is getting nasty." Boldly he added, "I don't blame them. It looks like money and threats are the real law in San Francisco."

Jack ignored the sheriff's jibe. He hustled Kathy out the rear of the courtroom. They went down a short hall and into the muddy alley in the back, where Kathy's carriage was waiting, polished to perfection. The brilliant sunshine had disappeared. There was a strong northeast wind, under a lowering sky. Kathy heard the angry crowd out front. Jack handed her into the carriage, then climbed in himself. "The Black Jack," he told Charles, the driver.

Charles drove the carriage down the alley. Past the block of buildings, he turned onto the plank street. Down the street the mob saw them. Men ran after the carriage, cursing and throwing rocks, bricks, and pieces of wood. Kathy heard Charles swear as something hit him. Something else crashed off the carriage door. Kathy glimpsed angry faces alongside. Then the carriage picked up speed, and the mob was left behind.

Jack leaned over Kathy. "Are you all right?"

Kathy nodded.

Through the opening behind the driver's box, Jack shouted, "How about you, Charles? You all right?"

"Yes, Mr. Jack," replied a pained voice. "I caught me a rock on the ear, is all."

They rode on. Jack put his arms around Kathy and kissed her cheek. "Don't let those people upset you. The *Alta*'s got them worked up. They're mad now, but on payday they'll be in the club spending their money like always. And fighting in line to buy tickets to your next show. Did I tell you? The plans for the theater are complete. I'll have the builder bring them by the house this week, to show you. I bought the property on Washington Street. We can start construction any time. I've found a play for you, too—*Mary Barton*. It's a stage version of the novel with songs. I think it's tremendous. I've been thinking about taking you on a singing tour of the East as well. It might be good for us to get away from San Francisco for a while."

Kathy said nothing. Her mind was occupied with other things.

The carriage drew up on the Square in front of The Black Jack. "Ah, here we are," Jack said.

He exited the carriage to a roar of acclaim from his friends and cronies. He handed Kathy out. She looked at the carriage where the thrown object had struck it. The shiny black door was dented and splintered, right across the gilded KM. There was blood on Charles's overcoat from his lacerated ear. Then Jack led Kathy inside.

The party was already in progress. White-jacketed bartenders dispensed champagne and whiskey. Food was set up on long tables. Brandy had prepared everything beforehand, so certain was she of the trial's outcome.

Jack moved through the crowd like a conquering prince. "Cheer up, Kathy," he said. "We won. You're supposed to be happy."

"I am," she said quietly.

"You have a funny way of showing it. Here, have some champagne." He handed her a glass. "There's some people I have to say hello to. Wait here, I'll be right back."

He went off, leaving Kathy alone. She sipped her champagne.

"Hello," said a voice. It was Brandy.

"Hello," Kathy replied. "Congratulations."

"Thanks," Brandy said. "Why aren't you celebrating?"

"I can't help thinking about what really happened to Judge Mason. And those witnesses at the trial. What about the one they couldn't find, the German?"

Brandy tried to make light of the subject. "Oh, he probably left town like the other fellow. You know what a transient city San Francisco is."

"That's not what really happened, is it?" Kathy said.

Brandy lowered her eyes. "I don't know. I don't want to know."

"Did you offer him a bribe?"

Brandy sighed. "Yes, but he wouldn't take it. He swore he'd testify. It was his duty, he said."

"Then what?" Kathy said.

"I offered him more money. But he wouldn't budge."

"And?"

"Then Juan took over."

Kathy went cold inside. She said, "You know, I never asked Jack what Juan does for him. I don't think I want to ask now."

"You may be right," Brandy told her.

Kathy said, "You were willing to buy Jack's life with the life of another man?"

"Yes," Brandy admitted. "I was. I wasn't going to let Jack hang. I'm sorry if that conflicts with your ideas of decency. It conflicts with mine, too, but I can't change the way I am, or the way I feel about Jack."

Kathy's lips tightened.

Brandy went on. "Don't think too badly of me, Kathy. I like you. You're a good woman. You're good for Jack. You're better for him than I could have been, I know that."

Brandy was going to say more, when one of the bartenders came over. "Brandy, Espenshade wants his money. He's leaving."

"Didn't stay long, did he?" Brandy remarked. "Is he afraid we have something that might rub off on him? All right, I'm coming." To Kathy she said, "Excuse me."

While Brandy went to pay the lawyer, Kathy looked around. The club was packed, but the crowd was more notable for who wasn't there. Espenshade wasn't the only one who didn't want to be tainted by this company. There were no politicians of note, no civic leaders or prominent businessmen. No respectable people. This was Jack's crowd. This was what Kathy had become part of. The flash dressers, the shady speculators, the gamblers and confidence men. The whores. Kathy's mother wouldn't have let these people in her house back door, much less the front.

Kathy's eyes rested on Juan Menendez. He was looking at her again with that strange expression. All that Jack had told her about Juan was that the two of them had put together some business deals in the diggings. Juan had a home out toward the Mission Dolores. It was not a mansion like Jack's, but Juan didn't have Jack's extravagant taste.

Kathy finished her drink. She was fed up with a lot of things, and this was one of them. She crossed the room to Juan, who bowed. "Señora Marlow."

Kathy was blunt. "Why do you keep looking at me?" she asked.

Juan spread his arms. "Ah, señora, I apologize. It is because I have seen you before, but I don't know where, and I keep trying to remember."

"Is that all?" Kathy was relieved. "I thought you had some deep, dark motive." She shook her head. "I don't know where it could have been. I was in San Francisco only two days on my first visit. In the camps I lived in Kate's Bar, near the Merced."

"I have not been to Kate's Bar," Juan said. "But I do not think it was in the camps that I saw you. Something . . . something about you is so familiar, yet I cannot put my finger on it. When did you come to California?"

"In forty-nine," Kathy said. "In May. Actually it was the end of February when we left Panama, but May when we got here."

Juan stiffened. "Panama?"

"Yes, we sailed from there. I thought we'd never get here. We had to go nearly to Hawaii to pick up a favorable wind."

A note of urgency entered Juan's voice. "And the name of your ship, señora?"

Kathy thought. "You know, I can't remember. It's been so . . ."

"The name, señora. Please."

"Something classical . . . the *Achilles*. Of course, that's it—the *Achilles*. How could I have forgotten?"

Juan's heart stopped. His jaw clenched so tightly, he thought it would break. Of course. He pictured her on that rolling deck, smiling easily, her face to the wind. Her hairstyle and clothes were different now, but it was her. This was the gringo woman who had taken the cabin from him and Elena.

"Yes," he said softly. "Of course. That was where I saw you. You were with two men."

"That's right. One of them was Jack, as a matter of fact. Don't tell me you were on the ship, too?"

Jack.

It all came together for Juan. Jack Marlow and this woman. They had been in it together. They had caused him and Elena to lose their cabin. If not for them, Juan's son would still be alive. Elena would be alive. Everything that had happened was their fault. He could almost laugh at the injustice of it all. He had helped to make

Jack rich. He had helped keep him from the hangman's rope. He had helped Jack and this *puta*. The people who had ruined his life.

"Yes," he said. "I was on the ship."

He could have killed her right there. He could have killed them both. It would have been easy. No, he thought. He would do it right. He would make theirs a fitting death, a death to be remembered by all San Francisco, all of California. He would give the gringos something they would never forget.

Kathy said, "Why are you smiling? Is something funny?"

Juan said, "No, señora. I was just thinking of something. You would not understand." He had waited a long time for his revenge. Soon he was going to have it.

Just then Jack returned from greeting his friends. He was laughing and a little drunk. There was a bright light in his eye. Ignoring Juan, he stood before Kathy. He looked into her eyes and ran his fingers up under her dark hair. In a husky voice he said, "Let's go home."

60

They drove back to the Nob Hill mansion. Kathy sat silently in a corner of the carriage as it rumbled over the street planking. Jack put his arm around her, caressing her shoulder and the back of her neck.

"Damn party," he swore. "I only went as a favor to Brandy, for getting me off. What I really wanted was to be alone with you."

Kathy stared out the carriage window. The gray sky of the short, fading afternoon mirrored her feelings. The northeast wind blew sand against the window.

"What were you talking to Juan about?" Jack said.

"Nothing." Kathy was in no mood for conversation. It didn't seem important that they'd been on the ship with Juan. She'd tell Jack later. If there was a later.

Inside the house, they went to the parlor. Jack called for champagne, then dismissed the servants for the evening. He poured a glass of champagne for Kathy, then he raised the bottle to his lips and drank. Liquid foamed up over the top and ran down his chin. He wiped it on his coat sleeve.

He put the bottle down and pulled Kathy to him. He kissed her hungrily. "I've missed you so much," he said.

Kathy pushed him away.

"What's wrong?" he said.

She stepped out of his embrace. "Jack, I know what you did."

"What do you mean?"

"I know you murdered Judge Mason. I know it wasn't self-defense."

Jack's dark brow clouded. "You've been talking to Brandy."

"It's not her fault. She thought I already knew."

Jack said nothing.

"Why, Jack? Why did you do it?"

"I couldn't let him talk about you the way he did. I wanted him to apologize to you, but he wouldn't. He went on again about how you were a whore. He made a crack about you having sex with animals. Animals, Kathy. Nobody says that about you and gets away with it. I—I lost my head. I'm sorry."

"You should never have gone after him," Kathy said.

"We've been through all this before," Jack replied. He moved toward her impatiently. "Come on. We've got a lot of catching up to do."

She backed up. "You never told me you owned part of a brothel."

"You never asked."

"All your great investments. Transportation, you said. Plank roads, you said. You never said anything about whores. What else have you invested in that I don't know about?"

"A few things. Nothing you . . ."

"Uh-huh," she said.

Jack caught up to her. He took her shoulders. "Let's not ruin a good night by arguing."

"Have you killed any other men?" she asked.

If he hadn't been drunk, he might have lied about it, but suddenly he didn't care. "All right, maybe I have. What of it? It was business."

"Business?"

"I'm in a tough racket, Kathy. When I first got here, I was

involved in a war with the Australians from Clark's Point. We had to kill some people. That's what war is all about.''

"How many did you kill in this 'business'?'' Kathy said.

"Maybe ten. Juan did most of it.''

"And you personally?''

"Three. Two in self-defense. They weren't the first men I've shot, and they probably won't be the last. I told you once before I'd do whatever I had to to get to the top.''

Kathy turned away. There were tears in her eyes. It was worse than she had imagined. She said, "Jack, I want a divorce.''

Jack was stunned. "What?''

"Divorce. San Francisco is the easiest city in the world to get one. It can be done quickly and quietly.''

Jack moved toward her. "Kathy, I don't understand . . .''

"I can't live with a murderer, Jack. I certainly can't love one.''

"But I did it for you. Everything I've done has been for you.''

"No. Whatever you've done, has been for yourself.''

"That's not true. Loving you may be the only decent thing I've done in my life, but I do love you.''

"Committing murder for love—you call that decent? My God, Jack, can't you see what you've become?''

"You knew I was no saint when you married me,'' Jack told her.

"No saint, yes. But not a murderer. I want a divorce.''

"No, dammit.'' Jack grabbed her. He kissed her. He pushed her down onto the bed.

She rolled away from him with a little cry.

Enraged, he lunged after her. He caught her and dragged her down. He pinned her wrists to the bed. He lowered himself onto her and forced his lips onto hers. She struggled beneath his powerful grip, but she could not move.

After a second, he raised his head. His dark eyes were inches from hers. His nostrils flared. "I could make you,'' he breathed. "There's not a court in this country that would hold me wrong.''

"Try it,'' she said, still struggling to get away.

Jack released his grip on her wrists. They were red where he'd been holding her down. He got off the bed. He smoothed back his dark hair. "No,'' he said. "I'm a gentleman now. I don't do those things. I'll wait for you to come to me of your own will. I'll wait if it takes fifty years. I'll never give you your freedom.''

Kathy sat up, rubbing her wrists, defiant. "I'll leave. I'll run away.''

"No, you won't. The servants will have orders to keep you here. When you go out, Juan will watch you. If you do escape, I'll track you down. I'll use all my resources and those of the law to do it. You're mine, Kathy, and you're going to stay that way. You'll never belong to anyone else."

He stormed out of the room, slamming the door. He locked the door from the outside, turning the silver handle. Shaking with rage, he went down the broad staircase to the parlor, where he drank champagne until he passed out.

61

Wade Rawson down the ramp of the river steamer *Antelope* moved slowly, knapsack slung over one shoulder. He was worn out, broke, another piece of flotsam washed down from the mines. The dog Roland trotted by his side.

The *Antelope* was tied up at the Central Wharf. It was a gray, cold afternoon in late January. There had been storms all the way from Sacramento, and Wade was glad to see the rain end.

People moved past Wade on the ramp—businessmen, couples, families who had been on excursions. There were miners, too, like Wade. Some were leaving California for good. Some had given up mining and had decided to seek work in the city. Others had come to spend the winter before returning to the mountains. Still others were sick and had come to the city to get well, or to die. One fellow made it no farther than the foot of the ramp. He sat on a bollard, shivering, blanket wrapped around him, lank hair hanging over his face. His bare feet were covered with mud. Wade would have liked to help him, but there was nothing he could do. There were plenty of miners in similar shape.

Wade had come to San Francisco to find Kathy. This was where she was supposed to be singing now. How long was it since he should have met her? Over a year. He wondered if she had given up on him. For a while he had given up on himself.

After being shot by the claim jumpers, he had lain by the cabin for two days, near death, with only the dog to protect him from marauding animals. Then he'd been found by a party of Indians driven from their hunting grounds by miners. Some of the Indians had wanted to kill him, but one, a chief named Flacco, had taken pity on him. He had ordered a litter made for Wade, and the Indians had carried him to one of their villages, at the head of the valley called Yosemite. There, they had nursed him back to health. Wade had stayed with the Indians for four months. Later, he'd searched for Jean-Claude's killers, but the search had been fruitless. Had he been searching for the killers, he now wondered, or for his own peace of mind? If not for him, Jean-Claude would still be alive. Every time he looked into Roland's brown eyes, he was reminded of that. First his greed had killed Ralph Bannister, now Jean-Claude. But there would be no more. He was done mining.

Right now he needed a place to stay. He had only a few dollars. He went up Sansome Street. The street had not been there when he was last in San Francisco; this had all been part of the cove. The sidewalks were jammed with merchandise, forcing pedestrians to detour into the street, which was a quagmire of seemingly bottomless mud. Wagons and horses plowed slowly through the gelatinous muck, while people on foot tried to make their way around them. A man on the *Antelope* had told Wade that there were cast iron stoves under the mud, even dead animals, but he didn't know whether to believe it. The street was full of horse manure. It stank to high heaven. Wade couldn't imagine what it must be like in summer. He saw an urchin drop his lollipop in the mire. The boy picked up the lollipop, brushed it off, and stuck it back in his mouth.

Wade got a room, or, rather, he and Roland shared a room with five other men at a seedy hotel in North Beach. Then he started in search of Kathy. The wind gusted off the bay. Wade had no coat; he tried to ignore the cold. Asking around, he learned that Kathy's show had ended its run. She was building her own theater, though—the Playhouse. Wade was told to try there for word of her.

The theater was on Washington Street, just behind Portsmouth Square. The walls and roof were up. Only the inside remained to be finished. Posters announced the grand opening, and Kathy's role in *Mary Barton*.

Nobody was working because of the weather. The front doors were locked. "Come on, Roland," Wade said. They went around back. Wade found an open door where the artists' entrance would be. He went in. The dog padded after.

The rear of the theater was a bewildering maze of narrow passageways, unfinished rooms, and piled equipment—rope, canvas, trunks, and crates. It smelled of new wood and paint.

"There has to be somebody around here," Wade said to the dog.

Rounding a corner, he bumped into a watchman.

"Who the hell are you?" the watchman said. He pointed with his lantern. "What's this dog doing in here?"

"He's all right," Wade said. "He goes where I go."

The watchman cried, "Tom!"

A second watchman appeared. Both were big, burly men. They would probably be bouncers when the theater opened. "What is it?" Tom said.

"We got us a prowler. With a dog."

"What do you want here?" Tom asked Wade.

"I'm trying to find Kate Beddoes," Wade said.

"Ain't everybody?" Tom said. "Go on, get out."

"I'm a friend of Mrs. Beddoes's," Wade explained.

"Sure, and I'm President Fillmore. I ain't gonna tell you again, pal—get out."

The two guards advanced on Wade. Roland growled at them, and they stopped.

Wade said, "How about a message? Can I leave a message?"

"The post office is the place for messages," the first watchman said. "They get paid for delivering them. There's no bums allowed in here. Or their mutts."

The watchman drew a pistol and pointed it at Roland. "Now, get that goddamn . . ."

"What's the problem?" said a smooth voice from behind.

Roland looked at the newcomer coming down the hall. His growl deepened and took on a warning note.

The newcomer wore a pearl-gray suit and a black hat. At first Wade thought it was Mr. Levelleire, come back from the dead. Then he looked closer, dumbfounded.

"Jack?" he said.

Jack Marlow stopped. His face went pale. His mouth slackened. In a low voice he said, "Wade. I thought you were dead."

Wade grinned. "So did I, for a while. Where'd you hear that, anyway?"

"It was . . . it was all over the camps. The man who killed Simon St. Clair. You're famous, college boy." Jack recovered his composure and threw his arms around Wade. "God, it's good to see you again."

At that gesture, the dog leapt at Jack, biting his leg. "Ow!" Jack yelled.

"Roland!" said Wade. "Stop it!"

Wade grabbed the dog by its collar. With difficulty he pulled the animal off Jack. "Roland! Roland!" He jerked the dog's head until it paid attention. "Stop it! Do you hear me?"

The dog sat, ears flat, looking at Jack and snarling. His lips curled back, showing his teeth.

Wade held the animal back. "Sorry, Jack, I don't know what's wrong with him. He's usually friendly."

Jack winced with pain. He tested his bitten leg gingerly in the narrow hallway. "I know I'm no animal lover, but this is ridiculous."

Both guards had their pistols out now. "Want us to fix him, boss?" said the first one.

"No, no," Jack told him. "Put those things away. Go on, leave us alone. This man is my best friend."

The guards looked at each other. Then they put their weapons in their coats and continued their rounds.

Roland was still watching Jack, growling deep in his throat. Jack took a step back. He grinned good-naturedly, rubbing his leg. "I've thought about you a hundred times since we split up."

"I've thought about you, too," Wade said. "You look like you've done all right for yourself."

Jack's grin broadened. "You bet. I told you town was the place to make your pile. What about you? It doesn't look like you found that Big Lump."

"I found it," Wade said. "Somebody took it from me."

"What happened? I heard your partner died. Frenchman, wasn't he?"

"Belgian. This was his dog."

"What about you?" Jack said.

"I got shot and left for dead. Indians saved me."

Jack whistled. "You're lucky. I wouldn't expect them to do that for a white man."

"They were good people. The only problem I had was that they wanted the dog as payment for what they'd done for me."

"Why? Because he's a good hunter?"

"No, they wanted to eat him. I had a hell of a time talking them out of it. Finally I took them back to my old camp. All the area around there was being worked by then, but I found a bag of my hidden gold that the claim jumpers had missed. My partner must have left one unrevealed, hoping I'd find it. There's a town there now, so I used the gold to buy food for the Indians. That made them happy. While I was there, I saw a doctor. He cut out one of my bullets. I've still got the other one in me. I guess I'll carry it to my grave."

Wade paused. "After that, I tried to find the men who killed my partner."

"Any luck?"

Wade shook his head. "Cold trail. I learned that Juan Soto might have been involved, but that doesn't mean anything. They blame every crime on Juan Soto up there. You know that. Anyway, he's supposed to be dead, too."

"I heard," Jack said. "They put a big reward on his head and sent some war hero and a bunch of Rangers after him. They caught him near the Tuolomne and cut off his head. It's on display in Sacramento."

Wade nodded. "I saw it on my way down here."

"You sound skeptical."

"Come on, Jack. Those 'Rangers' probably took the first Mexican they could find, cut off his head, said it was Juan Soto, and rode away with the reward. Nobody knows what Soto looks like, so who's to know the difference?"

Jack scratched his chin. "Where do you think Soto is?"

"Back in Mexico, probably. I don't care anymore. It's all behind me."

The dog was lying down now, watching Jack's every move. A low growl rumbled from its throat. "Well, it's good to have you in San Francisco," Jack told Wade, "though I'm not so sure about the dog. What are you doing here, at the Playhouse?"

"Looking for Kathy. It's a long story, but she and I are going to be married. What are *you* doing here?"

Jack replied hesitatingly. "I own the place. My wife and I."

"You're married?"

"That's the way most people get a wife."

"Great, Jack. Congratulations. But this is supposed to be Kathy's theater. If you own it, you must know where she is. She must have told you about us.''

Jack nodded slowly. "She told me."

"Where is she, then? Come on, Jack, tell me. Roland, shut up, will you?"

Jack said, "Why don't you come home with me first? Meet my wife."

"I want to find Kathy first. I'm over a year late catching up to her."

"No, come with me. It's almost dark, and you'll need something to eat. You look like you haven't had a good meal in months. I'll take you to Kathy later."

"Later tonight?"

"I promise."

Wade thought. "All right, but I can't stay long."

"Fine," Jack said. "Come on, let's get out of here."

They went outside, to a shiny black carriage. One door of the carriage had recently been repainted, but Wade took no note of the KM on it.

Roland didn't want to get into the carriage. Wade had to lift him in. He held the muddy dog on his lap. The dog still growled menacingly at Jack, and Wade clamped a hand over his muzzle.

"Once around the Square," Jack told the driver.

Wade nestled on the plush leather with the dog. "It's been along time since I sat on anything this nice," he said. "You get all this money running a theater?"

"No, the theater's a sideline. You'll see my main source of income in a minute."

The carriage turned into crowded Portsmouth Square. Jack pointed to a large, brightly lit building with crowds of men coming and going through the doors.

Wade read the sign. "The Black Jack. That's yours?"

Jack nodded, grinning proudly.

"You own a gambling hall?"

"You've got it, college boy. Black Jack Marlow, they call me now."

"Well, you always liked the cards," Wade said.

The carriage went up California Street to the mansion. "Welcome to my humble abode," Jack said.

"My God," Wade breathed as they got out. He looked from the house to the view of San Francisco and the harbor sprawled below him, lights winking in the deepening dusk. He shook his head. "It's a long way from Calosoco."

Jack said, "Charles, here, can take your dog around back to the stables. We'll send some beef out for him. Maybe that'll put me on his good list."

"All right," Wade said.

The driver, Charles, got down from the carriage. "Come on, dog," he said.

Roland looked at Wade, who pointed. "Go on." Wagging his tail, the dog went with the driver.

"What's he got that I don't have?" Jack wondered aloud, watching them.

Jack and Wade walked up to the ornately carved oak doors, Jack limping where the dog had bitten him. The butler let them in and took Jack's coat. To Wade he said, "Your coat, sir?"

"Don't have one," Wade told him. "Mule ate it."

"Yes, sir," said the solemn-faced butler.

Jack said, "Send for Mrs. Marlow, will you, please, Henry?"

The butler bowed and moved off. Jack and Wade went into the parlor. "Drink?" Jack said.

Wade nodded. Jack poured some port into a glass of cut crystal. Wade sipped the sweet drink. He looked around the expensively furnished parlor with its marble fireplace and heavy furniture. There were light footsteps, and Jack said, "There's somebody I want you to meet, dear."

Wade turned to see Kathy standing in the doorway. "Wade!" she cried.

62

Wade wanted to cross the room and throw his arms around Kathy. He saw that she wanted to do the same. But they didn't. They couldn't.

"You're Jack's wife?" Wade said, disbelieving.

The joy drained from Kathy's face. She nodded.

Wade turned to Jack. "Why didn't you tell me?"

Jack looked embarrassed. "I don't know. I should have. I wanted it to be a surprise, but I guess the surprise wasn't in very good taste."

Kathy's face was bleak. "I—I can't believe it," she told Wade. "You're supposed to be . . ."

"To be dead," Wade said. "I know."

"That's what Jack told me."

"I told you what I'd heard," Jack reminded her.

Kathy went on, never taking her eyes off Wade. "All that time, and I didn't hear from you. I thought maybe you'd met another woman, or lost interest in me, or . . ."

"Didn't you get my letter?" Wade said.

Kathy looked puzzled. "No."

"I sent it last March."

Kathy shrugged helplessly. "I never got it. And I always let the Civic Opera in Stockton know where I'd be."

Wade swore to himself. "I can't imagine what happened to it." Billy hadn't seemed like the type who would take the money and not deliver. Some accident must have befallen him. Briefly, Wade described to Kathy how he'd found the rich vein, how he'd stayed too long and been rescued by Jean-Claude, then decided to go back for more gold. He told her how he'd realized his mistake and been ready to leave, when he and Jean-Claude were attacked by the claim jumpers. "That was in June. Jean-Claude was killed and I was shot twice. I've been recovering from the wounds most of the time since."

Kathy looked concerned.

Jack poured himself another glass of port. "In the meantime, Kathy came to San Francisco. We met, fell in love, and got married." He smiled possessively at Kathy, then dropped the smile, as if he didn't want Wade to think he was gloating. "I'm sorry, Wade. These things happen."

"Yeah," said Wade.

Wade looked at Kathy. Was she really in love with Jack? Not by the look on her face, she wasn't. She looked like the victim of a cruel trick. Wade felt the same way. He and Kathy were back where they had started. They were in love, and she was married to another man. It was like a Chinese box. You opened it, and there was the same puzzle all over again.

The butler, Henry, came in. "Supper, sir," he announced. The butler wasn't English, but he gave a good imitation.

"Very well," Jack told him.

Henry said, "Will you dress, sir?"

Jack looked at Wade in his rough miner's garb and grinned. "Under the circumstances, I don't think that will be necessary, Henry. We'll dine informally tonight."

"Very good, sir."

To Wade and Kathy, Jack said, "Shall we?"

Wade and Kathy started into the dining room. Jack paused. In a low voice he said to Henry, "Send for Juan."

63

The three of them dined alone, sitting at one end of the long mahogany table. There was little conversation. Wade and Kathy had much they wanted to say, but not around Jack. Kathy sawed listlessly at her chop until it lay on her plate in tatters, like the tatters of her marriage, the tatters of her life. Wade picked at his food. He did not feel like eating.

Jack sat at the head of the table, wearing his Montgomery Street clothes, smelling of hair tonic and bath powder. He attempted to lighten the mood. "Well," he said, "here we are, together again. It's like old times, isn't it?"

"There are a few differences," Kathy pointed out.

"That's right. There's no jungle, no fever, and Cristobal and his merry men aren't chasing us."

"And you're married to Kathy," Wade added.

"Yes, there's that. And I'm rich."

Wade still had a hard time getting used to Jack's new style of speaking and dress. He had transformed himself. He used to wear homespun; now he looked and sounded like a real gentleman. Wade wondered who had taught him. He couldn't have picked it up by himself.

Wade cast a furtive glance at Kathy. Her eyes moved toward him as well.

Jack said, "Look, Wade, there's no hard feelings about what's happened, I hope? It's not like I tricked Kathy away from you, or anything."

"No," Wade told him. "No hard feelings."

"We're still friends?"

"Of course."

"Good. Have some wine. This stuff costs me a fortune, so it must be good."

He poured Wade a glass of burgundy and said, "What will you do now? Go back to the mines?"

Wade shook his head. "No. Even if I wanted to—and I don't—it's changed up there. It's big corporations now—stamping mills and men working for wages. The day of the independent prospector is about over."

"What, then?" Jack said.

Wade sighed. "I don't know. Go back east, maybe."

"No!" Kathy said.

Jack threw a quick look at her.

Kathy went on hastily. "I mean, you should think before you leave San Francisco. There's lots of opportunities here. Lots of jobs. It's a great place to get ahead."

"I don't know, dear," Jack said, very serious, his brows knit. "Business is slack now. A lot of merchants are worried. The boom is slowing down."

"There's always opportunity for an intelligent, enterprising man," Kathy said. "Perhaps we could lend Wade money to get started."

"Perhaps," Jack said. "We'll talk about it another time. Right now I must be getting to the club. Want to come, Wade? You've never seen anything like The Black Jack in full swing, I can assure you."

Wade said, "No, thanks. I'm not up for it right now. Maybe another time."

"Of course. I'll give you a ride to your rooms, then."

Wade noticed there was no offer to stay at the mansion, where they must surely have extra space. Kathy looked like she wanted to make the offer, but she didn't. Was she afraid? Wade said, "I think I'll walk. I haven't been to San Francisco in two and a half years. I'm curious to look around."

"Where are you staying?"

"The Bay City Hotel, in North Beach."

"Be careful. That's a dangerous area after dark."

"I'll be all right. I've got Roland."

"Who is Roland?" Kathy said.

Jack laughed. "Wade's man-eating dog."

"He belonged to my partner, Jean-Claude," Wade explained. "He stayed by me when I was shot. He kept wolves and coyotes and God knows what else off me till the Indians found me."

Jack said, "He's out back, eating our beef. It's his reward for giving me this chomp in the leg." He lifted his trousers, showing Kathy the blood-crusted teeth marks in his long drawers.

Kathy's eyes widened.

"If you see me foaming at the mouth tomorrow, you'll know he's rabid."

"Don't worry," Wade said. "He's all right."

Wade rose to say good-bye. Jack shook his hand. "We'll see you soon—won't we, Kathy? Tomorrow, maybe. I'll take you to the club then, and no excuses."

"All right," Wade said.

Kathy took both Wade's hands. She pecked his cheek. As she did, she whispered in his ear, "I have to talk to you." She glanced sideways to see if Jack had heard, but he gave no evidence of it.

Jack laughed. "You won't mind if I don't walk you to the stables. I don't fancy another confrontation with your pet."

Wade laughed. "I don't blame you. I still can't understand why he doesn't like you." The two men shook hands again. "Tomorrow, then," Wade said.

"Count on it," Jack told him.

Wade went back to the stables and collected Roland, who was begging table scraps and playing fetch with the servants. Wade and the dog set off down the graveled drive in the dark. They passed a man on horseback coming in.

The rider tied his horse in front of the house. He rapped on the door and was admitted by the butler.

Jack was in the billiard room, waiting. He had seen Kathy whisper to Wade, and he was troubled. As long as Wade was in San Francisco, he was a threat to the marriage. He was a threat if he learned how Jack had made his pile, too, and that had Jack more worried. He was glad that damned dog couldn't talk. He'd had to pretend he'd thought it funny when the beast had bitten him. He'd wanted to shoot it.

He looked up as the rider came into the room. "Ah, there you are, Juan. I've got a job for you."

64

Wade waited in the dark street at the foot of Nob Hill until Jack's carriage had passed, on its way to the club. Then he walked back to the mansion, the dog Roland at his side.

Wade banged the heavy brass knocker on the front door. Henry, the butler, answered. Wade smiled sheepishly. "I left my knapsack here."

"I don't recall you with a knapsack, sir," Henry said.

"No, I brought it, I'm certain."

"I'll have a look, sir. You may come inside, but leave your dog on the porch.

"Roland, stay," said Wade. He followed the butler inside.

"Wait here, sir," the butler said, indicating the entrance hall.

"I'll go with you," Wade suggested. "Help you look."

Henry turned a cold eye on him. "That won't be necessary, sir."

Henry started for the parlor. "Friendly fellow," Wade murmured.

Wade was alone in the entrance hall, facing the grand staircase. Where would Kathy be? Upstairs, maybe, in her room. He started for the staircase.

"Where are you going, señor?" said a voice.

Wade stopped. He turned to face a Latin man, well-dressed, wearing two-toned riding boots, a small ring in his left ear. The man had come from the drawing room.

Wade forced a surprised smile. "Hello. I'm a friend of Kathy Beddoes—Mrs. Marlow. I want to talk to her."

"That is not possible, señor. She cannot come."

The man's hair was combed straight back. His dark eyes were

not friendly. His face was intelligent, cultured. He looked vaguely
familiar.

"It's all right," Wade assured him. "I'm a friend of Jack's, too.
Ask Mrs. Marlow, she'll vouch for me. Wade Rawson is my name."

"You will have to leave."

"I can't do that, not right now. Henry, the butler, is looking for
my . . ."

Suddenly, Wade remembered where he'd seen that face before.
"Jesus," he blurted out, "I know you now."

The man stiffened. He looked even more unfriendly, if that was
possible. "Yes, señor?"

"Your name's Juan, isn't it?"

"Yes. Juan Menendez."

Wade couldn't recall the last name. It didn't matter. He wished
he hadn't brought it up at all. "Your wife was hung in Oro Fino."

The man looked surprised, as if he'd expected Wade to say something else.

Wade went on. "I—I tried to stop the men who did it. I wasn't
any help. I'm sorry, I shouldn't have mentioned it. I just never
expected to see you again, especially not here."

Juan studied him. "Yes," he said slowly, "I remember you."

"You're a friend of Jack's?"

"We are associates in business."

Just then the butler returned. "Your bag isn't here, sir," he said.
"My first assumption was correct."

Wade shook his head. "Funny, I could have sworn I left it here.
Oh, well. Listen, Henry, tell Mrs. Marlow I'd like to see her for a
minute, would you?"

"I'm sorry, sir. Mrs. Marlow can't see you. You'll have to
leave."

"I just want to ask her something. What's wrong with you people? It's not like I'm a stranger."

"As I said, sir, it's impossible."

Henry led Wade to the front door. "You're not very hospitable,"
Wade said. "I'll tell Jack."

"It's his orders, sir."

For the first time, Juan smiled. Henry opened the door.

Roland was sitting outside. As the door opened, Roland snapped
upright, nose pointed at Juan. He growled. The hackles rose on his
back.

"Not again," Wade groaned. "What's wrong with this animal?"

The dog lowered its head, ready to attack. Wade quickly knelt and restrained him. Behind Wade, Henry said dryly, "If I might suggest, sir. Perhaps a leash would be appropriate?"

"Thanks," Wade told him. "Just close the door, will you?"

"Good night, sir," said Henry. The heavy door shut quietly.

Wade let the dog go. Roland rushed to the door, barking, pawing at the thick oak, sniffing along the side and bottom for a way in.

"What do you have against that fellow?" Wade said. "You've never even seen him before." He shook his head. "I don't know what's gotten into you."

Wade stepped back, looking at the house. Was there a way to break in undetected? There didn't seem to be. The dog stopped barking. Wade walked around the side of the house.

Above him, a window slid open.

"Wade!" came a loud whisper. It was Kathy.

Wade stepped back, looking up. In the darkness he saw her outlined against a faint light.

"Wade," she went on, hurrying her words. "Jack's keeping me here against my will. I want a divorce, but he won't let me have one. He won't let me go anywhere by myself because he's afraid I'll run away. Wade, he killed a man for—"

Kathy stepped back—or was pulled back—from the window. The window slid shut again. The house was quiet.

After a moment Wade turned away. There was nothing more he could do there, not right then. He and the dog walked down the drive. Below them, the lights of San Francisco and the harbor blazed in nighttime splendor. Wade thought about what he had just heard. He thought about what he should do next.

Behind Wade, in the house, Juan Soto was also thinking. He was reliving the day of Elena's death. In his mind's eye he pictured the big miner Wade, the one who had yelled at Elena's murderers, the one who had tried to stop them. He pictured Wade's dark-haired partner as well, the one with the pistol. The partner had been bearded, wasted by bad food and fever, but . . . could it have been Jack Marlow? If it had been, why had Jack never told him that he had been in Oro Fino that day? And if it had been Jack, could this Wade be the third person from the ship *Achilles*? Surely God had heard Juan's prayers to deliver all three of his tormentors to Juan for justice.

Jack had told Juan that Wade was the miner whose partner they had killed near Tough Luck. He had told Juan that Wade must be eliminated. If Wade learned the truth, Juan and Jack could hang.

Juan did not care if he hanged, as long as he had revenge against Jack and the woman Kathy first. He would, in fact, do the deed tonight if Jack returned early from the club and the wind backed into the south or southwest. Right now the wind was wrong for what Juan intended. He had planned a spectacular act in Elena's memory. He could not bring Elena back to life, but he would give the gringos something to remember her by. They would remember him, too— he must find a way to let them know who had done this.

But first . . .

First he must settle accounts with the man called Wade. Not for Jack. For himself.

65

Wade wandered the crowded, muddy streets, trudging up and down the city's hills. San Francisco had changed so much, it was as if he'd never been there before. The dog Roland trotted ahead of him, fascinated by the endless variety of new smells and sounds. Now and then he paused to eat something out of the street or off the sidewalk.

Wade was thinking about Kathy, about what she had told him from the window. What should he do about her? What could he do?

His thoughts were interrupted by music, by the calls of whores and pimps, or by more bizarre approaches. "She's doing it on the bar right now, sir. Come and watch. Only an ounce of gold will get you in. A rare bargain for such an attraction, you'll agree."

A cold wind blew off the bay. Without a coat, Wade shivered. Once he stopped in a saloon for a toddy to warm up. Nobody complained when Roland came into the saloon with him. The bartender asked if he wanted a drink for the dog as well. San Francisco was that kind of town.

For all his thinking, Wade could arrive at no plan. He would have to confront Jack tomorrow and take the situation as it developed. It was not a confrontation to which he looked forward.

He started back to his hotel, located in the narrow ramshackle streets of North Beach. He believed what Jack had said about the neighborhood being dangerous. The only lights were those that shone through cracks in doors or windows. His ears were assaulted by strange music and foreign accents. The smells of exotic cooking wafted around him.

Roland had been walking ahead. Suddenly he stopped and looked at something in the dark. He came back and sat in front of Wade, ears alert, still looking forward.

Wade's senses came alive. He peered up the crowded street. He saw nothing wrong.

In front of Wade, a man stepped out of a narrow passageway between buildings. The man was lean and sharp-featured, the kind who wouldn't look you in the eye. He said, ''Trouble you for a dollar, mister?''

Before Wade could answer, two more men came from behind him on either side. They grabbed Wade's elbows and pushed him into the narrow passageway. In the lean man's hand, a knife gleamed.

Roland leapt at the lean man, sinking his teeth into the man's ankle. The man yelled. Wade twisted violently, throwing off his other two assailants.

There was vicious snarling and yelling as the lean man tried to shake Roland off. Wade fought the other two men in the dark. There were shuffling feet, grunting, thuds as bodies slammed into flimsy wooden walls. Wade punched one man off him. He grappled with the other. He grabbed his upper arm and swung him into the building. He knew that whatever happened, he mustn't go down. The first man was back on him. Wade hit him with a left hand, then a right, unable to get leverage on his punches in the narrow passage. He threw a shoulder into the man, knocking him away even as the second man grabbed him from behind. Wade staggered backward, rammed the second man into the building, once, twice, until he let go. Then he turned and punched him, grazing him in the dark. The first man bulled into Wade, missed him in the darkness and confusion, and slid off Wade's shoulder into his companion. Wade shoved them both together and stumbled for the alley.

He hurried down the dark passageway. He reached the alley, hesitated the briefest second, and turned left. He couldn't run at full speed. The alley was thick with mud; it sucked at his ankles. He banged into wooden crates; he tripped over empty bottles. He heard his two attackers behind him. He didn't have a pistol. He didn't have any weapon. He didn't know what had happened to Roland.

He made for the end of the block, hoping to get to the street and find help. His lungs were on fire. His heart was pumping like it would explode.

At the end of the alley a shadow loomed, dimly seen in the dark. A man. Was it help? Wade's senses told him no.

The man blocked the end of the alley. Wade put his shoulder down and barreled into him. The man was strong. He took Wade's charge, and the two of them careened into some construction equipment at the rear of a building. They fell over something hard. A wheelbarrow. Wade disengaged himself. He struck out at the man, hit nothing but darkness. He overbalanced and fell into the wheelbarrow, which had tipped over. Something had spilled out of it. Bricks. Wade picked one up. He scrambled to his feet and swung the brick at a dark form coming in at him. There was a sickening crunch. The man groaned and sank to the ground. The force of the blow loosened the unwieldy brick in Wade's hand. Before he could get a better grip on it, someone else was on him. The two men wrestled, slipping in the mud. The man knocked the brick from Wade's hand. Wade punched out. He hit something sharp, the man's teeth. He cut his hand, heard another groan. Someone pinned his arms from the rear. Wade tried to turn. The man had him tight. Wade kicked out. He struggled in the man's grip. Something whistled through the air. There were bright lights, pain. Blackness.

"Is he dead, then?" said the man with the sap, an Irishman. The Irishman was bent double, catching his breath, spitting blood. Wade had rearranged his front teeth, and that didn't make him happy.

The man who'd been holding Wade's arm knelt and put his head to Wade's chest. "No," he said. "Son of a bitch damn near broke my back. How's Toby?"

In the dark the Irishman examined the fellow who'd been hit with the brick. He felt his head. "Messed up bad, he is, wid a skull like porridge, and blood comin' out his ear."

"What about Mulhern?" said the second man, a Missourian named Odie.

"No sign o' him."

They heard a faint growling. They looked back toward the passageway. Light reflected off a pair of yellowish-green eyes moving back and forth in the darkness, just out of reach.

"It's that damn dog," said Odie. He picked up one of the bricks and threw it. It thunked in the mud. He threw another. There was a yelp, and the glowing eyes vanished up the alley.

Odie turned back to Wade. He drew a knife. "Now for this one."

"Wait," said a voice.

Another shadow loomed out of the darkness. It resolved itself into a man of medium height, well dressed, with a Latin accent. The ring in his ear glinted faintly.

"Come on, Juano," said the Irishman. "Let's be killing him and get out of here before somebody comes."

Juan knelt beside the unconscious Wade. There was blood all over Wade's face from the sap. Juan remembered how Wade had been hit above the eye by the bottle in Oro Fino.

"I've been thinking," he said. "Perhaps we will not kill him after all."

"What's wrong wid ye, man? The boss said the plan was—"

"I know what the plan was. I am changing it. This man once tried to help me. I am going to return the favor."

"What will ye do, then?"

"You'll see. You two put him in that barrow. Throw this tarp over him."

The two men looked at each other. Then they heaved Wade up. "Where're we going?" said Odie.

"Clark's Point."

Less than an hour later a rowboat made its way through the crowded anchorage off Clark's Point. Juan Menendez was at the tiller. Wade, still unconscious, was bundled in the bow. Odie and the Irishman manned the oars. Toby had been left in the alley to die. The other man, Mulhern, had his leg chewed to shreds by the dog and was out of action for the foreseeable future.

Fog rose from the bay. The oars rose and dipped in the oily water. So much garbage had been dumped in the bay that it smelled like a sewer. Juan steered the rowboat toward a shadowy three-master, riding low at its anchor. As they drew close, he cried, "Ahoy, the *Archer*."

After a second a voice replied out of the mist. "What d'ye want?"

"At the Seaman's Home they say you need crew." The Seaman's Home was a hotel owned by Juan and Jack that specialized in kidnapping sailors and supplying them to unscrupulous sea captains who paid well for the service. Ship's crews were always in short supply because of desertions by gold-mad sailors.

There was a pause. Then another voice called from the ship, a voice with authority. "How many do you have for us?"

"One."

"Come alongside."

"Up oars," Juan told the rowers. He maneuvered the boat until it bumped alongside the lee of the three-master. A line was lowered over the side. Odie and the Irishman made the line fast under Wade's arms, and he was hauled aboard while Juan clambered up the gangway.

Wade lay on the deck, just beginning to stir in the frigid salt air. The first mate, a hard-bitten man, stood over him. "A good-looking specimen," he told Juan. "I'll make a sailor of him if I have to wear out a rope's end to do it. How much d'you want for him?"

Juan smiled. "He is free to you. A gift."

The mate rubbed his chin. "You must want him out of town bad."

"He is lucky to be getting out alive," Juan said.

Juan knelt on the damp deck, beside Wade. Above them, the yards creaked. Wade moaned, rolling his head, which was crusted with dried blood. Juan said, "Good-bye, señor. In a few hours you will be on your way to Shanghai. After that, it is a voyage around the world." He looked up, "I am correct?"

The mate nodded.

To Wade, Juan said, "Do well, amigo. You would be wise not to return here."

He stood. "Adios," he said to the mate. "A prosperous voyage." Then he swung over the gangway and was gone. He had much to do.

On the deck Wade was coming to. The mate lashed his back again and again with a knotted rope's end. "Get up, you. Get up!"

66

The *Archer* was ready for sea. She would sail on the last of the evening tide. The breeze had fallen off and backed into the southwest; it swirled the heavy fog that lay over the bay. Harbormaster's crews stood by in long boats, ready to warp the vessel out of its anchorage.

"Hands to the capstan!" shouted the captain from the quarterdeck.

Wade emerged from the forecastle. He was barefoot, clad only in shirt and trousers. He was still groggy. His head throbbed from the blow he'd taken from the sap. There was dried blood on his face. The backs of his fingers were cut from hitting the Irishman's teeth. He had a dozen other hurts and bruises.

"You," snapped the mate, grabbing his arm and pushing him forward, "get to the capstan." Wade made his way unsteadily toward the ship's bow. Each step made his head hurt more.

"Lively there!" said the mate. He gave Wade's back a blow with the knotted rope's end. Another. Wade winced. He could feel new welts rising alongside the others he'd received since coming aboard. The mate watched him closely, lest he attempt to dive overboard and escape.

"Prepare to weigh anchor!" the captain cried.

Wade braced himself against one of the capstan's spokes, following the other sailors' example.

From overside came the *phut, phut, phut* of a small steam engine. It was coming toward them through the fog. It sounded like a launch.

"Ahoy the *Archer*!" came a call. "Belay, there!"

The captain, a choleric Marylander named Albemarle, shouted back through his speaking trumpet, "On whose orders?"

"The sheriff of San Francisco County and the Committee of Vigilance," came the reply.

The captain raised his trumpet again. "I must catch the tide, sir. I have no time for you."

Wade saw a dim flash through the fog. He heard a muffled rifle shot.

"That was across your bows, sir. Belay, or we'll put a volley into you and impound what's left. I have twenty armed men on board."

The captain was livid with rage, but he had no choice. "Stand fast," he ordered the crew. "Come alongside," he shouted to the launch.

At the capstan, Wade shivered. He wondered what it all meant.

The launch made fast alongside. There was the sound of feet on the boarding ladder, and a group of armed men appeared. They were civilians, wearing top hats and suits. A couple had on heavy coats against the cold. There were pistols in their belts. In their hands were shotguns and the Springfield army rifles that had proved so effective in the Mexican War.

Captain Albemarle hastened down the companionway to the ship's waist. "I must protest this intrusion, sir."

"Protest all you want," said the vigilantes' leader. He was a dark, humorless fellow with thin lips, a pointed nose, and shrewd, grasping eyes. He and his fellow committee members wore badges with the "all-seeing" eye. Two other members of the boarding party had lawman's badges pinned to their vests. One was a smallish, intense man. The other man was big and roughly handsome; of all the boarding party, he looked like he'd rather be somewhere else.

"I'm Sheriff Hays," said the smaller man, who carried a brace of pistols in a sash around his waist. "I understand you have a crewman abducted this evening against his will."

The captain spluttered, "I never—"

"That's me," said Wade, stepping away from the capstan. The mate growled and gripped his rope's end, but there was nothing he could do.

Hays showed the captain a piece of paper. "I have a warrant to remove this man from your ship."

"Let me get my boots," Wade said.

Wade retrieved his boots from the crew's quarters in the fo'c'sle. He'd put them on later. He hurried back on deck. The captain was still protesting. "You're leaving me short-handed, sir."

"I'm leaving you your ship, sir," said the ex–Texas Ranger. "Be glad I don't throw you in jail and have you charged with kidnapping."

"I had no way of knowing—"

"You knew," Hays said. He looked around the deck. "Anyone else here against their will?"

No answer.

"All right, let's *vamos*." To Wade he said, "You first."

Wade tossed his boots over the side into the launch. Then he snapped his fingers. "Oops. I forgot something."

"What's that?" said the sheriff.

"This." Wade turned, and he punched the mate on the jaw, knocking him into the scuppers. Wade waved to the rest of the crew and the captain. "Have a good trip, boys!" He scrambled over the ship's side and into the small steam launch.

The launch chugged away from the *Archer*. Through the fog Wade heard Captain Albemarle cursing as he gave the order to weigh anchor. Wade huddled against the cold. He turned his back to the breeze caused by the launch's passage through the water. He watched the *Archer* disappear into the fog, well aware how close he'd come to disappearing with it.

"Thanks," he told the vigilantes. He sat on a thwart and put on his boots. Somebody handed him a cup of hot coffee, and he sipped it gratefully.

"You're lucky we got there in time," said the vigilantes's shrewd-eyed leader. "A few more minutes and you'd have been on your way to China."

"How did you know they had me?" Wade said.

"One of our informants witnessed your kidnapping. He followed your abductors, saw you headed for the *Archer*, then came to us with the news. We came as soon as we could, Mr. . . . ?"

"Rawson. Wade Rawson."

The vigilantes looked at each other. One of them, a bluff, hearty fellow, said, "Not the Wade Rawson who killed Simon St. Clair?"

Wade wrinkled his brow. "That's me. Though it's not a deed I care to trade on."

Sheriff Hays said, "We'd heard you were dead, Mr. Rawson."

"A lot of people seem to have heard that. Fortunately for me, it's not true."

The vigilantes' leader looked uncharacteristically happy. "Well, this is a stroke of luck for us—eh, boys?"

"Yes, indeed," replied the bluff fellow. "You're just the man we need, Rawson."

"Need?" said Wade.

"In the vigilantes," the leader said. He held out a hand. "I'm Sam Brannan."

Wade had heard of Sam Brannan. He was a merchant, one of the wealthiest men in San Francisco. Brannan introduced the others: George Oakes—he was the bluff fellow—Will Hays, and more. The names tripped by Wade. The only one he recognized was that of the sheriff's big deputy, Jake Moran.

"You're the war hero, the one who brought in the head of Juan Soto," Wade said.

Moran cleared his throat. Wade noticed that his hands were covered by burn scars. "I did what they paid me to," he said, somewhat defensively.

Brannan went on. "A man with your reputation for action would be an asset to us, Mr. Rawson. A tremendous asset."

"Why?" Wade said. "You've got all these men. You've got Sheriff Hays, here, and Mr. Moran."

Hays spoke up. "Jake and I are officers of the court. We can make sure we're in another part of the country when the vigilantes act, but we can't join them. Technically, they're breaking the law."

"You joined in just now," Wade said.

"We had a warrant," the sheriff reminded him.

Wade shook his head. "You boys have got me wrong. I'm no crusader for law and order. St. Clair pulled a gun on me. I shot him because I had no choice."

"That's good enough for us," said George Oakes. "Any man who stood up to Simon St. Clair is man enough to stand up to Black Jack Marlow."

"Jack!" said Wade.

"You know him?" said Oakes, surprised.

"Jack Marlow was my partner in the mines. We came to California together."

The members of the vigilance committee looked at each other once again.

Brannan said, "And yet you have the reputation of being honest, Mr. Rawson."

"Honest enough," Wade told him. He didn't mention that he'd been at Jack's house earlier that evening. "What's Jack done, anyway?"

"What hasn't he done? Prostitution, gambling, hijacking. It was

Jack Marlow's men who abducted you tonight. Our informant recognized their leader—a man named Juan Menendez.''

"Menendez!''

"You know him, too?'' said Brannan.

"We've been introduced. But . . .''

"Menendez and Marlow run the Seaman's Home, which is a front for kidnapping sailors.''

"That can't be right,'' Wade said. "This informant of yours must have been mistaken.'' None of this made sense to Wade. Why would Menendez have kidnapped him?

The launch was approaching the Market Street Wharf. It cut its engine. The breeze was freshening. The lights of San Francisco blazed through the dissipating fog. As the launch was tied up, Sam Brannan faced Wade intently. "In the list of Mr. Marlow's sins, did I mention murder? Last Christmas, Jack Marlow shot one of our most prominent citizens dead in the street, in front of witnesses. It wasn't the first man he's killed in San Francisco, either.''

"I don't believe it,'' Wade said. "If Jack murdered someone, why wasn't he arrested? Why wasn't he put on trial?''

Brannan was grim. "There was a trial, but Marlow's gang bought off the judge and jury. They intimidated or killed the witnesses. It was a farce. Marlow walked away, scot-free. The law is powerless against a man like that. And when the law fails, we go to work.''

Wade went cold. "What kind of work?''

"We're going to put Marlow and Menendez on trial again. Then we're going to hang them.''

"When?''

"Tonight. Our men are gathering at the Sansome Street fire station right now. We moved against a number of the city's malefactors last summer. For a while, crime died out. Then Marlow came to town, and things got worse than ever. We've been hesitant to act against him and Menendez because they're heavily armed, and there's likely to be a gun battle. But after this last outrage, we've no choice. Every honest citizen in San Francisco is behind us. We'd like to have you with us as well.''

Wade remembered the miners court at Oro Fino. He shook his head. "Sorry, boys. I'm against vigilante justice. I've seen it misfire before. I've seen an innocent person hang.''

George Oakes said, "Jack Marlow is not innocent.''

"The courts are the place to prove that,'' Wade told him.

"Marlow owns the courts,'' Oakes protested.

Wade would have none of it. "Sorry," he repeated.

Brannan and his companions were disappointed. Brannan said, "We could use you, Mr. Rawson. You're sure we can't change your mind?"

"I'm sure," Wade said. "But you certainly have my thanks for what you did for me tonight."

"We were glad to help," Brannan told him. "I only wish we could help the other poor souls Marlow has sold to these merchant skippers." Brannan looked at the vigilantes. "Come on, men. There's work to do. Sheriff, I believe you and Jake have to serve a writ at the Mission Dolores?"

"We were just leaving," Hays said.

The men climbed out of the launch. They left Wade by himself on the wharf.

Wade thought about what he had just heard. He knew that Jack could be pretty raw. He knew that Jack had broken the law before he came west. Still, he couldn't picture Jack doing the things the vigilantes had accused him of—murder, prostitution. They'd even made it sound as though Jack were behind his kidnapping. But it wasn't only the vigilantes who had talked against Jack. Kathy, also, had said—or tried to say—that Jack had killed a man, presumably over her.

Wade had to return to the house on Nob Hill. If he was going to confront Jack over this, it could no longer wait until morning. He had to do it now.

67

"When are they coming?" Jack asked.

"Tonight," Wade told him. "Right now."

Jack snorted cynically. "Knowing Sam Brannan, they'll have a few drinks before they do anything."

It was midnight. Jack had come home early from the club. He and Wade were in the billiard room of his house. For the second time that day, Jack had been surprised to see Wade alive. He'd heard Wade's story about being shanghaied onto the merchant ship, and he'd wondered what had possessed Juan to change his orders. Juan and his men were supposed to kill Wade, to make it look like a street robbery. Jack thought how lucky he now was that Juan had done it this way.

Wade looked a mess and felt as bad. He sipped the brandy that Jack had poured for him. The fiery liquid took the edge off his pain but not off his anger. "Jack, I have to know. The vigilantes said your friend Juan was the one who kidnapped me."

Jack forced himself to look incredulous. "What? Why would Juan kidnap *you*?"

"You tell me."

"You make it sound like I had something to do with it."

"Did you?" Wade said.

Jack tried to calm him down. "Look, Wade. The vigilantes are wrong about who grabbed you, that's all. I don't know who it was, but it wasn't Juan. It could have been anybody, especially in North Beach."

Wade drank more brandy. "They also say you killed a man last Christmas. Murdered him."

Jack sighed. He shook his head in despair. "They never give up. Yes, I killed that man, but it was in self-defense after he insulted Kathy."

"They say you rigged the trial, paid off the judge and jury."

"Nonsense. Brannan and his pompous friends can't stand the fact that I got off, that's all. They don't like me because I'm from the wrong side of town and I've got more money than they have. They can't forgive me for that. They'll do anything to bring me down."

"It looks like they might be successful," Wade said.

Jack smiled in spite of himself. "It does, doesn't it?"

"Jack, there's one thing more." Wade hesitated, then went on. "I—I came back here tonight, after you left for the club. I talked to Kathy. She told me you're holding her here against her will. She said she wants a divorce, and you won't give it to her."

Jack tried not to show his anger. He dropped his gaze. "Kathy and I haven't been getting along, not since I shot that fellow at Christmas. I think she half believes Brannan and the *Alta* crowd about that. If you don't mind, we'll talk about this later, after we get out of here."

"We?" Wade said.

"You're coming with us, aren't you? It won't be healthy for you to stick around." Jack grinned. "The three of us on the run. It'll be like—"

"Like old times," Wade said. He sipped more of the brandy. "I hadn't thought about joining you."

"Think about it quick, partner. If what you say is true, there ain't much time. Wait here while I get Kathy."

"What about Juan?"

Jack spoke over his shoulder. "He'll have to look out for himself. There's no time to find him."

Jack started out of the billiard room, then stopped. "By the way, where's your wonder dog?"

Wade shrugged. "No idea. I haven't seen him since the fight in the alley."

"Oh," said Jack. "I'm sorry." He left the room.

Jack took the grand staircase two steps at a time. He hurried down the carpeted hall. He found Kathy in the sitting room that opened off their bedroom. She was studying the script of *Mary Barton*. She barely looked up as Jack came in. Once she would have asked who had come to the house, but she no longer spoke to Jack.

Jack flung off his evening clothes. "Get dressed," he told her. "We're leaving. The vigilantes are on their way." He pulled out a suit of heavy corduroy, good for traveling, along with a pair of high-topped boots.

Kathy put down the book and stood. "What? Who told you this?"

"Wade. He's downstairs in the billiard room. They wanted him to join them. Hurry up and get changed."

"But . . . what do the vigilantes want?" she asked.

"They want to take me to the foot of Broadway and stretch my neck, like they did those poor bastards last summer. They may string you up beside me. Now, get some clothes on."

Kathy steeled herself. "I'm not going with you, Jack."

"You have to come with me. You're my wife."

"No, I don't. And you can't make me. You don't have the time."

Jack stuffed his pants into his boots. He threw on a flannel shirt. He grabbed her shoulders. His fingertips dug into her skin. He could force her, but she would scream, and that would bring Wade, and . . .

"Don't come, then," he said, pushing her away. "I won't stay here and be hung because of you. Go with Wade. That's what you want, isn't it?"

"Oh, Jack," Kathy said quietly.

"Isn't it!" he shouted.

Kathy didn't answer.

Jack put on his coat and a wide-brimmed hat. He threw open the door. He paused and looked back. His eyes met hers. He said, "I love you, you know."

"Yes," she said, "I know."

He left, closing the door behind him.

He went down the hall to the gun room. He started to take the brass-plated Colt pistol, then passed it up in favor of a pair of heavy .44s, the kind he used in the old days when things got rough. He loaded and capped them. Then he went quietly down a narrow staircase at the rear of the house. Wade would have a lot of explaining to do when the vigilantes found him here by himself. That would give Jack more time to get away.

Jack went to the stables, where he saddled his strongest horse. He mounted and rode down the hill into the city. Before he left San Francisco, he had to get his money.

68

Wade waited in the billiard room. He was sure he'd done the right thing by warning Jack about the vigilantes—Wade was against that kind of justice. But he was not sure he believed Jack's replies to his questions. He *wanted* to believe, but there were nagging doubts.

He heard Jack shout upstairs. He thought about going up, but he hesitated. Kathy and Jack were married. Was their argument his business? Time was running out, though. The vigilantes would be there soon.

He left the room and started down the hall.

"Wade?" It was Kathy's voice.

Wade ran into the entrance hall. Kathy was coming down the staircase. She wore a fur-trimmed dressing gown. Wade ran up the stairs to her. They embraced and kissed. They couldn't help themselves.

"Where's Jack?" Wade said, pulling away.

"Gone," said Kathy. "He must have taken the back way."

"You're not going with him?"

She looked into his eyes, and she smiled. "No."

He felt a warm rush. Then reality intruded, and he felt the cold knife of betrayal. "He's left us to be picked up by the vigilantes. He lied to me. Everything the vigilantes said about him was true."

He grabbed Kathy's shoulders. "We'd better get out. The vigilantes will know I warned him, and there's no telling what kind of mood that will put them in."

"Let me put on a dress and shoes, and get my coat," she said.

"Hurry."

Kathy ran back to the room. Wade waited for her at the head of the staircase. In a few minutes she was ready. She wore a plain dark dress, and she carried her heavy coat over her arm. Wade took her hand. They ran down the stairs and across the entrance hall toward the front door.

"What is the rush, my friends?" said a voice behind them. "Stay and enjoy the evening."

Wade and Kathy turned to see Juan Menendez holding a pistol on them. In his other hand he carried a length of rope.

Juan looked as surprised as they did. To Wade he said, "I thought you were on your way to China, señor."

"I took a detour," Wade told him. So Juan *had* kidnapped him. But why?

"It is a detour you shall live to regret," Juan promised. "I owed you one favor. You will get no more."

"Sending me to China was a favor?"

"Letting you live was the favor. Where is Señor Jack?"

"He's gone," Wade said. "He was about to be visited by the vigilantes."

"A pity. I had hoped to have him here. But our paths will cross again."

"They're looking for you, too," Wade added.

"Let them. They will find something infinitely more exciting.

Indeed, all San Francisco will soon enjoy my little entertainment.''

Wade and Kathy stood powerless before the revolver's muzzle. Kathy fiddled nervously with the coat over her arm. Suddenly she lifted her head. "I smell something. Smoke."

Juan laughed. "Very good, señora."

"My God—the house is on fire!"

Juan laughed again.

The implication sank in on Kathy. "You—you started it."

Juan nodded. "In the library. It should burn well there, don't you think?"

The smell of smoke grew stronger.

"But why . . ?" Kathy said.

"In memory of a lady," Juan told her. "A lady whom you and your two friends forced from her cabin on the ship from Panama."

It took Kathy a second to remember. Then she said, "But it was a man who gave me that cabin. Jack told me."

"It was my wife!" Juan thundered. "And she did not give you the cabin. She was forced from it, chased out like an animal. She was pregnant." Juan waved the pistol, tears in his eyes. "Because of you we had to stay on the deck. Because of you my Elena lost the baby."

"Christ," whispered Wade. He'd heard that one of the *Achilles*'s passengers had suffered a miscarriage, but he'd never known the full story.

Juan regained control of himself. "Later, Elena was hung. In a mining camp called Oro Fino. For defending herself from a man who tried to rape her. The gringos said she was a whore, and she should die. They made me watch."

Kathy was fiddling with her coat again. She said, "I'm sorry— we're sorry—for what happened, but we had nothing to do with it.''

"Liar!" Juan said. "It is your fault, and you will pay."

"You're mad," Kathy told him.

"On the contrary," said Juan, "I am quite sane. I have dreamed of this moment for two and a half years. I have prayed for it. There were times when I thought it would never come, but always I kept hoping. And now my prayers have been answered."

Juan coughed. Tendrils of smoke were creeping into the hallway. There was an ominous crackling from the rear of the great house.

Kathy shifted the heavy coat on her arm. "We've got to get out of here."

"Oh, no," Juan said. "You are going to watch my production from the best seats in the house. As a theatrical person, Mrs. Marlow, you will appreciate that. You should find it quite stimulating."

Kathy turned anxiously toward the growing fire. "Please, Juan. Can't you understand—what happened to your family was not our fault."

"Tell that to Elena when you see her." Juan said. He waved the length of rope. "Now, sit in those chairs, please."

There were footsteps from the rear of the house. The butler, Henry, burst into the entrance hall. His face was smoke-blackened, his coat off, his shirt undone. "Mrs. Marlow, the house is on fire. Someone has killed Charles, and—"

He stopped when he saw Juan. Juan turned, pointed his pistol, and shot him. The butler's front foot went up in the air as if he were trying to kick the ceiling, and he fell on his back.

"Your employment is terminated," Juan said.

At that moment Kathy reached her free hand into a pocket of her coat. She pulled out a small pistol and cocked it. Juan turned back. He saw the pistol. He tried to fire his own weapon, but he was too late. Kathy fired first. Juan staggered backward. There was a small hole in his chest. Blood welled from it. He tried to raise the pistol. Kathy fired again. Juan grunted. He dropped the pistol. He went to his knees. He looked up at Kathy as though he wanted to say something, then he fell to the floor.

Wade rushed across the entranceway. He kicked the pistol away from Juan's hand. "So that's why you were playing with the coat," he told Kathy.

"I was trying to maneuver the pocket to where I could reach it," she explained. She was badly shaken. In her hand the brass-plated pistol was still pointed at the fallen Juan.

Wade looked at Kathy's weapon, and he suddenly went cold inside. "Let me have that," he said.

She handed it to him. "I thought we might need a gun. I didn't think we'd need it before we even got out of the house."

Wade examined the pocket Colt. He forgot the oncoming roar of the fire. Everything seemed to be spinning.

"Where did you get this?" he asked Kathy.

"It's Jack's. You gave it to him when you two split up." She saw the look on Wade's face, and she added, "That's what he told me."

Wade said, "Kathy, this pistol was taken from my cabin at the rich vein by the men who robbed me and killed my partner."

He and Kathy exchanged looks.

Kathy said, "You mean Jack robbed you?"

"He must have." All at once everything was clear to Wade. "That's why Juan kidnapped me. Jack told him to. Jack wanted me out of the way. He was afraid I'd find out what really happened."

Kathy's voice was hushed. She could hardly believe it. "That's where Jack got his money, then. Not from gambling."

"God, and I warned him about the vigilantes. I should have been marching at their head. No. No, I shouldn't. I have to deal with Jack by myself."

The entrance hall had become clouded with smoke. Their eyes watered; they stung. They saw flames now. "Come on," Wade said, "let's get out of here."

He checked Henry the butler, but Henry was dead. Juan was still breathing, barely. Wade grabbed him by the belt and dragged him through the front doors.

Outside, Wade straightened, breathing deeply of the cold night air. He looked up and saw the mansion on fire. Flames leapt among the billowing smoke. There was a strong smell of burning wood. The rest of the servants were crowded before him on the graveled drive. Frightened horses ran everywhere—Juan must have opened the stable gates before he set the fire, to save them.

Juan lay on the ground, groaning. He wouldn't last long. Wade knelt beside him. He slapped his face, bringing him to. "Wake up. Wake up, damn you."

Juan's eyes fluttered. They focused precariously on Wade.

Wade said, "Did you and Jack rob a claim at the head of the Mariposa last June? Did you?"

Juan answered weakly. "Yes."

"You killed a man and shot his partner?"

"It was you. Jack told me."

"Who tortured my friend?"

"I—I did it. I enjoyed it." Juan laughed. He raised a hand. He beckoned Wade closer. His voice was fading. "My name"—he shook his head—"not Menendez. Soto."

"Soto?" Wade said. "You're Juan Soto—the bandit?"

Juan nodded.

Wade said, "So Moran and his Rangers didn't get the right man after all."

Juan pointed at the fire. "Tell them, señor. Tell them who did this. Tell them why." He gasped, collecting his fading strength. He managed a grin. "Tell them . . . not Mexican. Chilean." There was a rattle in his throat, and he fell back, still grinning.

Wade stood. He twirled the pocket Colt's cylinder. Three loads left. That was enough. He stuck the pistol in his belt. Behind him, flames and sparks shot into the night sky. Timber crashed. The heat from the burning house was intense.

He turned to Kathy, putting his hands on her shoulders. "Wait for me on Telegraph Hill. You'll be safe there."

"Where are you going?" she said.

"After Jack."

"But he's left town by now."

"I don't think so."

He turned away and started down the hill toward the city. "Wade!" Kathy cried, but he paid no attention.

The wind was blowing out of the southwest. The fog was gone. Showers of sparks drifted high over Wade's head, landing in the packed buildings on Powell Street. Bits of flaming debris fell around him. Below, a point of light flared. It went out, then flared again more brightly. It began to spread.

San Francisco was on fire.

69

At the bottom of the hill, Wade turned down Powell Street. The fire was spreading rapidly in the stiff wind. The great city bell had begun to ring, summoning the fire companies.

Wade headed for Portsmouth Square. From the hill he had seen a commotion there. The vigilantes must have decided to seek Jack at the club first. Wade hoped that his guess was right and Jack hadn't left town. He wanted to kill Jack. He had never wanted to kill anyone before, but he had never hated anyone the way he hated Jack right now.

Wade was hard pressed to keep ahead of the fire. Buildings were going up in flames one after the other, a block at a time. The city was a tinderbox. Even the brick buildings had walls and ceilings of cloth as well as timber supports. There was a continuous popping as the dry, resinous wood exploded. The flames swirled higher, driven by the wind. The street was full of people. Some ran from the fire. Others ran toward it, to save valuables from homes and offices. Still others ran in aimless panic. Frightened animals careened down the street, many dragging wagons. A man was run down and vanished in the confusion. People scooped mud out of the street and slapped it on their houses, trying to save them. One merchant splashed vinegar from wooden casks on his store. Draymen brought up wagons. They negotiated with building owners to haul off their goods, haggling over prices. Meanwhile, the roar of the flames grew louder. A pall of smoke was blown by the wind over the city and the bay. It blocked out the stars. The great bell kept ringing, its deep peals underlying all other sound.

" 'Way there! 'Way there!"

The first fire company was coming, turning onto Powell Street. The firemen pulled the engine by the lead ropes. Boys ran before them with lanterns to light the way so the men wouldn't fall into holes in the street. They found the street blocked by the draymen.

" 'Way there! 'Way there! Move those wagons!"

The draymen refused. The firemen yelled at them, cursed them. The draymen took offense, and a series of fistfights erupted while the flames raced past the combatants.

The air was pierced by a thin, high-pitched wail, the screams of all the city merged into one. Beneath the scream were the deeper roar of flames, the rumble of collapsing bricks, the explosions of blasting powder as men frantically tried to clear fire breaks by blowing up buildings in the fire's path. Other men cut building supports with axes and pulled the structures down with ropes. They were too late. The conflagration had grown too large. The wind blew sparks and burning embers into the packed wooden structures beyond. A man whose shirt had caught fire rolled in the street. There were screams of people trapped in burning buildings. Everywhere were horses, wagons, confusion.

Wade turned off Powell Street, down Clay. He could barely breathe because of the intense heat and smoke. He was battling a mob. People were running, hysterical. More fire companies passed, yelling to people and vehicles to get out of the way. By the time

Wade reached Portsmouth Square, the fire was all around. Its flames backlighted the three-story buildings on the square. The city was bathed in a flickering red light. Wade glanced behind him. Jack's Nob Hill mansion burned like a beacon atop the inferno of the city. Juan had gotten his memorial to Elena.

There was a great crowd in the relative safety of the square. Wade saw the white armbands of the vigilantes everywhere. Many carried rifles, some with fixed bayonets. More vigilantes poured out of The Black Jack and formed in the square. All the windows and doors of the club had been broken. Everything inside looked to be smashed as well.

"There's no time to do more," shouted Sam Brannan to his men. "We've got a bigger problem on our hands now. We'll find Marlow later." The vigilantes were dismissed and left the square to help fight the fire or save their property, as they saw fit.

Wade looked for Jack. He counted on Jack being around somewhere. He counted on Jack's greed. Jack wouldn't leave San Francisco without his money. Wade bet that he kept a bundle at the club for just such an emergency as this. If the vigilantes had gotten to the club first, Jack would simply wait until they had left to make his move.

Wade pressed among the heads and bodies, amid the smell of smoke and sweat. There—was that Jack? He lost the man again in the tide of humanity. He dodged around people, pushed through them. Yes—it was Jack, in the middle of the crowd, facing the club. It seemed a brazen move, but the vigilantes were looking for an elegant gambler in a top hat. Neither they nor anyone else was likely to pay much attention to a slouch-hatted miner in rough corduroy.

Wade pushed toward Jack. He put his hand on his pistol butt. He wished he'd reloaded the weapon. That had been a mistake, but there was nothing he could do about it now.

Suddenly, there was a tremendous explosion. The force of it knocked Wade flat. A searing blast of heat swept over him. The breath was sucked from his lungs. The fire must have reached a store of blasting powder. A towering column of black smoke rose just behind the square. Wade saw blank spaces where buildings had been turned into matchsticks. The smoke rose hundreds of feet into the air. The city behind the square was a solid sheet of flame.

Wade pushed himself unsteadily to his feet. The explosion had terrified the crowd in the square. There were screams, yells, people streaming in all directions. The vigilantes were gone. Wade looked for Jack in front of The Black Jack. He didn't see him. Then he glimpsed Jack in the doorway of the brick house next door.

Wade labored through the mob. He was dripping with sweat. His cheeks grew hot from the flames. Smoke burned his eyes; it filled his lungs. Sparks and embers fell around him. They burned holes in his shirt. The fire roared like a living thing, like a great beast let loose upon the city.

Wade went into the brick house, which was filling with smoke. Girls in various stages of undress ran past him, outside, carrying their meager possessions. With a shock he realized this must be a whorehouse. It was the last place he had expected to end up. He stood aside to let the girls by. Then he went forward.

He pulled the pistol from his belt. He went from room to room, throwing open the doors. Jack wasn't there.

He started up the stairs cautiously, pistol pointed forward. Nobody seemed to be left in the house. Then a door opened, and Jack appeared at the head of the stairs. Two heavy bags of gold were thrown over each shoulder. Another bag dangled from his hand.

Jack saw Wade and stopped. The two men looked at each other. The roar of the fire was all around them. It was hot in the building. The city bell was clanging; the outside air rang with screams and cries of fear.

"You know, don't you?" Jack said, wheezing from the smoke.

"Yes," Wade said.

"I didn't want to kill anybody, Wade. I didn't want you hurt. You've got to believe that."

Wade started up the stairs.

Jack took a step back. "I don't want to shoot you, but I will if I have to. I worked too hard to get this money, I did too many things I didn't like. I'm not leaving without it."

Wade kept coming.

"We can work out a deal, Wade. We're friends."

"No," Wade said.

"The hell with you, then." Jack raised one of his .44s and fired. The bullet gouged splinters out of the polished banister near Wade's head. Wade ducked, then started back up the stairs. Jack fired again and ran along the landing. Wade had only three shots. He held his fire.

Jack made for the stairs to the third floor, hampered by the heavy bags of gold. He stopped and fired again. The bullet thunked in

front of Wade. Wade kept coming. Jack snapped off another shot
and went up the stairs. Wade fired his .31 and missed.

Wade ran up the stairs after Jack. He neared the top. He peeked
around cautiously. Jack was waiting for him. Both men fired simultaneously, jerking backward. Both men missed. Jack lumbered
down the hall, making for the steps at the rear of the house. Wade
followed. He fired his last shot. He hit one of the sacks of gold. He
swore and threw away his empty pistol. He lowered his head and
charged. Jack stopped at the head of the rear stairs, breathing heavily from carrying the gold. He turned and fired. Wade felt the bullet
clip his hair. Jack threw the pistol down, drew his other one. Before
he could fire, Wade launched himself through the air. He hit Jack
in the chest, and both men tumbled to the bottom of the stairs.

Kathy fought her way through the crowd. She hoped she wasn't
too late. She was afraid for Wade, afraid he'd get hurt. She didn't
care what happened to Jack. Let him get away, as long as Wade
was all right.

It was hard to move in the press of people, animals, and vehicles.
The fire was all around her. She pulled her coat over her head. A
building collapsed in front of her, spilling bricks and burning timber in her path. She went around. People lay in the street, dead, or
unconscious from inhaling smoke. Kathy heard the explosions of
gunpowder, the popping of wood. A nearby window blew out in a
shower of glass. The street was littered with bodies, with water,
mud, debris. In the red light and flickering shadows, it looked like
a scene from hell.

Portsmouth Square was clearing out. Most of the buildings were
on fire. She went to The Black Jack. Inside, she stopped. The floor
was a lake of spilled liquor and broken bottles. The mirrors were
smashed, the curtains torn down. The crystal chandeliers were shattered. The gaming tables were overturned and broken. Chips and
cards were everywhere.

"Is everybody out?" called a voice from upstairs. It was Brandy.
She came down, outwardly calm, making sure the building was
empty. Her red hair had come unpinned. One of her red stockings
was torn. The low-cut blue dress was dirty.

"Brandy," said Kathy. "What happened here?"

If Brandy was surprised to see Kathy, she didn't show it. She
said, "The vigilantes came looking for Jack. I thought for a while

they were going to kill me. They might have if, the fire hadn't started.''

''Brandy, where *is* Jack?''

''I don't know.''

''He said he was getting out of town. Wade's gone after him. Wade's his old friend. He knows that Jack killed his partner. He wants to kill him in revenge.''

''He knows *what*?'' Brandy said.

''Jack killed Wade's partner. Last spring. He and Juan murdered him and took all their gold. They shot Wade and left him for dead.''

Brandy swore. ''I knew that bastard Juan would get Jack in trouble.''

''We've got to find them before they kill each other. Do you know where Jack could have gone?''

''He'll have gone after his money,'' Brandy said. She grabbed Kathy's hand and led her out the front door. ''Come on.''

Wade and Jack lay at the bottom of the stairs. The rear landing was full of smoke. The heat was intense. The building was on fire.

Both men were dazed and hurt from the fall. They got up stiffly. Jack looked around for his pistol, didn't see it. Wade came after him. Jack lashed out with a fist, stopping him. He put his hands around Wade's throat and pinned him to the wall. He held him there, straining, the muscles on his neck standing out, sweat running down his smoke-blackened face. Wade gasped for breath. He hammered Jack's forearms, trying to break the iron grip on his throat. He placed the flat of his hand beneath Jack's chin and pushed. Slowly, Jack's head moved back. Wade felt Jack's grip relax. He punched out, hit Jack in the nose. Jack's grip relaxed more. Wade punched again. Jack stumbled backward.

Wade wanted to lunge at him, but he was out of breath, exhausted. So was Jack. They faced each other on the landing, heaving, choking in the smoke. Wade staggered after Jack. They grappled. Wade flung Jack against the wall so hard that he heard wood crack. He swung a right, opened a gash beneath Jack's left eye. Jack recovered and punched Wade in the stomach. Wade doubled over. Jack hit him in the jaw, knocking him backward on the narrow landing. Wade lost his footing and fell partway down the next flight of stairs. Jack picked up one of the heavy sacks of gold. He came down, swung the sack, hit Wade's shoulder, and knocked him farther down the stairs. He followed Wade and hit him again, in the head. Wade's brain was jarred. Jack pounded him again and again. Wade tried to cover his head. Jack hit him lower down, in the ribs, knocking the breath out of him with a whoosh. Desperate, Wade lashed out with his legs. He caught Jack's ankles and tripped him. Jack fell over Wade and down the stairs past him.

Jack reached the bottom of the stairs. He stooped for the bag of gold. Wade half staggered, half fell down the stairs after him. Jack took the gold, ran through the hall for the front door. Wade chased him. He tackled him from behind. They crashed off the wall, breaking a mirror and side table as they fell to the floor.

Sobbing, gasping for breath, both men stood. They could hardly raise their arms. Smoke wreathed around them. Burning cinders fell from the ceiling. Wade took a deep breath. In what seemed like slow motion, he punched Jack in the jaw, knocking him through the doorway into the parlor. He followed him, ramming his head into Jack's stomach. They fell into a table, breaking it, and went to the floor.

They lay there, breathing heavily. The carpet sizzled from burning embers. Outside, the city bell still rang. It seemed as though it had been ringing for hours. Slowly, Wade got to his knees. The scalp cut he'd gotten from the sap had opened up again. Blood dripped into his eyes. He tried to wipe it out. Jack picked up a broken table leg. He swung it. Wade saw it coming too late. The table leg hit him alongside the head. He dropped to the floor. Jack crawled over as Wade rolled onto his back. The broken edge of the table leg was sharp and jagged. Jack aimed it like a spear. He drove it at Wade's face. Wade caught Jack's wrists. Both men strained to the utmost, strength against strength. The splintered wood came closer, until it was an inch from Wade's eye. Suddenly Wade moved his head and relaxed his grip. The table leg plunged to the floor, just missing him. Wade reached over and hit Jack alongside the face. Again. Jack wobbled. Wade hit him again and pushed him off. Jack fell on his side. Wade smashed Jack's face. Jack went down. Wade fell on him. He hit him again and again. Jack was helpless to fight back. Wade no longer knew what he was doing. He struck out blindly in anger and frustration at being betrayed.

"Wade!" It was Kathy. She and a red-haired woman grabbed his arms and pulled him off. "Enough!" Kathy yelled. Jack's face was splashed with blood. The skin on Wade's knuckles was torn off.

"Let him go!" Kathy cried. "Get out of here before you get killed."

The red-haired woman bent over Jack. "Jack. Jack, wake up." The roar of the fire was all-consuming. The smoke was so thick, they could hardly see. Heat radiated from the walls as through they were about to explode.

Jack came to. He looked at the red-haired woman. "Brandy," he said, dazed.

"Get up," she told him. "Hurry!"

She tried to pull Jack to his feet, but he was heavy. Wade helped her. A minute ago he had wanted to kill Jack; now it did not seem important. Their eyes met as Jack stumbled to his feet.

"Get out of here!" Kathy yelled, pushing them. A few feet away a ceiling beam fell with a crash.

The four of them staggered out of the parlor. In the thick smoke they felt their way to the parlor door. Brandy went last, pushing Jack before her. She tripped over something and fell. When she straightened, she could no longer see. She didn't know where the others had gone. The smoke grew thicker and thicker. Brandy bent over, coughing. She started for the door. Flaming timbers crashed in front of her, blocking her way. She raised her hands, warding off the flames. She tried to go around, but a section of the ceiling fell at her feet. Another section fell behind her. She was trapped.

Kathy and Wade made it out the front door of the house. Jack came behind. The three of them sobbed for joy at breathing the relatively fresh air of the square. Wade and Jack sank to their hands and knees, hardly able to move, bloody and torn.

"Jack!" It was Brandy's voice from inside the burning house. "Jack!"

Jack looked at the flaming structure. He looked at Wade and Kathy. Then he heaved himself to his feet and started back into the building.

Wade grabbed Jack's arm. "No."

Jack shook him off and kept going. Wade started to follow, but Kathy held him back. "Let him go."

Jack fought his way through the smoke-filled hallway. "Brandy, where are you?"

"Here," she cried.

Burning timbers blocked Jack's path. He pulled them aside. The flesh roasted off his hands, but he paid no attention. The heat was worse than anything he had ever experienced. It was like breathing fire into his lungs. He pulled away more burning debris. Embers and cinders fell all around him. His coat was smoldering. The whole building would go in a minute.

"Jack!" Brandy cried again. She was off to the left.

He moved toward her voice. The heat singed his face. He choked from the thick smoke. He bent over, barely able to move forward, barely able to remain conscious. His eyes were full of tears and smoke; he couldn't see. He went by sound alone.

"Brandy?" he shouted.

"Here I am."

He stumbled into a last barricade of burning timbers. He heaved them aside. There she was. He crawled over a heap of broken furniture and other debris from the floor above. Brandy reached out a hand. Jack took it.

"It's all right," he said. "I've got you."

There was an awesome roar, and the building collapsed in flames on top of them.

70

Wade and Kathy sat near the top of Telegraph Hill, watching the fire consume the city.

Wade was smoke-blackened and bloody. His clothes were torn and burned. His right hand was swollen so badly he could not close it. It hurt his battered ribs to breathe. His eyes were sunken; he slumped with exhaustion. Kathy had thrown her coat around her shoulders. The top buttons of her dark dress were undone. Her unpinned hair hung in disarray.

"Thinking about Jack?" Kathy said.

Wade nodded. "And about that girl, Brandy. She must have loved him."

"She did. I think Jack realized at the end that he loved her, too. I think that's why he went back for her."

There were many people on the hill—men, women, a few children. They carried possessions in carpetbags, sacks, or wheelbarrows. Here and there makeshift tents had sprung up. Vendors went through the crowd selling water to the thirsty refugees for a dollar a drink.

They were safe here. There were no structures to catch fire, and the chaparral had been cut away long before. Below them the night presented a fearsome spectacle, as the roaring ocean of flame devoured everything in its path. Street after street went up—Sansome, Battery, Broadway, Vallejo, Union. The Black Jack was gone, so was Kathy's theater. The business district on Montgomery was a smoldering ruin. Ships in the harbor could be seen standing in deep water to avoid the sparks and drifting embers. There were collisions. Masts came down, riggings became entangled. From the dying city came shouts, screams, the bells of the fire companies, the explosions of blasting powder. The city bell had stopped ringing, melted by the flames. Over everything hung the acrid smells of smoke and charred wood.

"The city's being destroyed," Wade said. "People's hopes and dreams."

"And tomorrow they'll start rebuilding," Kathy said.

"There will be a lot to do—then, and for a long time to come."

"They'll do it. And the new city will be bigger and better than the old."

Wade looked at her. "Shall we stay and help them?"

Kathy slipped her arm through his. "Do you want to?"

"Yes, I do." Then he warned, "We'll be starting with nothing."

"We've got each other. That's all we need."

Suddenly there was a bark. A shadow bounded up the hill and lunged at them.

"Roland!" Wade cried.

The dog was overjoyed to see Wade again. He stood with his forepaws on Wade's shoulders, licking Wade's face and mouth. The dog was dirty, and his fur was singed in places, but otherwise he looked all right. "This is the dog I told you about," Wade explained as best he could under the assault.

"Hello, Roland," Kathy said. She reached over and scratched the dog's neck. Roland began licking her, too. Then he snuggled between them, his eager tail thumping each of them in turn.

Wade looked at Kathy, and he grinned. "You know, we could be in for an interesting wedding night."

About the Author

Robert W. Broomall has been a journalist, draftee, bartender, and civil servant. His main interests are travel and history, especially that of the Old West and Middle Ages.

Broomall has written several Westerns for Fawcett, including *Dead Man's Town*, *The Bank Robber*, *Dead Man's Canyon*, and *Dead Man's Crossing*, as well as the historical novels *Texas Kingdoms* and *California Kingdoms*. He lives in Maryland with his wife and children.